Vexed 2:

Twisted Faith

Vexed 2:
Twisted Faith

Honey

URBAN BOOKS

www.urbanbooks.net

Urban Books, LLC
300 Farmingdale Road, N.Y.-Route 109
Farmingdale, NY 11735

Vexed 2: Twisted Faith Copyright © 2020 Honey

ISBN 13: 978-1-64556-121-7
ISBN 10: 1-64556-121-6

First Trade Paperback Printing December 2020
Printed in the United States of America

10 9 8 7 6 5 4 3 2 1

*This is a work of fiction. Any references or similarities
to actual events, real people, living or dead, or to real
locales are intended to give the novel a sense of reality.
Any similarity in other names, characters, places, and
incidents is entirely coincidental.*

Distributed by Kensington Publishing Corp.
Submit Orders to:
Customer Service
400 Hahn Road
Westminster, MD 21157-4627
Phone: 1-800-733-3000
Fax: 1-800-659-2436

Chapter One

"Do you truly believe that Jesus died for your sins, Jayla? Do you believe His blood has cleansed you from all unrighteousness?"

"Yes, Pastor Monroe, I believe it. I . . . I asked the Lord to forgive me, and I believe He has."

"Hallelujah! You're born again! All of your sins have been washed away by the precious blood of Jesus Christ." The pastor wrapped his arms around his new convert.

"Thank you, Jesus," Jay whispered through a steady flow of tears. She relaxed in the warmth of Pastor Monroe's embrace and rested her head on his shoulder.

"Whatever crime you committed to bring you to this terrible place is no longer important. It's in the past. From this day forward, you are a new creature. You're no longer walking in darkness. You are a daughter of God's marvelous light."

Jay stepped backward to look into the pastor's steel gray eyes. He held her loosely in his arms. "Thank you so much for praying for me, Pastor Monroe. I needed it. I've been very depressed in recent weeks, worrying about my health and missing my family. Two years in prison has taken its toll on me. Sometimes I feel like I'd be better off dead." Jay's voice broke as a fresh surge of tears spilled down her face.

"Shh," the pastor whispered in her ear, pulling her closer in his arms. "You have no use for a grave. There is so much more here on earth for you to live for. God has great things in store for you in spite of your present circumstances. Let me help you find your calling, won't you?"

"Yes, sir."

"Great. I will speak with your correctional counselor to see if you and I can have private sessions. Until then, continue to read Scriptures daily in the Bible I gave you last week. You must pray often, Jayla. Talking consistently to God will give you strength to persevere during your darkest hours. Keep coming to chapel. I will always have a Word from the Lord for you and the other women confined to this facility. That is my calling. I'm going to help you find yours, even while you're behind prison bars. Go in peace, my sister."

Pastor Monroe hugged Jay once again before she turned to leave the small chapel.

"I saw you crying and waving your hands in the air the other night, acting like you had caught the Holy Ghost or something. What was that all about, King?"

Jay looked up from the ledger she was working on. She slid it to the side of her desk. "What are you talking about, Odette? Don't tell me you ain't ever been to church before."

"Yeah, I've been a few times, but I'm not all that religious. But you were acting all sanctified." Odette laughed.

"Laugh all you want, but that was a powerful service. I felt the Spirit, and I ain't ashamed of it. Did you know my father was a Pentecostal pastor? I was born and raised in the church."

"You were raised in the church, huh? Well, don't the Bible say it's a sin to be gay? And I know murder breaks one of them commandments. You're serving time 'cause you paid someone to kill your brother."

"That's in the past. I'm not that person anymore. Anyway, don't you have some mopping or dusting to do? I'm trying to balance the supply budget for the warden. I can't do it with you in here harassing me."

"All right, Ms. Business Lady. I'm sorry I disturbed you. Not everybody can sit behind a desk and do easy work in prison like you. Some of us have to do the hard shit. I'm out."

Jay rolled her eyes to the ceiling. "Close the door behind you."

Crunching numbers and balancing budgets was easy to Jay. Her Howard University master's degree in business had come in handy before prison, and it was benefitting her on the inside as well. Years ago, when she had worked as the executive manager of a five-star resort in Montego Bay, Jamaica, life was sweet. Back then, she had plenty of money, designer clothes, expensive jewelry, and more women than she had time or energy for. Those were the good ol' days. If only Jay had stayed on the island and not moved back home to Atlanta, she would've been a free member of society. Leaving Jamaica with her former lover Jill to take a job in her hometown was the beginning of her decline.

Jay frowned and closed her eyes at the painful memories. Jill. It was her betrayal that had caused Jay to lose touch with reality. Her brother, Zach, was the other backstabber. He and Jill had carried on a secret affair behind Jay's back. No sister deserved to be humiliated and disrespected by the big brother she'd once looked up to. Blood was supposed to be sacred. Zach had had no right whatsoever to touch Jill, because she was Jay's lover. Brothers didn't betray their little sisters in the neighborhood they came from. They were expected to be their protectors and confidants. Zach used to be Jay's hero. Now he wanted nothing to do with her. It felt like she didn't even have a brother anymore. To Zachary Sean King, Jayla Simone King was dead.

"I don't wanna hear it, Aunt Jackie. Didn't I tell you the last time Jay wrote you a letter that I wasn't interested in anything she had to say?"

"But she sounds so remorseful now. She's not the same person, Zach. Jay has accepted Jesus into her heart, and she attends chapel twice a week. The prison chaplain has been counseling her."

Zach ignored his aunt. He loved her like crazy, but he didn't share her feelings for his sister. Zach wasn't even sure if he had any feelings for her. Jay had paid a man, whom she'd thought was a professional killer, to put a bullet in the back of his head. What the hell kind of feelings was he supposed to have for a sister who would do some evil shit like that?

Yeah, Zach had betrayed Jay in the worst possible way. He had slept with Jill while they were still in a relationship. And they had conceived their son, Zachary Junior, as a result of the affair. Then they got married. Zach acknowledged his sins and asked Jay to forgive him, but she'd refused. She became bitter and vengeful, and she ultimately ordered a hit on him. That was why Jay was now serving time in federal prison. Thank God the dude she had hired to take Zach out was an undercover cop. Otherwise, Jill now would have been a widow, and Zachary Junior would have been fatherless. Zion, their baby girl, never would have been born.

If Jay had suddenly found jailhouse religion, Zach didn't give a damn. He still wanted nothing to do with her. She had caused him and his family more pain than he felt they deserved. He, Jill, and their two children had moved on from their nightmare of Jay and her evil deeds.

Aunt Jackie was still flapping her gums about Jay's spiritual transformation, and Zach continued to block out her words. He was watching his children play with toys and ABC blocks in the middle of the floor of his den. Jill was doing her thing in the kitchen. The aroma drifted into the den, causing Zach's stomach to growl.

"How much longer until dinner, baby?"

Jill poked her head into the den. "It'll be ready when it's ready." With a smile and a wink, she disappeared into the kitchen again.

"Zachary Sean King, are you ignoring me? I delivered a personal message to you from Jay, and you haven't said a word. She says she loves you and misses you very much. What do you have to say about that?"

"You don't wanna hear what I'd like to say to Jay, Auntie. Plus, I can't curse in front of the kiddies."

Chapter Two

Jay fumbled with the buttons on her ugly prison-issued blue shirt. The absence of the tips of two fingers on her right hand made the simple task difficult. The nurse had told her that the results from her blood work would be back from the lab in five to seven working days. Life with low-functioning kidneys and a diseased liver was rough for a chick in prison. Jay was on a lot of medication, and she had to limit her liquid intake. The staff doctor's goal was to delay dialysis for as long as he could, but eventually Jay would need it in order to live. Years of excessive drinking had caught up with her. Her quality of life was slowly depreciating.

The reality of Jay's medical condition weighed heavily on her mind. She was only a few months shy of her thirty-fourth birthday, yet she was in the early stages of cirrhosis of the liver, and her kidneys only functioned at 30 percent. It was quite depressing, but Jay had recently found hope in the kindness of Pastor Gavin Monroe.

The man had committed himself to helping her with her problems. Because of the charismatic Pentecostal pastor, Jay didn't have very many thoughts anymore about Zach and Jill or what they had done to her. She seldom thought about her ex-lover Venus and their daughter, Nahima. There had been a time when Jay constantly envisioned the day she'd be free so that she could make Zach, Jill, and Venus pay for how they had treated her. But since she had been attending Bible study and prayer meetings regularly in the chapel with Pastor Monroe, and having one-on-one counseling sessions with him, things had changed for the better. Jay's desire to get even with her brother and sister-in-law was gone. She actually missed Zach. The other day she'd started writing him a letter asking for his and Jill's forgiveness, but she didn't finish it. Mr. Callahan, the warden, had sent for her to make some changes to the inmate payroll account.

Jay would finish the letter to Zach, but not now. She was on her way to the chapel. It was her job to place the Bibles and hymn books in every other chair before service. Because of her budgeting expertise, there had been enough money in the prison's miscellaneous fund for the purchasing department to buy sixty new Bibles and hymnals for the inmates.

"Psst, King, tell me about Pastor Monroe. He's one sexy-ass preacher. Maxwell said he's the real deal. That chick swears he ain't fake. Is he really holy and tight with the Man Upstairs? Or is he freaky and slick like Bishop Long or Reverend Haggard?"

Jay closed her Bible and eased to the end of her cot to whisper across the narrow hall. "Pastor Monroe is a genuine man of God. He ain't fake. It's not about getting rich or laid for him. His mission is to save souls. That's it."

"Well, he's fine as hell. And I like me some white dudes. They be all sensitive and shit. Maybe I need to put in a request for some counseling so he can lay hands on me." Shanika laughed. "I want his good-looking ass to lay hands all over me, chile."

"Like I said, he ain't like that."

"How do you know, King? You ain't into men. I bet if you offered the pastor some pussy, he'd be all up in you. Can't no white man—preacher or not—resist some wet, hot chocolate pussy. It ain't natural. Since slavery, crackers have had a weakness for black women. That ain't gonna ever change."

"I'm not interested in sleeping with Pastor Monroe or any other man or woman. You shouldn't be thinking about anything sexual either, Shanika. Fornication is a sin. Besides, Pastor Monroe is a happily married man. He ain't about money or sex. The man has been called to save worthless sinners. That's all he's interested in."

"You mean to tell me you ain't ever noticed how tall he is? Dude obviously works out, 'cause he's got some tight biceps and a six-pack. I wanna run my fingers all through his thick black hair. Woo, Lawd! His mustache and beard turn me on. I bet he's got hair everywhere. I like hairy-ass men."

"I'm done with this conversation. You keep that non-sense over there in your cell. I'm about to read my Bible."

"You go right ahead, Mother Teresa. I'm about to get my freak on with my vibrator. But in my head, I'll be fucking that sexy white preacher with all that pretty hair."

"Vibrator? How did you get one of those up in here?"

"That's easy. Captain Floyd will turn his head and close his eyes to anything as long as you suck his dick every once in a while."

"You got issues." Jay frowned and shook her head. "I'm gonna pray for you."

Jay added the final numbers and hit the equals key on the calculator again. She blew air from her cheeks and massaged her temples. Something was definitely wrong with the quarterly financial report. She had crunched the same numbers five times. They just did not add up cor-rectly. The amount of inmate labor hours and the total of daily wages they'd been paid did not match. According to Jay's calculations, the women had not received their fair share of money for the work they had done. Someone in the accounting department at Leesworth Women's Federal Corrections Facility was padding the books. They wanted it to appear as though the inmates were earning fair wages for their labor.

Didn't they realize that a simple audit would quickly uncover the shoddy accounting? Maybe they did, but they weren't concerned because the errors would all be charged to Jay. She would be blamed for falsifying financial records. That could mean more criminal charges. Jay wasn't feeling that.

She added the numbers one last time and got the same results. What was she going to do to cover herself in the event of an audit?

"I wish you could attend one of the services at the prison, Holly. Some of the women have a thirst for the Word. I've watched them grow spiritually. There's one young lady named Ivy Maxwell. She has an anointed voice. She leads the praise and worship music before my sermons."

"What is she serving time for?"

"You know I don't know that, sweetheart. I've chosen not to ask the women what crimes they've committed. I don't want to give the devil any room to cloud my mind with judgment. I'm their spiritual leader, not their judge."

Holly Monroe pushed her wire-framed glasses up the bridge of her narrow nose. With great concern, she studied her husband's face across the dinner table. He was the love of her life. She and Gavin had been inseparable since the day they met over twenty years ago on the campus of Oral Roberts University. It was love at first sight for Holly

Elizabeth Blake. Her public speaking classmate had been clueless about her crush on him. Gavin was fascinated with her incredible oratory skills. It was the magnet that drew them together. Gavin had only wanted a friend, but Holly was in search of love from a godly man.

"Don't be naive, honey," Holly warned her husband. "Those women are con artists, violent robbers, and murderers. They can be deceitful."

"God knows their hearts, Holly. He knows mine, too. I only want to do for those women what I couldn't do for Sandy. All she needed was the love of Jesus and her family. I wasn't there for her. And because I wasn't, she left this world without ever knowing Christ as her Lord and Savior."

As great an orator and debater as Holly was, she could never win points in a discussion about Gavin's late sister. Sandy was a sensitive subject she treaded very lightly upon. She had died of a heroin overdose after many years of battling multiple addictions. Sandy had been six months pregnant at the time she'd injected herself with the lethal dose of drugs. Gavin was pastoring his first church fresh out of seminary. His older sister had reached out to him the night before she'd robbed their grandmother at gunpoint in order to buy her final supply of drugs. Gavin was preparing to preach a sermon at his church and had promised to call Sandy after the service. The following morning, when he made the call from his home in Scottsdale, Arizona, it was too late. Sandy's lifeless, pregnant body was already at the City of Atlanta morgue.

It had been fifteen years since Sandy's tragic death. Yet her loving brother, Pastor Gavin Monroe, was still trying to rid himself of the guilt he carried. He was seeking redemption by helping other women who reminded him so much of Sandy. The pastor's primary ministry

was his church, Marvelous Light Pentecostal Church, in
northwest Atlanta. However, his passion was the prison
ministry he had established at Leesworth two years ago.
He had founded Another Chance Women's Fellowship
with memories of Sandy in mind. She had been in and
out of prison for the better part of her life due to drug
addiction and chronic depression, which caused her to
do the craziest things to earn money to support her drug
habit.

Gavin believed he could have saved Sandy if he had
been home in Atlanta. Instead, he had been in Arizona,
fully immersed in his church. His costly mistake, according to him, was that he had confined God to a
building with a steeple and stained-glass windows. Gavin
admitted that he'd forgotten to evangelize outside of the
boundaries of church, especially to women with issues.
They needed God the most.

"I will attend service with you one day soon, honey. The
moment I find a break in my schedule, I'll go with you."

"Thanks, babe. It would mean a lot to me. I want you
to meet Ivy, Erica, Sophia, and my favorite inmate of
all, Jayla. She's the one I've asked the women at our
church to collect personal items for. Her family isn't
very involved in her life. She's dealing with some serious
health issues, also. The poor soul is depressed and ill, but
her faith is strong."

"Like I said, once my students get settled, I'll go to the
prison with you."

Chapter Three

"Oh, so you think I'm wrong?" Zach stared at his best friend, Dex, through the thick clouds of steam.

"Nah, I don't think you were wrong for refusing Jay's phone call. But why did you have to send her letter back to the prison unopened? I can understand why you and Jill didn't wanna read it, but you could've simply thrown it away. Sending it back was kinda crass for a dude like you."

"I want Jay to leave us the hell alone!" Zach lowered his voice when two gentlemen joined him and Dex in the gym's steam room. "Now that I returned the letter and refused her phone call, maybe she'll stop trying to contact me. I've moved on, Dex. Life is good. There is no room in my world for Jay."

"I feel you, but—"

"But what? You think I should've spared Jay's feelings? Did she spare mine when she paid that dude to smoke me? Did she give a damn about Jill's feelings when she kidnapped her in Jamaica and was seconds away from blowing her damn brains out?"

"Nah, Jay didn't care about anybody back then except herself."

"And right now, Zach only cares about Jill, our children, and the people who truly love us."

"I'm sorry, Jayla. I know this is hard for you, but you mustn't lose your faith. God is able to heal all diseases, and He is a comforter."

"Why is God punishing me, Pastor Monroe? I've confessed all my sins and repented." Jay wiped her tears with a flimsy tissue. "I reached out to my brother. He won't take my phone calls. Look at this." From her breast pocket, Jay removed the unopened letter Zach had sent back to the prison. "He didn't even open it!"

The pastor pulled a distraught Jay into his arms. "I will pray for reconciliation between you and Zachary. But right now, your health is more important."

"I know. The doctor prescribed a new medication for me. He wants to do some more blood work and testing in two weeks to see if my kidneys have responded to the new treatment. I don't wanna die, Pastor. I want God to heal me."

"He will if we only believe. Bow your head, Jayla. I want to pray for you."

Pastor Monroe prayed for Jay with her still nestled in his arms. With each soothing word, she felt a semblance of relief. Her tears subsided as she envisioned the doctor giving her good news about her health in the weeks to come. But in the midst of the spiritual moment, thoughts surfaced of Zach and how he had rejected her genuine remorse. How could he have been so cruel? She had forgiven him and Jill for their betrayal. Why were they still holding on to the past and what she had done to them? They had unforgiving spirits. Jay was serving a total of seventeen years in prison for ordering a hit on Zach and escaping from jail. Wasn't that punishment enough?

"God bless you, Jayla," she heard Pastor Monroe say. He dropped his arms to his sides.

"Thank you for your listening ear and a shoulder to cry on. And most of all, thanks for praying for me once again. I always feel better after one of your prayers."

The pastor smiled, and for the first time, Jay noticed how handsome he was. Shanika was right. For a white dude, he was delicious eye candy. Jay couldn't remember the last time she had been attracted to any member of the opposite sex. It was probably way back in sixth grade, when she'd had a crush on Tyrone Williams III. That was a long time ago. And she had never had sexual intercourse with a man in her life. Jay blinked and shook her head to redirect her thoughts. Satan was causing her sudden attraction to Pastor Monroe. He was tempting her.

"Are you all right, Jayla? Should I call for the nurse?"

"Yes, sir. Um, I mean, no, sir." Jay closed her eyes and shook her head again, totally confused. "I don't need the nurse. I'm fine."

"I could stay a little longer with you. We can read some Scriptures."

"I would like that."

Jay was excited about her visit from Aunt Jackie. It had been over six months since she'd last made the trip to the North Georgia prison. Her aunt was the only person other than Pastor Monroe who was on Jay's visitation list. Her father, Reverend Wallace F. King, had requested to visit her several times during her early days at Leesworth. Each time, Jay had refused to put him on her visitation list. Since her spiritual conversion, she had written a letter to her father in Raleigh, North Carolina, asking for his forgiveness for the many years she had hated him because of her mother's death.

Reverend King had killed his wife of ten years by putting a bullet in her heart, but it was a mistake. Belva Jayne King had been accidentally killed by her husband in an act of jealous rage. He had discovered his wife having sex in a hotel room one afternoon with his best friend, Claudius Henry. The good reverend had every intention of wounding his lowdown friend, but not his wife. The first lady was shot by accident.

Over the years, Jay had heard the story of that tragic day many times from family members. They'd all told her that her father had not intentionally killed her mother, but she had harbored hatred for him in her heart anyway. She had no memories of her beautiful mother. Jay had been only 2 years old when she'd died. Nearly thirty-two years later, she was ready to release the bitterness she had for her father and establish a relationship with him. It was time to let go of the past and move forward.

"King, your visitor is here. Let's go."

Jay snapped from her thoughts about her estranged father and left her cell with the guard. She followed the white stocky dude to the visitation area.

Aunt Jackie was hard to miss. She was a full-figured chick, but she had great fashion sense. Dressed in a bright orange jogging suit, her flawless coffee complexion glowed. Her salt-and-pepper sister locks had grown down her back. That pretty smile Aunt Jackie always had for Jay whenever she visited brought tears to her eyes.

"I'm glad to see you, Auntie. You look so good." Jay hugged her aunt tight and kissed her plump cheek. "You smell good, too."

"Thank you, Jay. I'm glad to see you too. How are you, baby?"

"I'm hanging in here as best I can. Let's sit down."

Jay and Aunt Jackie found a table in the middle of the crowded visitation room and took seats. They talked non-stop for the first hour of the two-hour visit. Aunt Jackie brought Jay up to speed on Uncle Bubba, Aunt Hattie Jean, Aunt Bertha, and a few other relatives. She didn't mention a word about Zach, Jill, or their children. She didn't speak about Jay's daughter, Nahima, either. That precious child had become an off-limits subject over the years.

"Someday, I hope to have a relationship with Zach, Jill, and my niece and nephew. I'm praying for their forgiveness. I would also like Nahima to know who I am when she gets older. She's my daughter no matter how much I've denied her. I was such a fool."

"You can't change the past. All we have is today. When Nahima is older and mature enough to handle the truth, it'll be up to Venus and Charles to decide if she should learn anything about you. They are her legal parents. As far as Zach and Jill are concerned, it's gonna take a miracle to bring you all back together."

"Well, I happen to believe in miracles."

"You are a miracle. Everything about you has changed. If God changed your heart, He can do anything. You even look different. I love how you're letting your hair grow out. It's pretty."

Jay raked her fingers through her naturally wavy hair. For many years she'd worn it cropped and tapered close to her head. Today it rested on her shoulders in a mass of thick black waves parted down the middle. "I don't trust the bootleg barbers and hairstylists here. I manage my hair on my own."

"Well, I like it. How is your health? Is the new medicine working?"

"I'm not sure. I feel okay today. I'll see the doctor next week. Say a prayer that he'll have good news for me."

Chapter Four

"Nooo!" Jay screamed and sat straight up in her bed.

She looked around her cell, shaking and breathing like she'd just run a marathon. Tears blurred her vision as she stared into the darkness. Jay bit down on her lip to hold back her sobs. The thin prison sheet clung to her body, drenched with perspiration. How many nights would she dream the same horrific dream? Was God trying to tell her something? For the fourth night in a row, Jay had been snatched from a restless sleep because of a recurring nightmare. The vivid, true-to-life scene of her dying alone in a hospital prison terrified her. She could not see Zach, Jill, nor Venus, but their voices—mocking her with laughter—were relentless.

Jay shivered against a sudden chill. She closed her eyes as she recalled the details of her nightmare. She had been charged with falsifying Leesworth's financial records. All of the money withheld from the inmates had been discovered in an account at a small bank in Atlanta with her name on it. Over $10,000 stolen from the prison's miscellaneous fund had been traced to the account as well. Jay had been sentenced to five additional years at Leesworth because of it. Aunt Jackie no longer wanted to be a part of her life. She was disappointed with Jay for stealing from her fellow inmates. No one believed she'd been set up, not even Pastor Monroe. He had also turned his back on Jay. She was left with no one to care for her while she slowly died a miserable death from cirrhosis of the liver and kidney failure.

In the dream, Jay lay helpless and frail, chained to a hospital bed, dying alone. Taunting and harsh words from Zach, Jill, and Venus floated around her lonely hospital room, followed by laughter. They were mocking her, finding pleasure in her demise. Even Nahima came to Jay as a baby in the dream every night. She cried and whined nonstop at the top of her little lungs. The whimpering and wailing was annoying, punishing even.

"Why is this happening?" Jay cried. She pulled her knees up to her chest and wrapped her arms around them. Rocking back and forth, she sobbed into the silent darkness. "God, please help me. I'm not a sinner anymore. I haven't done anything wrong. Please deliver me from hurt, harm, and evil."

"Come on in, Ms. King, and have a seat."

Jay eyed Mr. Callahan, the prison warden, suspiciously. She took a seat in one of the wingback chairs facing his desk. "Captain Floyd said you wanted to see me. Is there something wrong, sir?"

"I don't know. Is there?"

Suddenly, Jay's lips and throat felt extremely dry. She was thirsty, but due to the condition of her kidneys, her liquid intake was limited. She would sell locks of her hair for a cool glass of water right now. Jay cleared her throat. Her eyes rested on her hands folded on her lap. "If this is about the expenditure report, I promise you it's correct. All the highlighted areas represent errors I found in the accounting. They're not my errors, though. Someone upstairs in the business office doesn't know how to add. They should learn how to categorize transactions, too." Jay laughed nervously. "They don't seem to know the difference between expenditures, income, and profits."

The warden stood from his seat behind his desk and stuffed his hands inside his pants pockets. "So, you found errors and corrected them?"

"Yes, sir, I did. The funny thing is whoever made all the mistakes cheated us inmates outta a lotta wages. I indicated that in my report with red ink."

"I guess I should thank you for bringing the matter to my attention. I was totally unaware of the inefficiency in the business office." The warden rounded his desk and extended his hand to Jay. "I appreciate your hard work and honesty, Ms. King."

Jay stared at Warden Callahan's hand for a few seconds and blinked before she took it. She lifted her eyes to stare into the warden's face. He was a middle-aged brother, handsome by most women's standards. He was a typical Kappa pretty boy with fair skin and curly hair. Standing over six feet tall, he was usually even-tempered and pleasant. When Warden Callahan rubbed the back of Jay's flesh with the pad of his thumb, she slid her hand free from his grip.

"Is that all, sir?"

"For now. I'll keep a closer eye on the business office personnel from here on out. Don't worry about the inmates' wages. I'll make sure they get what they deserve."

Jay left Warden Callahan's office and headed back downstairs to her small workspace. She couldn't exactly call it an office. It used to be a supply closet. But at least inside of her makeshift office she did accurate work and kept impeccable records. Those dummies upstairs in the business office couldn't even do basic math. For seventy-one cents an hour, Jay performed all of her duties to perfection and corrected their countless mistakes. Maybe there would be an improvement in their work now that she had brought their shortcomings to Warden Callahan's attention.

Nahima was in possession of the ball, dribbling it carefully down the soccer field toward the goal. She was a bit clumsy, but she was far ahead of her closest opponent. Scoring a goal was inevitable. Zach could feel it in the pit of his stomach. He jumped up with his 2-year-old daughter, Zion, in his arms. "Stay with it, pumpkin! You're almost there!"

"She's gonna score, man! Look at her!" Dex shaded his eyes from the sun with his hand.

Venus placed both her hands over her mouth and watched her little girl run and kick the ball with the inside of her foot. It went past a little chubby boy's slow defensive effort and into the goal. Venus screamed and pumped her fist in the air. "That's my baby!"

"What about me? I'm her daddy. I taught her that move." Charles Morris Jr. kissed his wife on the cheek and started clapping his hands. He smiled and stuck his chest out a few inches with obvious pride. "Way to go, Nahima! You did it just like Daddy showed you."

Zach looked at his two friends with admiration. They were raising his biological niece with all the love they would give to their own child. Nahima Angelique Lawson Morris was 7 years old. Her short and innocent life had been plagued by controversy and chaos, but she was oblivious to all of it. Zach had made certain that his niece never experienced a single moment of pain or confusion because of the circumstances of her conception.

For four years, Jay and Venus had lived together as lovers. Nahima was supposed to have been their love child. Thousands of dollars, careful consideration, and planning had gone into her conception. Jay's eggs were fertilized with sperm donated by Venus's cousin, Whitaker. Then the zygotes were implanted in Venus's barren womb via in vitro fertilization. This ensured that

Nahima would be biologically connected to both Jay and Venus. That had been the plan from the very beginning. However, she was actually Jay's daughter.

As fate would have it, Venus eventually became Nahima's permanent and legal guardian after she and Jay went through a very bitter breakup, followed by a bogus lawsuit. A superior court judge had ordered Venus to pay Jay $25,000 to compensate for losses she'd encountered during their four-year relationship. The cost of the in vitro fertilization was also included in the judgment. Jay had only sued Venus out of spite and in retaliation to her severing all ties with her. The demise of their relationship had stemmed from Nahima's very complicated conception. Venus had wanted the child more than Jay had. Actually, Jay hadn't been interested in becoming a parent at all. She had only gone along with the deal to please Venus. But as the pregnancy progressed, Jay became jealous and more resistant to the idea of a child entering the scene. She'd realized she couldn't compete with a baby for Venus's affections and attention.

The untimely death of Venus's cousin, Whitaker, Nahima's biological father, had proved to be the breaking point. It caused Venus to go into premature labor, and Nahima was born by emergency cesarean section nine weeks early. While the baby fought to overcome major respiratory problems, Jay kept her distance from the hospital, leaving Venus alone to care for Nahima. But Zach was there through it all, overseeing his niece's care even after she was released from the hospital.

When Jay made no attempt to bond with her daughter or show any interest in her, Venus asked her to leave the home they'd shared for four years. Soon afterward, the lawsuit was filed. Once the judge awarded Jay a settlement, she left Atlanta for Jamaica, swearing she would never return. But she did four years later, when she'd learned Venus was engaged to marry Charles. Her intention had been to stop the wedding, but she'd failed. Jay had brought Jill with her to Atlanta, unaware that Zach had fallen in love with her while visiting them in Jamaica a few months earlier.

Against Zach's better judgment, he'd allowed Jay and Jill to live with him temporarily upon their relocation to Atlanta. His feelings and attraction for Jill began to flourish the moment she and his sister settled into his home. Several weeks after fighting temptation, Zach lost control one night in a moment of smoldering passion. He and Jill crossed the line, catapulting their once-innocent relationship into a steamy, forbidden affair. Neither of them had planned to betray Jay. It just happened.

Zach had only meant to comfort Jill after she'd overheard an extremely heated argument between him and his sister. Nahima had been at the root of the verbal exchange. Everything that Jay had withheld from Jill about the little girl came to light. Most significantly, Nahima's true pedigree was revealed. Before that night, Jill had believed the child was Zach's goddaughter. She'd had no idea that Nahima was Jay's biological child. It stunned Jill to no end how much Jay despised the little girl and blamed her for destroying her relationship with Venus. What kind of woman could hate her own child? The lies and secrets surrounding Nahima overtook Jill. She was an emotional wreck.

In an innocent and sincere attempt to console Jill, Zach's emotions and body betrayed him. He comforted her in the most effective and gratifying way a man could. Zach made sweet, passionate love to Jill. From that moment, they formed an unbreakable bond, which Jay considered the knife in her back. Everything that happened that fateful night between Zach, Jill, and Jay had been set into motion all because of the deep-seated bitterness toward an innocent and precious child. Nahima, according to Jay, represented everything that had ever gone wrong in her life. But today, the little girl was the recipient of lots of love from those who cared deeply for her.

Zach dismissed the unpleasant thoughts of the past as he watched Nahima's teammates shower her with congratulatory hugs and cheers. Her personal fan club, made up of her family and friends, celebrated her goal in rare form. Zachary Jr. was the leader of the pack. He worshipped his older cousin. They were very close. Their similar facial features were so striking that they could've easily passed for brother and sister rather than cousins. Nahima and Zachary Jr. shared the same caramel complexion, dark brown eyes, and naturally wavy hair. Their good looks had been handed down to Zach and Jay from their father, Reverend Wallace King.

Chapter Five

"Where are you going, Gavin? I thought you would stay in this morning because of the thunderstorm. It'll be raining cats and dogs all day, according to the weatherman. Come back to bed."

Gavin rushed to his sock drawer and searched through it until he found a pair of gray socks. He sat on the edge of the bed to put them on his feet. "Two of the inmates need me today. Ivy is appearing before the parole board as we speak. I must be there in case things don't go the way she'd like them to. Jayla is expecting test results from the doctor this afternoon. We've prayed for her healing, but God has the final word. Either way, she'll need me. She doesn't have anyone else. I'll be home after Bible study."

Holly snatched the covers from her body and scooted down the length of the bed to sit next to her husband. She kissed his cheek and rubbed his back. "I need you, sweetheart. Please come back to bed. We could spend the entire day together, and then you can go to the prison this evening for Bible study and prayer. I'll even go with you." She kissed him again and slid her hand from his back to his chest.

"I can't, Holly. We'll have to pretend like we're newlyweds some other time."

Gavin left the bed and went to the walk-in closet to find his shoes. He put them on. Holly watched him gather his wallet and prison identification badge and head for their bedroom door. She was disappointed, but not only with Gavin. Holly was disappointed with herself for not being able to be the kind of wife her husband deserved.

She and Gavin had been married for eighteen and a half years, and she had yet to give him the one thing he wanted more than anything else. Holly could not give her husband the baby he desired. According to a host of gynecologists and fertility specialists, there was no medical reason why she could not conceive a child. Other medical experts had tested Gavin more times than he had wanted, and they determined that he was capable of fathering a child. Their failure to successfully conceive remained a biological mystery.

Gavin and Holly had tried all they could, including in vitro fertilization, artificial insemination, and various fertility drugs. Nothing had worked. They'd considered adoption at one point but decided against it in favor of one final attempt at in vitro fertilization. When that failed, Gavin swore they would never again try anything other than natural conception. He told Holly if it was God's will for them to have a child, He would allow it to come to pass.

"I'll be home by seven." Gavin turned, placed a soft kiss on Holly's cheek, and patted the top of her head. "Don't bother to cook. I'll grab a salad on my way in."

"Oh, girl, I'm so happy for you!" Jay squeezed Ivy in a bear hug. "God heard and answered your prayer. You're a free woman! How does it feel?"

Ivy ran her hand over her long cornrows and smiled. "It feels like heaven! I can't wait to get outta this place. My sister and her boyfriend are on their way. We're gonna party like crazy tonight. My cousin, Tequila, is gonna hook me up with a weave and a fresh new outfit so we can hit Club Nuevo in Ridgewood. Some fine brother is gonna get him a piece of this ass tonight. It's been five years since I had a man inside of me."

"What are you talking about? What about your commitment to the Lord? It's because of Him that you were granted parole. How can you be so ungrateful?"

Ivy pushed Jay's hands away from her shoulders and glared at her. "I don't wanna hear that shit! I did what I had to do to get my ass up outta here. I sang some hymns and a few worship songs to make myself look good. I've been singing all my damn life in church, at parties, and in clubs. In here I did it for a white preacher and a bunch of fake-ass female convicts. My voice served its purpose. Hell, you even enjoyed it. You used to cry and shout every damn time I busted a note."

"So, it wasn't real?"

"It was real all right. It was real enough to convince the parole board that I deserved to get up outta here. I never should've been convicted in the first place. If I had been a dumb, blue-eyed blonde, nobody would've blamed me for putting a bullet in ol' dude's head. When a white woman shoots her abusive boyfriend, and he ends up paralyzed for life, she's a fucking hero. She walks free, writes self-help books, and appears on talk shows for the rest of her life. But not Ivy Leontine Maxwell, the black bitch from Bankhead. My young white court-appointed lawyer didn't give a damn about me. That's why them eight crackers and four Uncle Tom niggas found me guilty."

"But that's all in the past. You found Jesus right here in Leesworth. He set you free from your sins and from prison. Don't turn your back on Him, Ivy, please."

"Get away from me! I ain't trying to hear that shit. You keep reading the Bible and praying to God with that white preacher all you want. If you believe that nonsense, it's on you. If you were smart, you would be trying to find a way to get up outta here early, or them bad kidneys and fucked-up liver of yours are gonna kill you right here in this hellhole. Think about it." Ivy pointed her finger in Jay's face, less than an inch from her nose. "Use that white preacher like I did to get the hell outta here."

***

Dr. Yusuf did not have good news for Jay. Although her kidneys had improved slightly as a result of the new medication, her liver was a different story. The cirrhosis had spread from the right lobe of her liver to the quadrate lobe. Dr. Yusuf had prescribed a new medication to strengthen the other two lobes and something for depression before he left her alone in the examining room. He'd explained that he wanted to leave the prison ahead of the thunderstorm, which had been upgraded to a possible tornado. The kind middle-aged doctor from Pakistan may have left too late, though. The lights inside the building had flickered on and off several times while Jay was changing from a hospital gown back into her blue sweat suit.

She sat on the examining table and cried over her deteriorating health. A tap on the door startled her. "Come in."

The door opened slowly, and in walked Pastor Monroe. The sight of him wearing a sincere smile gave Jay a dose of comfort, but with it came a rush of tears. No matter how concerned or supportive the pastor was, he couldn't erase all the damage her years of heavy drinking had caused to her liver and kidneys. Jay doubled over and began to sob hysterically.

"It's going to be all right, Jayla," Pastor Monroe whispered soothingly, rushing to her side. "Tell me exactly what the doctor said."

"I'm gonna die in this place! I'll never get better because I was such an evil and manipulative person. My liver is in bad shape. I'm reap . . . reaping everything I sowed, Pastor." Jay stood and reached out to him.

Pastor Monroe gathered Jay in his arms. "It's okay to cry. Just let it all out, sweetheart. That's it. Weeping cleanses the soul. You have every right to cry."

Chapter Six

The lights in the examining room flickered a few more times before total darkness swallowed them. Jay was physically and emotionally drained. She collapsed in the comfort of Pastor Monroe's embrace. His biceps flexed as he tightened his arms around her trembling body. Jay felt the pastor's compassion for her state of mind. She sensed his concern for her health. Jay felt his love. It was what she needed more than anything at that moment. Her whole world was turned upside down. Besides Aunt Jackie, Pastor Monroe was the only person who cared about Jay. Everyone else had abandoned her, and it was her fault. She was responsible for Zach, Venus, and her father walking out of her life. And Nahima didn't even know who she was. It was what she'd wanted back then.

If only Jay could change the past and reverse the many bad decisions she'd made, her life would be so much different. Her worst mistake was rejecting Nahima. That precious child had been conceived by no act of her own. She was innocent and in no way responsible for the bad blood between Jay and Venus. Yet her mother, her biological mother, had chosen not to be a part of her life. But Venus hadn't. She'd loved, cherished, and nurtured the baby like she was God's greatest creation. And after all was said and done, she'd chosen Nahima over Jay.

Years later, Zach did the same thing by turning his back on his flesh and blood to be with Jill. That was real love. Actually, it was something far greater than love. Zach, Jill, and Venus had all willingly given their souls to another human being. For just once in her now-limited lifetime, Jay longed for someone who would value her enough to turn his back on the world, someone willing to ignore all things sacred and logical just to be with her. She needed that kind of love more than she needed her next breath. Jay needed an emotional and physical connection to someone who would reciprocate. And she was willing to do anything to have it.

Jay lifted her face so she could see Pastor Monroe's eyes, but the darkness was too thick. She inhaled the subtle scent of his aftershave lotion and closed her eyes. It felt good to be held. The gentle way the pastor rocked Jay in his arms gave her more than comfort. It was a gesture of compassion. He didn't care that she was a convicted criminal or what laws she had broken. It didn't matter to him, as he'd told her so many times. Pastor Monroe was a godly man, and she was a worthless criminal. Yet he had no reservations about showing her genuine affection.

Suddenly, Jay kissed the pastor full on his lips. It was an impulsive move, but also deliberate, calculated even. Her kiss was tender at first, then urgent and aggressive. Boldly, she eased her tongue inside his mouth. Pastor Monroe received it. He didn't pull away. His hands roamed from Jay's back, eventually finding her slender waist and then moving lower to her butt. He groped and squeezed it, pulling her body closer to his. Jay moaned when she felt the evidence of his desire pressing into her pelvis. She gasped and moaned into Pastor Monroe's mouth when the moisture of her arousal saturated the crotch of her panties. Jay was helpless and out of control. The new and unfamiliar sensations moving throughout her body both scared and excited her. The lights flickered on and off again, seconds before they spread brightness throughout the room.

"I'm sorry, Jayla." The pastor released her from his embrace and stepped away from her. "I didn't mean to . . . I was wrong. Please forgive me."

"No, it was my fault. I'm so emotional right now. My test results and the storm—"

"I'll leave you alone now," Pastor Monroe interrupted. His usual soothing and controlled voice had dropped to a mysterious bass tone. His breathing had become heavy and choppy. "I'm going to the chapel to pray and prepare for Bible study. I hope you'll be there."

The rhythm of Holly's heartbeat tripled. Her husband never failed to please her in bed. He was the only man she had ever been intimate with. She beamed with pride whenever she addressed the Sisterhood Ministry at church, constantly boasting that their pastor was her first and only love. Holly wondered how the women would react if she were to tell them just how skillful and thorough her husband was in bed.

Gavin's performance was exceptional on that stormy night. From the moment he exited the shower and joined Holly in their bed, he had been aroused and energetic like a stud. He was aggressive but pleasingly so. Holly couldn't recall the last time he'd performed oral sex on her. It had been a few anniversaries ago, if her memory served her correctly. Now as the rain continued to fall, Gavin's strokes in and out of her body seemed to match the rhythmic sounds of the drops pounding against the windowpane. Beads of sweat fell from his brow onto Holly's face. The moonlight peeping through the mini blinds allowed her to see Gavin's facial expression. It was intense and foreign. Everything about his countenance was different. His eyes bore into hers as if he were seeing her for the very first time. She felt special, rejuvenated.

Holly fell over the edge with pleasure. She screamed out her passion in a single word. "Gavin!"

Seconds later, she felt her husband release his seed into her womb. He groaned from deep within his gut. His climax was strong, rocking their bed as the storm continued to rage into the night. Gavin lifted his body and rolled away from Holly. Puzzled, she reached for him. She inched up behind him, pressing her body to his back. Gavin's entire body became tense when Holly wrapped her arms around him.

"I'm tired, Holly. It was a long day."

"I just wanted us to pray. This time it could happen, you know? Halle Berry had her first child at forty, and another one in her mid-forties. Kelly Preston and John Travolta had their third child when she forty-seven. And what about Diana Ross? She had two babies—"

"How many times have we gone over this? If God wants us to have a child, we will have one. I'd like to go to sleep now if you don't mind. I'm expected at the church at sunrise for men's fellowship."

It wasn't Jay's recurring nightmare that kept her awake that night. It wasn't the thunderstorm either. The disturbing news about her health had floated to the back of her mind, overshadowed by the passionate moment she'd shared with Pastor Monroe. The steamy memory would not let her rest. It had held her prisoner all through her prayer meeting and Bible study. The man of God whom Jay had grown to love and respect as her spiritual mentor had suddenly become the object of her desire. By some inexplicable force of nature, Jay, for the first time in her life, was sexually attracted to a man. It wasn't her imagination. Her feelings were real. There was an emotional and a physical connection stirring within, pulling her toward a man. But Pastor Monroe wasn't just any man. He was a good man and a pastor. And he was married.

Jay rolled over onto her back. It was quiet on the block. All of the other inmates were sleeping soundly while she was up trying to wrap her mind around what she had experienced with Pastor Monroe. Jay had kissed him. Yes, she had initiated contact with him, but he had returned her affection without hesitation. What had the kiss meant to him, though? Did he have secret intimate feelings for her?

Before their lips touched, Jay had never thought of the pastor as a man per se. Sure, Shanika thought he was good-looking. And maybe Jay had noticed his muscles and the size of his hands since her horny friend had pointed them out to her. But the thought of being intimate with the pastor had never crossed her mind before the kiss. And what a kiss it was. Just thinking back to the way Pastor Monroe had caressed her body and the feel of his tongue dancing with hers caused Jay to squirm. The new feelings she'd developed for the pastor were sinful. God was not pleased with the lust that had settled in her mind or her body. Now that she had tasted Pastor Monroe's brand of passion, she wanted more of it.

"Dear God, forgive me. I have sinned against you, my wife, and a troubled woman. Please remove from my flesh this lust I have for Jayla so that I may continue to minister to her and the other women at Leesworth as you have commanded. Strengthen me, so that I will forever live in your favor. Amen."

Pastor Monroe wiped the tears from his eyes and stood up. He had been kneeling in prayer at the altar inside his church since before dawn. After he'd made love to his wife the night before, sleep had escaped him. He'd wrestled with guilt, shame, and lust all night. It was horrible enough that he had kissed Jayla, but every time he looked at her during Bible study at the prison, he was reminded of the kiss they had shared, and he wanted to kiss her again. After the service, his sins followed him home and into his bedroom. While the pastor was making love to his wife, his mind was on Jayla. It was her pretty caramel-colored face he saw and her name he almost called out when he reached his climax. In his mind, he had made mad, sizzling love to Jayla last night. And although that thought disturbed him, it was the best sex he had ever experienced with Holly or any other woman before her. That single sinful moment with Jayla had inspired him to do things with his wife that he'd lost the desire for years ago. When it was all over, a sobering dose of guilt snatched Pastor Monroe away from his erotic fantasy. It wasn't Jayla, the woman he'd lusted for, whose eyes he looked into. Staring back at him was Holly, the woman God had blessed him with—his wife, whom he loved dearly.

As Pastor Monroe headed for his office in the back of the church to prepare for men's fellowship, he carried thoughts of Jayla with him. He had prayed and asked God to take away the lust he had for her. Only time would tell if He had.

Chapter Seven

"Nahima, can you answer the phone, pumpkin? Your little cousin has a loaded diaper. Uncle Z's hands are full."

Zach wrinkled his nose as he changed Zion's diaper. The toddler wiggled and whined, unhappy that her daddy was too slow at his task. She wanted to get down from the sofa to join Zachary Jr. in front of the television.

"It's Papa, Uncle Z. He wants to talk to you."

"I'm almost done."

Zach headed for the Diaper Genie to discard the smelly diaper, and Zion made a mad dash toward her big brother. Nahima handed her uncle the phone after he cleaned his hands with sanitizer.

"Talk to me, Pops."

Wallace King's first announcement to his son was a pleasant one. He had plans to visit Atlanta the following week to see Zach, Jill, and his three grandchildren. After that, father and son caught up on each other's lives since their last conversation a few days ago. Then Wallace dropped the bomb on Zach. On his way back home to Raleigh, he was going to Leesworth to visit Jay. She had placed his name on her visitation list, and Wallace had agreed to meet with her.

"Suit yourself. If you wanna subject yourself to Jay's abuse, then you go right ahead. Just don't call me crying when she spits in your face again."

"Jayla is not the person she was before, son. She's changed. I hear it in her voice. She begged for my forgiveness, and I obliged her. It was the Christian thing to do. And I am her father. I receive at least one letter a week from Jayla nowadays. Her faith is strong even though her health is on a slow decline. That's why it is so important that her family be reunited around her. Jayla needs me. She needs you too."

"Jay could have had me, Jill, and Nahima in her life, but she rejected us. She made a conscious decision to live her life without us in it. We've all accepted the situation and moved on. If you and Aunt Jackie wish to have a relationship with Jay, I won't stand in the way. But don't expect anything from Jill or me. We're fine without her."

"Is that you, King?" Shanika walked closer to Jay to check her out. "What's up with the new hairdo and jogging suit? And are you wearing makeup?"

"It's only a little mascara and lip gloss. I just felt like looking pretty today. So, I decided to check out the new hairstylist downstairs from C13." Jay shook her head from side to side. Her shiny, bone-straight tresses floated across her face. "What do you think?"

"She's pretty good. The sista's got you looking like a model. You kinda remind me of Will Smith's wife. I didn't realize your hair was that long. You should wear it straight more often instead of wavy and wild."

Jay smiled and ran her fingers through her hair. "I think I'll do that. Well, I'd better head to my office. I've got a lotta work to do. Warden Callahan is negotiating a deal with the CEO of the Kemp Corporation. They make shipping crates for a few major discount retail chains. If he lands the contract, there'll be better jobs for all of us around here. And better jobs mean more money."

"I'm on my way to the laundry room to do inventory. Thanks to you, Ms. Budget Queen, we got new blankets. Girl, you're a genius."

Jay ran her fingers through her hair one last time and wet her lips with the tip of her tongue before she knocked on the office door. She took a deep breath and released it slowly.

"Come in."

The sound of his voice was no longer just inspiring. It had become arousing. She heard it whispering her name in her dreams every night. The memory of its soothing richness distracted Jay at work and even when she attempted to read her daily Scriptures. Something was definitely wrong about her newfound attraction to Pastor Monroe, but it felt so right.

"Good afternoon," Jay said when she entered the room. She looked around to avoid eye contact with Pastor Monroe. "I'm sorry I'm late. There was a problem with that old copy machine upstairs, but Warden Callahan wanted the weekly vouchers today." She laughed nervously and tucked a few loose strands of hair behind her ear.

"That's okay. Have a seat so we can get started."

Jay sat in the chair in front of Pastor Monroe's desk. Her eyes rested on her Bible, which she held in her hand. To say that she was nervous only told half the story. Her heart was about to explode. She was frightened to death. There were so many questions that needed answers. Would they discuss the kiss, or would they both pretend it had never happened? Did the pastor have regrets, or had what they shared meant as much to him as it had to her?"

"We need to talk," they blurted out at the same time.

"You go first, Pastor Monroe."

"No, Jayla, I'd like to hear what you have to say."

Jay cleared her throat. "I . . . I can't explain why I kissed you. It just kinda happened. But it won't ever happen again, I promise, unless you want it to."

"I'm a married man. I'm also a pastor and a trusted professional counselor assigned to this facility. I should not have indulged you in any way. I owe you an apology. I'm very sorry for violating you. We both allowed our emotions to lead us down the wrong path. It must never happen again. Do you understand?"

"Yes, sir."

"Good. We're going to study from the book of Galatians today, but as usual, we'll start with confessions and prayer."

The sitcom Holly usually watched on Tuesday nights was a major disappointment. She'd prepared for her weekly dose of comedy with her nightly cup of cinnamon tea and a stack of English essays to grade in the den. With her wire-framed glasses perched on the edge of her nose, she skimmed her students' compositions, reading their ideas about the influence of social media on the baby boomer generation. Holly found the essays far more entertaining than her favorite sitcom. The story line lacked its usual quirkiness, and it was hard to follow.

Gavin had retreated to his study after dinner. He'd been quiet all evening after returning home from the prison. Something was bothering him. He couldn't fool Holly. She knew her husband better than anyone else. His mood was somber and his countenance distant. Everything was running smoothly at the church, so there had to be something going on with the women at Leesworth. Gavin's involvement with the inmates ran deep. They were much more to him than convicts. He considered the women to be his spiritual daughters or sisters. Whenever one of them had an issue, it affected Gavin a great deal. That was the type of man he was. He had a huge heart for the less fortunate. He went out of his way to help those who most people in his position would turn their backs on.

Yes, if one of the women at Leesworth had a problem, Gavin was on a mission to take care of it. Holly wanted to help him if she could. She abandoned the stack of essays and the television to join her husband in the study.

Holly tapped softly on the door before she entered the room. "Are you okay, honey?"

"I'm fine." Gavin looked up and offered her a half smile. "I'm preparing for my counseling session with my lone death row inmate tomorrow morning. She's a mother and grandmother. Her time is winding down. She's exhausted all of her appeals. The governor won't pardon her. Then there's service in the evening. We're still trying to find someone to replace Ivy. What a voice. We miss her terribly."

"Maybe I could come along and bring my guitar. I can't sing a lick, but—"

"No, not tomorrow." Gavin sat up straight in his chair, shaking his head.

"And why not?"

"Um, you haven't been cleared yet. And . . . and I haven't prepared the women. Some of them are really shy. Thanks for offering, but let's make plans for you to join us later. Maybe one day next month?"

"Okay. Whatever you think is best, Gavin."

Chapter Eight

"Shanika, what were you doing in Captain Floyd's office? And what took you so long?"

"You don't wanna know, Mother Teresa. Let's go eat."

Jay picked up her pace to catch up with her friend. "Were you in there having sex with him?"

"I was sealing a deal. I have a son to think about. My cousin ain't doing right by Malcolm. Until his daddy comes back from Afghanistan and moves him to Savannah with him and his wife, Shanika gotta do what she gotta do."

Jay snatched Shanika's arm and spun her around to face her. The two women stood toe-to-toe in the empty hallway. "You don't have to let Floyd use you for nickels and dimes, girl. He should be ashamed of himself. If Callahan ever finds out what he's doing—"

"Callahan? Are you serious? That dude has fucked more inmates up in here than Floyd, Jamison, and Rockwell put together. Leesworth ain't nothing but a well-organized brothel. Warden Callahan is everybody's pimp. You're the only chick up in here who ain't fucking somebody for something. But don't trip. Before you got all sanctified, I know you were licking Private Freeman. She was crazy about some King. You had that ugly bitch sprung."

"Lower your voice." Jay looked around. Luckily, they were still alone. "I did some things when I first got here that I'm not proud of, but I wasn't being manipulated."

"You were an inmate hooking up with a prison staff member, right?"

"Yeah."

"Then you were being manipulated just like me and every other chick up in here who's spreading her legs for some bastard in a uniform. Unless you're fucking for love, it don't mean a damn thing. You're just sealing some kinda deal."

As Jay and Shanika got closer to the cafeteria, they heard what sounded like a confrontation. It wasn't the regular mealtime chatter. Two inmates were screaming and cursing so loudly that they could be heard above everyone else. There were several other voices responding to it. Jay stopped at the door, but Shanika ran inside to check things out.

Two women—a Puerto Rican and a heavyset white chick—were up in each other's face. They were surrounded by a bunch of inmates who were cheering them on.

"I knew this was gonna happen sooner or later!" Shanika yelled over her shoulder at Jay. "Gomez and Clowers have been beefing for weeks."

Jay walked closer to Shanika. "What's up with them?"

"They just don't like each other. You know how it is. Gomez is the leader of the Hispanic chicks, and Clowers heads up the trailer-trash troop. Look at them. There's about to be a war up in here. Let's get our food. Odette and Erica are at our table."

"Okay, break it up, you two!" Corporal Jamison burst through the crowd and jumped between Gomez and Clowers, waving a metal defense baton high in the air. His towering stature was imposing as he stood between the much-shorter women. A few other guards followed him. They pushed back the huddle of women who were encouraging the fight.

"I'm coming for your ass later, Clowers! This shit ain't over, *mami!* You better watch your fucking back!"

"Come and get it, bitch, anytime! I ain't going nowhere! I've got seven to ten, baby. All I need is five minutes with you!"

Lust of the flesh, the single most powerful temptation known to humanity, had nearly destroyed many men before Pastor Monroe. Adam had eaten the apple offered to him by Eve out of weakness, changing God's divine plan for all mankind. David had fallen victim to his lust for Bathsheba. Because of his humiliating fall from grace, he penned the fifty-first Psalm. Sampson lost his locks of hair, wherein his strength lay, all because of the beautiful Delilah. Thousands of years later, Thomas Jefferson could not resist his desire for Sally Hemings any more than JFK could keep his hands off of Marilyn Monroe. Bill Clinton was impeached because Monica Lewinsky performed oral sex on him in the Oval Office and he chose to lie about it to the entire world. Tiger Woods had finally made a comeback on the greens, but his unquenchable thirst for multiple women had cost him his wife, millions of dollars, and respect.

Pastor Monroe did not want to follow in the footsteps of men who had been overcome by lust, but he was slowly being consumed. He recognized it. He felt himself losing the battle, but he had no control over it. He wanted Jay in a way he'd never wanted any other woman. She invaded his waking thoughts as well as his dreams. The part of her that was vulnerable and needed him was the magnet that pulled him deeper into her emotional clutches.

Jay was also very beautiful and shapely. A few days before, when she'd walked into his office wearing a new hairstyle and makeup, he nearly came unraveled. The whole time they studied Scriptures and discussed her upcoming visit with her father, Pastor Monroe's eyes were fixated on Jayla's lips and breasts. His imagination worked overtime, flashing scene after scene of him making love to her in every position possible. Nothing they'd read in the Scriptures or talked about could erase the fantasy.

The pastor's throbbing erection had lasted long after their counseling session ended. That was why he had decided to discontinue his private meetings with Jayla. Instead, Pastor Monroe had presented a proposal to the prison's board, asking permission to hold group sessions with her and four more of his Leesworth clients together. That way, he could still counsel Jayla as she continued working through her emotional issues, but he would be safe from temptation.

Pastor Monroe removed Jayla's chart from his file cabinet. Flipping through it, he wondered if she would be upset because of the decision he'd made regarding her private sessions. There was no need for an explanation. Jayla was well aware of what was happening between them. The fire that had been ignited by a single kiss was explosive. If the lights had not been restored, causing them to return to their senses, only God knows how far they would've gone. Pastor Monroe shuddered at the possibilities.

When Jayla had presented him with the option of kissing her again during their last meeting, he was tempted to take her in his arms again right then and there. Fortunately, his head took control over his weak flesh, and he told her that nothing like that could ever happen again. Although his words were in direct contradiction to his feelings, Pastor Monroe knew he had done the right thing. Somehow, he would make Jayla agree that group counseling would be better for both of them. Hopefully, today would be the last time they would ever meet alone.

The alarm blared in the middle of Jay's counseling session with Pastor Monroe. They had already discussed the discontinuation of private sessions in favor of group counseling. Jay was disappointed with the pastor's decision, but she agreed it was for the best. An important discussion was interrupted by the alarm and the warden's intercom announcement telling everyone to stay right where they were. They had been exploring some things that Pastor Monroe felt Jay needed to say to her father during his visit the following day. She was nervous, and the pastor had been encouraging her when the alarm first sounded.

Loud screaming and heavy footsteps running up and down the hallway scared Jay. It sounded like a riot. Pastor Monroe left his desk to lock the door. The commotion grew louder. Neither of them had any idea what was going on. Someone pounded on the locked door and gave it a hard kick. Jay screamed, ran behind Pastor Monroe's desk, and crouched down beside his chair.

Warden Callahan repeated his announcement. All inmates and prison staff were on lockdown. No one could enter or leave the building.

"What do you suppose is happening, Jayla?"

"I don't know. Maybe someone escaped or they found some serious contraband. It's so noisy out there. Is that a dog barking?"

"It sounds like it. This isn't good at all. I'd better call my wife to let her know I'll be late." Pastor Monroe picked up the phone from his desk and held it to his ear. There was no dial tone. Cell phones weren't allowed inside the prison, so as usual he had left his in his car. "The phones aren't working."

Jay gasped and covered her head when someone kicked the door several times. More voices and the sound of feet pounding against the floor echoed in the hallway. The dog was still barking, too.

"Jayla, get up from the floor, sweetheart. Go relax on the couch. You're safe with me. I won't let anything happen to you. We'll stay in here until the warden says it's safe to leave."

Jay did as Pastor Monroe had said. She took a seat on the couch on the other side of the room.

Chapter Nine

Thirty minutes had passed. The scene outside had obviously lost some of its fizzle. The dogs were no longer barking, and fewer people seemed to be roaming the hall. Warden Callahan had not given permission for anyone to move from their location. Less than ten minutes before, he had repeated his initial announcement to remain in place until further notice.

Jay and Pastor Monroe had resumed their session. Both were seated comfortably on the couch, engrossed in a role-play exercise. The pastor was pretending to be Jay's estranged father. He quietly listened to her explain why she needed him in her life.

"As a child, I often wondered what it would feel like to have a daddy at home to protect me. Uncle Bubba came around as often as he could, but it wasn't enough. He wasn't you. When Aunt Jackie married Uncle Julius, it was cool. He moved us into a house and spent lots of time with me."

"Was he kind to you?"

Jay nodded. "He was very kind to me and Zach. He took me to the father-daughter dance when I was in middle school. That was one of the best nights of my life. He gave me flowers and took me to dinner at Red Lobster." Jay smiled. "I made a bad grade on a math test once because I didn't study. I was too busy on the phone trying to hook up my best friend, Kara, with a dude named O.C."

"What happened when Aunt Jackie saw the failing grade?"

"She never saw it. Uncle Julius signed that sucker. Then we reviewed all my wrong answers and corrected them."

"Your Uncle Julius seems like he was a wonderful man."

"He was. And when he died, my whole world crumbled. I felt like everyone who had ever loved me left me for some reason. Either they died, went to prison, or in Zach's case, went away to school. I took it pretty hard when my brother left for college. If he had been around when Uncle Julius had his heart attack, I think I could've handled it better. I needed Zach, but he wasn't there. He came home for the funeral and then rushed right back to Tallahassee. I need him now too, but he hates me."

"How do you feel about Zach today?"

"It doesn't matter how I feel. I'm dead to him."

"What is your greatest fear?"

"I'm afraid that I'll die alone in prison without ever knowing how it feels to love somebody and have them love me back."

Pastor Monroe blinked. Jay's sincerity had touched him. She was vulnerable, honest, and open. She deserved to be loved, even if it was only for a little while. Her desire to be loved broke his resolve, and his need to love her took over. The overwhelming temptation and the visions of him loving her completely returned, but there was no way for him to escape this time. Pastor Monroe swallowed hard. It was a losing battle. He reached out and held Jayla's face gently with his hands. Her eyes closed, and he felt her body tremble at his touch.

"Love me," Jay whispered.

When their lips touched, the familiarity was there, but it felt like the very first time just the same. Slowly and methodically, Pastor Monroe snaked his tongue in and out of Jay's mouth while he fumbled with the buttons on her blue prison-issued shirt. Jay tugged away on his collar, determined to relieve him of his tie. The emergency alarm blared again, and Warden Callahan's voice followed. He repeated his instruction for all inmates and staff to remain in their current locations. Order had not been fully restored at Leesworth. Jay sighed and then moaned when Pastor Monroe fondled her bare right breast. They still had time. There would no interruptions.

Jay's shirt hit the floor. She threw her head back and tried to suppress her whimpers, but the feel of the pastor's wet, warm tongue licking her hardened nipples was driving her insane. Her fingers ran through his thick black hair as he worshipped one breast and then the other. Pastor Monroe stopped shortly to ease Jay onto her back, where her head relaxed comfortably on the couch's armrest. Then he lowered himself to his knees and removed Jay's loose-fitting jeans and plain white panties.

When she was completely naked, Pastor Monroe stood to his full height, his eyes never leaving Jay's body. Minutes, it seemed, ticked by. Neither of them spoke. If ever there was a moment to turn back, to say no and deny themselves the fulfillment of their cravings, surely it was now. Pastor Monroe closed his eyes as if listening and waiting for some sort of sign. He needed a reason not to take Jay as he had done in his dreams countless times. The way he felt about her and his appreciation for her naked body lying before him—ready and waiting—were good enough reasons to have his way with her. Knowing that what he wanted to do would go against his spiritual principles as a man, husband, and pastor no longer convicted him. Pastor Monroe was caught up. He wanted Jay, and he couldn't stop himself from having her. His faith was twisted, and he was helpless to make it right.

Jay reached her arms out, welcoming him, and that was all it took. Pastor Monroe stripped naked quickly. He positioned his body on top of Jay's, careful not to burden her with his full weight. Kissing and touching her smooth skin everywhere he pleased was more satisfying than he had imagined. The scent of foreplay filled the air in the small room. Its sweetness intensified his arousal. He had to taste her. In every dream, it was what he had done. Now that he had her in his arms, he wanted to execute every act he had envisioned.

Jay moaned out her pleasure. The pastor's lips and tongue kissing and licking her wetness were apparently too much. With each flick of his tongue, Jay seemed to soar higher. Sensations the likes of which Pastor Monroe had never experienced before caused his body to tingle and hum. Jay squirmed and purred as an invisible whirlwind swept them up and spun them around. They were on the edge, breathless and dancing in a rhythm so smooth and so sweet that she swore she was floating on air. And then it happened. Warm ripples of sheer satisfaction spread throughout her body, weaving through the feathery locks of her hair down to the soles of her feet. An orgasm of maximum gratification propelled her to the mountaintop.

As foreplay ended, preparing her for the main event, Pastor Monroe snaked up Jay's body. He kissed her deeply and passionately on her open mouth as he settled between her legs to enter her. She was wet, warm, and welcoming. He thrust his hardness at her entrance, and she extended the gap between her legs, wanting very much to feel him inside of her. Determined yet gentle, he pushed and rotated his hips to join them.

"I need to tell you—"

"Shh. I . . . I understand, sweetheart."

Did he? Jay closed her eyes. He had no idea. Grimacing against the pain but anticipating the pleasure, she lifted her hips to meet Pastor Monroe's powerful thrust.

He kissed Jay's lips the moment he buried himself inside of her. His lips left hers to place tender kisses on her cheeks, where tears trickled down her face. Pastor Monroe didn't move immediately. He paused to savor the moment they became one. The connection was more fulfilling than he had anticipated. Not even his wildest and most erotic fantasy could compare to the feeling of being joined flesh to flesh with Jay. As sinful and forbidden as adultery was, the contentment far outweighed the transgression for now. It was an out-of-body experience, one he'd cherish for life and never forget.

In Jay's teary eyes he saw her need to be loved, and in his heart, he had the capacity to oblige her, if only this once. With care he began to move slowly and gently in and out of her. Smooth and purposeful strokes intended to touch her soul were met by even thrusts. Gazes locked, searching deep inside of each other's hearts, only enhanced their lovemaking. The tight fit of their bodies was perfect. Jay's walls were filled to capacity, and her warmth and wetness captivated Pastor Monroe.

Jay's baby-like coos were released between kisses. Each time she looked into his steel gray eyes she saw raw desire. Pastor Monroe felt something real for her. She wasn't imagining it. Why else would he be making love to her right now? Jay reached up and held his face in her palms. This time when they kissed, her soul left her body. She cried out seconds before her body convulsed, quivering through another orgasm so strong that she felt sparks of electricity prickling every inch of her flesh.

"Jay . . . *Jayla!*" Pastor Monroe responded. "Oh, my sweet Jayla!" He kissed her eyes, nose, lips, and neck as he rode out the magnificent wave. "Mm, Jayla," he mumbled repeatedly through kisses.

Pastor Monroe rolled onto his back with Jay cradled to his chest like a precious treasure. He drifted off to sleep with her resting comfortably on top of his body, completely satiated. It seemed like merely seconds later that Warden Callahan's voice boomed over the speakers, announcing that the crisis was over. Inmates had ten minutes to report to their cells for a mandatory head count and lockdown.

Chapter Ten

Pastor Monroe rested his head against the wall of the shower as the hot water pounded against his body. Blood slid from his genitals, mixing in with the water, and vanished down the drain. He'd helped Jay clean herself as best he could with half a box of tissues from his desk. She kept apologizing for soiling the couch and scaring him to death. A lot of blood had poured down her thighs. Pastor Monroe wasn't sure what to make of it. Jay didn't offer an explanation either. They'd worked together in silence as guards marched up and down the hall, knocking on doors in search of inmates.

Fortunately, Jay was able to leave his office undetected. Pastor Monroe had stayed behind for nearly an hour trying desperately to gather his thoughts. He and Jay had made love. He accepted that. The guilt and shame of it all had not settled in yet. What he couldn't comprehend was the blood and the resistance he'd met at the onset of intercourse. Jay was a very beautiful woman in her mid-thirties. Surely she had been intimate with a man before, if not several men.

"Gavin, honey, are you okay? You've been in here for a while. Is everything all right?"

"I'm fine, Holly. I'm just meditating. Go back to bed."

"I watched the news. They reported on the massive fight at the prison until all of the women involved were separated and in isolation. I was worried sick about you. Why didn't you call me?"

Pastor Monroe turned the water off and stepped out of the shower. Holly handed him a black-and-white striped towel. "The phones were shut down. You know cell phones aren't allowed on the premises. I was never in harm's way. I was locked inside my office the entire time. The warden kept us informed over the security system."

"Were you afraid?"

"Why would I have been afraid? I was secure in my locked office. I fell asleep eventually. Before long, the warden announced that the coast was clear. I left the building and drove to the grocery store to buy some fruit. Now I'm home. Case closed."

Jay thanked Shanika for the three sanitary pads and tossed them on her cot. She turned and stood at attention in front of her cell, waiting to answer roll call. All the guards had funky attitudes. It wouldn't take much for them to throw someone in the hole for breathing too loud this evening. The fight between Gomez and Clowers had evolved into a prison-wide battle. For reasons unknown, dozens of inmates had jumped on one bandwagon or the other. Some were just fighting for the hell of it. There had been no real allegiance to Gomez or Clowers.

While Jay was making love with Pastor Monroe in his office, safe from all the chaos, her girls hadn't been so lucky. Odette and Erica were hiding out in the cleaning supply closet, sweating and on the brink of dehydration because of the heat. Shanika's situation wasn't as bad as theirs. She at least had the comfort of air conditioning and the television in the laundry room. Of course, she had locked the door to protect herself as well as Lizzie and Pat, the two older women she worked with. The three young white chicks who handled the steamer were scared to death. They cried and screamed every time someone tried to break into the laundry room to escape the madness.

Sophia was missing, though. Even now, as Jay and Shanika stood across the hall from each other waiting to be counted present for roll call, neither of them had any idea where the only Hispanic chick in their crew was. There was a strong possibility she had been mistakenly thrown into isolation with Gomez and her gang.

Sophia's mother was white, and her dad was Cuban. She was the spitting image of Mr. Mendez, and she spoke fluent Spanish. Gomez had been sweating her about hooking up with her gang, but Sophia wasn't down with them or the way they handled business at Leesworth. They were messy and always starting trouble. Gomez had been in more fights than any other inmate. Sophia was too cool to roll with her and her crew. She had just a year left on her ten-year sentence. Pastor Monroe was one of her biggest supporters. A lady in his church had already agreed to hire her at her restaurant once she was released. There was no way Sophia would jeopardize her freedom by associating with a menace like Gomez.

"King 187532368!"

"I'm present, sir!" Jay responded to her name and identification number.

Captain Floyd and two less-experienced guards marched down the hall, barking at all the inmates on C17. Everyone but Sophia was present and accounted for. And of course Clowers and her homegirls were missing in action, too. More than likely, they were all in isolation. The unlucky ones were probably in the infirmary if Gomez had gotten her hands on them. She was known to draw blood if given the opportunity.

Gomez and most of her crew lived on C19. The only thing Jay had heard about them was that they had started the brawl in the recreation room and decided to run and hide after it was over. They bombarded unauthorized areas of the building and fought some of the guards, too, before they finally came out of hiding and surrendered.

When the lights went out, Shanika whistled for Jay's attention. "We need to find out where Sophia is as soon as possible. Something ain't right. No one from the kitchen has seen our girl. She was at work when the fight first started. Where the hell could she be?"

"I don't know. I just hope God is watching over her."

"I do too. Hey, why did you need those girlie goodies from me? I thought you were on the rag two weeks ago."

"I don't know. I just started cramping all of a sudden. It's probably because of the stress from the fight. I was terrified."

"Oh yeah? Where did you hide out?"

"Oh, um, I was in counseling."

"You and the preacher were locked in his office?"

"Nah, nah . . . um, I took cover in his office. He managed to get out. I think he was upstairs with the warden. I'm not sure." Jay faked a yawn. "I'm sleepy, Shanika. Good night."

"I am too. Good night."

It was another restless night for Jay. The magnitude of what she had experienced in Pastor Monroe's arms came crashing down on her at once. It was heavy. Her emotions were mixed. She felt a sense of sinfulness mixed with satisfaction. She had embraced her womanly essence because it was new and refreshing, but she wanted to forget about the wantonness that came along with it. Jay didn't regret making love with Pastor Monroe, but she couldn't escape the guilt or shame of her sin.

Her faith and her relationship with God had sustained her over the past few months. Pastor Monroe had taught her to rely solely on the Word of God in every aspect of her life, no matter how grim things may appear.

But the instant he'd touched her and she'd begged him to love her, every morsel of her spirituality flew out the window. Apparently, the good pastor's Christianity did, too. They willingly crossed the line, dismissing their commitments to God. They'd risked getting caught, too. Jay forgot about her declining health, and Pastor Monroe gave no thought to his marriage.

And neither of them had remembered the importance of protection.

"Ah, my baby girl, I'm so glad you invited me here." Wallace allowed his tears to fall unchecked as he enfolded Jay in his arms. "I have prayed for this day."

"I'm happy that you agreed to see me, Daddy. It must've been difficult for you to come here after all I've done, and not just to Zach and Jill. I've been awful to you, too."

"Hush now, Jayla. I didn't come here to relive the past. I'm concerned about your health and your spiritual life." Wallace released Jay and took a step back. He smiled at her, although he was still crying.

Jay wiped her eyes and blew her nose with a tissue. She motioned toward a pair of vacant chairs at a table in the middle of the crowded visitation room. Wallace followed her. They greeted the other inmate and her visitors before they took their seats.

"My health is stable for the time being. The jury's still out on the new medication. I'll see Dr. Yusuf Wednesday afternoon. I'm praying for good news. Yes, my faith is still strong. What else do I have?"

"You have your father. I'm in it for the long haul. We've allowed too much time and pettiness to separate us. I'm sorry."

"You don't owe me any more apologies. I'm the one who's sorry. I've been such a fool over the years. I shredded every letter you wrote me. I spit in your face and cursed you when you visited me at my job in Atlanta. Then I showed out on you at the courthouse during my trial. Are you sure you're over all of my foolishness?"

Wallace smiled and squeezed Jay's hand. "The past is all forgiven and forgotten, Jayla. From this day forward, you and I will enjoy a fresh, new start after thirty-two long years."

Chapter Eleven

In light of the recent violence at Leesworth, Warden Callahan had issued a ban on all group gatherings with the exception of Bible study and prayer. The sewing club, reading circle, aerobics class, and all other group activities had been suspended until further notice from the warden. The proposal for group counseling that Pastor Monroe had submitted was denied, but he could continue individual sessions with his clients and services in the chapel under tight security.

Pastor Monroe crumpled the official denial and tossed it in the trashcan. He wanted to do the right thing. Group sessions would've been the perfect solution to ensure that he and Jay never found themselves alone again. It wouldn't have stopped him from thinking about her or suppressed his desire to make love to her again, but at least it would have limited their opportunities to touch each other. The fight had destroyed his plan to keep his distance from Jay while still providing her with the counseling she needed in a group setting. He couldn't close her case. Jay wasn't ready to be released from counseling yet. Her health issues were much too serious.

Was the counseling situation punishment for making love to Jay, or was it a test? Maybe God was giving Pastor Monroe a second chance to exercise faith and self-control where Jay was concerned. He was weak with lust. His feelings for Jay had become a thorn in his flesh. She was his greatest temptation, but he was determined to resist her at any cost. Prayer and meditation were the only ways to do that.

"It's not my business what you ladies do with your bodies around here. I've seen worse things than this since I've been at Leesworth. I've nursed nipple bites, rectal tears, and all kinds of sexually transmitted diseases. An inmate in C21 had a vibrator stuck so far up her tutti-frutti that she had to be hospitalized." Nurse Williamson clapped her hands and laughed.

"That's nasty." Jay frowned.

"What you have here are a few vaginal lacerations, honey. A little feminine balm should take care of them. It ain't my business how you got them. All I'm supposed to do is treat you. Here you are," she said, handing Jay a tube of generic vaginal ointment. "Apply it three times a day for the next few days or until you feel some relief. Warm compresses will help too."

"Thank you, Nurse Williamson."

"There's no need to thank me. I'm just doing my job. Dr. Yusuf will be in shortly."

Jay looked up from the spreadsheet on her desk, surprised to see Pastor Monroe in her office.

"I got permission to have our session outside near the garden. I hope you don't mind. It's a beautiful day. I thought a little walk would do us both some good."

"I don't mind."

Jay followed Pastor Monroe out into the hallway. They walked side by side in complete silence. When they reached the security office near the exit, Pastor Monroe displayed his ID badge and handed the permission slip to the guard. A female sergeant recorded Jay's inmate number and waved them through. She and the pastor walked outside into the balmy afternoon weather.

"How are you, Jayla?"

"I'm okay, I guess. I saw the doctor today. My health is pretty much the same. Nothing has changed over the last three and a half weeks."

"Did he do a full examination? I was concerned about you after we . . ."

"Oh, I talked to Nurse Williamson about that. She gave me a tube of cream."

Pastor Monroe nodded. Then he stopped walking. Jay did too. Their eyes met for the very first time since they'd made love.

"I didn't mean to hurt you."

"I know. I tried to tell you. I should've made you listen to me."

"What are you talking about, Jayla? What should you have told me?"

Jay looked around, uncertain of how to explain her situation. It was complicated. She wasn't sure how much she should reveal about her past life. Pastor Monroe had promised to never judge her about anything, no matter how unpleasant it was. Jay didn't want to tarnish his image of her. She had genuine feelings for him, and something told her he cared a great deal about her as well.

"Can we sit down over there?" Jay asked, pointing to a metal bench near the vegetable garden.

"Are you really okay? You can tell me the truth. I don't want any secrets between us." He placed his hand on the small of her back and led her to the bench.

"I tried to tell you that I had never been with a man before."

Shocked, Pastor Monroe stretched his eyes. "How is that possible? You're halfway through your thirties."

"I'm a lesbian, all right? At least I used to be." Jay broke down in tears. "I don't know anything anymore. All I'm sure about at this moment is the way I feel about you. I love you. I know I'm not supposed to, but I do."

"Dear God, Jayla, I had no idea. When I saw the blood, I assumed that it was because you had been celibate since you've been at Leesworth. This is terrible."

Jay searched his eyes. "So, you wish we hadn't made love? Because if that's what you're saying, it's worse than terrible! I thought you cared about me!" Jay stood abruptly. "I'm not some whore you can just use and toss aside like trash!"

"Please sit down. You're way off base. I didn't use you. And I've never thought of you as a whore."

"Then why did you say it was terrible, like you hate that it ever happened?"

"I have no regrets. I care very deeply for you. I shouldn't, but it's too late now. We've sinned, though. Awfully so, in fact. We can't continue to give way to our flesh. Do you understand that?"

Jay nodded and sniffed back tears. "What are we gonna do? I don't wanna sin, but I can't control the way I feel for you."

"We're going to confess our sins to God and never allow ourselves to be overcome by temptation again. No one can ever know what we did. There is too much at stake."

"What am I supposed to do with my feelings? Do you really think we can pretend that we never made love?"

"No, we can't. But we must do everything within our power, with the help of God, to make sure that we never make love again."

Chapter Twelve

Pastor Monroe's fingers weaved through Jay's full head of hair and massaged her scalp gently. He moaned and sang her name softly as she slithered her tongue up and down his dick. Her moist, hot mouth applied the perfect amount of pressure to make his toes curl. Over and over again, she alternated light to medium suction with expert snaking motions of her tongue. Her fingertips caressed his testicles lightly, enhancing his pleasure. She sucked the full length of him at a moderate tempo, like a sweet candy cane. The sounds her skills were causing him to make took her performance to the next level.

His body stiffened and Jay relaxed her cheeks and raised her head. She stood and straddled Pastor Monroe, who sat totally naked on the couch, trying to catch his breath. Jay rubbed her erect nipples across his open mouth. A faint purr rolled off her lips when he extended his tongue and circled her left areola. He sucked and teased it. Jay rubbed her drenched and swollen clit against the head of the pastor's penis, causing more of her moisture to gush forth like a waterfall. He grabbed her hips and pulled her center down toward his crotch. Carefully, he thrust his lower body upward to meet his target and slid inside of Jay.

Smooth and steady, their joint bodies rocked to their own rhythm. It was a timeless, unhurried ride. Jay rested her left cheek on the top of his head and held on. In sweet, slow motion, they danced the ancient dance of lovers and communicated their feelings with hums and grunts. When Jay's inner muscles began to contract, she threw her head back and belted out her love for the one and only man she'd ever shared her body with.

Pastor Monroe stood up, Jay still in his arms, without breaking the connection. He hurried to his desk and sat her on top of it. He pumped in and out of her body vigorously, like a freight train at maximum speed, until he released a rushing stream into her. For seconds, they were motionless, sweat pouring down their bodies. Only the sound of their ragged breathing floated about the room.

During their last counseling session, they'd prayed a prayer of forgiveness and vowed to never touch each other again. They were supposed to deny the desires of their bodies but never their feelings for one another. Pastor Monroe had had every intention of keeping his promise to God and his commitment to his wife, but he was too weak to resist Jay. One simple kiss sent him into a downward spiral, totally out of control. Moments later, he and Jay were naked in an embrace, loving each other like there would be no tomorrow.

Pastor Monroe found Holly in their bedroom, rocking in one of the companion recliners. The room was dark aside from the light of the muted television. When she opened her eyes, he immediately noticed how red and swollen they were. She had been crying.

"What's the matter, babe?" He reached down and stroked her cheek.

Holly reached inside the pocket of her yellow bathrobe and pulled something out. She handed it to her husband. It was a pregnancy test. Like the hundreds she had taken over their eighteen and a half years of marriage, it was negative. There would be no baby in the Monroe home anytime soon.

"We are good people, Gavin. We live just like the Bible says we should live. There are people out there who do not have a conscience. They are wicked! How can they have gobs of children, but we can't have just one, huh? I want a baby!"

"Calm down. In God's divine time, He will give us a child."

"I am a forty-one-year-old Christian woman who is married to a pastor. I have a master's degree. I'm a college professor, for Christ's sake! We live in a quarter-of-a-million-dollar home. We own stock in Disney, Proctor & Gamble, and Pepsi. There is enough money in our investment account to take care of a dozen children! Where is our baby?"

Holly's uncontrollable sobbing broke her husband's heart. It had been a couple of years since she'd reacted this way to a negative pregnancy test. He had no idea what had triggered such an emotional reaction this evening. She was hysterical.

Pastor Monroe kneeled next to the recliner and took her hand. "I know you've heard this speech more times than you care to recall, but you have to exercise faith. Abraham was a hundred years old and Sarah was ninety when God blessed them with Isaac."

Holly snatched her hand away. "I don't give a damn about Abraham or Sarah! I want a baby. Don't you understand? I feel like I'm losing my mind!"

Pastor Monroe lifted Holly from her seat and held her in his arms. She cried pitifully and melted into her husband's strength. When her sobs faded to whimpers, he carried Holly to their bed and laid her down. He sat on the side of the bed and rubbed her back until she fell asleep.

***

Although they never discussed it, Pastor Monroe and Jay finally stopped fighting their feelings for each other. There was an unspoken agreement between them. They were caught up in an outright whirlwind affair. Love had overruled everything, including their faith. Their counseling sessions had been replaced by hot and steamy sexual rendezvous every Wednesday afternoon. By the time Bible study rolled around in the evenings, they were on their knees asking God for forgiveness. Sin versus salvation was their ongoing struggle, but it was a secret to everyone else.

Poor Holly was clueless, fighting her own battles with infertility and depression. Her quest to give her husband the child he wanted was her top priority once again. Over the years, her efforts to become pregnant had often consumed her. Then there had been times when she totally left the situation in God's hands and exercised unwavering faith. Since the last negative pregnancy test results, she had transformed into a very desperate woman. Holly Monroe was once again obsessed with becoming pregnant, and her anxiety was wreaking havoc on her marriage. As her marriage suffered, the relationship between her husband and his prison lover flourished.

The once-dedicated pastor and husband took extreme measures to spend as much time at Leesworth with Jay as possible. Together they recruited new members for Another Chance Women's Fellowship, so their prayer and Bible study group was growing. A young recovering drug addict named Bria had replaced Ivy as the song leader. Sophia brought more Hispanic inmates into the group. She translated Pastor Monroe's sermons and lessons into Spanish so the new members could benefit from them. Even after she'd been beaten brutally in the Leesworth gang war for no reason, Sophia hobbled around on her broken leg, doing the Lord's work.

Pastor Monroe's outreach ministry at the prison was growing, but it was all for the wrong reasons. He and Jay were actively recruiting more inmates to divert attention from their affair, and it was working. While she walked around like a prison evangelist, witnessing to her fellow inmates about Jesus, no one suspected that she was screwing Pastor Monroe. Souls were being saved because of their efforts, but they were drifting further and further away from God.

"Professor Monroe, you do understand that this particular drug has not yet been approved by the Food and Drug Administration, don't you?"

"I understand, but I don't care."

"Some women in Canada and England have experienced success, but I must warn you that some extreme side effects have been recorded."

Holly sat up straight and slammed both of her palms on Dr. Cameron's desk. "Look, I have done my research. I know the risks. I'll take my chances. Give me the disclaimer so I can sign it. I want the damn drugs today!"

"Fine. I want to monitor you though. I insist. There is a clause in the disclaimer that spells it out in plain English. If I give you the injections, you must come in once a week for blood work and partial examinations. That's the only way I'll agree to this." The doctor handed Holly the five-page disclaimer.

She snatched it and rummaged through her purse for a pen but couldn't find one. Holly became visibly frustrated. She searched Dr. Cameron's desk frantically. He had extended his hand, offering her a pen, but she didn't notice his kind gesture until he cleared his throat.

"Thank you," Holly whispered, grabbing hold of the pen. She quickly flipped to the last page of the disclaimer

and scribbled her signature on the line. She stood and removed the jacket of her navy blue business suit and flung
it over the back of her chair. "I'm ready," she announced,
rolling up the sleeve of her white blouse.

For three weeks, Holly went to Dr. Cameron's office for
the fertility injections. Pastor Monroe was none the wiser.
He had his own secret life with Jay while Holly had hers
with the fertility specialist. Each had ventured off into
their private worlds. Holly was doing what she thought
would strengthen their marriage. The pastor's secret
indulgence strongly defied the principles of the life they
had built together. His affair was pulling him away from
Holly and gradually destroying their marriage. He was
so out of tune with what was going on with his wife that
he missed the changes in her physical and psychological
states.

In addition to the outbreak of irritating rashes all
over her arms and legs, she was experiencing a dramatic
downward shift in weight. She was having drastic mood
swings, too. Holly's students and colleagues had all taken
notice, but her sudden symptoms went completely over
Pastor Monroe's head. He'd missed the vaginal dryness,
too, because they'd only made love twice since the night
of the storm nearly two months ago. Holly's side effects
from the new fertility drugs slipped under her husband's
radar totally. That was, until the morning he found her
sprawled out on the floor of the master bathroom.

"Holly? Holly, what's wrong?" Pastor Monroe dropped
to his knees and pulled her into his arms. He pried her
eyes open with his fingers. Her pupils were dilated. Sweat
was streaming down her face. "Holly, wake up! Talk to
me!" He shook her and placed his ear to her mouth to see
if she was breathing.

"Mmm . . ." Her head rolled from side to side. She coughed. "Mmm . . . mmm . . ."

"Thank God! You're alive!"

Relieved that she was responsive, Pastor Monroe laid Holly carefully on her back so that she could continue to take in air. He rushed to the bedroom to call 911.

Chapter Thirteen

Pastor Monroe kissed Holly's moist forehead and stroked her pale cheek with the back of his hand. He turned to Martha, his mother-in-law. "I'll be back later this evening."

"Where are you going?"

"I'm late for work." He checked his watch. "I still have time to make it to my afternoon session if I hurry."

Martha stood and crossed the private hospital room. She stopped in front of her son-in-law. "What about your wife?" she asked, tilting her head in Holly's direction.

"The emergency physician said she'll be fine. I ought to sue Dr. Cameron for giving her experimental drugs without my permission. She could have died!"

"She's already dead emotionally because she can't give you a child. That's what this was all about, Gavin. She wants to have a baby, your baby."

"I know, but I never would've agreed to more fertility drugs, especially if they weren't FDA approved. I told Holly no more drugs! She and I had an agreement. I don't know my wife anymore. Her obsession to become pregnant has turned her into a lunatic. She's not the woman I married."

Martha placed her hand on Gavin's heart. "Yes, she is. Holly is the same young girl who stole your heart back in college. She loves you more than life itself. It was because of her that you were able to complete your graduate degree and build your ministry. Don't you understand?

My daughter loves you so much that she risked her life to give you the baby you've always wanted."

"Well, I never thought she would've taken it this far. We're not only partners in marriage. We were supposed to be partners in faith, too. Somewhere along the way Holly lost hers."

Pastor Monroe got to Leesworth a few minutes before prayer and Bible study was to begin. He'd called ahead and canceled all of his counseling appointments but confirmed that evening service in the chapel would go on as scheduled. After a long conversation with his mother-in-law, he decided to stick around the hospital just in case Holly woke up. She didn't. She rested peacefully throughout the day.

Bria, the new praise and worship leader, was standing at the front of the chapel, leading the women in the final verse of "Amazing Grace." Pastor Monroe rushed in and headed straight for the podium. When the song ended, Bria handed the microphone to the pastor and smiled.

"Good evening, my dear sisters and daughters in Christ. Forgive me for my tardiness. I had a family emergency. I solicit your prayers for my wife, Holly, this evening. She took ill early this morning and had to be rushed to the hospital." He paused when his eyes landed on Jay. Her gaze dropped to the floor. "Now please stand and recite the Believer's Confession with me."

Pastor Monroe paced the floor of his office impatiently. Jay had promised that she would find a way somehow to meet him there before she reported to her cell. He wanted to see her. His hands needed to touch her before his day ended.

The pastor looked up when he heard the doorknob turn. Jay slipped inside the room quietly. The second the door closed behind her, Pastor Monroe pulled her into his arms and kissed her hungrily. She threw her arms around his neck and returned his kiss with an urgency of her own. Then without warning, she wiggled and shoved him away.

Breathing heavily, he reached for her again. "Come here. I missed you today. I couldn't get you out of my mind."

"Gavin, stop it! Baby, we need to talk, and there ain't much time. I'm pregnant."

Jill let out a soft scream and pressed her hands to her chest. Someone knocking at the door frightened her. She did a swift about-face and looked into Zach's eyes. He smiled that smile at her that never failed to turn her on. Her pulse quickened. Jill ran to the front door of the dance studio to let Zach in.

"I didn't mean to scare you, baby. I wanted to surprise you." Zach looked around the room. "Where is the security guard?"

"It was time for him to leave. He tried to bully me into leaving too, but I refused. My creative juices were flowing. I thought you were hanging out with Dex."

"I'm gonna meet him and Charles at Floyd's House of Floetry for drinks and appetizers in a little while. I wanted to come by here and check up on my wife. I saw you doing your thang, baby! Can't nobody dance like you! But I don't like you here by yourself at night."

"Were you watching me dance?"

"Yep, and it gave me a woody, too. But don't change the subject. You shouldn't be here at night without Red or Marco around to protect you. This ain't Jamaica.

There're some sick fools roaming around the ATL. If they see a fine sista up in here shaking her ass all alone, they'll do anything to get at you. Promise me that you won't stay here by yourself again."

"I promise, Zachary, but I am a big girl. I can take care of myself, ya know?"

Zach shook his head, unwilling to budge on the issue. "I made a mistake once. It almost cost you your life. That ain't gonna happen again, not as long as I'm alive." He tapped Jill playfully on her ass. "Come on, let me walk you to your car. After I hang out with my boys for a few hours, I'm coming home to do some nasty shit to you."

Aunt Jackie never missed choir rehearsal. Even if it was an extra one that Brother Slocomb, the eccentric minister of music at Refuge Pentecostal Temple, suddenly sprung on them, Jackie Dudley Brown showed up. But this particular Saturday morning she would be a no-show. Jay had called Thursday afternoon from Leesworth, completely distraught. She'd been bawling so hard that Aunt Jackie couldn't make out what she was trying to tell her.

Jayla Simone King was not a crier. Anyone who truly knew her could say amen to that. Jay was simply an unemotional person with a strong will. Whenever she had lowered her guard and expressed her feelings in the past, it was explosive anger. Very seldom did she display sadness. It went against her nature. So, when she called Aunt Jackie, crying and stumbling over her words, she knew something was terribly wrong. She agreed to make the trip to Leesworth Saturday morning to check on her niece.

Aunt Jackie had called and spoken with Wallace to see if he had any idea what was going on with Jay. He didn't have a clue. Obviously, Zach had no idea what was up with his sister either, but he got a call too. As expected, he didn't want to discuss anything about Jay. He did, however, offer to take Aunt Jackie's Buick LaCrosse for a tune-up and tire rotation at the dealership before the long drive. He slipped her some pocket money, too, when he came back with her whip in tip-top shape.

"Please be careful, Auntie. And don't be speeding. For what it's worth, I hope Jay's okay. Don't tell her I said that, but I really mean it."

"All right. I'll call you when I arrive at the prison."

"And you better call me when you're heading back, too. You know how much I worry about you." Zach pecked his aunt on her plump cheek.

"Yes, sir," she said and started laughing.

Chapter Fourteen

Jay looked like certified crap when Aunt Jackie first laid eyes on her. She hurried over to her niece and threw her stubby arms around her. A round of heartfelt sobs overtook Jay when her aunt embraced her. She was pitiful and unable to speak for a while. She rested her head on Aunt Jackie's shoulder and cried like a baby.

"Come, Jay, let's sit down and talk. Auntie is here."

Hand in hand, they searched the visitation room for two chairs. Jay's body was shaking like a leaf on a tree. Aunt Jackie tightened her grip on her hand and led her to the back of the room. An inmate and her two visitors were looking through a stack of pictures. Their entire conversation was in Spanish. Aunt Jackie waved and smiled at them before she sat down. Jay slumped down in the chair next to her aunt.

"Okay now, what are all those tears for?"

Jay rubbed both hands down her face, wiping away moisture from her eyes and nose as best she could. "I messed up. I really did it this time, Aunt Jackie. Even in prison, I've managed to do the worst possible thing ever. I was born a complete failure. No wonder everybody leaves me behind. They know I'll eventually screw up their lives one way or another."

"You're not making any sense, sweet pea. Take a deep breath and tell Auntie what it is you've done that's so terrible."

Jay did a visual sweep around the room. She didn't want anyone to hear her revelation. So far, she, Pastor Monroe, and Nurse Williamson were the only two people at Leesworth who knew about her pregnancy. She hadn't even told Dr. Yusuf yet, although Pastor Monroe had begged her to. She blew out a shaky breath and lowered her head. "I'm pregnant. God have mercy on me, I'm seven weeks pregnant!"

"What? You can't be! How in the world did that happen? Were you raped?"

"Nobody raped me. I got involved with someone. I won't tell you who he is, so don't even ask me. I need you to promise me that you won't tell anyone. I haven't made up my mind what I'm gonna do yet."

"Honey," Aunt Jackie whispered, squeezing her niece's badly damaged hand, "what are your choices? You can't raise a baby in prison, and I know you're not considering having an abortion."

Jay removed her hand from her aunt's grasp and looked away. "Are you judging me? You have no idea how I feel, so don't be judging me. You don't have a right to do that."

"I ain't judging you, chile. I'm in shock. But even so, I don't want you to have an abortion. We're Christian folk. We don't believe in killing babies."

"But I don't wanna ruin the father's life. He's married but he loves me, Aunt Jackie. I love him too, more than I thought was possible. We didn't mean to fall in love. It just happened. Now I know exactly how Zach felt about Jill. Some things in life are beyond our control."

"Does he love you enough to take your child and raise it if you decide to go through with the pregnancy?"

"We haven't talked about that yet. I'm not sure if I wanna put that kinda pressure on him. Like I told you, he's married. And his wife has been sick recently. Asking him to take his outside child home to his wife is pretty heavy. We'll discuss our situation Monday and make a decision. There's one thing I won't agree to under any circumstances though."

"And what's that?"

"I won't expose him. I love him too much to ruin his life. If anyone finds out what we've done, he will lose everything. Before I reveal the name of my child's father, I'll terminate the pregnancy."

Pastor Monroe tucked an extra pillow under Holly's head and kissed her cheek. "Have a good night, babe."

"Won't you lie with me for a while?"

"I'm not sleepy. I'll be tossing and turning. You'll never fall asleep with me in here. I'm going in the den to watch Trinity Broadcast Network. Somebody's preaching a good sermon tonight, I'm sure."

Holly sat up. "You're still angry with me. Don't deny it, Gavin. Ever since I left the hospital, you've been moping around and keeping your distance from me. I was wrong to take those fertility injections, but I've apologized a thousand times. When are you going to get over it?"

"I am over it already, Holly. I'm just wondering what I'll have to get over the next time you decide to try something stupid to get pregnant."

"Nothing. I'm done. I really mean it this time. If we can't conceive a child the regular, old-fashioned way, then we won't have one at all."

"I'm glad you've come to your senses. Another episode like your latest one would've driven me right out the door." Pastor Monroe sighed and walked toward the bedroom door. "Get some rest. I'll see you in the morning."

He headed for the den, but not to watch the Trinity Broadcast Network. He definitely needed a Word from the Lord, but it would've fallen on deaf ears. Pastor Monroe was too distracted to receive a sermon. His dilemma with Jay and her pregnancy were consuming him. Here she was, carrying his child after a very brief affair, but in eighteen and a half years of marriage, Holly hadn't become pregnant a single time. Finally he had fathered a child, but it was with the wrong woman, and the circumstances were totally screwed up. There was no way that he and Jay could have a child together. It would destroy his ministry and his marriage. He would lose his counseling license, too. But how could he kill his baby?

Running his fingers through his hair in frustration, Pastor Monroe took a seat on the sofa. He sat in complete darkness, weighing the limited options he and Jay had. Abortion was still a very reasonable possibility. Or maybe her aunt would be willing to take the baby and raise it. Her father and his wife could take responsibility for the child as well if they wanted to. Regardless, Jay would eventually have to reveal the name of her child's father to the officials at Leesworth. The fact that she was an inmate would require that she do so. There would be a thorough investigation. Ethics charges would be brought against him for participating in a sexual relationship with an inmate committed to the penal system in the state of Georgia. If that were to happen, he would lose everything . . . but he would finally have a child.

Jay read the note from Warden Callahan attached to an in-house funds request. What he had asked her to do didn't make sense. He wanted her to approve and release the money for 1,000 new blankets. Then she was expected to submit the request to the purchasing clerk to have a $3,100 check cut and made payable to the Odyssey Supper Club in Buckhead.

For starters, all Leesworth inmates had just received new blankets a couple of months before. And why $3,100? The prison had only paid the Army Surplus Warehouse a dollar and a quarter apiece for the 2,100 new blankets. Jay couldn't even imagine why the check would go to some fancy Buckhead establishment. Callahan was obviously up to no good again. Not only did he like to roll around between the sheets with pretty inmates, but he didn't have a problem stealing their hard-earned wages, too.

Like all the other questionable financial transactions that had come across Jay's desk, she marked it with a special symbol and logged it in her personal journal. Then she headed downstairs to the outdated Xerox machine to make a copy for her records.

Chapter Fifteen

"You worry too much, Zach. It's just a little tingling in my left arm and shoulder. My carpal tunnel syndrome is probably coming back. I've already made an appointment with Dr. Troutman. He'll see me tomorrow morning at nine fifteen." Aunt Jackie bent over and picked up the sprinkler off the ground.

Zach continued his lecture in her ear through the Bluetooth he'd bought her for Christmas. "I'm worried about you. You need to take better care of yourself. Jill and I want you around to watch the kids grow up. They need their nana. What happened with that diet you were on? You were doing so well."

Aunt Jackie repositioned the sprinkler on the other side of her yard and turned it on. She let out a high-pitched shriek and wobbled away from the spray of water as fast as she could. "Boy, don't you start talking about my weight now! I have big bones like my mama. Not everybody was meant to be skinny like my daddy and Belva."

"My mom was petite, but I don't expect you to ever be skinny, Auntie. I just want you healthy. From now on, I'm gonna pick you up every Tuesday and Thursday so you can come and work out at the gym with me."

"I ain't going to the gym with a bunch of health fanatics. I'm outside right now getting some fresh air and exercise. You're acting like I'm ninety-five years old and weigh five hundred pounds. Remember, I'm only a few years older than you, Zach. And I wear my size twenty-two figure well, thank you very much. To be honest, I think the trip to Leesworth and back wore me out. That's all. You never asked me how Jay was doing."

"I sure didn't."

"Your sister is dealing with some serious issues right now. I really wish you would reach out to her. Jay needs all the support she can get."

"Jay doesn't need me. She has you, my father, and Jesus. She'll be all right."

A few minutes later, Aunt Jackie ended her call with Zach. With God's help, she had kept Jay's secret as she'd promised. She almost blurted it out a couple of times during the conversation. It wasn't easy holding something as sensitive as a jailhouse pregnancy, of all things, locked up inside. The stress was weighing Aunt Jackie down. She didn't know how much longer she could deal with it by herself. At times she felt like she would explode if she didn't reach out to someone for help, but Jay had confided in her about her pregnancy, and she'd begged her not to tell a soul. Therefore, Aunt Jackie was bound by her word. The only person she was able to talk to about Jay's problem was the Lord, and she had been wearing His ear out. Every time she thought about her niece walking around in prison carrying some slick, no-good married man's baby, tears came to her eyes. All she could do was pray.

Mrs. Taylor, Aunt Jackie's busybody neighbor, came out on her front porch. That was her cue to go back inside her house. She waved at the older woman and started toward her steps.

Like a bolt of lightning, the tingling in her left arm and shoulder hit her, but it was different from all the other times. It hurt and she couldn't breathe. The sharp stabs of pain spread from Aunt Jackie's arm to her chest. She tried to yell out to Mrs. Taylor for help, but she couldn't. The earth was spinning out of control, and all the air was leaving her lungs. Her meaty legs suddenly became rubbery and gave way. She fell forward in the grass. The water from the sprinkler fell down on her like rain.

"Jackie, are you all right, sugar?" Mrs. Taylor hurried down her steps, leaning on her wooden cane. "Carl Lee, call 911!" she yelled over her shoulder toward her front door. "Hurry up! Something is wrong with Jackie over here!"

Pastor Monroe rubbed his hand over Jay's flat belly and kissed her lips. "You have great faith in your aunt. I'm glad to know that she can be trusted, but I think you're fooling yourself about the warden. He won't thumb his nose at an inmate who managed to get pregnant in his prison. That's a very serious matter. Every man on his staff will be a suspect. They won't take too well to the suspicion. There'll be all kinds of rumors and finger-pointing. Things are bound to get ugly around here."

"I still won't tell Callahan anything, no matter what. He won't be able to force me to talk. Trust me."

"How are you so sure? Where is all of this newfound confidence coming from?"

"I know certain things about Callahan," Jay said, sitting up. She slid her arms through the sleeves of her shirt. "I've got enough stuff on him to make him keep away from me for the rest of my sentence. He'll be afraid to even speak to me. Callahan is foul. He operates a crooked prison, and I can prove it."

"I hope you're right."

"Stop worrying, Gavin. I got you. Don't you know how much I love you? I'll never expose you. Just promise me that you'll always be a part of our child's life."

"Of course I will, but I'll have to go through your aunt. And Holly can't ever find out."

"You won't have to worry about Aunt Jackie. Our secret will be safe with her. She'll allow you to see our baby whenever you want to. You can be the godfather." Jay laughed.

Pastor Monroe laced his fingers through Jay's on her left hand and held their hands to his lips. He kissed her knuckles. "What do you see?" he asked.

"What are you talking about?"

"Look at the difference in our complexions. Once our baby is born, everyone will know he belongs to me."

"There're over a hundred white male guards and staff members in this place. No one except you and me will know for sure who my baby's father is. What do you think Callahan is gonna do, huh? You think he'll line up every white male employee and make them take a DNA test? He won't, because he knows I'll blow him outta the water if he does anything stupid. Callahan will protect my privacy because he needs me to protect his."

Jill raced toward the entrance of the cardiac intensive care unit. She pushed the glass double doors and rushed to the nurse's station. "Excuse me, ma'am, I'm Jillian King. I'm looking for my aunt. She was brought here by ambulance a little while ago. Her name is Jackie Dudley Brown."

"Have a seat, ma'am. Someone will be with you shortly."

Jill stared at the gray-headed, portly white woman like she had lost her damn mind. "You don't understand. My aunt had a heart attack. I need to be with her and my husband. He's back there somewhere. You may know him. He's a nurse here and—"

"Jill!" Zach rushed over and wrapped his arms around her.

"Is she your wife, Zach?" The nurse watched them with compassion in her eyes. "I didn't know. Go back to your aunt, honey, and take your wife with you. Go on now."

Zach and Jill hurried to the waiting area closest to Aunt Jackie's room. Dr. Boulder, a cardiologist, approached them with an update.

"I'll be honest, Mr. King. It's iffy at best from here on out. Your aunt's heart is in bad shape, but something tells me that she's a fighter. She's critical but stable right now." He placed his hand on Zach's shoulder. "I've done all I can do. It's in the hands of someone greater than you and me. Let's hope for a miracle."

Thanks to the speedy response by Mrs. Taylor, the emergency medical unit had arrived quickly at Aunt Jackie's house and saved her life. She had suffered a massive heart attack and was knocking on death's door when the technicians reached her. Carl Lee, Mrs. Taylor's 30-year-old grandson, called Grady Memorial Hospital and went through hell and high water before he was finally connected with Zach. Once he gave Zach the disturbing news, he left his sick babies in the neonatal intensive care unit upstairs and rushed to Aunt Jackie's bedside. He didn't leave her until he went searching for Jill.

Chapter Sixteen

The burden of telling Jay about Aunt Jackie fell on Wallace's shoulders. It was one of the most difficult messages he ever had to deliver to anyone. He didn't delay his call to Leesworth, because time was of the utmost importance. Once he explained the situation to Jay's corrections counselor, the kind man assured him that she would be allowed an emergency phone call by the end of the day.

As expected, Jay was completely devastated by the news. She dropped to her knees at the end of the phone call and screamed until her voice grew hoarse. The evening nurse, a young woman named Yana from the Philippines, insisted that she spend the night in the infirmary for observation. She wanted to give Jay some medication to help her relax, but of course she refused it. No matter how upset she was, she didn't want to risk putting anything into her system that could possibly harm her baby. Jay didn't need medicine to comfort her. She needed her man. Pastor Monroe was the one and only person who could console her.

"Excuse me, Yana, I don't mean to disturb you, but I'm an emotional wreck. I can't sleep. Is there any way you could call someone for me?"

"Who would you like to speak with, Ms. King?"

Jay burst into tears. "I need to speak with Pastor Monroe, please. I won't tell anyone, I promise. I'm one of his clients. You can check my record. I'm in individual counseling with him three times a week. Please, Yana, if I don't speak with him tonight, I think I'll lose my mind."

Yana searched the support staff's directory and found the pastor's home telephone number. She dialed it and was greeted by Holly. In brief, she explained the situation and asked if her husband could take a crisis call from one of the women under his care at the prison. Yana handed Jay the phone and stepped outside so she could speak with her counselor in private.

"Gavin, I need you," Jay wailed as soon as she heard his voice. "My aunt had a heart attack! My father said she's in critical condition. The doctor doesn't even know if she'll live. She can't die. She just can't! If Aunt Jackie passes away, who'll take care of our baby?"

"I'm sorry about your aunt. I wish I could be there for you right now, but I can't. I'll come to the prison early to-morrow morning. I need you to calm down. You mustn't upset the baby. Please try to get some rest. God will take care of your aunt, and I'll be there bright and early to take care of you and our baby. I love you. Good night."

Holly stood outside the closed door of her husband's study. She pressed her ear against it, trying her best to hear his side of the conversation. In all his time at Leesworth, he had never received a call after hours. Yana, the nurse, had explained that there was an emergency with one of his clients at the prison. Apparently, the woman was in crisis. Holly closed her eyes and whispered a prayer for the poor soul. Whatever problem she was facing, God would be able to solve it. And with a special man of God like her sweet Gavin in her corner, Holly was sure the woman would be fine.

Whatever was going on with Jay had stressed Aunt Jackie out so much that she'd had a heart attack. The churning in Zach's gut told him so. He was guilty of many things, but being a fool was not one of them. Ever since Aunt Jackie had returned from her visit with Jay, he'd noticed something different about her demeanor. She seemed worried about something, preoccupied even. Before her spur-of-the-moment trip to Leesworth, Aunt Jackie wasn't complaining about tingling sensations or shortness of breath. Hell, she'd been overweight all her life, and arthritis wasn't new to her. She didn't have high blood pressure, diabetes, or heart disease. It had been five years since her surgery on her left wrist to relieve carpal tunnel syndrome. There had been no indication that it had come back. None of her past or present health conditions had sent his dear, sweet aunt into a massive heart attack. Something traumatic or someone was responsible.

It was Jay's fault that Aunt Jackie was lying in intensive care, fighting for her life. Zach believed it as sure as he believed there was a God in heaven. He couldn't prove his suspicions, but he couldn't shake them either. If his father wasn't willing to find out what had happened between Aunt Jackie and Jay during their last visit at the prison, he would. His sister was the last person in the world he wanted to see. Honestly, his life had improved since he had cut Jay off completely, but if making a trip to Leesworth to confront her crazy ass about what she had said or done to Aunt Jackie was the only way to get answers, Zach was down with it.

He looked around the hospital room. Cards, balloons, and stuffed animals were everywhere. The Inspirational Voices, the choir Aunt Jackie had sung in since she was a teenager at Refuge Pentecostal Temple, had sent a huge GET WELL banner. The nurses had been kind enough to hang it above her door. Jill had taken dozens of green plants and flowers that church members had sent to the hospital home with her. They weren't allowed in Aunt Jackie's room because of the ventilator.

"What did Jay say to you? What did that fool do?" Zach squeezed his aunt's hand. "I know she did something crazy, and you couldn't handle it, could you? Why do you always get caught up in Jay's mess?"

"Mr. King, visitation hours are almost over. You have five more minutes."

Zach turned around and faced the nurse. "Yeah, I know. I haven't been home in two days. I've been camping out in the waiting area. I'm funking up the place. I guess I'll go home to my wife and babies tonight."

"Good night. I'll see you tomorrow afternoon."

"Jay is psychotic, Dex! I knew that bitch hadn't changed. That's why I shut her ass out. All those letters and phone calls begging me to forgive her and accept her back into my life were a bunch of bullshit! I submitted an online request to her corrections officer a month ago, asking to be placed on Jay's visitation list. I haven't gotten a response yet."

"That's weird, because I thought Jay wanted to see you. Wasn't she begging you to visit her a while back?"

Zach nodded and took a sip of his guava juice. "Yep, but I didn't want anything to do with her crazy ass back then. Now I need to see Jay. I wanna know what went down between her and Aunt Jackie during their visit. Something significant happened. I can feel it in my gut."

"Whatever went down, Aunt Jackie didn't want you to know about it. If she did, wouldn't she have told you when she got back?"

"That's what I don't understand. Why would Auntie keep a secret so disturbing for Jay that it nearly killed her? It irks the hell outta me, man. She's lying up in a hospital bed, unable to speak or move, all because of some shit my sister did, and I don't know what it is."

"Aunt Jackie can't tell you, and Jay refuses to tell you."

"Well, my dad is going to Leesworth Saturday to surprise Jay. She hasn't called or written him a letter since he broke the news to her about Aunt Jackie's heart attack. That's guilt. Jay knows her actions nearly took my aunt out. That's why she's distanced herself from my father and why she refuses to see me."

"Do you think your dad can get Jay to tell him what happened?"

"I don't know, but I sure as hell hope so."

The alarm chirped, and the front door slammed shut. Zach and Dex looked toward the entrance of the den. Jill walked in with a sleeping Zion in tow. Zachary Jr. was on her heels.

"Daddy, Daddy, I was good at school!"

"Is that so? What about your sister?"

Jill handed Zach their daughter and kissed him on the cheek. "She was sweet, as usual." She turned to Dex. "How are you, sir? I hope you're staying for dinner. It'll be ready in about thirty minutes."

"Nah, Ramona is expecting me," Dex said, standing up. "I better get there on time. That woman is mean as the devil when she's pregnant. After this one, I'm getting the old snip."

"Ouch!" Zach closed his eyes and covered his crotch with both hands.

Jill laughed and headed to the kitchen.

"Tell Ramona I said hello. I'll update you on Jay as soon as I hear from my father."

Chapter Seventeen

Jay was not happy to see her father. That was the first thing Wallace noticed when she entered the visitation room. Her facial expression gave her away. She had put on a noticeable amount of weight, too. Wallace was shocked. He stood from his seat. When he reached out his arms to hug his daughter, she gave him a half smile and hugged him back. Wallace pulled out an empty chair for her.

"I had no idea you were coming today. I was resting. I don't feel well." Jay took the offered seat.

"I haven't heard from you in a while, sweetheart. Is there something wrong?"

Jay shook her head and lowered her eyes. "I haven't been feeling well lately. That's all. Dr Yusuf said my health is stable for the most part. At least it hasn't gotten any worse. It's Aunt Jackie. I'm so worried about her. I can't function, Daddy."

"It seems like you've found comfort in food." Wallace chuckled lightly.

"Yeah, I have. This is the heaviest I've ever been in my life. Aunt Jackie always thought I was too skinny. Now that I've picked up weight, she . . . she can't even see me." Tears began to stream down Jay's face. "If she doesn't make it, I'll lose it. I swear I will."

Wallace draped his arm around Jay's shoulders. "We all have to continue to pray. Faith goes a long way. Jackie has shown some signs of improvement, according to Zach."

"I know. Mr. Green, my corrections counselor, told me that she opens her eyes more often and responds to the doctors, nurses, and Zach by blinking. And she cries sometimes. But he said she just lies there, unable to move or speak. It breaks my heart." Jay swiped at a new stream of tears.

"Your aunt is a strong woman, Jayla. She raised you and your brother single-handedly when she was only a few years older than both of you. Jackie has insurmountable faith, too. You know that. She will pull through this and have a glorious testimony."

"I hope so. Because if she doesn't, I don't know what will happen with my b . . ." Jay's voice trailed off before she let the cat out of the bag.

"What did you say?"

"I said I don't know what will happen with my battle. You know, my health battle, Daddy. This whole thing with Aunt Jackie is affecting my health."

"I'm sure it is." Wallace leaned back to stare into his daughter's eyes. "Zach has this idea that your aunt was troubled about something. He feels she was under a lot of stress because of you."

"Zach hates me so much that he'll blame me for anything. If there's a tornado in Oklahoma City, he'll say it's my fault. The Falcons didn't advance in the playoffs. I guess I'm responsible for that, too. God forbid if they cancel *Law & Order: SVU*. Zach will blame it on me."

"We all know about your call to Jackie. You were very upset and asked that she visit you right away. She shared that with your brother and me. Now what I'd like to know is what happened while your aunt was here. Why were you so shaken up? What was the emergency, sweetheart? Whatever it was, it took its toll on Jackie."

"Did Aunt Jackie say that? Did she tell you or Zach that my life here in this godforsaken place suddenly became her burden?" Jay pushed back from the table and stood above her father. "She didn't tell you or my brother anything, did she? Zach needs someone to blame for the most tragic event in our lives since you killed our mother. It's so easy for him to point his finger at me while I'm sick and locked up. What's even sadder is that you joined his team in this blame game. I'm outta here."

Jay left the table with Wallace jumping up after her. She never looked back at her father even when he called her name repeatedly. Embarrassed, Wallace turned around and faced the many curious eyes watching him. He stuffed his hands in the pockets of his khaki pants and left the visitation room.

Zach hung up the phone with Wallace more convinced than ever that Jay was hiding something. According to his father, she had danced all around his direct question about what had taken place between her and Aunt Jackie during their last meeting. Instead of telling Wallace what they had discussed, Jay became angry and very defensive. Then she stormed off, ending the visit abruptly.

Guilty! That single word had taken hold of Zach's psyche and wouldn't let go. But as much as he wanted answers to solve the mystery surrounding Aunt Jackie's heart attack, he didn't have time to investigate. There were more pressing issues to deal with. For instance, Aunt Jackie's condition was stable, but she still couldn't talk. She wasn't eating either. Dr. Boulder had written an order for a feeding tube to be inserted in her abdomen in the morning.

Then there was the decision of whether Aunt Jackie should be admitted to a rehabilitation facility once she was released from the hospital. Her brain function was normal. A series of extensive tests had determined that, but she had yet to speak or move her hands. Day in and day out, Aunt Jackie lay in the hospital bed in her standard private room, sleeping or staring into space. She was alive, but in most ways lifeless. The situation was overwhelming for Zach, yet he was committed to his aunt regardless.

Jill, Dex, Venus, and several members of the Dudley family did their part to help Zach care for Aunt Jackie. They took turns sitting with her at night and visited her throughout the day. Aunt Hattie Jean tended to her laundry to make sure she wore a fresh nightgown every day. She despised the ugly hospital gowns and had forbidden all the nurses from putting them on her baby sister. Uncle Bubba kept Aunt Jackie's house in order by collecting her mail, maintaining the lawn, and airing the place out once a week. Zach took responsibility for all of his aunt's bills. He wouldn't have it any other way.

Aunt Jackie's recovery was Zach's top priority. But the question of why she had even taken ill in the first place was constantly on his mind.

"Warden Callahan is going to find out that I'm pregnant today. Dr. Yusuf said he can't put it off any longer. He and the nurses have taken care of me with the strictest confidentiality for four months now. Now I'm beginning to show. It's amazing that no one around here has noticed."

"Is Dr. Yusuf going to meet with the warden?"

"Nah. He recorded the pregnancy in my medical file as a first-time discovery yesterday. By policy, all new diagnoses on inmates must be reported to Callahan within twenty-four hours. My time is up. He'll know by the end of the day." Jay rested her head on her man's shoulder and closed her eyes. She liked the feel of his hand rubbing her baby bump.

"What is the worst-case scenario?"

"Callahan will send for me and ask me who my child's father is."

"And what will you tell him?"

"Nothing. I'll imply that I got raped by one of his guards. Believe me, that's Callahan's worst nightmare. It'll look bad if he has to explain to the governor how an inmate in his prison got pregnant by one of his guards. When I tell him I don't wanna press charges and that my family is gonna take the baby, he'll let it go. He will sweep it under the rug with everything else he doesn't want to deal with. Callahan has the power to do that."

"He also has the power to destroy me."

Pastor Monroe stood from the couch and started pacing. Jay watched him struggle to process her plan. He was worried, but she was confident that everything would work out. Callahan was cocky and predictable. He cared more about money, power, and connections than anything else. He wouldn't dare allow a pregnant inmate to destroy his illegal empire. Men like him would agree to anything to stay on top.

Jay cared about the father of her baby. He was her main concern. She would do anything to protect him and their unborn child. Nothing and no one else, not even Aunt Jackie, mattered at the moment. Jay was fearless when it came to the man she loved and the child they had created together. She wasn't afraid to take on Callahan. She had the goods on him plus a backup plan. So, if he wanted to play hardball with Jayla Simone King, he could bring it on.

"Sit down, baby." Jay patted the space on the couch where the pastor had been sitting. He sat and threw his arm around her shoulders, pulling her close. "You're gonna have to trust me on this. It may appear that Callahan has the upper hand, but he doesn't. I do. I have his corrupt behind by the balls. If he sneezes hard, I'll snatch them off and feed them to the stray dogs. The warden doesn't know it yet, but I can tear his kingdom down. If he comes after you or me, I'll show him."

Chapter Eighteen

"So, Ms. King is pregnant," Warden Callahan said in his empty office. He flipped through her medical file one last time before he pushed it to the side of his desk. He leaned back in his leather wingback chair and raised his long legs. He propped his feet on top of the desk. With his hands clasped together behind his head, he allowed his mind to recall his earlier conversation with Jay. She had come to his office at his request and sat down across from him as cool as a cucumber. Pregnant, missing fingers, and all, she was still sexy as hell. Maybe he should have fucked her before one of his guards got a hold of her.

If Callahan's memory served him correctly, his inmate treasurer was into women when she first came to Leesworth. She'd been sentenced to more than ten years in prison for ordering a hit on her brother. Big brother had stolen baby sister's bitch, and she lost her damn mind. Once she got settled into the system, she sought out Private Freeman and damn near licked her bowlegged. Yeah, he knew all about Jay's little fling with his junior guard, but he was cool with it. Callahan didn't mind prison staff and inmates mixing it up as long as they were discreet. But some guard had gotten a little careless with his dick by knocking up Jay, and the warden was pissed the hell off.

Right now, Jay was claiming that she didn't want to expose the guard for fear of a big scandal. Supposedly, someone in her family had already agreed to take the child and care for it until Jay was paroled. That was a joke. More than likely, Jay would die at Leesworth because of her serious health problems, and she had the nerve to be pregnant on top of it.

Her medical condition had already cost the prison more money than any other inmate housed there in the ten years Callahan had been in charge. Her medications ran over $700 a month. Plus, she was in counseling three times a week, and Dr. Yusuf did blood work on her often. Now the prison would be financially responsible for her prenatal care. Callahan would much rather pay for another abortion than labor and delivery, but when he presented Jay with the option to terminate her pregnancy, she became visibly shaken. She told Callahan, in no uncertain terms, that she wanted her baby and abortion was out of the question.

Callahan stood up and looked out of his window. A bunch of inmates were out in the courtyard. There was a basketball game in full swing on the blacktop, and a lot of women were working in the vegetable garden. The health addicts were jogging around the track or exercising in the middle of it.

Jay's reaction to a possible abortion was eating away at Callahan. Her outburst had stunned him. She had allowed her emotions to slip through her usually hardcore exterior. Her weak side showed up. For some reason Jay wanted her child. Callahan had never met an inmate who wanted to give birth to a staff member's bastard. Even he had fathered a couple of basketball teams over his years at Leesworth, and he had done so with a very diverse group of inmates.

Callahan didn't discriminate when it came to prison pussy. As long as an inmate had a clean bill of health, he would nail it. And each time one of the women had become pregnant from that potent Callahan seed, she didn't put up a fight about getting rid of the baby. But Jay was adamant about having her child, which was very unusual. Maybe it was a love child, and she really hadn't been raped at all. Or she had plans to use the baby as justification to get an emergency medical parole hearing. Either way, the warden was suspicious of Jay's pregnancy. He was going to keep a close eye on her from now on. All of her interactions and activities would be monitored around the clock regularly. Callahan wanted to know who had fathered Jay's baby and why she was hell-bent on having the little bastard.

"How is your client?"

Pastor Monroe's fork, spearing a juicy piece of steak, stopped in midair just inches from his lips. He cocked his head to the side and studied Holly's face for a few seconds. "Which one of my clients?"

"Oh, I don't know her name, honey. I'm referring to the one who called you in the middle of the night a couple months ago. How is she doing?"

"She's fine."

"I prayed for her," Holly said as her husband chewed his food. "She must've really been in crisis if the officials at the prison allowed her to call her mental health counselor after hours. You never told me what was going on with her."

"It was nothing really. She got some bad news from home about one of her family members. The assistant warden in charge that night thought it would be best if I spoke to her. I did what I could and followed up with her the next morning."

"Is she one of the women who attends prayer and Bible study, or is she only receiving individual counseling?"

"She's a part of the ministry, and I counsel her." He placed his fork on the edge of his plate. "Where are all

these questions coming from, Holly? And why are you
so concerned now? A few months ago, you weren't the
slightest bit interested in my ministry at Leesworth or
the inmates. I used to talk to you about them all the time
and beg you to come with me to service. You were too
busy then. Now you want to know about every inmate
and her situation." He snorted and shook his head.

"You're wrong, honey. I was always interested. The
timing was just all wrong back then. My schedule is much
lighter now. So, I downloaded a volunteer's application
from Leesworth last week. Other than drug testing, I've
been cleared. I should be able to attend service with you
next Wednesday night."

Warden Callahan submitted two more major requests
for funds for Jay to process. Once again, she followed his
instructions to the letter. Then she made copies of everything and filed them away in her personal records. One of
the bogus transactions involved a winery near Dahlonega,
Georgia. Callahan had authorized a check for payment
to Gallagher's Winery and Vineyard in the amount of
$4,000. Jay's brain went into overload. What did the
warden need 500 bottles of wine for? 300 bottles of
white wine and 200 bottles of merlot would be shipped to
an address in Alpharetta in a few weeks. Maybe Callahan
was having a big party or opening a club. Regardless of
his intentions, he was up to no good. He was purchasing
the wine with stolen funds that belonged to the State of
Georgia and the inmates at Leesworth.

It really didn't matter to Jay, though. Her hands were
clean. She was an insignificant inmate following the
instructions of the warden. All of her ducks were in a row.
When the shit hit the fan, which Jay was sure it would
someday in the near future, her ass would be covered.

Chapter Nineteen

"Ms. Brown, I know you can hear me. I want to know if you understand my words. Do you know these two people standing here with me?" Dr. Boulder watched Aunt Jackie's eyes float over to Zach and Jill. She blinked once, which was the signal for yes. Two blinks meant no.

"She recognizes us, Zachary! She understands." Jill stepped closer to the bed.

"If this person is Zach, I want you to blink once. If you think this is Jill, blink twice."

Two quick blinks was the correct signal. Aunt Jackie knew who Jill was. The two women cried and shared a happy moment when Zach clapped his hands and cheered to celebrate the highlight of his day. He followed Dr. Boulder out into the hallway, leaving Jill and Aunt Jackie alone.

"It's psychological, Mr. King. Your aunt's brain function is normal. She suffered no brain damage, even though she stopped breathing after the heart attack for a little over a minute. It was a miracle if I've ever witnessed one. But besides the damage to her heart and the strain on her lungs, she is in full recovery mode."

"What are you trying to tell me?"

"I'm no psychologist or psychiatrist, but I think it's all in her head. Ms. Brown doesn't know that she can actually speak or process thoughts, but she can. It's almost as if she doesn't want to talk or even think. She may be suffering from post-traumatic stress disorder in the aftermath of the heart attack. Anyway, I want her to continue physical and occupational therapy three times a week. I'm going to add speech therapy, too. Also, I'm going to have Dr. Capone come in. I'm sure you've heard of him. He's one of the top psychiatrists in the state."

"Yeah, I know him. His reputation is second to none."

"I'm certain he'll be able to unleash whatever is holding your aunt back from speaking in no time at all." The doctor checked his watch. "Well, I've got to run now. We'll talk again soon, Mr. King."

Zach stood in the hallway, relieved that Aunt Jackie's physical condition was improving. When she made the distinction between him and Jill, he almost did a dance right there in the hospital room. Zach should've been calling Aunt Hattie Jean and Uncle Bubba to tell them the good news, but he was stuck on Dr. Boulder's theory. Aunt Jackie did not want to talk. She had placed a psychological block on her speech. Zach believed the doctor. His assessment made perfect sense. Before the heart attack, Aunt Jackie had chosen not to speak about Jay's secret. Now after that same secret had almost cost her her life, she couldn't speak because her mind would not allow her to.

The more Zach thought about the situation, the angrier he got. He made up his mind that he would be placed on Jay's visitation list at Leesworth one way or another. He didn't give a damn what he had to do. Zach was going to come face-to-face with Jay and demand that she tell him what the hell she had done to traumatize their aunt.

"I'm pissed off with you, King. How could you not tell me? I'm supposed to be your girl."

"Stop being so doggone dramatic, Shanika. I'm stressed out enough already. The situation is very complicated. I had to work out some things first."

Shanika peeped outside the laundry room before she closed the door. She turned around and faced her friend. "It wasn't complicated when you were lying up with some lowlife guard. I can't believe you were walking around here pretending to be so holier-than-thou while you were getting your freak on. You had me fooled. I thought you were real."

"Hey, I am real! I mean . . . I was real." Jay closed her eyes and rubbed her stomach. "I wasn't faking. Things aren't always as simple as they seem. I didn't get pregnant the way everyone thinks I did. You'll be the first person in this place I'll tell the whole truth to when the time is right, but I can't say anything now."

"I'm gonna hold you to that. All of the guards and a bunch of nosy-ass inmates are running around whispering and making up shit. They think I know the deal 'cause we're tight. I told Floyd and Jamison that I don't know shit! I'm kinda glad you didn't tell me. That way, they can't torture me into saying anything."

"Just keep them outta your face. Continue to tell the truth. You don't know anything. All you need to say is that I'm definitely pregnant, and I won't tell you who the baby's father is."

Shanika hugged Jay and kissed her face. "You're my girl, King. I got you."

Callahan turned off the security monitor when Jay left the laundry room. He'd watched her and Shanika Dixon's private conversation like a hawk. They made sure they spoke in hushed tones so the newly installed security system wasn't able to pick up a single word either of them had said.

Callahan had stuck to his plan to keep a close watch on Jay. So far, he'd come up with nothing. She had a pretty straight schedule. She reported to her office at the same time every day. She ate with the same women at each meal, and they sat at the same table. Counseling and Bible study were her only two activities outside of work. She didn't seem too familiar or friendly with any of the guards, especially not the males.

Callahan concluded that Jay was smart and sneaky. She was knocked up, and no one knew who was responsible except her and the perpetrator. Whoever he was, he was one lucky son of a bitch. Callahan's dick got hard just thinking about how good a fuck Jay probably was, but he didn't want her now. Someone else had already spoiled the goods. If he couldn't taste it first, he didn't want to taste it at all. Callahan didn't have an appetite for leftover prison pussy. Now that Jay was pregnant, she was no longer on his list of potential bed companions. The only thing she was good for now was processing checks so he could get his hands on all the money he needed.

Callahan didn't really give a damn about who had fathered Jay's child anyway. It was more a matter of curiosity. No warden appreciated certain activities going on in his prison without his knowledge. It made him look weak and dumb. Jerome "J.C." Callahan couldn't live with that kind of reputation hanging around his neck. That was why he was determined to find out who had gotten his prison business guru pregnant. He would deal with the worthless son of a bitch and then blackmail both of them into submission.

It had been nearly five months since Aunt Jackie's heart attack. She had left the hospital a few weeks before and was recuperating at home. Zach was paying for around-the-clock medical services from a home healthcare agency that provided her with premium care.

Although she was in all kinds of therapy every week, she still had not spoken or taken her first step. Zach was frustrated. He wanted his aunt back. Life wasn't the same without her smile and her laughter. Everyone missed Aunt Jackie's sharp sense of humor and good cooking. Zach knew his old auntie was locked up somewhere inside of her body and mind. He couldn't understand why she just wouldn't jump out.

The speech therapist had mentioned introducing Aunt Jackie to sign language as a form of communication. She was now moving her hands to make signals and grunting to get attention. She seldom smiled, but Zachary Jr. and Zion never failed to make her happy. However, whenever Zach brought Nahima over, all Aunt Jackie seemed to do was cry. The child would climb in her lap and rest there for long periods of time, hugging and kissing her nana. Aunt Jackie would respond by rubbing Nahima's back as tears rolled down her face. No one was able to interpret her emotions, not even Dr. Capone. He concluded that Nahima reminded her of Jay, the niece she was unable to visit due to her illness.

Zach disagreed, but he didn't bother to mention it to Dr. Capone. Nahima was indeed the spitting image of Jay, but that wasn't the reason her presence saddened Aunt Jackie. It was something much deeper than that. Zach had a feeling that Nahima reminded Aunt Jackie of Jay's secret. It may have even had something to do with the child. Who knew for certain about anything when it came to his wicked sister? The woman was a trickster, a con artist, and a master manipulator. Jay wasn't above using Nahima or anyone else for her own selfish gain. Her secret could very well include the little girl she had abandoned and forgotten since birth. Zach made a mental note to discuss the possibilities with Venus and Charles.

In the meantime, a meeting with Jay, or at least a simple phone conversation with her, was at the top of Zach's agenda. Wallace had been writing letters and sending her cards lately, but she hadn't responded. He'd also spoken to Mr. Green, Jay's corrections counselor, a few times to check on her. The man had reported that she was doing great. When Wallace asked about her health, Mr. Green told him he was not at liberty to discuss that matter without the inmate's consent. He was equally evasive whenever Zach called to inquire about his request for visitation with Jay. Each time, he was informed that his application had not been processed yet. He claimed he didn't know what was taking so long. The truth of the matter was that Jay did not wish to see Zach. And her actions indicated guilt in his opinion.

Chapter Twenty

"Ms. King, did you hear what I said? Your brother called again this afternoon. He wants you to approve him for visitation."

Jay sucked her teeth and rolled her eyes. "I don't wanna see Zach," she snapped. "When I was writing and calling him every week, begging him to come and visit me, he gave me his butt to kiss. He wouldn't even accept my calls that I was paying for. Did I tell you he sent my last letter back to the prison unopened?"

Mr. Green nodded and followed Jay to the next row of chairs. He had found her inside the chapel, placing Bibles and hymn books in the chairs in preparation for evening service. "Your brother is very persistent. He wants to see you, but a phone call would suffice. Can you at least call him?"

"I ain't got time for Zach, just like he didn't have time for me. Now we're even."

"He said he has news about your aunt. Don't you even want to know how she's doing?"

Jay stopped and stared at Mr. Green, speechless. "How did his voice sound? Was it shaking? Could you tell if he was crying?" Jay sat down with a short stack of Bibles in her hands. "I pray for my auntie every day and night. Lord, I hope she's not dead."

"I think your brother would've told me that. Don't you?"

"Maybe he did, but you don't wanna tell me. How do I know that you're not running some sick game on me?

Aunt Jackie could be dead right now! How could you not tell me, Mr. Green?"

"Look, as far as I know, your aunt is very much alive. I have no reason to think otherwise, but there's only one way to find out for sure. Call your brother."

Jay's curiosity caused her to sneak peeps at Holly all throughout prayer and Bible study. No matter how hard she tried to focus on the music and the sermon, she couldn't keep her eyes off the plain-Jane-looking chick. As Pastor Monroe gave the benediction, Jay leaned forward to check out his wife. The group had formed a big circle around the pastor. Everyone was holding hands. Jay's roaming eyes were the only ones open in the entire room. They were homed in on Holly.

She wasn't pretty, and she had a boyish figure. Where were her breasts and hips? God had definitely cheated her out of a nice body. Her butt was flat as an ironing board. No wonder Pastor Monroe liked to squeeze the junk in Jay's trunk all the time. And he loved to hit it from behind. He put a capital D in doggie style. Whenever they made love in that position, he would grip Jay's ass tight with both hands and ride her like a stud on a stallion until the earth tilted on its axis.

The group said, "Amen," in unison, snapping Jay from her pleasant but sinful thoughts. Her body wanted to rush over to Pastor Monroe and give him a hug like she and the other women in the group normally did, but her mind told her to be cool and stand down. She started collecting the Bibles and hymn books and stacking them on the bookshelf. Shanika and Sophia walked over to help their pregnant friend.

"So that's his wife? She looks like Miss Jane Hathaway on *The Beverly Hillbillies*. The only difference is her long hair. Miss Jane's hair was short. And she didn't wear glasses." Shanika giggled.

"She's not pretty, but she seems sweet."

Jay ignored her girls. She continued stacking the books quietly, but she stole frequent glances at Pastor Monroe and Holly out of the corner of her eye. He was introducing his wife to the other inmates. Jay was jealous, angry, and hurt. The pastor had given her no warning whatsoever that Holly would be at the service. At least she would've been able to prepare mentally if he had. When he acknowledged the only stranger in the room as his wife, Professor Holly Monroe, before he began his sermon, Jay had almost fainted. The baby even responded with series of hard kicks. Mother and child were pissed off that Daddy's wife had come to the prison.

"As fine as the pastor is, I thought he would have a pretty wife with some fashion sense. Miss Jane's dress looks like it came from the Goodwill."

"Be quiet, Shanika. Here they come," Sophia whispered.

Jay turned around and watched her lover and his wife close the distance between them. She wanted to break out in a sprint and get as far away from them as she could, but she couldn't move. Something held her in place. Jay didn't want to meet the woman he slept with every night, but she felt compelled to make her acquaintance. They had something in common. Holly and Jay were in love with the same man. He owned the keys to their hearts. Each woman had a claim to him. Pastor Monroe may have been Holly's husband of eighteen years and counting, but he was the father of Jay's unborn child.

Jay took in a few long breaths and exhaled slowly. Her hands began to tremble, so she placed the Bibles in a nearby chair. The baby started kicking again. Jay rubbed her belly nervously.

"Ladies, I want you to meet Holly." Pastor Monroe draped his arm loosely around his wife's shoulders.

Sophia reached out to Holly for a friendly handshake. "It's a pleasure to meet you, ma'am. I'm Sophia Mendez."

"I've heard good things about you, Sophia," Holly said, shaking her hand.

"I'm Shanika Dixon." She waved at Holly and smiled.

"It's a pleasure to meet you, Shanika."

"I feel the same way."

Jay stood silently, eyeing Holly from head to toe. Pastor Monroe watched, obviously nervous, his arm still wrapped around his wife's shoulders. He had to feel every bit as uncomfortable as Jay did. This was a meeting neither of them was prepared for. The three points of their unique love triangle had come together in a potentially telling moment. Tension and uncertainty hung over them like a dark cloud. The silence was deafening. Shanika, Sophia, and Holly were innocent and oblivious to the awkwardness of the chance meeting.

Jay found her voice. "I'm Jayla, but everyone calls me Jay." She extended her hand.

Holly didn't take Jay's hand right away. She didn't see it. Her eyes had dropped to Jay's very noticeable baby bump. As she stared, Pastor Monroe squirmed with anxiety. His eyes shifted back and forth between a shocked Holly and Jay, who fidgeted timidly.

"Holly, Jay is the young lady the women at church sent a care package to."

"Um, yes . . . I remember now. I'm glad we were able to help, dear." Instead of shaking Jay's hand, Holly stepped away from her husband and hugged her.

Jay returned Holly's affection. "Thank you," she mumbled for a lack of anything better to say.

"You are most certainly welcome. If there is anything else you need, please let Gavin know. The ladies and I would be more than happy to help you again."

Gavin takes care of all my needs, boo! I don't need anything from you or your church ladies. Those icy words were on the tip of Jay's tongue. Her hormones and mounting anger had kicked in. Her brain fought hard to suppress what was inside of her heart.

Pastor Monroe must've sensed that Jay was on the edge. He placed his hand on Holly's shoulder and spoke quickly. "It's getting late. I don't want you ladies to miss curfew. I'm going to walk Holly to the security office before I head back to mine to tidy up. I need to check my calendar, too."

Holly looked at Jay, Shanika, and Sophia. "Good night. It was a pleasure to meet all of you."

Chapter Twenty-one

"How could you let her come here without warning me, Gavin? I felt like such a fool, standing there all big and pregnant with your child, in front of your precious wife! I didn't deserve that. Why didn't you tell me she was coming this evening?"

It broke Pastor Monroe's heart to see Jay so upset. She was crying pitifully. Her feelings were truly hurt. The emotional outburst wasn't good for the baby. He wanted Jay to calm down and listen to what he had to say. He wasn't going to make any excuses for what had happened. He owed her the truth.

Pastor Monroe took a seat on the edge of his desk and spread his arms wide. "Come here, Jayla, please."

Jay folded her arms across her swollen breasts and shook her head. "No."

"All right, you can hold on to your bitterness if you'd like, but at least listen to me. I asked Holly not to come here tonight, but she insisted. She had already been cleared for access to Leesworth. I don't know what brought about her sudden interest in the inmates' fellowship. When I left this morning, I was under the assumption that she would not attend a service until after I had spoken to the women, more specifically you."

"It hurt my feelings to see her here. I wasn't prepared. The way she looked at me made me feel like I'm nothing. Everybody knows she's your wife. You claim that you love me. I'm carrying your child, but I can't tell anybody. I can't compete with Holly. She wins."

Gavin stood up, and in one giant step, he closed the gap between them. He pulled Jay into his arms. "I love you, Jayla. And I love our baby. I would never, ever do anything intentionally to hurt either one of you. In a perfect world, you and I would be together waiting for the arrival of our child. But nothing is perfect. We have to accept life the way it is." He pulled back and made eye contact with Jay. "Believe in me and believe in our love, okay?"

"Okay, I can do that. But I don't ever wanna see Holly here again. Do whatever you have to do to keep her away from Leesworth. I don't care. Just make sure our paths never cross again."

Uncle Bubba and Aunt Hattie Jean were sorting through Aunt Jackie's mail, separating all her bills from the rest of the envelopes. Over the months since her heart attack, a mountain of catalogues, magazines, and a variety of newsletters had accumulated. Zach had told Uncle Bubba to store them in a cardboard box in the laundry room. He said he would get around to sorting through everything soon. His work schedule and taking care of Aunt Jackie took up most of his time. The box was overflowing.

Among the stacks of mail were three big brown envelopes from Jay. Uncle Bubba recalled that the first one was delivered a few days after Aunt Jackie had been hospitalized. He'd mentioned it to Zach, but at the time, he was so distraught over his aunt that he hadn't paid much attention. Uncle Bubba never mentioned the envelope again.

Since then, two other envelopes had been delivered from Leesworth. Aunt Jackie couldn't read them, and everyone knew that Zach wanted nothing to do with Jay.

So, Uncle Bubba threw both envelopes in the box for safe keeping, in hopes that one day Aunt Jackie would be able to read again. When that day came, she would be happy to hear from her troubled, incarcerated niece.

Aunt Hattie Jean reached over her husband's shoulder and removed the three envelopes from the box. "What are these?" she asked, examining them closely. "Are they from Jay?"

"Yeah, she sent them. I don't know why, though. She knows Jackie ain't in no condition to be reading nothing."

"Humph, Jay don't know how my baby sister is doing. She ain't been in touch with anybody, not even her daddy. He's been writing her, but she won't write the man back. Zach's been calling the prison and talking to Jay's counselor. He wants to talk to her and update her on Jackie's condition. That chile won't give her brother the time of day."

"That's Jay."

"It sure is. Well, I'm gonna leave these here envelopes on the kitchen table with Jackie's bills so Zach can see 'em. Maybe he'll read 'em, and maybe he won't. I'll leave 'em there just the same."

Holly had waited up for Gavin to come home last night, but she fell asleep before he arrived. When she woke up in the morning, he had already left the house for men's devotion at the church. Holly had hoped to talk to Gavin about prayer and Bible study at the prison. She had enjoyed the service and meeting the women he ministered to. They were nothing like she had imagined. Holly was ashamed to admit that she'd expected a group of rough-looking women covered with tattoos and scars. She was surprised by how attractive and well-spoken some of them were. She fell in love with Bria the moment she'd opened her mouth to sing. She was anointed with the voice of an angel. Sophia gave a beautiful testimony about how life in prison had changed after she committed her life to the Lord. There wasn't a dry eye in the chapel when she left the podium and took her seat.

The inmates had been very attentive during Gavin's Bible lesson. They'd hung on to his every word and answered his questions confidently and correctly. It made Holly proud to know that her husband was making such an impact on women with troubled pasts. As tragic as Sandy's life had been, she had not died in vain. Because of her struggles with depression and addiction, Gavin had established a ministry to help women just like her. He'd committed his life to saving them because he'd failed to save his sister and her unborn child.

For some reason, Jay reminded Holly a lot of Sandy. No, they did not look alike. Jay was African American. She was very pretty, too. Holly wasn't sure if she had battled drug addiction. She didn't even know what crimes she'd committed that had landed her in prison. Actually, the only two things Holly knew about Jay were that Gavin was dedicated to her and she was pregnant.

When Holly first noticed Jay's protruding belly, she was taken aback. Quite naturally, she became curious. Why had God blessed a prisoner, who was facing a grim future, with a child but not her and Gavin? They had the resources and stability to take care of two or three babies. Jay didn't. Sometimes life was so unfair, even for Christians. God certainly did work in mysterious ways.

Chapter Twenty-two

"Nahima, get your little cousins and take them in the den, pumpkin. I can't concentrate with you guys running around in here. And don't make too much noise. Your nana is sleeping."

"Okay."

The three cousins, who could've easily passed for siblings, ran from the kitchen into the den. They left Zach and Jill at the table to add up Aunt Jackie's monthly household expenditures and home healthcare bills. A twenty-four-hour certified nurse's assistant seven days a week was costing Zach a grip, but he never complained. He had sold the most valuable stock in his investment portfolio to pay for his aunt's medical care. Medicaid and Medicare covered more than 85 percent of all of her therapy, which included her weekly sessions with Dr. Capone.

"If I allow another two hundred and fifty dollars for groceries, the total for this month will be $2,771."

"Correct," Jill confirmed. "What about her hair, Zachary? I'd like Fatima to come over to shampoo it."

"Go ahead and make the appointment. Have we covered everything now?"

"I think so. Oh, wait." Jill left the table and walked over to the counter. She picked up the three brown envelopes. "Aunt Hattie Jean called. She told me to make sure you saw these. They're from Jay."

Zach eyed the envelopes suspiciously. "Why the hell would Jay be writing Auntie in her condition? Hasn't she done enough damage already?"

"This first one came shortly after Aunt Jackie took ill." Jill waved it before Zach's face. "Uncle Bubba said it was postmarked before her heart attack."

Zach grabbed the envelope and tore into it. There were a few documents stapled together inside. A handwritten letter was on top of them. Zach ignored the documents and placed them on the table. Jill stood above her husband, peering over his shoulder. They both read the letter in silence until they saw the words "pregnant" and "baby."

"What the fuck? Jay is pregnant? This is the secret that nearly killed Aunt Jackie! I swear, baby, I feel like bombing every damn building at Leesworth."

Zach tossed and turned the better half of the night. His head felt like it was about to explode with all the questions about Jay floating around inside. After his sister had ordered a hit on him, he'd realized she was in need of psychological help. Then she topped that by escaping from prison and terrorizing him and his family. When Jay kidnapped Jill in Jamaica and held her captive, Zach was forced to accept the life-changing reality that his sister was severely deranged. He had run out of words to describe Jay in light of her shocking pregnancy.

How the hell did a lesbian with no maternal instincts all of a sudden fall in love with a white married preacher and get pregnant with his child? And it had all happened in prison. The situation blew Zach's mind. The thought of Jay being pregnant and alone was unbelievable. No wonder Aunt Jackie had suffered a heart attack. It was some heavy shit to process. Only Jay would get herself tangled up in some madness like a prison pregnancy by a married preacher. In the letter, she claimed they were in love and committed to each other. *Well, Reverend Slick Dick needs to pour some of that love and commitment on his child.* There was no way in hell Aunt Jackie could take legal guardianship of an infant as Jay had written and asked her to. Even if she were perfectly healthy, Zach would not allow it. She had already devoted her life to two children. It wouldn't be fair for her to sacrifice her retirement for years running behind another snotty-nosed kid.

Even from a prison cell way up in North Georgia, Jay was fucking with Zach's head and screwing up other people's lives. A preacher stood to lose his wife, congregation, and counseling credentials because of her. And an innocent child would be born in a prison hospital to a crazy woman, only to be snatched away and placed in the child welfare system indefinitely. Worst of all, a sweet, caring Christian woman who was once full of life was now living in a state of physical and mental disability.

"That's your fifth drink, Zachary. No more, sweetheart. No more."

"Ain't you my designated driver?" Zach held up his keys and dangled them in Jill's face. "I drink and you drive." He doubled over in his seat and laughed.

Jill snatched the keys and stuffed them inside her purse. She was vexed. Zach had chosen the wrong night to get wasted. They were hanging out with their closest friends, which was something they hadn't done in quite a while. Dex and Ramona had invited them, Charles, and Venus over for dinner. It was couples' night. Wallace and Patricia were in town for a brief visit. They were at Zach and Jill's house watching all three of the grandchildren. Of course, Wallace Jr., the proud 9-year-old uncle of the trio, was there as well. Instead of enjoying the company of their good friends and Ramona's delicious cooking, Zach was trying to bury his sorrows in a liquor bottle.

On the flip side of the situation, Jill fully understood her husband's pain. He was under undue stress. Zach was very bitter and depressed because of Aunt Jackie's stagnant recovery and Jay's situation. He was dealing with everything the best way he knew how. Emotion suppression had worked for him as a child after the death of his mother and his father's arrest. Zach had shared with Jill how his sadness was often mixed with confusion, fear, and the unrealistic notion that his mother would return soon and bring his father with her. So instead of crying and embracing the pain, he held it all inside because there was no need for it. He was waiting for his beautiful mother to come home and fix the mess she and his daddy had made of their family, but that day never came. Zach was almost 9 years old when, out of the blue, he finally got it. Death was the end. His mother was never coming back, and neither was his father. Zach finally unleashed all the tears, pain, and anger he had locked deep inside. The little boy mourned at last.

Aunt Jackie's questionable recovery and Jay's role in it had presented Zach with a reason to mourn all over again, but he refused to. He didn't want to. Emotion suppression was easier. Zach wanted to avoid the pain. He didn't want to feel anything. Between his family, work, and taking care of Aunt Jackie, he'd found a place to bury all of his emotions. Zach would not allow himself to become vulnerable again like he had after Jay had arranged his murder. There was no time, space, or reason for him to endure any more hurt because of his sister. This time Jay would not win.

Jill, his rock, was his saving grace, but she was also his conscience. She understood his inner turmoil, and she felt his pain, but there was no place in their lives for destructive behavior. Their children and Nahima needed him. Aunt Jackie did too.

"We're leaving, Ramona and Dex." Jill stood and walked over to her friends. "The children are at home with Papa and Grammy Pat. Little Zachary is a handful by himself. It's time to relieve the grandparents of their babysitting duties. And look at Zachary." Jill tilted her head in his direction. "He's had way too much to drink."

"Look, cut him some slack. He's just—"

"No, Dex, I will not cut him any slack. Zachary is a man with a family and many other responsibilities. There is no room on his agenda for pity parties and foolishness. I will call you to let you know that we've made it home safely." Jill turned and retraced her steps to the sofa. "Get up, Zachary! We're going home."

Chapter Twenty-three

"Dear God, Holly, I don't want to see my credit card statement this month. How much damage did you do?" Pastor Monroe dropped his briefcase on the far end of the sofa away from all the shopping bags.

"I didn't do so bad."

"Didn't you go shopping with Trudy a few weeks ago? What was the occasion today?"

Holly picked up one of the shopping bags and pulled out a sweatshirt. "Only a few of these items are for me, honey."

"And who might the rest of them belong to?"

"Jay, your client at the prison. Most of these things are for her."

"Why did you buy all of this stuff for her without first checking with me?"

"Before you blow a gasket, hear me out. I told a few women at church about her condition, and we decided to collect some maternity clothes for her so she can be comfortable. What you see here is our contribution. I was careful to only buy items that were on the approved list in the social service department at the prison. I think I did quite well." Holly held up a pair of maternity jeans. "Aren't these nice?"

"I guess so. I'm going to the kitchen to make a sandwich."

***

Jay read the scathing letter she had received from Zach one more time and burst into tears. "I hate you! Ugh!" She buried her face into her pillow.

Zach knew all about the baby and Gavin. He had obviously read the letter she had written to Aunt Jackie asking her to take the baby and care for it until she was released from prison. Because of the heart attack, that was no longer an option. Aunt Jackie couldn't take Jay's baby even if she wanted to. She was in no condition to do so, and Zach was 100 percent against the arrangement. He had made that perfectly clear in his letter.

Zach had accused Jay of being selfish and manipulative. He'd implied that she may have gotten pregnant on purpose just for the hell of it. Then Zach stuck a knife in Jay's heart. In the harshest language imaginable, he told her how the shock and stress of her pregnancy had been too much for Aunt Jackie to handle. He blamed her for almost killing their auntie. Those words hurt Jay more than anything. She didn't think Zach could be so cruel. Then, as if his attacks and accusations weren't enough, he promised that he would never forgive Jay for what she had done. He said her baby would suffer for her sins, both past and present, in foster care.

The thought of her and Gavin's child growing up in the homes of strangers tore Jay's heart into tiny pieces. It opened the emotional floodgates, and she couldn't stop her tears from falling.

"King, are you all right over there, girl? You sound like you're having a nervous breakdown. Tell me what your brother said in that letter. You need to get it out. It ain't good to hold all that stuff inside."

"He . . . he blames me for my aunt's heart attack. He said I . . . I almost killed her. I didn't mean to hurt her, Shanika. I would never do something like that intentionally, but I had to tell Aunt Jackie about the baby. Who else was there? I asked her not to tell anyone else until I figured out what I was gonna do."

"What are you gonna do? What are your plans for the baby?"

"I don't know, but I don't want my child growing up in foster care."

"What about the father? Maybe he'll take the baby."

"He can't!"

"All right then, ask your daddy and his wife. Or maybe your ex will take your baby and raise it with Nahima."

"I haven't spoken to my father in months. I've been avoiding him. Venus and her husband ain't gonna hardly help me out. I can't blame them though."

"Pray on it and go to sleep. Then run it by Pastor Monroe tomorrow. There might be someone in his church willing to take care of the kid until you get outta here."

Jay rolled over on her side with her face to the concrete wall. The truth was there was nobody who could take her baby for her. Aunt Jackie was sick, and her father was too old. She had cut him off anyway. None of her other relatives cared about her. Jay hadn't heard from any of them since she'd been at Leesworth. Zach wanted her baby to go into the system, so he wouldn't lift a finger to help her, and asking Gavin to take his child was totally out of the question. Jay couldn't and wouldn't do that to him. The only way she would even consider Gavin as a placement for their child was if . . .

Jay sat up straight. She had an idea. It wasn't perfect. There were a few kinks that needed to be worked out, but it was her only hope. For the sake of her baby, she had to give it a try. If she could get the right people involved, there was a fifty-fifty chance that her baby would have a home after all.

"Shanika, are you still awake over there?"

"Yeah, I'm up. I can't sleep because I'm worried about you."

"I think I may have a solution to my problem, but I'm gonna need your help."

"I'm in, girl. Just tell me what you need me to do."

Warden Callahan was tempted to throw in the towel on his mission. He was no closer to finding out who had fathered Jay's child than he was in the beginning. Even with all the extra pairs of eyes on her, he hadn't received a single report about anything unusual in her weekly routine. Jay's day-to-day pattern was predictable, right down to the second. Installing additional cameras and audio recording devices in her office and the other areas she frequented had been a total waste of time and money.

There were only two places where Jay spent lots of time at Leesworth that Callahan had not bugged. Both locations were completely off-limits. Dr. Yusuf's office and the counselor's office were both protected by strict privacy laws in the state of Georgia. All inmates had the same medical confidentiality rights as free members of society. Therefore, Callahan had avoided the violation. No matter what type of information he would gain from the doctor or the counselor's office via secret cameras or audio recording devices, it would never be permissible in a court of law or in in-house prison proceedings. To the contrary, the gathering of such information would be considered illegal.

But the warden wasn't looking for anything to use against Jay and the father of her child for official purposes. He had a very personal agenda. The identity of the man who had impregnated Callahan's silent embezzlement partner was extremely important to him. The bastard had chosen the wrong inmate to have his way with, and he'd made a fool of the warden. No one at Leesworth would embarrass him and get away with it, and because Jay refused to name her rapist, she would suffer with him once he was identified.

Callahan buzzed Cherell, his loyal assistant. "Tell Captain Floyd to go ahead with the project we spoke about this morning. Let him know I expect a report on my desk by the end of the week."

The warden leaned back in his chair, a satisfied smirk on his face. He couldn't wait to see what the new spyware would reveal in the counselor's office. Jay hadn't confided in her friend Shanika Dixon or anyone else in their clique about her child's paternity. The name wasn't listed in her medical file either. Floyd and Jamison had already done some snooping around to determine that. What better person was there for Jay to place her confidence in than her mental health counselor? Pastor Monroe knew something. He counseled Jay three times a week, and she attended his Wednesday evening services in the chapel. She had definitely shared some valuable information with the good preacher, and Callahan wanted to know all about it. He hoped the mystery that had nagged him for months would be solved by the weekend.

Chapter Twenty-four

"What's gonna happen to Jay's baby, dude?"

Zach placed his lunch on the cafeteria table and shrugged. "Hell, I don't know, and I don't give a damn. Jay and her prison love child are not my problem."

"Daaamn!" Dex stretched his eyes at his best friend of over twenty years and shook his head. "Since when did you become so coldblooded? No matter what Jay did to you, Jill, and Nahima, she's still your sister. And that makes her child your niece or nephew. The baby is as innocent as Nahima, Zach. He or she has nothing to do with the beef between you and Jay."

"You're wrong," Zach said, pointing his fork at Dex from across the table. "Nahima is a product of a carefully planned conception between a couple who was truly in love. Jay got knocked up with some white bootlegged preacher's kid in prison because of her own selfish agenda. The pregnancy has a purpose, and it has nothing to do with loving that preacher or with her biological clock. Jay hates children. You know that. Stop being naive. It ain't manly."

"All I'm saying is the baby your sister is carrying is your innocent flesh and blood. It will be Nahima's baby sister or brother. It would be tragic for those two children to grow up in this world without ever knowing about each other. You could make the difference, Zach. Aunt Jackie can't take Jay's baby, but you can."

"I don't want Jay's baby. A situation like that would
tie us together for the rest of our lives. I can't handle
that. My commitment is to my two children and Nahima.
You and Jill can take your bullshit guilt trips somewhere
else. Jay needs to make that preacher man up and take
his baby. It's his responsibility, not mine. Reverend
Slick Dick knew he had a wife when he was breaking in a
prison lesbian."

"Well, I think you're dead wrong for turning your back
on that baby. Aunt Jackie would want you to step up and
do the right thing. I hope your conscience eats your ass
alive every day until you change your mind."

Jay and Shanika left the library and quietly headed
for the cafeteria, each in her own thoughts. For two days
they had met there to research the adoption process in
Georgia. Neither had had any idea that there were so
many different types of adoptions. Jay had narrowed the
list down to three possible options that would best suit
her case.

A private open adoption was her preference. It was
simple and in Jay's best interest as a mother. If Pastor
Monroe and Holly would agree to the terms, they would
gain full custody of the baby, but Jay would have some
semblance of involvement in her child's life. Naturally,
it would be little to none in light of her living situation,
but from a legal standpoint, she would still be recognized
as the child's biological mother. All terms in a private
open adoption in the Peach State between the birth and
adoptive parents were negotiable at the discretion of all
parties involved.

Jay wanted Pastor Monroe to take their child and
raise it with Holly but under the pretense that another
man was the child's biological father. In other words,

Professor Monroe would have no knowledge whatsoever that the child was actually her husband's flesh and blood. Pastor Monroe would present the idea of adopting Jay's child as a mercy mission to save the poor baby from going into the child welfare system, but first Jay would have to convince him to go along with her plan. She hadn't spoken to him about it yet. Their counseling session was scheduled for after lunch. Jay planned to make her pitch to him then.

"Take three more steps, Ms. Brown. I know you can do it. Come on now."

Aunt Jackie gritted her teeth. She placed her left foot in front of her right one and grunted. Then she stopped and looked down at her feet. Her legs were rubbery. They were still very weak. It was only the third day that she had taken steps with her walker. Yesterday she'd taken ten. Paris, her cute little physical therapist, had raised the bar. She wanted Aunt Jackie to take fifteen steps today.

"Uh-uh." Aunt Jackie shook her head. "Uh-uh."

"Oh, yes, sweetie, you can do it, and you will. Come on now. We're all waiting for you."

Aunt Hattie Jean walked over and stood next to Paris. Marsha, the certified nurse's assistant, watched from her seat on the sofa.

"Go ahead and take the steps, Jackie. I'm still your big sister. Don't let me get a switch at you."

"Ugh!" Aunt Jackie took another step and rolled her eyes at her sister. She took one more.

"Give us a bonus step, and I'll leave you alone until tomorrow," Paris coaxed. "Ms. Hattie Jean will serve you some lunch, and then you can take a nap. What do you say?"

Aunt Jackie frowned and nodded. Then she took one last step. Her cheering squad gave her a round of applause. Marsha and Paris helped her to her recliner, and Aunt Hattie Jean went to the kitchen to get her lunch and call Zach. She had to wait a little while before he answered, but she'd expected as much because he was at work.

"Talk to me."

"Boy, that ain't no way to answer the phone at your job. You know better than that. If Jackie's health weren't so poor, she'd whip your ass."

"I knew it was you, Aunt Hattie Jean. You call me every day at the same time to give me a therapy report. How was it today?"

"She took sixteen steps. I knew she could do it. Now if we could just get her to stop all of that crazy sign language and start talking."

"Dr. Capone and the speech therapist are working on that. They both think Aunt Jackie will talk sooner rather than later. Remember, it's totally psychological. Dr. Capone believes trauma robbed her of her speech and something equally impactful will cause it to come back. Her birthday is coming up soon. Maybe I should throw her a big surprise party. That might make her talk."

"I still say if we starve her for a day or two, she'll start talking. Even when she was on the feeding tube, Jackie didn't skip a meal. She ain't lost very much weight since the heart attack. Let's starve her, Zach."

Zach laughed. "We are not gonna starve her. Aunt Jackie will start talking soon."

Chapter Twenty-five

Warden Callahan jumped up from the chair behind his desk and lunged at the two guards in his office. He shoved Captain Floyd clean across the floor. Then he stepped to Corporal Jamison and looked up. The man was six or seven inches taller than the warden, but he had fear in his eyes.

"You big, stupid motherfucker! How the hell did you install the spyware in the wrong office?" He turned to Captain Floyd. "I put you in charge. You were supposed to make sure everything was in order. We've wasted an entire week. All I have is a tape filled with hours and hours of absolutely nothing!"

"I was busy taking care of the other things you put me in charge of, sir. I had to supervise those two important deliveries. You said no one could do it except me."

The warden rubbed the top of his head several times in frustration. "Yeah, I guess I gave you more than you could handle. And you thought that idiot could take up the slack."

"Yes, sir, I did," the captain mumbled.

The warden rounded his desk and sat down behind it. "We're going to try this again. I want both of you to stay late this evening. Go and remove the devices from the social worker's office and install them in the damn counselor's office. Do you two understand?"

"Yes, sir."

***

Jay was on her way to Pastor Monroe's office for a counseling session. Although he loved her very much, he wasn't thrilled about facing her this particular day. Every time they were together, Jay asked him if Holly had made a decision about the adoption yet. And each time he told her a lie. Holly didn't want Jay's baby unless she would agree to a private closed adoption. She did not want the child to know the identity of its biological mother or father until the age of 18. Eventually, they would have to tell the child that he or she had been adopted. Holly just didn't want the child to know the names of his or her parents until after their eighteenth birthday. She was against the child having contact with the biological parents or any member of their family. Everything Holly wanted was in direct contradiction to Jay's wishes.

Pastor Monroe wanted his child, but he couldn't override Holly's wishes any more than he could force her to abide by Jay's terms. He was stuck in the middle between his wife, whom he was committed to, and the mother of his child, the woman he truly loved. And in the midst of it all was his innocent, unborn son or daughter. Pastor Monroe's dilemma was more complicated than any other he had ever faced, but he had a possible solution, and he prayed to God that it would work. He just needed Jay on board.

As if on cue, she rushed into his office. When the door closed behind her, she waddled around his desk and sat on his lap. "I missed you," she said with her lips pressed against his.

"I missed you too." He rubbed her belly filled with his child.

"Did you feel the baby move?"

"Yeah, I think we have a dancer or a soccer player in there. Come and let's talk on the couch."

Jay stood up. "Is there something wrong? You seem sad." They walked to the couch together and sat down.

"Holly wants the baby, but she insists that the adoption be a closed one. That's the only way she'll go through with it."

"I won't do that. It'll defeat the purpose. The adoption has to be open so you and the baby can come here to visit me. I want to be able to send pictures and cards so my child can know who its mother is. I don't mind the baby calling Holly Mommy, but he or she will know that I'm Mommy too. When I get outta here, I want a relationship with my child."

"I understand, sweetheart, but Holly will not go along with an open adoption."

"What kind of woman would want to deny a mother access to her own child? That is so selfish!"

"Holly isn't selfish at all. She's been generous to you, and she'll be more than generous to our child. She simply won't agree to your proposal."

"So, she gave me some clothes and personal items. That doesn't make her a saint, Gavin. Our baby ain't some object. It's our flesh and blood. And I can't believe you would sit here in my face and defend Holly's selfishness."

"Holly is not selfish," he shot back, slightly annoyed.

Jay jumped up from the couch. "Holly is selfish, inconsiderate, and heartless. If I didn't love you, I'd be happy to tell her in her face exactly what I think of her. She's jealous, Gavin. She's jealous that I'm able to give you the one thing that she can't. It makes no difference that she doesn't know you're the actual father. I'm still able to give you the baby she can't! I'm leaving now. I don't feel like talking anymore."

"Don't you want to hear about my plan that could possibly solve our problem?"

"No, I've heard enough from you today. Go home to your wife."

***

Holly grabbed a roll from the platter and began to butter it. "I don't want a black baby, Trudy. I can't have a little nappy-headed nigger running around calling me Mommy. What would the other church members think? And the mother is a convicted felon. God only knows what she's serving time for. She could be a murderer. You know those people have a high propensity for violence. That type of behavior is hereditary."

"How does Pastor feel about it?"

"For some reason he wants that baby in the worst way. He has begged and bargained with me to no end. I had to lie to him. I told him I would take the baby if Jayla would agree to a closed adoption. Of course she won't. You know how black mothers are. They can be poor as a pauper and as ignorant as a beast, but they'll cling to their babies. They'll be living in a hole in the wall with ten kids by ten different men, but they will keep every one of those pickaninnies instead of giving a few to someone who can provide for them and teach them some good sense."

"Do you think Pastor will drop the subject now?"

Holly took a sip of tea. "Dear God, I hope so."

Ten minutes into Jay's counseling session with Pastor Monroe, Captain Floyd realized he had forgotten to turn the spyware on. He ran to the office he shared with Corporal Jamison. When he sat down at his desk and turned the monitor on, he was surprised to see Pastor Monroe in his office alone. Jay was nowhere in sight. Where the hell was she? She never missed counseling. The captain swiveled around in his chair a few times. He would have a little talk with Dixon to see if she knew what was going on with her friend.

Chapter Twenty-six

"Are you sure it's a boy, Dr. Yusuf?"

"It is a boy indeed, Ms. King. And he will arrive in ten weeks. I've known the baby's gender for some time now. You forbade me to tell you. I hope you're happy that you're having a son."

Jay nodded and slid down from the examination table. She took the sonogram picture the doctor offered her and studied it. "Yeah, I'm happy, but I've got a lot on my mind."

"Is there anything I can do to help?"

"Nah, my situation is complicated. Thanks for offering, though."

"I'll leave you alone now to get dressed."

I'm having a boy. Jay's thought was a bittersweet one. If Nahima had been a little boy, it may have made a world of difference. A son could've possibly saved her and Venus's troubled relationship and the course of Jay's life. She had never wanted a child, period. Motherhood didn't seem the slightest bit appealing to Jay back then. Nahima was conceived out of her love for Venus. A baby was supposed to have been the symbol to mark the success of their relationship, to complete their family. Unfortunately, it was Nahima, or what she represented, that ultimately tore Jay and Venus apart. Her presence threatened their relationship. Nahima robbed Jay of all the love and attention that Venus once had only for her. Jay wasn't able to compete with her own daughter.

But many times over the years, she often wondered how things would've turned out if Nahima had been a little boy. The entire time Venus was pregnant, Jay prayed for a son. It wasn't meant to be.

Now that Jay's son was going to make his debut to the world in ten weeks, she had mixed emotions. She was happy to know that she was carrying a boy, but the circumstances were so screwed up. She couldn't raise her son in prison, and she refused to expose his father. How could Jay be completely happy when the future of her baby's welfare was so uncertain? The more she toiled over the possibilities, the more sense Pastor Monroe's suggestion made. They had made up during their last session together. He apologized to Jay for defending Holly and for falling short of convincing her to go along with the open adoption.

He offered a suggestion that he truly believed would remedy the situation. He asked Jay to reach out to Zach. In his opinion, a face-to-face conversation between the King siblings was long overdue. Pastor Monroe had no knowledge of their history, but he knew they were estranged. Regardless of what had transpired between the brother and sister, he felt that an innocent baby could bring them back together.

He helped Jay write a letter to Zach, asking him to come visit her at Leesworth. To ensure that her brother would receive the letter, they addressed it to Dex and asked that he hand deliver it to his best friend. The letter was stamped, sealed, and tucked under the flimsy mattress of Jay's bed in her cell. She was afraid to mail it. Rejection was a bitter pill to swallow.

Dex, no doubt, would make sure Zach received the letter, but he couldn't force him to respond. And her brother definitely couldn't respond without first reading the letter. Jay had already placed Zach's name on her visitation list. Now all she needed to do was send the letter inviting him to Leesworth for a visit. If he decided to come, she would beg for forgiveness for everything she'd ever done to him, Jill, Nahima, and Aunt Jackie. Then she would ask Zach to take custody of her son the moment he was born.

"Stop it, baby, I need to get dressed. There is a pile of work on my desk."

Pastor Monroe teased Jay's nipple with the pad of his thumb and kissed her stomach. She tried to wiggle away from him, but he had her pinned down on the couch in his office. "You're so sexy pregnant. Your body is exquisite. I've never made love to a pregnant woman before. I can't get enough of you, Jayla."

"Well, I just gave you plenty of me. Now move so I can get up and back to work." Jay pushed his arm away playfully and sat up on the couch. "I mailed Zach's letter to Dex this morning. I'm praying that he'll come to visit me soon."

"You've both acted childishly in recent months. First, Zach sent your letter back unopened. Then, after your aunt's heart attack, he wanted to reconnect with you, but you refused. Now you want Zach to visit you. I'm curious about what went on between you and your brother in the past, but I really don't want to know. My hope is that the two of you reconcile. Then I want Zach to take custody of our son until you're released from prison."

"And when I'm free, you, our son, and I will be a family."

"Hi, Cherell, I need to see Warden Callahan please."

The dutiful administrative assistant smiled, displaying a pretty set of pearly white teeth. The top two in the front adorned with gold stood out. One outlined a heart and the other one flaunted the letter C for Cherell. The shiny gold teeth combined with the specks of bronze hair in her micro braids made an interesting combination. Regardless, Cherell was a very attractive brown-skinned girl in Jay's eyes. She was cute but very ghetto.

"The warden ain't here today, Ms. King. He won't be back until Monday morning. Can I help you with something?"

"I'm sure you can. Who would be able to read his writing better than you?" Jay handed Cherell the request form. "He wants a check to be made payable to Jeff or Jett. I can't make it out. And does the person have a last name by any chance?"

Grabbing a pen from her desk, Cherell giggled. "Oops, my bad, girl, I wrote that. That's Jefferson's Premium Meat Warehouse. The warden calls the owner Jeff since they're close friends and all." Cherell corrected the mistake on the form and handed it back to Jay. "I fixed it."

"Thank you."

Jay left Callahan's office and headed to the copier. She didn't have a clue what the warden had purchased from his good friend Jeff, but it was expensive. $2,300 worth of any cut of beef could feed all the starving children in the slums of Kingston, Jamaica. Jay wondered who Callahan was planning to feed.

Zach tossed the letter on the coffee table and picked up his half-empty Heineken bottle. He took a long swig.

"Oh, hell nah, Negro, you're gonna finish reading it." Dex snatched the letter up and slapped it on his boy's chest.

"I should've known something was up with you. Ramona is due any damn minute now, and you're over here harassing me. Talking about you wanna hang out with me on a weeknight because you're stressed out. You brought your ass to my crib so you could drink up all my beer and hit me with Jay's bullshit!"

"Don't worry about Ramona and the baby. Her parents are at our house with her. And Jay's letter ain't no bullshit. She's ready to talk to you face-to-face after almost three years. A few months ago, you were bitching because you couldn't get Jay to call or put you on her visitation list. Well, you got your wish. Your sister wants to see you. Take your ass on up to Leesworth and find out what she wants to talk about. I'm surprised Jay wants to see you after that letter you sent cursing her out."

"Jay is up to something like she always is. I wouldn't be surprised if her crazy ass wants to ask me to give her a kidney. Hell, knowing Jay, she might be getting married. Reverend Slick Dick probably told wifey about his prison love child and she divorced him."

"Or maybe Jay just wants to apologize for everything she's ever done to you."

Chapter Twenty-seven

Cherell buzzed Warden Callahan's desk. His temper went from zero to fifty in a matter of seconds. He'd asked not to be disturbed while he read over the contract from the CEO of the Kemp Corporation. He was eager to finalize the deal with them. But they'd been back and forth over a few issues, money being the most pressing one of all.

"What is it, Cherell?"

"Corporal Jamison is here to see you. He said it's important."

Blowing out a gush of hot air, the warden dropped the contract on his desk. "Send him in."

The corporal walked in wide-eyed and anxious, clutching something in his hand. He planted his six-foot six frame and medium build in the middle of the warden's office like a tree. Jamison had had his share of romps in the sack with some of the inmates. Those who preferred darker brothers threw their panties at him all the time. Warden Callahan knew all about it.

"Good morning, sir. I have the disc from the counselor's office. I made sure the camera was on a few minutes ahead of time before all three meetings King had with him. I didn't look at it, though." Jamison laughed nervously. "You didn't tell me to."

"Give it here." The warden snatched the tape. "I'll watch it later. I've got more important matters to take care of."

"Yes, sir. Should I turn the spyware on again today when King has her counseling session with the preacher?"

"I'll let Floyd know, and he'll give you instructions. You may leave now."

As soon as Jamison left, Callahan put the DVD on his desk. Then he sat down and picked up the contract. Mr. Kemp was trying to play hardball. Just who the fuck did he think he was dealing with? J.C. Callahan was nobody's punk or fool. If Kemp Corporation wanted the Leesworth inmates to help assemble its shipping crates, they would have to pay them more than eighty-seven cents a day. How the hell was he supposed to get his cut if that was all Mr. Kemp was offering? No, he would have to up his offer to a dollar and a nickel a day per inmate, just like Warden Callahan's secret financial advisor, Ms. King, had suggested very early on in the negotiations. She was one smart woman. Her expertise with numbers had helped to make things a lot easier for the warden around Leesworth. The woman really knew her stuff.

Callahan eyed the DVD. Yes, Jayla King was smart. She was smart enough to get knocked up in prison right under his nose. And she wouldn't reveal the name of the baby's father, all under the guise that she was doing the prison a favor by saving it from a nasty scandal. Callahan stood and picked up the disc. He walked over to the DVD player, popped it inside, and turned on the television. He folded his arms across his chest and watched the screen.

"Boring," the warden yelled at the television after some time. He grabbed the remote control and fast-forwarded the tape. "Let's see what happened Wednesday, shall we?"

The warden took a seat on the edge of his desk. On the screen, Pastor Monroe looked up and smiled when Jay entered his office. He left his seat behind his desk and met her in the middle of the room. They embraced, but not in a simple or friendly kind of way. There was chemistry and familiarity between them.

Callahan shot up from his desk when the pastor's hands palmed Jay's tight, round ass and pulled her closer. Then he kissed her deeply and hungrily. Within seconds, they were tugging at each other's clothes and kissing each other everywhere.

The warden was speechless and aroused. He developed an erection the size and stiffness of a mountain when he saw Jay's naked, pregnant body. Pastor Monroe lifted her effortlessly off her feet and carried her to the couch. He sat down with her high in his arms. Elevating her hips, he pulled her to sit on his shoulders. Her wetness was directly in his face, obviously where he wanted it to be. Jay threw her head back and moaned when the pastor dipped his tongue into her honey pot. But it wasn't just for a taste of her sweetness. He devoured her like a ravenous animal would a juicy piece of meat until she screamed and fell apart.

"Well, well, well . . ." Warden Callahan whispered. His pants were unzipped, exposing himself. He'd begun a slow and thorough massage on his hardness as the footage continued to roll. "The mystery has been solved."

Their eyes met and locked. Jay had to remind herself to breathe. She remained seated at the table, not trusting her legs to sustain her on her swollen feet. She was beyond nervous with each step Zach took bringing them closer and closer together. Even with the many voices talking and laughing in the jam-packed visitation room, Jay heard nothing. Tension-filled silence rang in her ears. Time and motion stood still when Zach stopped in front of the table where she sat

"What's up, Jay? You wanted to see me, so I'm here."

Jay licked her lips. Her mouth suddenly felt dry, and her throat was tight. She'd practiced her greeting a thousand times in her head, but she couldn't remember a single word. She decided to say what came naturally. "Have a seat, Zach. I'm glad you came. How are you?"

Zach pulled out the chair directly across from his sister and lowered his tall, muscular frame into it. "I'm fine."

"I am too, I guess. As far as my health is concerned, the doctor says I'm stable for now. My back is giving me grief, though. That's an expected symptom of my condition. How is Aunt Jackie?"

"Her health is improving gradually since she damn near died. She's still not talking, though. Why am I here?"

"Zach, I'm so sorry for ordering a hit on you. There's no excuse for what I did. I was wrong. I was wrong to kidnap Jill in Jamaica, too. She didn't deserve that. I know it's asking a lot, but I want you to forgive me. We'll probably never be close again. I'm sure you don't even consider me your sister anymore, and I understand. But I've had time to do lots of soul-searching since I've been here. I take full responsibility for my present circumstances. There's no one to blame but Jay. I pray that one day you and Jill will find it in your hearts to forgive me."

"That's a tough one. I've tried to forgive you. God knows I have. But the memories of all the lies, deception, and schemes haunt me like a never-ending nightmare. And then you got yourself pregnant by some other woman's husband. The man's a preacher at that. He was helping you find something besides Jesus. The news about your pregnancy almost took our aunt out. How the hell do you think that makes me feel?"

"It was never my intention to hurt Aunt Jackie. I needed someone to talk to, a person who loved me who I could trust. I didn't want to tell Daddy. Aunt Jackie was the only person I could confide in, but I didn't mean to stress her out. I live with the guilt of causing her heart attack every day. I'm sorry."

"It's your pattern, Jay. You fuck up and leave a pile of shit behind for someone else to clean up, just like a dog. First it was Venus and Nahima. Then you moved on to Jill. After her, you came at me—viciously. You wanted me dead. And in between all of your attacks on the people you claimed to have loved, you left innocent casualties in the aftermath. Nina, Ayla, and that poor white chick were victims you used to get to your next level of craziness. You've got a pool of blood on your hands."

Jay nodded and maintained direct eye contact with her brother. "My sins are piled high, but I've been forgiven. God and I have an understanding about my past. Now I'm asking that you forgive me and meet me somewhere in the middle of a casual association and a general acquaintance. Like I said earlier, you don't consider me family anymore."

"Give me some time. Let me think and pray on it. That's about as good as you can get from me at this point in my life. Aunt Jackie is my primary concern right now. Plus, I have my wife, my kids, and Nahima to consider. Allow me time to process everything." Zach looked around the room filled with all types of people from every walk of life. Every race, ethnicity, and age was present. "Is there somewhere we can get something to drink around here? I'm thirsty."

Jay pushed her chair back and attempted to stand. "Yeah, we have a vending area—"

"Sit down. Just tell me where it is. You look like you're about to pop, girl. You'll only slow me down. I'll get a soda for me and whatever you want."

Jay relaxed in her seat and directed Zach to the vending area. Then she watched him walk away.

Chapter Twenty-eight

On their walk around the visitation room, Jay complained about severe back pain. It was her idea for them to walk and talk while he sipped on fruit punch and she finished off a bag of chips. Walking sometimes eased the tension in Jay's lower back, and Dr. Yusuf wanted her to exercise as much as possible every day.

"Let's sit down, Jay. You seem tired, and you're waddling like a wounded duck."

"You won't get an argument from me about that, but it's not so much that I'm tired. All the extra weight is killing my back."

Jay followed Zach back to the chairs they'd vacated. Once they took their seats, an awkward silence fell over them. During their walk around the visitation room, they'd maintained a safe conversation, approaching only subjects unrelated to their estrangement. Jay wasn't totally relaxed, but it felt good to be in Zach's presence. She had been such a fool to have ordered a hit on him. Regardless of his affair with Jill, she had no right to try to punish him with death. Jay's subsequent actions were desperate, impulsive, irrational attempts to escape justice. Unfortunately for her, she only managed to dig a deeper ditch for herself, and she eventually came face-to-face with a judge and jury after all.

"When is the baby due?" Zach's question snatched Jay from the past.

"Dr. Yusuf said February twenty-first."

"Are you ready?"

"I'm not afraid, if that's what you're asking. Labor and delivery are the only ways for this little fellow to get here." Jay rubbed her tummy affectionately. "Unless the doctor—"

"You're having a boy?"

Jay looked up at her brother and smiled. "Yeah, I'm gonna have a little boy." Her smile quickly faded as tears filled her eyes. "But he'll go into foster care unless someone in the family is willing to take him. Gavin—that's the baby's father—can't take him. I won't let him."

"Why not, Jay? It's his son too."

"Gavin is married and he's a pastor. If he acknowledges our son, he could lose his church and his professional license. His reputation would be ruined. For once in my life I wanna do right by someone who loves me. I love Gavin, Zach, and I'm not gonna expose him."

Zach stared at Jay for several seconds. She could tell he was thrown off by her commitment to her child's father, but it wasn't an act. It was a sincere gesture to spare the man she loved.

"Aunt Jackie would've taken your son in a heartbeat. Everyone else in the family is either too old or has more children or grandchildren than they can provide for."

Jay closed her eyes and sniffed back tears. "Can you and Jill please take my baby?" The words spilled out.

Zach should've seen it coming. He knew Jay better than anyone else dead or alive. He was no longer naive when it came to his sister. His instincts had warned him that there was a motive behind her urgent request to see him, and Dex had dropped a few hints about what Jay may have wanted from him. *Can you and Jill please take my baby?* Zach slapped the steering wheel with both hands when those words came back to him.

Jay was a bold-ass bitch. She had no right to ask anything of the brother she had paid some clown to take out, yet she had asked without hesitation. And she'd done more than just ask Zach. She'd presented a very compelling summation, justifying reasons why he and Jill should take custody of her son upon his birth. Extremely intelligent and eloquent, Jay could've easily been an attorney. If she'd represented herself in her murder-for-hire trial, there was a good chance she wouldn't have been sitting in jail. But she was in prison, and she would be for the next ten to fifteen years, depending on her health and behavior. Apparently, it wasn't very hard to conceive a child at Leesworth Women's Federal Corrections Facility, but raising one there was out of the question.

"I'm so damn tired of cleaning up your mess! Damn you, Jay! I ain't gonna raise your baby! I don't give a damn what anybody says. I won't do it! He ain't my fucking problem!" Zach yelled and cursed Jay as he cruised down the interstate on his way home.

"At least he didn't say no."

"And he didn't say he would either, Shanika. You don't know my brother. He can be stubborn. But when it comes to me, I can't even blame him."

"Can't he tell how much you've changed?"

Jay took the pillowcase Shanika had folded and placed on top of a tall pile of others. She grabbed one from the laundry cart and started folding it. "I believe he saw a difference in me other than my big belly, but when I asked him to take my baby, he completely shut down. It was like he checked out on me even before he left the building. I wish I could still read Zach's mind the way I used to when I was a little girl. He's a hard nut to crack now. I can tell you one thing I know for sure from the way he looked at me."

"What's that?"

"My brother still loves me. He couldn't hide it, no matter how hard he tried. Of course, he'd rather die and go to hell before he admits it, but I saw it in his eyes. It was there as plain as day."

"Well, if that's true, you ain't got nothing to worry about, girl. He's gonna take your little boy and love him the same way he loves his kids and Nahima."

"Lord, please let that be true."

Jill wasn't any more thrilled about the idea of taking custody of Jay's son than Zach was, but at least she was willing to consider it. He'd told her there wasn't a snowflake's chance in hell that they would take the baby. Jill understood the reason behind his decision, but Zach's attitude disturbed her a great deal. His bitterness had clouded his ability to think rationally. It was as if he'd forgotten that he and Jay had been loved and raised by Aunt Jackie when circumstances beyond their control took both of their parents away from them. She didn't hesitate to take them, even at the young and inexperienced age of twenty. Aunt Jackie confessed many, many times that she'd hated their father back then, but it didn't taint her feelings for Zach and Jay. They were her flesh and blood, born to her imperfect sister, who was doing the unthinkable at the time of her death. She had been very angry with Belva for placing herself in a situation that robbed her two innocent children of their mother.

Zach had an opportunity to do something quite similar to what Aunt Jackie had done for him and Jay. The situations were different in more than one way, but the main, underlying issue was identical. Another innocent

King child was in need of a home and someone to care for him in the absence of their parents. Sadly, no one was willing or available to open their arms to him.

"What is it tonight, Gavin? Do you have a headache? Are you tired? Is Sunday morning's sermon coming forth? Or is one of your precious convicts in crisis? I have had it with the excuses!"

Holly ripped the covers away from her body and left the bed. She snatched her silk lavender bathrobe from the bedpost to cover the matching negligee. She was about to freeze anyway from trying to be sexy for her husband. Frustrated to the maximum level, she stomped around the bedroom, blowing out the dozen or so magnolia-scented votive candles she'd lit in hopes of creating a romantic atmosphere. They'd missed the mark. The lingerie went unnoticed, as did Shania Twain's voice assuring him that he was "still the one." And the only thing the damn whipped cream had done was soil Holly's expensive satin sheets.

"Come back to bed, Holly. There's no need for you to be upset. This happens to couples all the time. Men my age sometimes have problems when they're operating under pressure."

"What kind of pressure are you under? Please tell me exactly what it is, because it's driving me batty as hell! How many times have you touched me in the past seven and a half months, huh? Maybe twice or three times tops? You must have the weight of the world on your shoulders. Whatever it is, I think it's only fair that you share it with your wife."

"Do you want to know why I don't want to touch you? Do you really, really want to know?"

"Yes."

"I don't enjoy it anymore!" Gavin jumped up from the bed. "Every time we make love, I say to myself, 'If she doesn't get pregnant, she's going to lose her mind. She'll take a dangerous drug behind my back or slip something in my food. Or maybe she'll go back to the little Asian guy and let him stick a thousand needles in her like she's a porcupine!' You've done it all before, even after promising me that you wouldn't. Having sex with you is no longer worth the stress. I'd rather have peace of mind."

Chapter Twenty-nine

Holly threw herself onto the bed when Gavin left their room in a huff. He'd grabbed a pillow and a blanket from the walk-in closet and run downstairs. It was still happening after over nineteen years of marriage. Their infertility issues had dragged them down into a funk once again, but this time it was their all-time worst. They'd never gone longer than six weeks without making love. Erectile dysfunction was a new issue altogether. Gavin was too young and healthy to be affected by that. And why hadn't he mentioned it months ago? She would've scheduled him an appointment to see Dr. Radcliffe.

Nothing about their marriage made sense anymore. Gavin was mean and moody most of the time. He had more compassion and tolerance for the inmates at Leesworth than he had for his own wife. He especially loved Sophia, Shanika, and Jay. The tobacco picker, druggie, and pregnant nigger were a delightful trio. The sun rose and shined on those three, but Jay was his favorite of all. He was willing to adopt her baby to save it from the child welfare system, and he expected the three of them to share the child. The idea was utterly ridiculous, and that was why she had rejected it.

Baby or no baby, Holly wanted her marriage to get back on track. Maybe she would have to resort to some of her old tactics. For starters, she needed to find a way to get Gavin to spend less time at the prison with those women. And if need be, she would lace his food as she'd done countless times in the past. Only this time it would be with the little blue pill and not a fertility hormone. Holly wasn't about to let erectile dysfunction ruin her chances of getting pregnant. She would save her marriage and give Gavin a child by any means necessary.

"Come on in, Ms. King. Have a seat."

Jay waddled into Warden Callahan's office on swollen legs and feet. Her lower back was aching, and she was grumpy as hell a little over a month before her due date. When Captain Floyd came to her office to tell her the warden wanted to see her, she was none too happy.

"Floyd said you wanted to ask me a question about the quarterly wages report. Is there something wrong, sir?"

"I'm not sure. I'll let you be the judge of that, Ms. King. You see, something very shocking has been brought to my attention recently. Even as the head honcho around here, some things slip past me. It's not easy to oversee a staff of 437 people and an inmate population of 2,000-plus women. No, no, no, it is an extremely difficult task, but I've done my best over the ten years I've been here. I've seen it all, or so I thought, until now. I'd like to show you something, if I may."

Jay watched the warden stroll over to the shelf where his television and DVD player sat. He turned and smiled at her before he aimed the remote control to start the show. Jay swallowed a grape-sized lump in her throat when she saw Pastor Monroe sitting at his desk. He was wearing his navy pinstriped suit, and his hair, beard, and mustache were freshly trimmed. The kiss, the fondling, and the foreplay rolled out in a blur. Jay dropped her head when she saw her naked body on the television screen.

Callahan had secretly recorded her and Pastor Monroe making love in his office. Not only was it illegal, but it was a gross invasion of their privacy. Sure, they were in violation of a list of policies, but they weren't the only ones. Jayla Simone King was nobody's bitch, not even Warden Callahan's. He thought he had her by the tit. It was time to hand him his balls. The big, bad, powerful warden was smiling now, but not for long.

"So now that you know who my baby's father is, what do you plan to do, sir?"

"I'll deal with his perverted ass first, and after you drop his little bastard, I'll deal with you. So, a tough, diehard dyke like you let some white punk-ass preacher break you in. You better be glad it was him and not me. I would've spread your hips from east to west."

"I think I—"

"Shut the fuck up, bitch!" He walked coolly over to Jay and stood above her chair. He bent down, placing a hand on each armrest. "You can forget about the good pastor. He's going to get a pink slip today. I still may press charges against him. I haven't decided yet. As for you, if you so much as sneeze too loud, I'll have you written up and transferred out of the state of Georgia quicker than you can blink. You go that?"

"Hell nah, Negro, I ain't got nothing! And I suggest that you back up off me."

Warden Callahan straightened his posture and lifted his hand to strike Jay.

"I wish you would hit me. I'll scream and act the fool so bad up in here that every guard in this damn building will come running. I'm thirty-five weeks pregnant. You'll be somebody's cellmate in your own prison before nightfall. And I've got the goods on you anyway."

The warden lowered his hand. "What the hell are you talking about?"

"I have an entire file filled with bogus receipts, vouchers, request forms, and checks to show the governor how you're paying for your daughter's wedding. That dumb, ugly heifer flunked outta Bethune-Cookman University and got knocked up, but Daddy is still gonna throw her the wedding of the century with dirty money. You ought to be ashamed of yourself, stealing from the State and the inmates."

Warden Callahan backed up nervously. It was Jay's turn to smile. She had his ass sweating and fidgeting like a crackhead on the prowl for a rock. He was thinking. The gloss in his eyes and the pulse beating fast in his throat were telling signs.

"You can't prove a damn thing." He laughed dryly. "And who the hell do you think will believe you over me? You said it yourself. The accounting department is always screwing up. I've never signed a request form for anything that wasn't related to expenses within the prison. Cherell completes and signs everything else."

"I've got a file, fool! The indisputable proof is in it. I have made copies of everything and coded all transactions. I know the vendors, delivery locations, and dates. Hell, I know your daughter's social security number and bra size, you stupid motherfucker."

Callahan burned a hole in the carpet pacing back and forth several times before he dropped down on the edge of his desk. Mr. Big Shot was flustered, shocked, and defeated. Jay could recognize that look on anyone. She'd worn it many times over the last three years. And just like the warden, she had brought it on herself by plotting to destroy someone's life. Then, as if he'd been struck by a bolt of lightning, Callahan reached over and grabbed the walkie-talkie from his desk. A wide grin had replaced his scowl.

"Floyd, where are you?" There was no immediate response. "Floyd, where the hell are you?"

After a static-filled pause, Floyd, in his deep Southern drawl, answered his boss. "I'm on rounds in the recreation area, sir."

"I want a shakedown in King's cell, pronto."

"In whose cell, sir?"

"Damn it! I want a shakedown in Jayla King's cell now! Any papers or books you find should be brought to my office immediately."

Chapter Thirty

"Who were you talking to?" Zach eased his arms around Jill's tiny waist and kissed the back of her neck. He pulled her back against his broad chest.

"It was Venus. We're planning an outing for the kids." Jill placed the cordless phone in its cradle. There was no other place she'd rather be than in her husband's arms. She shuddered when he licked her ear and blew warm air into it.

"I guess Charles and I will have to make plans to hang out while our wives and children do their thang. Too bad Dex can't roll with us anytime soon. He's on rocking chair and diaper duty. Our new goddaughter keeps him and Ramona up all night long, crying and nursing."

"I know. I feel sorry for them."

"You should feel sorry for yourself, because when the kids go to bed, I'm gonna keep you up all night long."

"Half the night would be much better. I have to rise very early in the morning. I promised Madame Helena that I would help judge solo performance auditions for the spring recital at eight o'clock."

"Okay, I'm going to bathe the kiddies and put them to bed early. I'll meet you in our room in thirty minutes." Zach swatted Jill on her ass. "Wear something sexy."

"Something sexy, eh?"

"Yeah, put some red polish on your toenails. That's sexy."

"What else should I wear?"

"Nothing. The red toenail polish is enough." Zach smiled and winked before he headed to the den to round up Zachary Jr. and Zion.

What Dr. Yusuf had initially diagnosed as typical pregnancy back pain due to excessive weight had turned out to be something more serious. Jay's kidney function had decreased drastically. They were weak. The pregnancy had limited their ability to properly filter Jay's system. Therefore, she had retained lots of water. Her legs, hands, and feet were terribly swollen. The back pain had worsened, and she was barely able to walk.

The warden had ordered an electric scooter for Jay to maneuver her way around the building. He allowed her to work in her cell whenever she felt up to working at all. Dr. Yusuf had informed Jay that if her condition did not improve by the end of the week, she would have to undergo an emergency cesarean section. There was a strong possibility that a dialysis routine would begin immediately after the baby's birth.

Jay was very depressed about her health. She was worried about her baby, too. Dr. Yusuf assured her that her son was fine and encouraged her to maintain a positive attitude. She attempted to hold it together, but it was hard. Pastor Monroe was supportive. He spent more time at Leesworth just to be close to her. He would be in the delivery room with her whenever the time came. Warden Callahan had already approved that request and many others from Jay. Pastor Monroe would be allowed to sign his son's birth certificate, and the record would be sealed. A prison social worker had been instructed to notify Zach the instant his nephew was born. He still hadn't agreed to take the baby, but Jay was hoping against hope that he would.

***

"You see, it was my intention from the very beginning to pay the money back, Ms. King. I didn't steal it. I borrowed it."

Jay leaned back in the comfortable chair on her electric scooter and looked over the ledger again. "But you'll be in the hole again next year. All you're doing is moving money around to cover what you stole. And you were willing to let Cherell or me take the fall in the event of an audit. That's why I covered myself. Did you think I was stupid?"

"No, I know how intelligent you are."

Jay laughed. "Is that why you had Floyd shake down my cell? Did you really think I only had one file? I've been sending copies of all of your illegal transactions to my Aunt Jackie for months. That file is more valuable than that nasty DVD from Gavin's office. Those documents are permissible in a court of law, but that DVD isn't. Have you destroyed it yet?"

"Yes, I have." The warden placed both of his palms on Jay's desk and leaned in. "Now when can I have that file?"

"I'm gonna let my aunt hold on to it for a little while longer. Everyone needs a little security, Warden Callahan."

Holly yawned and stretched her arms high above her head. Her eyes had grown blurry, watery, and itchy after hours of searching the internet. She wanted to know more about Jay, Sophia, and Shanika. Her husband was so in love with the three of them, and it was getting under Holly's skin. And there was another, nameless inmate who had recently joined the women's ministry at Leesworth. She was also in counseling with Pastor Monroe, and he'd quickly added her to his list of damsels in distress.

Apparently, the woman was as nutty as a fruitcake, and she was constantly on suicide watch. Every time she threatened to kill herself, he refused to leave her until she settled down. He had never worked overtime before. The other day he'd spent close to twenty-four hours at Leesworth before he came home to rest for a few hours. Then he showered, went back, and put in another sixteen hours of dedicated service for his precious convicts. The pastor had no clue what kind of women he was dealing with, yet he was committed to them wholeheartedly. That was why Holly had made it her mission to get the scoop on them.

She was surprised to find out Sophia Mendez was serving time for violent crimes. She had been convicted for her support role in an armed robbery, an attempted murder, and other related chargers. Fortunately for her, her ten-year sentence was coming to an end. Sophia's trial had been covered all over the news and in the *Atlanta Journal-Constitution*. Her love for a strung-out thug had led her down the wrong path. According to newspaper clippings, Sophia's fiancé, Emilio Castro, was a drug addict who was unable to hold down a job, so he robbed homes and businesses to support his habit.

Out of love, Sophia had helped her man rob the combined convenience store and check-cashing establishment where she had worked for six years. During what would eventually become a botched robbery, one of the store's owners pulled out a gun and tried to defend everything he and his family had worked hard for. Angry and agitated, Emilio shot the older Indian gentleman in the head at midrange, leaving him with severe brain damage. He then fled the store but was apprehended a few hours later.

Emilio confessed his crime to the authorities but implicated Sophia as the mastermind behind everything.

While he was deliberately throwing his silent partner in crime under the bus, she was at the hospital with her boss and his family. Sophia had purposely stayed behind at work as they had planned, pretending she wasn't a part of Emilio's robbery attempt. In fact, it was Sophia who had called for an ambulance and tended to her boss until help arrived. She was horrified, as she'd stated in her testimony during her trial. No one was supposed to have been wounded or killed. Sophia's confession and the testimony she gave against Emilio on behalf of the prosecution guaranteed her a ten-year prison sentence, rather than the fifteen to twenty years she could've served.

Holly couldn't dig up any dirt on Shanika or Jay. She didn't know their last names. Shanika had introduced herself to Holly after service at the prison that night. She'd said her whole name, too. How her last name had escaped Holly was a mystery. Jay didn't offer her last name or even a smile. "Guarded" was the one word Holly remembered about her attitude that night. It was weird. Holly had felt like she was being judged or inspected under Jay's penetrating gaze. The atmosphere was tense.

Holly was guilty of doing a little judging that night as well. Jay's baby bump had caught her totally off guard. Her husband had not mentioned that she was expecting, and when Holly had tried to fish for information about Jay's pregnancy, he had stayed pretty tight-lipped. Even when he presented her the adoption proposal, he wasn't very forthcoming. Holly didn't know much of anything about Jay or her situation except that she needed someone to take custody of her child to prevent him or her from going into foster care.

The lives of Jay and Shanika remained top secret to Holly. The relationship between them and Pastor Monroe did, too. Why he was hell-bent on playing such important roles in their lives drove Holly's curiosity straight through the roof. She was aware of the "Save Sandy" syndrome her husband suffered from, but there was more to it than that. The sudden emergence of the inmate with the severe mental health issues only added fuel to the fire. He was more passionate about his job and his ministry at Leesworth, as well as pastoring his church, than he was about his marriage.

Holly was fed up. She could deal with her husband's love for and commitment to his church, but his affection for those damned inmates at Leesworth had pushed her to her breaking point. If she could uncover their pasts and expose their crimes, Pastor Monroe would look at them with new and more perceptive eyes. Then he wouldn't be so sympathetic toward them. He would spend less time at the prison and more time at home with his wife. And the sexual-enhancement drugs and blue pills she planned to sprinkle in his food and drinks would soon help them conceive a baby.

There was only one way Holly could get her hands on the information she needed to tarnish Jay's and Shanika's images in her husband's eyes. She would have to reach out to his nemesis.

Connor Hayes was a recovering cocaine addict who had turned his life around. His private investigation firm had an impeccable reputation in the metro Atlanta area, having assisted hundreds of law firms and private citizens in solving major criminal cases. Connor was do-ing quite well for himself. He was now a devoted family man and a deacon in his church. His days of crime and drug use were long behind him. The sins of his past were forgiven and forgotten by most, but not by his former brother-in-law, Pastor Gavin Kyle Monroe.

It was because of Connor that Sandy became ad-dicted to all types of street drugs and prescription pills. Everyone in both of their families had been aware of

it. Connor had never denied that, while they were high
school sweethearts, he had introduced Sandy to alcohol,
ecstasy, and marijuana. They eventually got married
after dropping out of school in the eleventh grade, and
together they spiraled out of control in their extremely
toxic and drug-tainted relationship. Somehow, Connor
managed to escape from the world of addiction, leaving
Sandy trapped in its clutches. He claimed he reached
back and tried to help her several times, but there was
no hope. Sandy did not want to be rescued. Connor soon
divorced her, earned his GED, and went to college to
study criminal justice. Sandy sank deeper and deeper
into the dark world of drugs, depression, and abusive
relationships. Eventually, she lost the battle against
chemical dependency and her life.

Even after fifteen years since Sandy's death, her
brother still blamed Connor Hayes for her demise. He
never mentioned Connor's name, but those who had
firsthand knowledge of the situation knew how he felt
about his former brother-in-law. There was no love lost
between them. Holly had remained neutral in her opinion of Connor over the years. The little she knew about
him had been told to her by her husband and his family.
She had only spent time around Connor twice or maybe
three times in her life. It was during the very early years
of her relationship with Pastor Monroe. Over a decade
had passed since she'd run into him at a church conference. Conner had given her his business card during
one of those rare meetings. Holly never imagined she'd
have any use for it, but she did now. She wanted Connor
Hayes to dig up everything on Jay and Shanika. Money
was not a problem. Holly was willing to pay whatever
amount Connor would charge her to get the information
she needed.

Chapter Thirty-one

"I feel somewhat guilty, Zach. I can't deny it. The baby will be Nahima's little brother or sister. One day they should be introduced to one another, but I can't raise Jay's child. Biologically, Nahima's her little girl, but the circumstances are very different. I carried her for thirty-two weeks." Venus patted her flat stomach for effect. "I nursed and cared for her from the moment she entered the world. The bond was formed even before she was born. Nahima is my flesh and blood."

Zach stole a French fry from Venus's plate and nibbled it. "I understand. It'll be hard for you and Charles to bond with Jay's baby when neither of you have blood ties to him."

"Him? Is Jay gonna have a boy?"

"That's what she told me when I visited her."

"Wow! She wanted Nahima to be a boy. She was disappointed when the doctor told us that I was carrying a girl. It really shouldn't have mattered. It was still her child, regardless of the gender. Anyway, I can't believe Jay is having a boy."

"It's too bad the little dude is gonna grow up with strangers. My dad is considering taking the baby, but he's too damn old. Personally, I think it's rather selfish of him to impose an infant on Patricia anyway. And Jay has yet to even tell the old man she's pregnant. They haven't spoken in months. Daddy is just waiting for her call. Then he'll make the offer." Zach signaled the waiter for the check.

Just Ribs was his and Venus's favorite restaurant. It became their meeting spot back when she and Jay first started having problems. Venus had been pregnant with Nahima, and she needed a shoulder to lean on. Zach was the man for the job. It was at a table inside the small, family-owned rib joint that he'd made a vow to be the prominent male presence in Nahima's life. He had kept his word. Even after Charles adopted his niece and became her legal father, Uncle Z remained faithfully involved in every aspect of Nahima's life.

"What if Jay never calls your father?"

"Hell, I can't answer that one. All I know is that he and Patricia have been tossing the idea around about possibly taking the little boy until Jay is released from prison. That's about all they can do until they speak with Jay."

Conner Hayes, private investigator to Atlanta's elite, stared out over Peachtree Street through his window. It was busy and lively as usual. He enjoyed the luxury of having his office in the middle of a high-traffic business area. It helped him to build upon his already well-established clientele, which consisted of an assortment of patrons. His client list included everyone from suspicious housewives to paranoid rappers to rich and powerful politicians. No client or case surprised him. It seemed that even the least likely person at some point needed to know about someone else's affairs for one reason or the other.

Connor's first appointment of the day had been a true blast from the past. Holly Blake, now Holly Monroe, had sashayed into his office bright and early. She'd skipped all the customary pleasantries and catch-up chatter and gotten right down to business. Holly hired Connor to investigate two inmates at the Leesworth Women's Federal

Corrections Facility. It was odd because she didn't offer very much lead information for him to build a case on. It would basically be a blind, grassroots investigation. All Holly could tell Connor about inmates Shanika and Jayla was their race, physical descriptions, and an estimation of their ages. That was it in a nutshell. She had no clue why or how long either woman had been incarcerated or where they were from.

Connor was perplexed by Holly's pressing need to know everything about the two inmates. She'd explained that Gavin had developed a close relationship with the two women while working at Leesworth. They both were a part of his ministry at the prison. Jayla was also one of his mental health clients struggling with family issues, and she was pregnant. Surprisingly, Gavin had considered adopting her baby, but Holly was against it.

Outside of those little tidbits, she had offered Connor nothing in the form of background information on the women, and it was all he had to go on, but he had resources and manpower all across the state of Georgia. There wasn't a government agency or private business that he couldn't tap into. And for the handsome down payment Holly had so graciously given Connor as an incentive, there would be no stone left unturned. He assured her that he and his team of investigative experts would have something to report to her within seven to ten business days. Connor Hayes was a man of his word. He would deliver, and his gut told him that when he did, it wouldn't be anything that Gavin wanted Holly to know. Nothing would give Connor more pleasure than to stick it to his former brother-in-law for old times' sake.

"King, I think we need to take you to the clinic. You don't look so hot, girl. Come on, let's go." Shanika helped Jay to her feet.

"Let's get her on the scooter," Sophia said, massaging Jay's lower back. "I'm very concerned about her puffy hands and feet."

"Do you remember everything I told y'all?"

"We remember, King. We remember. Stop worrying. We got you."

Shanika and Sophia followed Jay as she whizzed her scooter through the tables in the cafeteria. They were worried. Jay felt sorry for them. Her two BFFs in the whole world had been by her side over the past week or so, waiting on her hand and foot. Bria came by whenever she could, and so did Odette, but Shanika and Sophia had been shackled to her like slaves on a ship. The warden had made concessions for the women to spend extended hours with Jay during her final days before she gave birth.

Dr. Yusuf was confident that the delivery would go well. The baby was healthy and in perfect position in her womb, and by the grace of God, Jay was holding up better than he had thought she would. In only two weeks she would have the baby. He wasn't sure if she would go into traditional labor or if he would have to perform a C-section. Either way, the little boy was coming soon.

When the women reached the double doors of the clinic, Shanika knelt beside Jay's scooter and searched her face. "Do you want me to have Callahan make the call now?"

"Uh-uh, I think it's too soon. I don't feel any contractions. I'm just tired, and my back is aching. I don't want him to come all this way for nothing."

"Who is he?" Sophia screamed. "I'm up to my ears with all of the secrecy. Why can't I know who he is? I am the baby's auntie and godmother, too. I demand to know who he is, right now!" Sophia went off into a tirade in Spanish.

Jay couldn't hold in her laughter. Even when she was in pain, Sophia had her cracking up. Shanika was laughing too. They were used to Sophia raising hell over the fact that they still had not revealed the identity of the baby's father to her. It seemed cruel and unfair in her opinion, but they were actually being good friends. Sophia was close to being released from Leesworth, and she had a good job waiting for her at an upscale restaurant thanks to Pastor Monroe. His church members had promised to hire her once she had completed her sentence. Sophia was going to join his church, too, and become involved. Jay didn't think she needed to know that her soon-to-be pastor had committed adultery and fathered her child. It would possibly cause her to stumble in her faith. Neither Jay nor Shanika wanted to see that happen. They wished only the best for their girlfriend.

Sophia zipped her lips when they entered the clinic. Nurse Williamson hurried from behind the counter when she saw them. "What's going on, ladies? Is it time?"

"No, ma'am, I don't think so. My back is hurting, as usual, and I don't have much energy."

"And she's not eating or drinking the way she should," Shanika pointed out. "She lost her appetite."

"Let's get her in an examination room so the doctor can check her out. He's with another patient right now, but I'll let him know Ms. King is here."

Chapter Thirty-two

"Hello."

"Mrs. Monroe, this is Valerie Stewart from the Leesworth Women's Federal Corrections Facility. I'm a deputy warden here. Please forgive me for calling your home this late, especially on a Friday evening."

"That's quite okay. I'm sure it's an emergency for my husband. Another suicide threat, I suppose?"

"Um . . . no, ma'am, not at all. Is Pastor Monroe available to speak with me?"

Holly's suspicions shot to high alert. It was ten minutes before ten o'clock, and the prison was calling, but it wasn't a suicide threat from his new client. What was the emergency then? If it wasn't a matter of life and death, why was Mrs. Stewart calling her husband?

"Mrs. Monroe, is the pastor home? If he's not, I'll try him on his cell. He assured Warden Callahan that he wanted to be alerted if there were any changes in this particular inmate's condition."

"Yes, he's here. I'll get him for you." Holly leaned over and pressed the button on the wall panel of their intercom system. She spoke into the speaker. "Gavin, there's an important call from the prison for you. It's Mrs. Stewart, the deputy warden."

He thanked Holly and picked up the phone in his study. Acute inquisitiveness grabbed hold of Holly and held her prisoner. It went against her principles as a Christian, a wife, and a first lady to eavesdrop on her husband's telephone call. But something uneasy was stirring inside of her, and she was powerless to do what she knew was right. She placed her hand over the mouthpiece of the phone and listened to the conversation between Gavin and Mrs. Stewart.

Shayla, the third-shift nurse's assistant who took care of Aunt Jackie, sat in the rocking chair next to the bed. The Bible in her lap was facedown. Shayla was confused and totally at a loss for words. She hated to call Zach or Aunt Hattie Jean so late, but she was running out of patience. For some strange reason that she couldn't begin to comprehend, Aunt Jackie was restless and combative. Evelyn, the second-shift NA, had experienced the same thing with her before Shayla got there. Aunt Jackie had refused to eat, and she didn't want to go to bed. When Shayla arrived, she and Evelyn forced her to lie down by threatening to call Zach. He would've contacted Wilma, the nurse on call at Agape Home Healthcare Agency, and asked her to come and give her a sedative. Aunt Jackie didn't want that at all.

Just when Shayla thought her usually sweet patient had settled in for the night, she started crying and motioning with her hands. She had snatched the covers from her body and was pointing to her walker.

"Why do you want to get up, Ms. Brown? Where do you want to go, darling? It's late, and you need your rest. Your nephew and his wife are bringing the children over to visit you in the morning. Your sister is coming to cook breakfast for everybody, too."

"Mmm, mmm," Aunt Jackie grunted. She pointed to her walker across the room again and attempted to stand.

Shayla got up from the rocking chair and reached for the phone. "I'm calling Zach. He needs to know what's going on here. He's gonna call the nurse and have her bring you a cocktail because you're showing out tonight."

"Uh-uh, uh-uh, uh-uh!" Aunt Jackie shook her head several times and waved both her hands.

"You don't want the nurse to come?"

Aunt Jackie shook her head from side to side. "Uh-uh."

"Okay, I won't call Zach if you get back in the bed and go to sleep." Shayla walked over to the bed and tucked Aunt Jackie in for the fourth time that night. "It's time for you to get some rest."

Inside Jay's room at the hospital, Pastor Monroe sat quietly in a chair, watching her sleep. The doctor had given her an injection for the back pain and another medication to help her sleep. The pastor was worried about Jay and the baby, but he was more concerned about what would happen after his son was born.

Jay hadn't heard from Zach. They didn't know if he and Jill were going to take custody of the baby. Time was running out, but Jay had faith in her brother. She believed Zach would do the right thing despite their strained relationship. It was what Aunt Jackie would want Zach to do, she'd explained. Their dear aunt would expect him to take his nephew and love him like he did his own children. Zach could be stubborn and harsh at times, but he loved Aunt Jackie to pieces, and he would do anything to please her. That's what Jay believed in her heart, and she had convinced Pastor Monroe to believe it too.

"I usually don't take business calls on the weekend, Holly. That's why I have assistants and associates. What can I do for you on a Saturday morning?"

"I'm sorry, Connor, but I wanted to know if you had come across any information on the two subjects you're investigating for me."

Connor leaned on his golf club and raised his other hand to his forehead. He shielded his eyes from the sun as he watched the long ball his friend had hit across the lush green course soar through the air. When the ball landed, he spoke into his Bluetooth. "My team assigned to your case is working on it. I'm sure they'll have something to report to me in our Monday morning discovery session. I'll give you a call after we meet. I've got to run now, Holly. I'll be in touch."

Holly slammed the phone down in its cradle and stuck the tip of her thumb in her mouth. She sank her teeth into her nail and chewed on it. It was a nasty habit she'd picked up in recent months. All of the time Gavin was spending at work and away from home was causing her to do things she'd never imagined doing before. He would have a conniption if he ever found out she had contacted Connor Hayes. Holly had surprised herself with that sneaky move. Then she topped it off by hiring the man to investigate a pair of prison inmates all because she was jealous of the relationship they had with her husband. But Gavin had pushed her into stooping so low. He had changed and placed others before her and their marriage. The prison officials were now calling him at all times of the night for secret missions for the women.

Holly had listened to the conversation between Gavin and the deputy warden that night when she'd called, but she couldn't comprehend a single thing they'd discussed. It sounded like they were speaking in code. No names were mentioned, and no emergency was identified, per se.

"Things appear serious, not critical. Inmate is in location one and in distress. Counselor's expertise is required immediately." Those were the words Holly heard Mrs.

Stewart say. Gavin didn't reply. He simply thanked the woman for calling. A few minutes later, he entered the kitchen carrying a duffel bag and announced that he had to report to Leesworth to handle an emergency.

Holly needed Connor and his staff to do the job she had paid them $3,500 to do. If they delivered, she would gladly pay the other half of the fee, plus a hefty tip.

Chapter Thirty-three

"Please lower your voice, Zachary. You're going to wake Aunt Jackie. You know she didn't sleep very well last night."

"I'm sorry, but I don't need this type of stress on me right now. My plate is full with work, taking care of my aunt, and spending time with you and the kids."

"How far apart are Jay's contractions?"

Zach looked at Aunt Hattie Jean like she was crazy, because he couldn't answer that question. He didn't even ask the nurse or the young lady who had called him later to update him on Jay's condition. His mind went blank after Mr. Frazier, one of the deputy wardens from Leesworth, called to inform him that Jay was in the early stages of labor and would be delivering the baby before the end of the day. When the man asked him how soon he could get there to sign the paperwork for the social worker, Zach told him he wasn't sure. He should've told the man the truth. He wasn't coming at all. Zach blinked when his aunt asked the question about Jay's contractions again.

"They didn't tell me how far apart her contractions were, and I didn't ask. Why is Jay doing this to me? She told those people at the prison that I'm taking her son, but I'm not! I never led her to believe I would."

"But, Zachary, he's—"

"No, Jill, I don't wanna hear it! I am not gonna take that baby! Every day I would have to look at him and be reminded of what his mother tried to do to me. My sister hated me so much that she wanted me dead. Then she almost killed you. I can't live with those thoughts every day for the next decade. Only a fool tortures himself."

"Zach, I'm not telling you to take the baby," Aunt Hattie Jean began. "I just want you to go to the prison hospital and check on your sister. Look at the baby and see if you can't love him like you do Nahima."

Zach hopped up from his seat at the kitchen table. "Let me say this one last time so everyone can hear me: I don't want Jay's son!"

"Take . . . ta . . . take the . . . the b . . . baby! Take the . . . the baby!"

Everyone turned toward the voice coming from the doorway. It was Aunt Jackie, standing with the support of her walker, crying and pleading. She wanted Zach to take Jay's baby. She spoke those words with clarity in a gravelly and shaky voice. She hadn't uttered a syllable in over six months. Her family was shocked to silence as she continued to beg Zach to take Jay's son. Aunt Jackie crossed the threshold slowly, still crying and pleading with her nephew. She inched at a snail's pace in his direction.

"Auntie, don't do this to me. Please don't. It ain't fair. Don't make me clean up another one of Jay's messes. I ain't gonna take him. Cry all you want, but I won't do it."

Everyone in the kitchen had focused their attention on Aunt Jackie. She was now at Zach's side. She tugged on his arm, but he wouldn't look at her. He couldn't. Since the day Aunt Jackie took him and Jay into her care, Zach had latched on to her with a love and commitment so strong that nothing could come between them. They hadn't agreed on every issue over the years, but their bond had endured the test of time. Together, aunt and nephew had overcome tragedy after tragedy and obstacle after obstacle, but the issue they now faced had the potential to rip them apart. Up until now, they had stood together on all matters concerning Jay. Today they were at odds. Each had taken a firm stand on the opposite side of the most crucial and controversial issue their family had faced since the murder of Belva Jayne Dudley.

Zach was now as emotional as Aunt Jackie. Fighting back tears, he kept his eyes straight ahead, refusing to look at her. He wanted Aunt Jackie to be quiet. For months he had prayed to God that He would bless her to speak again, but now that He had, Zach wanted her to shut the hell up. What she was crying and begging for was totally out of the question. His mind was made up, and it had been for months. Zach and Jill would not take Jay's baby. His decision was non-negotiable. It would be the first time ever that he wouldn't consider Aunt Jackie's feelings or opinion about something. Zach was going to act just like Jay this go-around. He would be selfish, heartless, and stubborn.

Jill, Aunt Hattie Jean, and Uncle Bubba watched Zach and Aunt Jackie standing side by side in a standoff of wills. Tension and raw emotion filled the time and space around the small kitchen. The sound of Aunt Jackie's sobbing appeal to Zach pinned everyone in place. She couldn't be ignored. Jill left her chair at the table and walked over to comfort Aunt Jackie. Her voice had weakened, but her will was still strong. She wanted Zach to take Jay's baby.

"I'm outta here," Zach announced to no one in particular. "It's getting crazy in this house. The last thing I want is for my sister to cause me to lose my damn mind."

With that said, Zach brushed Aunt Jackie's hand away from his arm. He still refused to look at her. He grabbed his jacket from the back of his chair and stormed out of the kitchen.

"Zachary!" Jill called out. She hurried after him. "Where are you going? What about me and the kids?"

"Fall back! I need some space."

"I haven't spoken to Zach since last night, Jill. Hush now. Don't cry. He'll come around. Do you want me to drive around and look for him?"

"No, don't do that, Dex. That won't be necessary. Thanks for offering, though. You need to spend your time away from work with Ramona and the girls. How are they?"

"Ramona and Abriah are cool. They're in the kitchen eating breakfast. I made waffles. Arianna is finally sleeping after whining half the night. Your goddaughter is rotten. That's enough about us. How are you? Are you gonna be okay?"

"I think so. I'm just glad that Aunt Jackie has settled down. She hasn't spoken since Zachary left. She's still crying, though. My heart goes out to her. She wants us to take Jay's baby, but Zachary doesn't want him."

"What do you want?"

"I want everyone to be happy. I would like our family to be at peace again."

"Do you think you and Zach should take Jay's son? Could you love him and care for him despite who his mother is?"

"Yes, we should take the baby. I could be a good mother to him, regardless of the circumstances, but I'm not sure about Zachary. He doesn't hate the child. All babies are innocent in his eyes. It's just hard for him to embrace what Jay's baby represents. She hurt him terribly, ya know?"

"I know."

"Zachary is not a wicked man. He's very kind and caring. This situation is a very complicated one. Zachary needs time to sort through a few things. Please don't judge him like our family has."

"I won't judge my boy. Nobody has the right to do that except God Almighty."

"Thank you, Dex. I must check on Aunt Jackie now. She and the children are watching a movie in the den. I'll call you later."

Holly wished she had called Leesworth before she drank three glasses of Moscato. Now she was too tipsy to drive up there and demand to see Gavin. The woman she had spoken with claimed he wasn't there. Holly didn't believe that. Gavin had called her twice last night to let her know he was okay. Both times the prison's name and number had appeared on the caller ID screen, and she'd heard the assistant warden ask that he come to the prison before he left. Gavin was at Leesworth. Holly had no idea what emergency had called him away from their home or which inmate it involved, but he was definitely at the prison. Apparently, the woman she had spoken with earlier didn't know where he was. Maybe he was with the client who was in crisis. What else could he have been doing?

Chapter Thirty-four

"You're my son," Pastor Monroe whispered softly as tears spilled from his steel gray eyes. He rocked the tiny infant in his arms and looked at him in awe. "I can't believe it. You definitely belong to me. You've got my eyes. Those are my grandmother's eyes."

The nurse tapped on the door before she entered the room. "Sir, do you have any idea how long it will be before Ms. King's family member arrives? The social worker is on the phone. She wants to know."

"I don't know, ma'am, but I'm sure Mr. King is en route."

"I'll tell the social worker that he's on his way."

Pastor Monroe looked over at Jay. She was resting. Labor and delivery had taken its toll on her. After six hours of excruciating pain, Dr. Yusuf decided to take Jay to surgery. Her blood pressure had spiked into the danger zone, and she had retained too much fluid to have a safe delivery. The doctor was afraid to risk the baby or Jay. An emergency C-section seemed appropriate in light of her delicate condition.

Exhausted, Jay had slept through the birth of her son, but Pastor Monroe didn't miss a single moment. He'd witnessed everything, starting with the ambulance ride from the prison to the hospital in the wee hours of the morning. He was nervous, but he didn't show it. Jay needed him to be strong and brave. She was depending on him to be her rock. He experienced his weakest moment when Dr. Yusuf made the decision to take the baby by cesarean section. Jay found her strength and courage and assured him that she and the baby would be fine.

Hidden behind a surgical mask and scrubs, Pastor Monroe was prepared to meet his son. He held Jay's hand and did everything in his power to keep her awake and alert, but the medication and the overexertion were slowly taking effect. Once the anesthesia kicked in, Jay clocked out, and Pastor Monroe was on his own. He witnessed the entire procedure. Nothing grossed him out. He found the birth of his son fascinating and beautiful.

Pastor Monroe looked at Jay again when the baby began to stir in his arms. She still hadn't met their son. He checked the clock on the wall. Where was Zach? He should've been there by now. It had been several hours since Shanika had called to tell him that Jay needed him to come to the hospital.

"Sir, the social worker is on her way here." The nurse had returned to the room. "I hope Ms. King's family member makes it in time."

Pastor Monroe kissed his son's pale little face and whispered a prayer. "He'll be here."

Zach increased the speed on his windshield wipers as he cruised up the interstate through the steady downpour of rain. The road sign a few miles back confirmed that he was a half hour away from his destination.

Thoughtlessly, he had hopped inside his SUV and peeled out of his old neighborhood without a clear plan. No one had ever described Zach as impulsive before, but that was exactly the kind of behavior he was exhibiting. He'd left Aunt Jackie's house without telling anyone, not even Jill, where he was going. Hell, he didn't even know himself at the time. Zach had wanted to escape from the madness. He needed to put as much distance as he could between himself and Aunt Jackie. Her crying and begging were messing with his head.

Zach had imagined that her first words would be, "Thank you, Jesus," or, "Praise the Lord." He wasn't prepared for the request she'd made. That's why he took off the way he did. He didn't want Aunt Jackie's emotional plea to cause him to reverse the decision he'd already made. If anyone could make him change his mind about anything, it was she. And Zach didn't need the pressure.

Since he'd left Aunt Jackie's house, he'd had lots of time to think. The drive and the soothing sound of the rain had helped him gather his wild thoughts. It was good for a man to get away every once in a while to talk to God and allow Him to speak back. It had been a long time since Zach had faced his Creator one-on-one without any distractions. The time and silence had been used wisely, and now he was at peace with himself and with God.

"Nooo, please don't take him! My brother is on his way," Jay screamed and cradled her son closer to her chest. "Please don't take my baby."

The social worker, a full-figured sista with a short afro, approached the bed. "I'm sorry, Ms. King. I've held this off longer than I should have. Time is up. I have to take the baby now. I cut you some slack yesterday by postponing the paperwork. You told me your brother would be here this morning. Where is he, ma'am?"

"The rain must've slowed him down. You can understand that. Just give him a few more minutes, please."

"I'm sorry, but I can't do that." She walked closer to the bed. "Ms. King, I must take him now."

Jay screamed and turned away from the woman. "You can't take him! He needs me! Please don't take my baby!"

Dr. Yusuf, two male attendants, and a nurse entered the room. Jay cradled her son in the crook of one arm and swung the other one to keep everyone away from her. The men rushed toward the bed and restrained her while the nurse carefully pried the baby out of her hold. Dr. Yusuf removed a syringe from his breast pocket. As Jay cried and fought against the attendants, the doctor injected her with a strong sedative. She whimpered a few times as her body went completely limp and fell back to rest on the mattress. Jay could no longer scream or put up a fight. Moments later her eyes closed.

Jill smiled when she opened the door and found a handsome white man standing on the other side. "May I help you, sir?"

"My name is Gavin Monroe, ma'am. Are you Mrs. Jillian King?"

"I am. Who are you?"

Pastor Monroe looked down at Zachary Jr., who had a death grip on his mother's legs. Then he looked up at Jill again. "Mrs. King, I'm Gavin Monroe, the father of Jayla's son."

"Oh, my," Jill said, pressing her palm against her chest.

"I'd like to come in and speak with you and your husband, please, if I may."

"Zachary isn't here right now."

"Thank God. Can I assume he's at the hospital?"

Jill shook her head slowly. "I'm afraid not, Mr. Monroe. My husband went to North Carolina, unexpectedly, to visit his father. He won't be back until tomorrow afternoon. I'm so sorry."

Pastor Monroe's countenance changed before Jill's very eyes. His shoulders slumped forward, and his face became flushed. The brightness in his eyes dimmed. He ran his fingers through his hair several times before he closed his sad eyes and took a deep breath. "Jayla was so sure that your husband would take our son. I believed he would because she did. There was no plan B, Mrs. King."

Jill stepped aside. "Come in, Mr. Monroe. Let's sit and talk."

Jay awoke the next morning with a hole in her heart. She was alone and very depressed. The physical pain from surgery didn't compare to the emotional pain she felt from losing her son. There was no greater love, no stronger bond than that of a mother and a child she had birthed from her womb. She now knew that firsthand. Although his conception was the result of an adulterous affair, little King Jalen Monroe was perfect in every way.

Jay cried the moment she laid eyes on him. It was instant euphoria. Pastor Monroe had handed him to her when she finally woke up a few hours after the delivery. It was a life-changing moment. Nothing had brought Jay more joy than meeting her son for the first time.

But now he was gone. Zach had not stepped up to the plate as Jay had expected him to. Obviously, Pastor Monroe's personal appeal to him had failed. Zach had decided to close his heart to his own flesh and blood. Maybe they were even now. Jay had paid to have her brother killed, and he had taken her heart away from her in retaliation, but had the score really been settled? Jay thought not. The playing field wasn't level from the start. Jay was incarcerated when she reached out to Zach for help. The stakes were much higher, too. Neither sex nor pride was up for grabs. It was all about the innocent life of a baby boy born into complex circumstances beyond his control.

Zach had hit Jay where it hurt the most. Her heart and soul had been ripped out of her body, and it hurt like hell. Jay didn't think she would ever recover from her loss. Zach had deliberately poured water on her head while she was drowning instead of throwing her a lifeline. He'd plucked an eye for an eye, even after Jay had begged for his forgiveness. Zach was the winner of their bitter rivalry, which he had started the moment he took Jill to bed four years ago. There never would've been any bad blood between them if he had never crossed the line. Zach's betrayal had caused the murder-for-hire scheme and Jay's prison escape to Jamaica. She'd still have ten fingers if Zach had stayed in his lane. And now her beautiful baby boy was gone. That was the greatest tragedy of all.

"I hate you, Zach! You're an evil bastard! I hope you rot in hell!"

Chapter Thirty-five

Zach pulled back the covers and slipped into bed behind Jill. He gathered her in his arms and kissed the back of her neck.

"You're late."

"Yeah, I should've called. I wanted to hang out with Wallace Jr. for a little while before I headed back. I went to eat lunch with him at his school. He's a smart kid."

"I saw a picture of Jay's son. He's very beautiful but tiny. His name is King Jalen Monroe."

Zach sat up, flipped on the bedside lamp, and stared down at his wife. "How did you see a picture of Jay's baby?"

"His father showed it to me."

"Where the hell did you see the kid's father?"

"He came here yesterday to talk to you."

"That man doesn't know me. What do we have to talk about?"

Jill sat up and placed her palm on the side of Zach's face. "He came to ask you to take custody of his son. The man loves Jay and their baby, but he's in a bit of a predicament right now. He promised to be the sole financial provider for his son and spend time with him every day. The only thing he wants from you and me is to allow the little one to live with us."

"Reverend Slick Dick is a punk! He wants to have his cake and eat it, too. If he loves Jay and their son so damn much, why won't he man up? He needs to tell his wife and the members of his church that he committed adultery with one of his incarcerated clients and knocked her up. Then he can take his son home and raise him with his wife. If she ain't down with playing step-mommy to his outside child, the good pastor can raise him alone. It's simple."

"It sounds simple. Mr. Monroe has broken laws and violated policies on his job by having a relationship with Jay. If he makes a public acknowledgment of his son, he could be arrested. Like Jay, he can't raise a baby from a prison cell."

Zach turned off the light and relaxed his head on his pillow. "Jay and Reverend Slick Dick should've thought about that before they started their little prison romance."

Connor was pretty damn proud of the three-man team he'd assigned the Holly Monroe case. They'd hit the jackpot. A few pieces of the puzzle were still missing, but Michael Stokes, the lead investigator, had done a fantastic job. The guy had the instincts of Sherlock Holmes and the hunger of a stray dog.

Like Connor, Michael had wasted his younger years drinking, drugging, and dealing with codependent women. He knew all the hot spots and crime-infested areas in Atlanta and the surrounding areas. Michael had contacts in high society as well as the underworld. Gavin Monroe had an unblemished reputation in both, so initially the case was stalled in park, but a chance meeting with former Leesworth inmate Ivy Maxwell set the investigation into motion. Connor hadn't expected that his past would somehow be intertwined. Fortunately, his name hadn't been mentioned, nor had he been referenced directly, but fragments of the life he had left far behind him had resurfaced in the case.

Michael Stokes met parolee Ivy Maxwell one night at Blue Rhapsody, a modest supper club in midtown. The talented, street-smart redbone from Bankhead was waiting tables and singing sets between comedy acts at the establishment. Ivy was gorgeous. That was the first thing that caught Michael's eye, but she was so much more than something nice to look at. Ivy's voice was smooth as velvet, and she was funny. She may have been a little rough around the edges, but Michael was drawn to her good looks, no-nonsense attitude, and raw sex appeal. He'd never put the moves on a black woman before, but Ivy got under his skin.

She had just finished singing a couple of Roberta Flack classics and was about to go backstage when Michael cornered her and asked that she join him at the bar. Sassy and in a hurry to get back to work, Ivy put her hands on her curvy hips and told Michael that if he wanted to spend time with her, she suggested that he move to section eight so she could serve him. Otherwise, he'd have to wait until Blue Rhapsody closed at three o'clock in the morning.

Michael was a smart man. He was also very headstrong. Whenever he wanted something or someone, he'd move heaven and hell to make it happen. He spent the rest of the evening at a table in section eight, enjoying snippets of Ivy's spicy charm. Her perfume and the sway of her hips were kicking Michael's ass. He admitted to Connor and his two coinvestigators that he was hooked after an hour or so.

He waited for Ivy to get off work to offer her a ride home. It took a little coaxing, but she eventually got into his shiny silver Mercedes and accompanied him to a nearby Waffle House. They talked until the sun came up, but neither Michael nor Ivy was ready to say good-bye. They ended up in a hotel room, having explosive sex late into the next afternoon. It marked the beginning of a friendly liaison between them.

Their steamy weekends hit a bump in the road when Michael learned that Ivy was on parole. She'd forgotten to mention that. It just didn't seem all that important, she'd said. Michael was a man first and foremost, which explained his insane infatuation for a woman he hardly knew, but his investigative instincts soon caught up with his sex drive and dominated it. A little snooping around and a few phone calls resulted in the full scoop on Ivy Leontine Maxwell. At the top of her rap sheet was an attempted murder charge. Everything else faded into the background. She didn't deny anything when Michael confronted her. In fact, she was proud of finally standing up to her abusive boyfriend, even though she had disabled him for life.

From that point on, Ivy shared details with Michael about her life at Leesworth. She talked about her friends and the corruption throughout the administration headed by Warden Callahan. She confessed how she had used Pastor Monroe to help influence the parole board to set her free. It was more than a coincidence that the pastor's name had landed on Michael's desk the week before his heart-to-heart conversation with Ivy. It was a miracle. The information Ivy provided Michael with proved one thing: Pastor Gavin Monroe was as straight as an arrow.

As far as she knew, he had never slept with an inmate or even flirted with one. All the women, including Ivy, respected the pastor and his ministry. They knew he wasn't a fake. He had a genuine passion for saving troubled women who reminded him of his late sister, Sandy. Pastor Monroe had shared the tragic story about his sister with the members of Another Chance Women's Fellowship at Leesworth. They knew it all too well. Sandy had been introduced to drugs and alcohol as a teenager by her high school sweetheart, and she developed an instant addiction to both. Her life went downhill from there. Sandy sank deeper into the drug world, upgrading to the heavier street substances. She was still in love with the man who had turned her on to drugs, and she was depressed that he had left her.

Whenever Pastor Monroe had mentioned his sister to Ivy and the other women, his emotions never failed to show. He loved her, but he couldn't save her. All the inmates knew they were extensions of Sandy in some peculiar way. Even the women who had never taken drugs felt a connection to her. Her spirit was very much alive in the ministry that her brother had established at the prison.

Ivy had benefitted from Another Chance in many ways, and she told Michael as much. She loved Pastor Monroe and was grateful to him for everything he had done for her. That was why she spoke highly of him. But she also pointed out his few character flaws. One was his inability to judge people. He had misjudged Ivy. He thought she was a saint, and that wasn't the case. She had been a fake, and he was clueless. The pastor's other flaw was his bitterness toward his former brother-in-law. It was buried deep in his heart. He had tried to hide it from the women in the fellowship, but he couldn't.

Connor grimaced. The guilt of Sandy's tragic life and death would forever haunt him. It was something he dealt with every day, but when Michael talked about him in his report, it was like rubbing salt in a fresh wound. Sure, he was the only one in the room who knew the identity of the man Gavin Monroe harbored such great contempt for, but that didn't lessen the burden. The guilt was still there, and it always would be, no matter what. Maybe Connor needed therapy to move past it. Then again, he wasn't sure if that would help at all. No amount of therapy would change the fact that he was responsible for Sandy's drug addiction, and it sure as hell couldn't bring her back.

Connor shook off his guilty past and went back to his desk. Holly was probably sitting by the phone, waiting for it to ring. Connor had the 411 on Shanika Antoinette Dixon and Jayla Simone King. They both had colorful pasts, to say the least. There were some similarities between the two ladies, but they were opposites in many other areas. For instance, Ms. Dixon was a con artist. She once led an identity theft ring made up of over thirty people. They all worked for the Unites States Postal Service. They bought and stole everything from social security numbers to credit card numbers. Ms. Dixon's biggest mistake was purchasing a Lincoln Navigator using a dead man's social security number. But that was nothing compared to what Ms. King had done. She was serving seven years for hiring an undercover police officer to kill her brother because he had stolen her lover. Then she'd escaped to Jamaica but was eventually captured and extradited back to the States.

Connor didn't think the information his team had dug up on Ms. Dixon or Ms. King was all that valuable. They were already in prison. He had no idea why Holly needed it in the first place. They were typical criminals. Gavin was being Gavin. He was trying to save Sandy via Ms. Dixon, Ms. King, and any other inmate under his care at Leesworth.

Connor was going to give Holly a file on each woman. In addition to the information that Ms. Maxwell had provided, the team had obtained both women's employment records and transcripts from their respective court trials. Ms. King's college transcripts were included, as well as copies of her two passports. Holly had paid for the information, and Connor was going to release it to her. She could now put her suspicions to rest. Gavin was not some perverted preacher preying on prison inmates after all. After Connor received the balance of his fee, he planned to close Holly's case at Hayes Investigations and Security Firm.

Chapter Thirty-six

"She won't eat. She took a few sips of juice. That's all. I'm worried about her."

"I am too, Sophia. I tried to call her brother again. No one will answer the phone. I think he and his wife are ignoring all calls from the prison. They're not gonna take the kid."

"It's a shame, because he's so cute. Jay has a thousand pictures of the little angel."

"Yeah, he is cute. He looks just like . . ."

"Like who? Who were you about to say? Tell me, Shanika!" Sophia threw her spoon down on her tray.

"The baby looks like his grandfather," she snapped. "You wouldn't know that, because you didn't see King's father when he visited her. I did."

"Her father is a white man? The baby is white as a cotton ball."

Shanika took a bite of her Spam sandwich. She needed time to think of a few good lies. Sophia was too damn perceptive. Hell, anybody with half a brain could look at Jay's son and notice that he was white. If they looked closer, those gray eyes would freak them out. Apparently, Sophia hadn't noticed them.

"You know damn well King's daddy ain't no cracker. He's just high yellow, you know? He's a redbone."

"Oh."

"Come on." Shanika grabbed her tray. "We need to let the nurse know about King. She's gonna waste away and lose her damn mind if she doesn't eat and get outta that damn cell."

"She needs to see Pastor Monroe and attend service so he can pray for her."

Hell nah! Pastor Monroe has seen more of our girl than he should have. He's seen things that nobody else has. He needs to pray for himself. Shanika laughed at her own thoughts. She liked the pastor, and she still had a little respect for him, but he and Jay had created more than just a son together. They had created one hot mess. And if Zach didn't stop acting a damn fool and petition the court to take custody of his nephew, things were bound to get worse.

"Gavin, please slow down! You ran that red light back there. We're already late." Holly rolled her eyes and folded her arms across her chest. "There's no need to rush now. Where were you anyway?"

"You know where I was, Holly. I was working."

"This dinner was planned three weeks in advance! Everyone is already there waiting for us. Trudy called fifteen minutes ago. What was so important that you couldn't get home before dark? Was one of your precious daughters threatening to hang herself again?"

"One of the inmates is having a really rough time right now. She's fallen into a very deep depression. I'm afraid she is going to have a nervous breakdown and will require hospitalization."

"Let's see. Who could that be? Is it Sophia, the armed robber? Oh, wait! Or is it Shanika, the expert identity thief who has stolen more credit cards and social security numbers than you can shake a stick at? I bet it's Jayla. Be careful now. If she gets upset, she might just steal a bunch of cash and hire someone to assassinate you."

Pastor Monroe took his eyes off the road and stared at Holly for a few seconds. The streetlights made it possible for him to see the smirk on her face. Holly was proud to rattle off the crimes of the women he ministered to every day. It was information that Pastor Monroe did not care to know, and Holly was aware of that. Her intentions had been cruel and spiteful.

"What are you talking about? How do you know what those women did? Who told you about their pasts?"

"It doesn't matter! I know everything about those con artists you devote all your time to. They're all using you, just like Ivy Maxwell did. Did you know she's a nightclub singer? Yeah, your praise and worship songbird isn't singing for the Lord anymore. No, she took her act to the Blue Rhapsody thanks to you, Pastor Monroe. All of that singing she did at the prison was just an act to make her look good for the parole board. You helped a woman who tried to kill a man get out of prison early. She didn't give a damn about you!"

Holly threw her head back and cackled like an evil character in a horror movie. Pastor Monroe didn't recognize the woman sitting next to him. It certainly wasn't his wife. There was a demon in the front passenger seat of his car. He snatched the steering wheel to pull over to the side of busy Piedmont Road. He ignored the drivers honking their horns in protest of his cutting across the lanes. The car came to a sudden stop in front of a jewelry store.

"You had no right to invade those women's privacy," he said just above a whisper. "What kind of monster are you?" Pastor Monroe quickly unfastened his seat belt and exited the car, leaving the motor running.

"Gavin! Gavin! Where the hell are you going?" Holly screamed just before the door slammed shut. "What's wrong with you? Come back here this instant!"

Pastor Monroe kept moving, walking farther and farther away from the car with Holly's voice echoing in the distance. He jogged across the street and vanished into the darkness.

Aunt Jackie held the picture of little King Jalen in her hand and wept. Her eyes were fixated on the precious baby. Aunt Hattie Jean had a picture too. The two sisters held hands and cried together. When the package from Leesworth had first arrived, they were excited. They thought that Jay had finally reached out to them after the many months she'd been out of touch, but the package was from her best friend, Shanika Dixon.

She'd sent the pictures and letter asking that someone in the family come to Leesworth to visit Jay. She was extremely depressed. Shanika also asked Aunt Jackie to encourage Zach to reconsider taking King Jalen. The child welfare agency had notified Jay that a hearing had been scheduled at the end of the baby's thirty-day stay in foster care to determine where he'd be placed permanently. King's foster parents were interested in adopting him, but if a suitable relative placement was available, it would take precedence over the foster parents' wishes.

"I want this baby, Hattie Jean. I want him here with me so bad."

She squeezed her sister's hand. "Now you know you can't take care of no baby, Jackie. You can't even take care of yourself, sweetie. I can't take him either. I gotta take care of you. I'm still praying that Zach will come to his senses. That boy is so stubborn."

"He calls me every day, but he refuses to discuss the baby or Jay with me. Zach won't even come over here because he's so afraid I'll beg him to take his sister's child. I shouldn't have to beg him. Zach knows how important family is. I taught him myself. I don't know what has gotten into that boy. He's acting just like Jay. I expect better from him!"

"Calm down. You can't get worked up over this. We all want the baby to be raised within the family, but I ain't gonna let you have another heart attack worrying about it. Let's just pray. This here letter says we have three weeks for God to change Zach's old, stubborn heart. It ain't over yet."

Chapter Thirty-seven

Gavin had been home. Holly could tell because some of his clothes and shoes were missing. All of his toiletries and his electric trimmer were gone, too. Holly hadn't seen Gavin or spoken to him in a week. She had no idea where he was staying. Whenever she called his cell phone, she got his voicemail. He was ignoring her. She was his wife, but he was treating her like crap, all because she had taken the time to find out exactly what types of women he was dealing with at Leesworth. He was so ungrateful. Didn't he realize she was trying to save him? Gavin was too kindhearted and trusting. Holly simply did not want to see him get hurt or abused by a bunch of worthless convicts. He had allowed his work to become personal, and that was unhealthy.

Hopefully, Holly would get a chance to speak with Gavin after Bible study at the church. She'd left several messages on his voicemail, asking him for a few minutes of his time. They needed to talk and clear the air. Holly had decided to apologize and beg for his forgiveness. Then things would get back to normal. If he wanted to continue to waste his time with the inmates, she would let him. Holly just wanted Gavin back home where he belonged.

"Caring for a newborn is a major responsibility, Wallace. Do you really think you're up to it? You were much younger when I had Wallace Jr."

"Aren't you gonna help me?"

"I'll help you as much as I can," Patricia told him truthfully. She wiped her mouth with a napkin and stared at her husband from across the table. "You know my situation, sweetie. I finally made partner at the firm. I thought my days of rocking babies and changing diapers were over. It's only because I love you that I'm agreeing to come out of baby retirement part-time."

"I appreciate your willingness to sacrifice for my grandson. Now if only I could speak with Jayla so we could get the process started. I left a thousand messages with her corrections counselor, asking her to contact me. I hope she's okay. It couldn't have been easy for her, giving up her child to strangers. When I was separated from her and Zach for all those years, I became numb. I didn't want to feel anything. It was too painful. But my children were with their family."

"And Jay has no idea who her son is with. She must be devastated. Maybe you should drive down to the prison Saturday to check on her."

"Maybe I will."

Sister Juanita Grant, the lead usher on third Sundays, had meant no harm. There was no way that she could've known there was friction between Zach and his aunts. When she escorted him and his family down the center aisle at Refuge Pentecostal Temple, she thought it was a great idea to seat them next to the Dudley sisters, Jackie and Hattie Jean. They were family. Zach looked like someone had sucker punched him in the gut the moment his and Aunt Jackie's eyes met. He stood as stiff as a board and in total shock, towering above her as she sat comfortably on the end of the pew. It was kind of awkward because it was her first Sunday back at church since her heart attack. Zach hadn't expected to see Aunt Jackie. She'd failed to mention during their last phone chat that she would be in service.

Zachary Jr. hopped up on Aunt Jackie's lap, and Zion tried to find a spot there as well, but Zach picked her up and handed her to her mother. The little princess was not too thrilled about that. Nahima kissed her aunt Jackie's cheek and scooted past her and Aunt Hattie Jean to take her seat. Zach was frozen in place with Jill behind him, nudging him and whispering in his ear. She wanted him to move on and sit down because people were staring at them. Zach bent over.

"Good morning, Auntie. You're looking mighty pretty." He pecked her on the cheek. "I didn't know you would be here today."

"It was time to get back to the house of God. I'm feeling well in my body, but my soul's a little weary. I've got family problems that I need to take to the Lord in prayer."

Zach tiptoed past Aunt Jackie. He didn't have a come-back for her comment, which was saturated with self-pity and sarcasm. Aunt Hattie Jean reached up and pinched him on his arm when he shuffled past her. He narrowed his eyes in response before he took his seat. Jill sat next to her husband, looking just like a fashion model in a chic red pantsuit. Zach draped his arm around her shoulders and focused his attention straight ahead.

The choir had just started singing a slow worship song. Their three-part harmony was flawless as usual. It gave Zach goose bumps. They sounded awesome. The only thing missing was Aunt Jackie's golden soprano voice. She'd sung lead on so many songs with the choir in the past. It just wasn't the same without her.

Zach leaned forward to sneak a peek at his aunt. Her eyes were closed, and her hands were lifted toward heaven in worship. And she was crying. The tears weren't tears of joy, though. Aunt Jackie was going through, as the old church mothers used to say. She'd told Zach that her soul needed healing, and she had come to the right place to get that special touch she was seeking. But if Aunt Jackie thought her healing would include a certain nephew of hers miraculously experiencing a change of heart and taking custody of her great-nephew, she was sadly mistaken. That just wasn't going to happen.

The song ended to a boisterous round of applause and a whole lot of shouting. Zach took another look at Aunt Jackie when the congregation settled down. She had opened her Bible and pressed it against her ample bosom. Her head was bowed low as Reverend Broadus led the congregation in a word of prayer before his sermon. Zach clamped his eyes shut and prayed that God would give Aunt Jackie peace and understanding to accept the decision he had made regarding Jay's son.

"Brothers and sisters, I'd like you to turn with me to the Book of Genesis, chapter twenty-five. When you find it, say amen."

The sound of pages flipping back and forth filled in the silence. Jill turned to the passage of Scripture, as the pastor had asked, even with Zion perched on her lap. She elbowed Zach to get his attention. She moved her Bible closer to him, encouraging him to read along with her. Voices saying, "Amen," all across the sanctuary assured Pastor Broadus that he could read the Scripture he had chosen for the day.

He asked the congregation to listen attentively as he read the story about twin brothers, Jacob and Esau. The account of their birth, manhood, and bitter estrangement was covered in the twenty-fifth, twenty-sixth, and twenty-seventh chapters of the Book of Genesis. Reverend Broadus skipped around the passages, focusing in on key verses. He gave extra attention to the verses in the twenty-seventh chapter, where Jacob cheated Esau out of his birthright with a bowl of stew. But the meat of the Scripture reading was in the thirty-second chapter. It detailed the reconciliation between the twin brothers many years after Jacob had betrayed Esau and scammed him out of his rightful inheritance.

Reverend Broadus closed his Bible and looked out over his congregation. Beads of sweat glistened on the top of his round, bald head. The good reverend leaned on the podium and spoke in his rich baritone voice. "The title of my sermon for the people of God this morning is 'Forgive and Let it Go.'"

Zach shifted uncomfortably in his seat when the congregation responded to the title of Reverend Broadus's sermon with applause. There was something about the way he had announced it that made Zach's stomach do a little flip. It felt like the topic was directed at him. There were over a thousand other people lining the pews, all decked out in their Sunday best, listening to the pastor preach. But Zach was experiencing a mild case of paranoia. Or it could've been that he was arrogant enough to think he had been singled out by Reverend Broadus and the sermon had been customized just for him. Either way, Zach had caught a squirming demon in his seat, and he couldn't keep still.

"I'll be back," he leaned in and whispered to Jill. And then to make his little escape look legitimate, he lifted Zion from her lap and made her his ally. He excused himself, moving in the opposite direction of his two aunts. It was easier on him mentally to disturb the people on the other end of the pew than to face the Dudley sisters, especially Aunt Jackie.

Chapter Thirty-eight

"Do you ever wonder what your fellow inmates are up to?"

Ivy rolled off of Michael's body and landed on her back. She stared up at the slowly spinning blades of the ceiling fan. "Yeah, I think about them. Do I miss them? Hell no, I don't miss anything or anybody at Leesworth."

"Have you ever thought about the pastor who helped you? What's his name again?"

"His name is Gavin Monroe, and he's just as white as you, but y'all don't look nothing alike. His features are darker. Look at you. You're all thin and pale, with your sandy brown hair." Ivy laughed but stopped quickly. "Yes, I've thought about the pastor from time to time since I've been out. He gave me his card with all of his contact information on it before I was released. I almost went to his church one Sunday, but I changed my mind."

"Why?" Michael asked, stroking Ivy's inner thigh softly.

She shrugged her shoulders and spread her legs wider when Michael's fingers got closer to her spot. "I guess it's because I feel guilty. That man was good to me. Shit, he was good to all of us. It was wrong for me to use him, but I wouldn't change a damn thing if I had to do it all over again."

Michael did a smooth flip and wedged his slender body between Ivy's thighs. "Are you using me, too?" He nibbled the side of her neck.

"Am I using you for what? You came sniffing after me. And you're the private investigator. How the hell do I know you're not using me to get information about how things go down at Leesworth?"

Michael's eyes, a light shade of brown, bore into Ivy's. Hers were dark brown and shaped like those of a doe. She was defensive by nature. Every time he said something that struck a chord, her eyes darkened, warning him that he was in serious trouble. Michael wanted to make love to Ivy again, but it wouldn't happen unless he said something quickly to assure her of his trust.

"I'm not investigating anyone at the prison, babe. I'm just curious. You said the pastor, a white guy, was cool, but you only used him to get what you wanted. I had to ask. I want to know if that's why you spend so much time with me. I wonder if there's something you may want from this white guy. That's all. I didn't mean to piss you off."

Ivy opened her mouth to give Michael one of her sassy responses, but he cut her off with a kiss. It was a wet and sloppy one, with lots of tongue action, too. He knew he'd accomplished his goal when she kissed him back with just as much fire as he was giving her. It was foolish to waste time and a nice hotel room arguing.

Michael's sole reason for bringing up Gavin Monroe was to plant a tiny seed inside Ivy's head. He wanted her to make contact with the preacher so he could have her tailed by one of his associates at Hayes Investigations and Security Firm. Then their interaction would be monitored to determine how close they really were. Had they bonded well enough during Ivy's time at Leesworth for the good pastor to confide in her about what was going on back there now? If that were the case, maybe the missing pieces to Holly Monroe's case would fall into place.

Mr. Hayes had officially closed the case, reporting to Mrs. Monroe that her husband only was doing the Lord's work with the women at the prison. But Michael had a hunch that they'd missed something. Ivy seemed confident that Gavin Monroe was an honest and sincere man of the cloth, and she was probably right, but there was something at Leesworth that kept the preacher there for extended periods of time and during odd hours. Call it nosiness or inquisitiveness. It was an itch that Michael couldn't scratch. With or without Ivy's help, he was determined to find out exactly who or what Gavin Monroe was so dedicated to at Leesworth Women's Federal Corrections Facility.

"Jayla," Pastor Monroe whispered and wrapped her securely in his arms. He allowed her to cry on his shoulder. He too was an emotional train wreck, but he had to be her rock.

"It's been almost two weeks. I'm gonna lose my mind. I haven't heard from Zach or my aunt or my father. They've all turned their backs on me and our son."

"That's not totally true. I've reached out to Mrs. Brown. She and your other aunt, Mrs. Blackmon, are very concerned about you and the baby."

Jay took a backward step to stare at Pastor Monroe in shock. "You spoke to Aunt Jackie?"

"Yes, I called her. Shanika sent her pictures of King. She's convinced that Zach will change his mind soon and take action to secure legal guardianship of the baby before it's too late. Your aunt is a woman of unwavering faith, Jayla. She's been praying and fasting over the situation. So have I, but I feel awfully unworthy of the Lord's mercy. My sins caused this dreadful predicament. Oh, I don't regret falling in love with you or creating our son, but—"

"But what's the use of us being in love when we can't be together? And why the hell did we have a son when neither one of us is at liberty to raise him? He's with strangers!"

"Zach is going to get King. Then I'll help him and Jill raise him until you're released. I'll take full responsibility for my son's finances. He won't need or want for anything. I'll be in his life. He'll know who I am before he gets too old."

Jay pulled away from Pastor Monroe and took a seat on the couch. "Go home to your wife, Gavin. Forget about me and King. Some kinda way, you're gonna have to pretend like we don't exist and act like we never did. I'm gonna ask Callahan to transfer me to another state. He'll make up something and make it look legit."

"No, you can't do that. I won't let you."

Jay folded her arms across her chest and shook her head. "I can't do this anymore. I have to save myself from losing my mind. If I go away and leave you, our son, and my past behind in Georgia, it'll ease the pain. As long as I'm here, I'll feed into the false hope that things will one day get better. That ain't gonna happen for me."

"There'll come a day when things will be just the way we want them to be."

"No, they won't! My kidneys are weak. I'll need dialysis soon. My liver is diseased. I'm facing at least ten more years in prison. And my son is lost to me forever. Where is God, Gavin, huh? I sure can't feel Him. Didn't He see them come in the hospital and snatch my baby away from me? How come He didn't tell Zach to save our baby from the system?"

"I don't know." The pastor sat down on the couch next to Jay. He placed his arm around her shoulders and pulled her body closer to his. "I wrote Zach and Jill a letter. They should've received it by now. I hope they respond soon."

"He won't respond, and he won't allow Jill to. He never called you after you visited Jill. Zach is punishing me. I'll make it easier for him. I'm leaving."

"You're not going anywhere. You're thinking and speaking impulsively. We have two more weeks. Let's exercise faith in God and in your brother."

"God? He don't care nothing about Jayla Simone King. If He did, why is my mama dead? How come my daddy, a pastor, killed her? Why did her trifling ass, the first lady of a church, commit adultery in the first place? And tell me, why did you, another pastor, cheat on your wife with me and get me pregnant with a child who was taken from me, Gavin? Tell me that, damn it!"

"No one is perfect, sweetheart. We all sin. It may not seem like it now, but God is real, and He will deliver us and our child from our unfortunate circumstances."

Chapter Thirty-nine

Jamal "Jack Man" Price and his wife, London, appeared to be the ideal couple with the perfect marriage. They lived the lavish lifestyle of the rich and famous in their fabulous mansion in an exclusive gated community in Alpharetta, Georgia. Like them, their neighbors were millionaires who were all about that privileged life. The grass was greener on their side of the track for sure. Nothing but ballers and entertainers made their homes behind the gates of the coveted Saint Croix Estates.

As a superstar wide receiver for the Atlanta Falcons, Jack Man was right at home with a few of his teammates, the starting point guard for the Atlanta Hawks, award-winning rapper Blaze, and pop diva Rain. There were some actors, music producers, and bestselling authors living in the neighborhood, as well as the country's premier African American movie director and screenwriter.

Mr. and Mrs. Price enjoyed the good life envied by many, and for the past two and a half weeks, they had enjoyed taking care of King Jalen. They hoped to adopt the little boy soon. Their court date was rapidly approaching, and their attorney had assured them that, so far, everything appeared to be in their favor. No one from the baby's family had expressed an interest in taking custody of him, not even the father, who had signed the birth certificate. For legal purposes, the names of the baby's parents had been blacked out on all of his paperwork

from the child welfare agency. The Prices had no idea
who they were or what the baby's last name was. All they
knew was King Jalen was an adorable little angel who
they wanted very much to become their son forever.

London, more so than her husband, was praying for
the adoption to go through, because she'd never birthed
a child. Jamal had three from a previous relationship.
He had undergone a vasectomy before he met London,
swearing that he had retired from the sport of baby
making. Child support payments were eating up most of
his earnings from his shoe and sports drink endorsement
deals. His $60 million contract with the Falcons was just
enough to cover his over-the-top expenses. That's exactly
why the instant Jamal realized he and his then–Atlanta
Falcon cheerleader girlfriend were locked into a long-
term relationship, he made it clear that he'd had the
old snip. At the time, London was cool with it because
she didn't want to ruin her size-four figure pushing out
babies anyway. Many hours of working out and healthy
eating had been invested in keeping her body in tiptop
shape. Back then, staying fit was more important than
having a baby.

However, since Jamal Jr., Jamilah, and Jamir had
grown older and more possessive of their father, London
had started feeling left out in the cold. It was bad enough
that she was the oddball. London was the only white person in the entire Price family. Everyone seemed to feed
her with a long-handle spoon. Jamal's mother, Sabrina,
couldn't stand her, and she didn't care who knew it.
Her grandchildren were certainly aware of her feelings
toward their dad's wife. They threw shade in London's
direction too, but Jamal didn't notice how his children
treated his wife.

He was too busy working out, making public appear-
ances, and sealing deals to maintain his baller's cash

flow after football. If the Jack Man had a clue as to how icy his sons and baby girl handled his wife, he would go ham on them. He truly loved London despite her many flaws. And because he genuinely cared for her, he often overlooked her quest to keep up with the Joneses, her lack of domesticity, and her sudden obsession with adopting a child.

The sole reason why Jamal Price had agreed to become a foster parent in the first place was to please London. They were only approved to take babies who were considered adoptable. King Jalen was just the second child placed in their care since they'd become foster parents a year and a half ago. The first child, a baby girl named Destiny, was a part of their family for three months before her paternal grandparents in Louisiana were granted custody of her. London and Jamal had bonded with the cute little infant, having picked her up from the hospital when she was only 3 days old. They were heartbroken when she left their home. That was why they were so eager to finalize King Jalen's adoption as soon as possible.

Jamal planned to switch the child's first and middle names around and call him Jalen King Price. Then his initials would be JKP, just like the other Price children and their superstar dad. He would be just as good-looking as the rest of the gang, too. The baby already looked like London had given birth to him. King Jalen and his foster mom had the same dark hair and full lips. The baby's lips were God-given, inherited from his birth mother. London's were silicone, compliments of Dr. Zurich Moss, cosmetic surgeon to Atlanta's elite. Little King Jalen's steel gray eyes could easily represent a combination of Jamal's black ones mixed with his wife's exotic hazel orbs. From his gorgeous features to his calm temperament, the baby was a perfect fit in the Price family. Jamal's and London's fingers were crossed, hoping that in a little over two weeks he would become a legal and permanent member of their household.

"Larry—he's the new butcher at Cohen's Market—gave me his secret recipe for the rub I used on this tenderloin." Holly carefully poured gravy over her husband's meat. "I hope you like it. It's a fine cut of beef. You'll find it to be quite tender. That's because of the marinade Trudy told me about. It is absolutely delicious."

Pastor Monroe nodded. Then he turned and watched Holly prance around the kitchen like she was floating on air. She was one happy woman now that her man was home. He had shown up unannounced around midnight two days before. He offered Holly a simple apology for blowing up and leaving her on the side of the road a couple weeks back, and she accepted it immediately with no questions asked.

That night her guilt was still raw. She admitted how wrong she was to pry into Jay's and Shanika's criminal backgrounds, but she didn't reveal where the information had come from, because he didn't ask. Pastor Monroe simply went into the master bathroom, showered, and joined Holly in their bed. They had sex minus the intimacy and passion. The chemistry between them was long gone, absolutely extinct. What they shared that night was merely a physical sign, a confirmation, that their strained marriage was still intact. It was on life support, but very much legal and ongoing.

"These were a labor of love," Holly said, returning to the table. She set a plate of hot bread in the center. "I know how much you love my mother's rolls. I followed her recipe down to the smallest grain of salt."

"Thank you."

Holly sat across from her husband and reached over to grab his hand. He whispered a short and sweet grace. Holly smiled and said, "Amen," before she finished piling food on his plate. Pastor Monroe looked on, knowing full well that he didn't have much of an appetite. His mind was filled with thoughts of his son and Jay. The situation was eating away at him on the inside. For once in his life, he was in desperate need of someone to talk to. His problems were too big for him to bear alone. The counselor needed counseling. If he didn't confess and release his frustrations to someone soon, he was going to lose his mind.

"Holly, I need to share something with you. I'm not sure how to begin, but—"

The phone rang. They both turned and stared at it in silence. For some reason, Holly seemed relieved by the interruption. Pastor Monroe wondered if she had some-how sensed that what he was about to say to her was unpleasant news that would change their lives forever. If she knew about Jay and his son, she had done an ex-cellent job suppressing it. If Holly had knowledge about his affair and King Jalen, surely she would've killed him by now. There was another reason why she welcomed the interruption of the phone. Maybe the tension and unease in the room were sure signs that any conversation between her and her husband wouldn't be a good one.

"I'll get it." Holly laughed nervously. "It's probably Trudy calling to see how the tenderloin turned out."

Chapter Forty

Ivy hung up the phone and hurried back to her work section, feeling proud of herself. Pastor Monroe had sounded excited to hear from her. The smile in his voice had made her day. He actually wanted Ivy to come to his church to sing a song for his congregation, and she had agreed to it without hesitation. One simple song was nothing in comparison to what he had done for her. To be honest, Ivy owed the man an entire concert. If it hadn't been for Gavin Monroe, her ass would still be at Leesworth doing laundry for eighty-eight cents a day. Only a true man of God would've presented the parole board with such a favorable reference on her behalf. Ivy owed Pastor Monroe for his contribution toward her second chance at life, and she was going to start paying off her debt because of the sweet man who had just walked in the door.

Michael winked as he made steps in Ivy's direction. The sight of him in a dark suit and wingtip shoes made her nipples stand at attention. He wasn't sexy in the traditional meaning of the word. She couldn't even truthfully say he was good-looking or had a banging body. But the white dude was smooth, and he didn't mind spending money on cute little trinkets to surprise a girl every now and then. The fact that he had transformed eating pussy into an art form only raised a sista's appreciation for Mr. Stokes to a whole other level. Ivy liked the arrangement she and Michael had. It was relaxed and casual with no strings attached. Neither of them saw any reason to define it or slap a label on it. They enjoyed each other's company, and because of that, they hooked up often.

"Hey, you."

Ivy gave Michael a sexy smile and quickly checked out her space. She didn't want any of the other waitresses all up in her business. They were a bunch of nosy busybody heifers. Most of them were haters, and she couldn't stand them. What Ivy and Michael had may not have been considered a love affair or even a romance, but it worked for them, and it was private. The last thing she wanted was some tramp from the Blue Rhapsody flowing into her mix.

"Hey," she whispered coolly, wiping off a table. "Have a seat. What can I get you?"

"For now, I'll have a screwdriver, but later on I want to screw you."

The spontaneous dampness in Ivy's crotch made her fidget. Her breath got caught in her throat. She had to wait a few moments before she was able to answer. "I'll get your drink. I'll make sure Max puts some extra ice in it so you won't catch afire before I get off. We won't shut down before three. Some rapper and his entourage are supposed to stop by for an autograph session. Gold diggers are gonna be up in here throwing their panties at them."

"What about your panties? Will they go sailing through the air?"

Ivy leaned over to whisper in Michael's ear, "I ain't wearing no panties."

"I see."

"No, you ain't seen nothing yet. Wait until this place closes. I'm gonna show you everything. Are we finally going to your house or is it still being remodeled?"

"Yeah, um, the crew painted upstairs today. The fumes will kill you, babe. We'll get a room downtown. You pick the spot."

"Fine. We'll go back to the Beacon. You know how I like their breakfast. You can feed me in bed."

"Is he asleep?"

"Yeah, he's out like a light." London untied the sash on her pink silk bathrobe to display her nakedness.

From his relaxed position on their king-size bed, Jamal's eyes roamed downward and homed in on the area between London's thighs. She'd had a Brazilian wax. A few inches up were the belly ring and heart tattoo with his name scrawled inside. Completely turned on, Jamal reached for London and pulled her down on top of him. Shit was about to get real serious in their bedroom now that little King Jalen had finally fallen asleep. He was a good baby. The only time he cried was when he was hungry for a bottle or had a loaded diaper. Otherwise, he slept peacefully like an angel. And during those chance moments when he was awake, he smiled and flashed his bright eyes at London from his baby swing.

As precious as King Jalen was, he required lots of attention. Jamal wasn't used to London devoting so much of her time to someone other than him. His kids were older and independent. On those weekends they spent at his house, they had their own activities. They usually hung out with their spoiled rich friends at the country club in the Saint Croix community. All three of the Price kids had their own agendas. The only thing they needed from their dad or London during their weekend visits was money, and there was plenty of that available. Time was the precious commodity that Jamal didn't have very much of. He was moving and shaking,

even in the off-season. London was usually with him
for companionship and to wait on him hand and foot.
There was no way she would be able to do that with a
newborn baby in tow. She'd already announced that she
didn't want a nanny to raise King Jalen. Her overbearing
mother would babysit for them whenever they needed
her to. London's obsession with the baby was causing
Jamal to have second thoughts about becoming a father
for the fourth and final time.

As the heat reached the boiling point in the Price
bedroom, Jamal tucked his dilemma regarding his foster
son in the back of his mind. London had pulled out the
chocolate syrup on a brother and was about to do her
thang. It was an X-rated scene. Thoughts of babies were
not permitted. Jamal grabbed two fistfuls of London's
hair when she went down on him. It had been a couple
of weeks since they'd been able to get buck wild. The
freakiness was long overdue. Jamal was humming and
bucking, enjoying his wife's skills. The bass in his growl
mixed in with the shrillness of King Jalen's wailing
floating through the baby monitor.

London's head popped up. "Oh, my God, the baby is
crying. Mommy's coming, sweetie!"

"Even if I wanted to transfer you out, I couldn't, Ms.
King. You have too many health problems. You're a
Georgia native, and your crimes were committed here.
No other corrections facility anywhere in this country
is going to take on an inmate from another state who
requires the costly amount of medical care you do. Hell, I
can hardly afford to keep you here at Leesworth."

"Have you put in any requests?"

Warden Callahan folded his arms across his chest and shook his head. "Nope. What for? I know how the system works. It all boils down to money. You're considered a financial liability in the eyes of any warden."

"If I'm such a burden, why do you want me here? You should be looking for some fool to take me off your hands. Put in some requests around the southeast region. Mississippi is the fattest state in the country. I bet they have some inmates whose conditions are worse than mine."

"Forget about it, Ms. King," the warden said, standing up behind his desk. "I'm going to keep you here with me. You're an asset to Leesworth. And honestly, you need to be near your family and the people who care for you."

Jay knew Warden Callahan was referring to Pastor Monroe. The two men had spoken at length. No doubt, the pastor had asked the warden not to transfer her out. He was keeping hope alive, even though time was winding down and he hadn't heard a single word from Zach. He was expecting a miracle when there was no sign of one in sight.

"I don't want anybody to care about me. I've tried love. It doesn't work. Faith and sacrifice don't either. I was better off the way I was. When my heart was closed, I couldn't feel anything. Now that it's open, it hurts like hell. Love cost me everything."

"I can't promise you anything, but I will always look out for you here. I know we went through a rough period, but we're cool now. You kept my secret and helped me fix a few things, and I did the same thing for you in return."

Jay laughed. "Man, we hated each other. You were out to destroy me, and I wanted your blood. We were forced to get along because of certain circumstances. It's not like you actually gave a damn about me."

"You're right, but now I genuinely care about what happens to you. Stay here at Leesworth where I can look out for your best interests. That white man cares about you. Let's hope he has enough Christianity in him to get a prayer through to heaven on behalf of your son."

"I'll stay. What other choice do I have?"

Chapter Forty-one

Ramona was tired of all the questions the dingy white chick kept asking her. Arianna had kept her and Dex up all night with her whining and screaming. All Ramona wanted was a few moments of solitude while she waited for Dr. Hussein to check her little one's tiny ears, but the dumb chick sitting next to her wouldn't shut her damn mouth. Her beautiful baby boy was wide awake. He had the most exotic eyes. They reminded Ramona of a pair of shiny quarters.

"How old is your little girl?" the woman asked.

Ramona rolled her eyes to the ceiling. "She's three months old."

"This little man is almost a month old. His daddy and I adore him to pieces. You should see his nursery. It is fabulous! Everything is red, black, and white with footballs everywhere. The room is a shrine to the Atlanta Falcons."

"Isn't he a little bit too young for that?"

"Oh, no, sweetie, we had to start him off early. You see, Jamal, that's my husband, he plays for the Atlanta Falcons. He's their star wide receiver. I'm sure you've heard of him. They call him the Jack Man because he used to be a thug in his hood back in the day."

Shocked shitless, Ramona's jaw dropped. It wasn't because she was impressed that she was having a conversation with a pro baller's trophy wife. She couldn't believe the dumb brunette Barbie had actually let the statement about her husband's past roll off her tongue.

Ramona felt like punching the brainless trick dead in her cosmetically enhanced mouth. She pulled her emotions back and recovered from the stun of stupidity.

"I don't watch football," Ramona lied as smooth as butter. "I couldn't name three Atlanta Falcons if my life depended on it."

"Oh, well. Anyway, we are spoiling our son rotten. His first photo session is scheduled for next week. I'm so excited. I want him to do baby food and diaper commercials. He's too cute to keep to ourselves."

"He is very handsome. And his eyes are gorgeous. Which side of the family did he inherit them from?"

The woman cuddled the baby closer to her perky bosom and shifted uncomfortably in her seat. "Oh, my great-grandfather on my mother's side was an Irishman. They came from him."

"Arianna," a nurse holding a chart in her hand called out. "Dr. Hussein can see you and your mommy now, sweet pea."

Ramona snatched up her purse and diaper bag quickly and turned to Ms. Clueless. "It was nice meeting you, Mrs., um . . ."

"It's London Price," she rushed to say with a wave of her hand. The gigantic diamond on her ring finger sparkled under the bright light. "And this future Hall of Famer and *GQ* model is Jalen King Price."

Jill zipped the children's suitcase closed and brushed past Zach, totally ignoring him. She headed for the walk-in closet and stood in front of her shoe rack. She grabbed two pairs of sandals and walked back into the master bedroom where Zach stood in the middle of the floor.

"Damn it, Jill! I don't understand why you're not excited about this trip. You complain about us not visiting your family enough. Hell, I thought you'd be happy about our impromptu getaway."

Jill dropped the shoes inside her suitcase and spun around to face her husband. "Why now, Zachary? Why are we going to Jamaica eight days before the custody hearing for Jay's son, huh? Have you even responded to the letter from the baby's father? Does he know you want nothing to do with your nephew?"

"I don't have to tell Reverend Slick Dick a damn thing. I don't remember him calling or writing me a letter informing me that he was about to knock up my sister."

"What did you say?" Jill inched toward Zach, closing the distance between them. "Repeat what you just said."

Regret of Zach's last statement was written all over his face. Jill read it in his eyes. The rigidness in his stance was confirmation. Zach had slipped and revealed that he had some type of feelings for Jay and her involvement with Gavin Monroe. He couldn't hide it, but he was giving it his best shot. With his signature coolness, he walked over to the recliner in the corner of the master suite and plopped down.

Jill could extract all kinds of emotions from him that no one else could, but she wasn't about to get him to confess that he was concerned about Jay. That was his most private secret. He was pissed off with Gavin Monroe, too. Jill had heard his rant several times over the past few weeks. No married preacher and professional counselor had the right to get involved with an inmate. As far as Zach was concerned, the entire situation was the shady preacher's fault. Somehow, he had convinced Jay that he loved her. And Jill had been fooled into his game because she believed him. Zach would not buy into it. He wasn't about to let Jay trap him either. Yes, he cared for her in his own peculiar way, Jill figured. He was sympathetic toward her and her son too, but he couldn't fall prey to the madness. That was the reason he had booked a family vacation to Jamaica on a whim. It was his escape from Jay, her baby, and Aunt Jackie. Zach didn't want to be in the country on the day of the custody hearing. No matter how things turned out, he would accept it as God's divine will. Who was he to interfere with that?

Jill asked Zach to repeat what he had said. This time she added a little spice to her voice. She was a perceptive woman. She knew her man better than he knew himself. Her insight often blew Zach's mind. Any other time he would appreciate how in sync she was with his feelings, but today it seemed to annoy the shit out of him. Jill planted her fists on her hips and waited for an answer. Zach couldn't ignore her, because she was standing directly in front of him, looking down in his face.

"Gavin Monroe and I don't have anything to talk about. That's all there is to it. We're going to Jamaica because my job has me stressed out. I had a baby die on me last week. You know how that affects me, Jill. I need to get away to regroup. And didn't I promise your dad that I would make sure you visited the island as often as possible?"

Jill pursed her lips and nodded. She changed her stance, shifting all her weight to one hip, which meant she didn't believe a damn word Zach had said. It was a clear signal that she was sure he read without any confusion. Jill's distrust in him at the moment was making Zach sweat.

"Zachary, we could visit my family later on, like during the summer. Why should we pull the kids out of school for a week to go now?"

"They're in preschool, baby," Zach reasoned. "What the hell are they gonna miss? A college entrance exam?

Finish packing. Our flight leaves tomorrow morning. I've got a few errands to run."

Ivy ended her solo performance and opened her eyes to a standing ovation. The all-white congregation at Marvelous Light Pentecostal Church had received her soulful rendition of "Amazing Grace" with great appreciation. It was the only hymn that Jaw Bone, the keyboard player from the Blue Rhapsody, knew by heart. He was sitting on the piano stool, grinning like a damn fool behind dark sunglasses. He was acting like he and Ivy had just finished a gig at the *BET Hip Hop Awards*. It was probably because he was high as hell. Ivy was surprised he'd even shown up, but he'd crept into the church a few minutes before it was time for her to sing, smelling like a blunt and wearing the same suit he'd had on the night before at the club. Even in his inebriated condition, Jaw Bone had tickled the ivory keys as skillfully as Liberace ever could.

The applause swelled, and it scared the shit out of Ivy. She hadn't expected such a spirited reaction from the prim and proper white people. There were lots of them in attendance, too, maybe a thousand or more. As her eyes roamed the crowd, she took in the smiles on the friendly faces. Hundreds were still clapping, while others were waving their hands and speaking in tongues. The sight brought stinging tears to Ivy's eyes, and she eventually allowed them to fall freely. They wanted another song. Too bad Jaw Bone's gospel repertoire was a song of one.

Ivy kissed her fingertips and waved to the audience before she started her descent down the pulpit stairs. Pastor Monroe, always the kind and thoughtful gentleman, hurried over from his huge, comfortable chair in the center of the stage to take Ivy's hand and escorted her down the steps. Before he released her hand, he pulled the former prison songbird into a warm embrace. The members of Marvelous Light Pentecostal Church let out a chorus of "amens" and "hallelujahs" all over the contemporary-style sanctuary.

As Ivy made her way back to her seat, she received hugs and compliments from several strangers. It was a humbling experience. The patrons at Blue Rhapsody had never responded to her singing with such appreciation. Only Michael made a big fuss over her performances. Ivy was enjoying her rock-star experience at the white megachurch. She flung her wavy auburn weave over her shoulders and continued toward her seat.

She wished Michael could see her softer, conservative side. The brown three-piece pantsuit had her feeling all stylish and sophisticated. Her cousin Laveta had warned her not to go overboard with her makeup and accessories. She didn't want her to scare the Christian crackers out of their church. Ivy took her cousin's advice and used the earth tones of brown, bronze, and yellow. She chose a classic pair of gold hoop earrings to complete her outfit. Ivy damn sure looked like a gospel singer, but she was far from it. If only the people whom she'd just fascinated with her voice knew exactly what type of chick she really was.

Ivy sat gracefully in her seat and reached for a Bible in the compartment on the back of the pew in front of her. Pastor Monroe was now standing in front of the podium, thanking her for singing so beautifully. Out of the corner of her eye, Ivy saw Jaw Bone making his smooth escape out a side door. She shook her head, but she couldn't judge the man because she was just as sinful as he was, maybe even more. At least Jaw Bone kept his lifestyle 100 percent at all times. Ivy was playing a role this morning. Her whole damn life was one big screenplay, but at least she was free, and she had the handsome man preaching in the pulpit to thank for that.

Chapter Forty-two

While Ivy sat listening attentively to the pastor's inspiring sermon, Holly was checking her out from head to toe. Gavin hadn't told her about his surprise guest soloist, and she was madder than a rattle snake. Unable to contain her anger another second, she signaled for the usher who was on pulpit duty.

"Yes, ma'am, First Lady, what can I do for you?" the young lady dressed in red whispered.

"Bring me a glass of ice water. And make sure the guest singer gets a visitor's card. I'd like her contact information for my personal records so I can keep in touch with her."

"Of course, First Lady, I'll do that right away. Is there anything else?"

Holly crossed her legs and waved her hand, dismissing the overly chipper usher. Her eyes homed in on Ivy again. Where had Gavin dug her up from after all these months? They'd obviously been in recent contact. He was prepared for her appearance. Mark, the assistant pastor, had escorted her straight to Gavin's office the moment she'd arrived. She'd stayed there, emerging just seconds before the praise team took to the stage to start the service. The attempted murderess feigned innocence all through the service, right up until Gavin stood and announced there was a guest singer in the house.

The introduction he gave her before presenting her to the congregation was a bit too tasteful for Holly. Not once did he mention how he'd met sister Ivy. She was his sister all right—the one who'd used him to get out of jail early. The sweet and wholesome words Gavin had used to introduce the ex-con-turned-nightclub-singer nearly caused Holly to puke. Sure, Ivy could sing. No one could deny that. But she was nothing but a piece of homemade ghetto trash dressed in an expensive borrowed—or stolen—designer suit. And she had made a huge mistake by walking back into Gavin's life for whatever reason she was cooking up. Ivy had used him once, but Holly refused to allow her to do it again.

"I'm not going to miss this place, but I'll miss you two so much. You're my sisters." Sophia wiped her eyes and looked at her two best friends in the world. "Please take care of yourselves."

"We will," Shanika mumbled through tears.

"Enjoy your freedom, girl. You deserve it. Don't ever come back here. Do you hear me?"

"I hear you, Jay. I'm praying that your brother will show up at court next week and take little King home with him. My faith is strong, my sister. I need you to agree in prayer with me, okay?"

Jay nodded, but she didn't have any more faith. She no longer believed in miracles either. Her heart had turned back to stone.

Sophia reached out and hugged her friend. Jay squeezed her back. Shanika threw her arms around both of them. The three friends held on to each other and cried until the loud buzzer sounded, alerting them that the security gate was about to open.

"I've got to go now. My father is here. I love you both so very much. I'll be in touch."

***

"Logan, please stop pulling your sister's hair. Daddy doesn't like that at all." Michael frowned and shifted his attention back to his phone conversation. Tommy, his co-worker, had called to give him a report on Ivy's reunion with Gavin Monroe.

"Is this a good time, Mike? It sounds like you have your hands full with your kids."

"I'm fine. Sherry is upstairs trying to put the twins to sleep in the nursery. I'm watching Logan and Summer while she does that. Go ahead. I'm listening."

"That Ivy is a hottie. I see why she has your nose wide open. And, man, can she sing!" Tommy let out a high-pitched whistle. "I almost cried when she sang 'Amazing Grace' like a pro."

"My Ivy is a woman of many skills. Did she spend any time with the pastor alone?"

"They hung out briefly. When she first got there, she went to his office. No one was in there with them, but I don't think they have a sexual history. I'm pretty sure your nigger side piece has told you the truth about her relationship with the good pastor. He was her minister while she was in lockup. He appears to be the real deal. His sermon was great. He talked a lot of faith mumbo jumbo and about miracles. The guy almost made a believer out of me."

"So, he's a straight arrow. It makes me wonder why his wife doesn't trust him."

"I don't know. She wasn't too thrilled about Ivy being at their church. She was clearly flustered. I got the distinct feeling that her husband forgot to tell her Ivy would be there. It was strange. Anyway, the pastor introduced your girl like they were old friends. He didn't mention Leesworth at all. I guess he didn't want his flock to know that Ivy is an ex-con."

"I can understand that. He didn't think it was important. Well, it seems like you had a dry run. I'm going to have to find out myself what Ivy and Gavin Monroe talked about in his office. If it amounted to nothing, I'll have to find a reason for her to visit the good pastor again so they'll have another chance to catch up."

"I think it's only an ear infection, Leo. Stop worrying. The doctor will give her some ear drops and maybe an antibiotic. It'll clear up in no time."

"You believe it's an ear infection, eh?" Leo asked, swinging his daughter in his arms.

"Yes, honey, a simple ear infection."

"Well, Leo will feel much better if a doctor comes to say so. Me Molina is frettin' sumtin' awful."

Nina, now known around Jamaica as Marta Fox Hines, rubbed her protruding belly and smiled. Her husband, Leo, was overly concerned about their 11-month-old daughter, Molina. She had a low-grade fever and a slightly inflamed inner right ear. The little girl had slept in her father's arms all night long, waking up and crying frequently, tugging on her tiny earlobe. Leo had insisted that he and Nina bring their daughter to the clinic very early the next morning.

Even after rising at the break of dawn to travel down from the mountains above Kingston to the lower lands, they'd met a large, impatient crowd in the waiting area of the clinic. The room was packed with other sick babies in the arms of frantic mothers, elderly patients, and pregnant women. Nina was expecting their second child in four months, but her pregnancy was progressing well. Her and Leo's concern this morning was for their fretful baby girl.

They'd arrived at the clinic at eight o'clock sharp. After waiting two and a half hours, a nurse finally came and took them to examination room seven. She managed to take Molina's temperature while she flailed her arms and screamed on her father's lap. Now the entire Hines family was sitting in the sterile Winnie-the-Pooh–inspired examination room, waiting to be seen by the doctor.

Nina chuckled at her husband. "You're so impatient. The doctor will be here soon, and Molina will be fine. I, on the other hand, have a full bladder. I'm not sure how much longer I can wait before I'll have to go to the restroom."

"Go on, my dear. Leo can take care of Molina and speak with the doctor. Go on now, before you wet yerself."

"No, I'll hold it. I want to be here when the doctor comes to examine her."

Zach was impressed by the new pediatric wing of the Johnson Medical Center in Kingston. His friend Dr. Harry Johnson was not only a great physician and advocate for the poor in his country but also an astute businessman. He had single-handedly wooed a group of very wealthy men and women from all across Europe and the United States to invest in the expansion of his medical clinic. There were ten examination rooms, a modern and well-equipped lab, and an imaging room. More construction was in the early planning stages.

"I'm impressed." Zach slapped his buddy on the back and grinned. "Your countrymen should be proud of you. Jill and her family are. You're making quality healthcare available to the poor people of Jamaica, while a group of heartless people known as conservatives in America—the wealthiest nation in the free world—don't give a damn about the less fortunate. Do you know how many people in America die each year of treatable diseases and injuries because they don't have healthcare coverage?"

"No, my friend, I can't imagine."

"Thousands, and it's a damn shame."

"It is indeed a shame in a country overflowing with wealth and resources." Dr. Johnson checked the time on his watch as he and Zach rounded the corner on their way to the reception area. The clinic's staff was located in the center, inside of a large office that was bustling with activity.

A medical clerk handed Dr. Johnson a few charts. "You have twin boys in room three for a well check, a five-year-old boy with asthma in room five, and a little girl with presumably an ear infection in room seven."

"Thank you, Viola." The doctor patted her shoulder. He turned to Zach when she returned to her desk.

"I'm about to head back to the resort. It's time for a nap. I came to the island to relax and regroup, and that's exactly what I've been doing."

"Oh, no, my friend, you'll have to nap later. I need your help right now. Go scrub up."

Zach held up both hands and shook his head. "Nah, Doc, I'm not working this go-around. Every time I come over here, you trick me into working. I'm on vacation."

"Viola," Dr. Johnson said, totally ignoring Zach, "give Mr. King the chart for the child with the ear infection. He'll do an assessment before I see her. Thank you."

The doctor left Zach standing in the middle of the office with his mouth wide open. He turned slowly to face Viola, who was waving the chart at him. Her smile was infectious.

"Come with me, Mr. King. I'll get you a lab coat, and you can scrub before you get started."

Chapter Forty-three

Zach gave the door three light taps before he opened it and walked into the room. "Is this Molina Hines?" His eyes were on the beautiful little girl, but the question was for her father.

"Yes, this is me Molina."

"I'm Zachary, sir." He extended his hand. The father accepted it with a firm grip. "I'm a nurse visiting from the United States. I'm helping Dr. Johnson today. He'll be in shortly."

"I am Leo, this little girl's papa. Her right ear is ailing her sumtin' terrible."

"Is that so, pumpkin?" Zach reached into the breast pocket of his borrowed lab coat and pulled out a pen light. "Can I have a look inside your ear, please?"

Molina poked out her bottom lip and rested her head on Leo's shoulder. Zach took advantage of the opportunity by shining the light inside her right ear so he could see what was causing her discomfort. As he was examining the baby's ear and speaking to her in a calm voice, Nina returned to the examination room. She had left, racing for the restroom a few minutes before Zach arrived. Her path crossed with Dr. Johnson's in the hallway on her way back. When she heard an unfamiliar male voice inside the examination room, she paused outside the cracked door.

Nina was surprised to see Zach examining her daughter. She never would have imagined running into him.

Over the past two and a half years, life in Jamaica had been peaceful and happy. Leo had done everything in his power to provide for Nina and protect her. When she became pregnant with Molina, they were able to contact her mother and stepsister in California to let them know that she was safe and doing well in Jamaica. Both women were happy to hear from Nina, but they knew it wasn't safe for her to contact them very often.

Nina felt very secure in her new life as a wife and mother. Up until she'd almost come face-to-face with Zach at the clinic, she'd had no worries. She was a bit shaken now as she stood frozen in place outside the examination room. Zach was actually touching her daughter under Leo's watchful eye. The whole scene was so shocking that Nina had to pee again. She watched Zach and Molina a few seconds longer before she made another mad dash for the restroom.

"Is there something wrong, Holly? You've been moping around for the past few days, barely talking. Are you sick?"

Holly closed her book and placed it on the end table. She removed her reading glasses and placed them there as well. "That evening when I prepared the tenderloin, you were about to tell me something, but the phone rang and interrupted you. We never got back around to our conversation. Were you going to tell me you'd been in contact with Ivy Maxwell?"

No, I was going to confess to you about my affair with Jayla and tell you about our son, was what Pastor Monroe wanted to say to Holly, but the timing was all wrong that evening. One of his most trusted deacons was under the care of a hospice, dying from a rare form of cancer. A young woman who had been released from

Leesworth two years ago had returned on more drug charges, but this time they were more severe. And worst of all, he had not heard a word from Zachary King. He'd spoken with his aunt, Ms. Brown, who informed him that her nephew and his family were out of the country and weren't expected to return until after King Jalen's custody hearing. It was not a good time for Holly's foolishness.

"Yes, I was going to tell you that Ivy had called to let me know that she was going to visit me at Marvelous Light. I encouraged her to join us for Sunday morning worship service and asked her to sing. Was that a problem for you?"

"It wasn't a problem, Gavin. I just wish you had warned me. I wasn't prepared. I felt like an outsider in my own church. It's painful enough that I'm all alone in this marriage. We don't even have children to fill in the lonely gaps."

"Don't start talking about babies. I'm not in a good headspace this evening. There's a lot going on at the church. The doctors have turned brother Melton over to hospice care. Millie and the children are devastated. I spent a lot of time with them today." He sighed and threw his head back against the headrest on the recliner. "And I had an inmate return to Leesworth. When she left two years ago, I thought she had turned her life around and was ready to take on the world. She came back today on the same charges she served time for before. She'll probably spend the next eight years of her life in prison."

"I'm sorry. I didn't know your day was so crappy. I won't talk about babies tonight. Heaven forbid I should want to discuss starting a family with my husband. I'm going to bed. If you care to join me before I fall asleep, I'll give you a decent blowjob to take the edge off. Good night."

***

Ivy took one last peek at her roast in the oven and turned it off. The aroma coming from her small kitchen was heavenly. She had prepared her first home-cooked meal for Michael ever. It was a special occasion. At last, she had moved into her own apartment. Michael had given her $2,000 to help her finally make the move from Laveta's crowded and cluttered house in Bankhead to a two-bedroom apartment in Ridgewood.

The neighborhood was a big improvement, and she had the privacy she'd dreamed about since being released from Leesworth. From now on, Michael wouldn't have to waste money on hotel rooms. He and Ivy could get their freak on in the queen-size bed he'd bought her. The entire cherry-wood ensemble was gorgeous. Michael had surprised Ivy and picked it out himself. He'd arranged for it to be delivered early one Saturday morning after he had dropped her off following one of their wild nights at the Beacon Hotel.

Ivy had prepared a soul-food spread to thank Michael for his kindness and to break in her new spot. She imagined they would be spending more time together now that she had her own place. Every weekend rendezvous at the Beacon had been sizzling hot, but now that Ivy had a love shack, she had a feeling she and Michael would get to work their magic on each other more often. Maybe they could pull a few all-nighters during the week. Then once the renovations on Michael's house were completed, Ivy would spend time with him there to switch up the scenery a bit. The thought of that made her whole body tingle with excitement.

"Damn it!" Ivy shouted and snapped her fingers when she realized she'd forgotten to put the dinner rolls in the oven. It was almost seven o'clock. Michael would be there soon.

Ivy searched her lower cabinets and found a cookie sheet. She rinsed and dried it in a hurry and placed the rolls on top. Then she removed the roast from the oven, placed it on the counter, and tossed the rolls inside. Ivy wanted dinner to be perfect because she wanted to impress Michael. He wasn't her man, per se, but he was the closest damn thing she had to one. And he was the only dude she was dealing with at the time. She wasn't sure what direction their fiery fling was heading in, but she was satisfied with where it was right now . . . well, almost. Ivy's only complaints were that she and Michael didn't spend enough time together, and she didn't know much about him. She didn't push him, though. She didn't want to scare him away. Maybe it was too early in the game for Michael to make his life an open book.

The sound of the doorbell rippling through the small apartment yanked Ivy back to her dinner date. She took off her apron. As she made her way down the small hallway, she froze at the sound of a key rattling in her lock. Ivy smiled. Michael was letting himself in. It reminded her of Dr. Cliff Huxtable returning home to Clair after a long day at the hospital. Life couldn't be any sweeter unless Michael were to invite her into his world and make her his special lady. The sexual affair was cool, but Ivy wanted more.

Chapter Forty-four

On the ride from the Johnson Medical Center back to the Blue Lagoon Resort, Zach found himself in the most emotionally challenging battle of his life. He was one disturbed brother. His buddy Roy was talking and pointing out new buildings and repairs in the road along the way, but his words sounded like a foreign language in Zach's ears.

His mind was on the six little orphans he had assisted Dr. Johnson in treating just before the clinic closed. All of them had contracted some type of gastrointestinal virus that caused frequent vomiting, chronic diarrhea, and severe dehydration. The youngest, a baby girl, had to be rushed to Kingston General Hospital. Her name was Cassidy, and she was 2 years old. The child appeared lifeless when a caretaker at the orphanage carried her inside the clinic and placed her in Zach's arms. The woman was crying and screaming in a pitiful voice, begging for him to save the little girl's life.

Apparently, some food that had been donated to Angel's Charity Orphanage from a local market was outdated and spoiled. The cook had complained to the head mistress at the orphanage about the foul smell of the chicken and vegetables when the food was delivered, but the woman ignored her. A soup prepared with the donated food items eventually made the little ones sick. Dr. Johnson became livid when the caretaker told him what had happened. He, Zach, and the nurses worked diligently to treat the children, but Cassidy's case required more than what he and his staff could provide at the clinic. She was so young and tiny. Her body was unable to respond to the medicine he had given her like the older children. Cassidy required hospitalization.

While Zach and the other nurses treated the children under Dr. Johnson's command, all he could think about was his children and Nahima. They were healthy and well cared for. More importantly, they were loved. The innocent and helpless children were fortunate to have been taken in by the staff at Angel's Charity Orphanage, but those people were not their family, and the facility was not a home. Zach couldn't help but wonder where the children's parents were and why they had abandoned them. Were they dead? That was the only way his children would be raised without him in their lives. It would take death to keep him away from Nahima, too. He loved his niece like there was no tomorrow, despite the fact that he and Jay were estranged. No matter what, Nahima was his flesh and blood, and she had not asked to be born into complex circumstances. She, like those six little orphans, was innocent.

And so was King Jalen.

"Why are you frettin', Nina? The man never saw yer face."

"I know he didn't see me, but what if he had?" Nina lifted her other foot so that Leo could rub it. The trip to and from the clinic had earned her a foot and ankle massage. "Do you think he would've recognized my face?"

"Maybe. Maybe not. You look different now, especially with yer big belly." Leo rubbed Nina's stomach and laughed. "Yer hair is short and black. It wasn't like that back then."

"The last time Zach saw me was when I testified at Jay's trial. My hair was long, curly, and auburn. I had wide hips and a waistline, too." Nina shuddered at the memories of being badgered and intimidated by the district attorney on the witness stand in front of a courtroom full of strangers, all because of Jay. "My life was one big disaster back then."

"And what do you think about yer life here with Leo now?"

Nina smiled and pressed her back into the stack of pillows her husband had placed behind her for comfort. Her eyes fluttered shut as he continued massaging her achy, swollen feet. "My life is perfect. I'm a lucky girl. Meeting you was the best thing that ever happened to me. Then when Molina came along . . . I can't describe how it felt the first time I held her in my arms. And now we're going to have a little boy."

Nina sat up straight in the bed and looked into the eyes of the man who had given her a second chance at life. "Leo, promise me that we will always be happy. When I saw Zach today, the whole scene shook me up. Seeing someone from my past, a person connected to Jay, reminded me of how differently things could've turned out back then. I could be in prison right now if it hadn't been for you. Just promise me that this happiness will last forever."

"As long as Leo is livin' and breathin', then Nina, Molina, and little Leo will be happy."

Ivy woke from a peaceful sleep and discovered she was in bed alone. After dinner, Michael had helped her wash the dishes and put the leftover food away. Then they retired to the bedroom to christen her brand-new bed.

Ivy rolled over and smiled as she inhaled the manly scent of Michael's body embedded in her sheets. He was in the shower. The thought of him naked with water running down his lean body heightened Ivy's feminine senses. She got up and tiptoed to the bathroom. She heard Michael humming off-key, softly. Feeling brazen and naughty, Ivy snatched back the shower curtain and wrapped her arms around Michael's waist. She pressed her cheek to his back, enjoying how good he made her feel. The humming stopped when her hand slid from his stomach to fondle his manhood. It hardened instantly as she stroked him the way he liked her to.

Michael threw his head back and released a breath. "We can't do this, babe. I've got to get out of here. I have an assignment."

"I hear you, but your dick didn't get the message." Skillfully, Ivy increased the pressure of her strokes and picked up just the right amount of speed.

The soap and the washcloth fell to the beige tile floor of the shower. Michael turned around and swept Ivy up into his arms. He carried her into the bedroom, both of their bodies dripping wet. He dropped her on the bed and started searching for his pants. When he found them, he pulled a condom from his pocket and tore into it with lightning speed. His hands trembled slightly as he rolled it over his hardness.

"Turn over. I'm feeling like a cowboy."

On command, Ivy flipped and assumed the position. She was wetter than a river and hot as lava. Michael had the ability to make her lose her damn mind in the bedroom. No other man could bring out the sexual beast in her the way he could. The dude had a marksman's aim and knew how to apply the perfect amount of force on his entry to make a sista dizzy with pleasure. Ivy almost went over the edge too soon when Michael smacked both her butt cheeks with his hands and told her how good her pussy was. But she held on for the ride, knowing it would only get better with each powerful thrust.

She responded to every stroke he gave her with a back push. Michael's voice switched from deep moans to full sentences filled with lies and promises to give Ivy the world as they headed down the stretch. To speed things up, he reached under Ivy and fondled her breasts, each thumb tormenting the hell out of one of her rock-hard nipples. Like a strike of lightning, her climax lit up her dark room and damn near knocked her out. All Ivy could do was hum and buck until the wave faded. Michael's hands left her breasts and grabbed her ass again. His thrusts had accelerated, and his words and thoughts had become unintelligible babbling mixed with moans and vulgar profanity. It was a perfect, unintentional Tarzan impersonation.

"I can't move," Michael mumbled in a hoarse voice before he collapsed on top of Ivy.

She pressed her face into the mattress and giggled. The weight of his body fully spread on top of hers felt good. She squealed when he buried his face in the crook of her neck and bit softly into her flesh. "Didn't I feed you good enough last night? You ate like a couple of men. Then you ate my pussy like it was dessert. Now you're biting me as if you're hungry again."

"I can't help it, babe. I like the way you taste." Michael laughed, rolled off of Ivy, and pulled her on top of him. He sighed when she rested her head on his chest. "I don't want anyone else tasting or touching you, so I hope you'll do what I asked you to do."

"What?"

"Call your preacher friend and make an appointment to meet with him. Ask the good pastor to help you find a job someplace in an office or a factory."

"But I love to sing. The only place Pastor Monroe can find me a job singing is in a church. I ain't trying to be no church singer. Now if he can get me a gig at one of those fancy clubs, singing for white folks, or in a recording studio, singing background for some bigwigs, I'll leave Blue Rhapsody in a heartbeat."

"Call him. You'll never know what he can do for you until you ask him."

Chapter Forty-five

"I don't know what I'm gonna do, Shanika. If I lose my son, I'll kill myself. I swear to God I will. I can't live without ever seeing him again."

"Have you talked to your auntie?"

Jay nodded and wiped her eyes with a crumpled tissue. "She is just as pitiful as I am. Zach's punk ass blamed me for her heart attack. What he's doing is gonna cause her to have another one. I hate that selfish bastard. He and Jill ain't coming back from Jamaica until after the hearing. Damn, I wish Fudge had been an actual hit man and smoked his ass for real."

"Stop talking like that, King." Shanika threw her arm around her girl's shoulders. "You don't mean that shit. How could Zach take your son and be dead at the same time?"

"Damn it, girl! If I had hired a real hit man and not some undercover cop, I wouldn't even be in prison. I never would've met you-know-who or gotten pregnant."

"Where is baby daddy anyway? He hasn't been to work in two or three days."

Jay looked toward the door of the laundry room. Then she lowered her voice. "He had a death at his church. One of his big, important members died. The funeral was this afternoon. He's going to the welfare office to speak to the social worker. He made an appointment with an attorney to see if the custody hearing can be delayed since Zach is out of the country. Gavin wants to talk with my brother, man to man, and ask him to take our son. Hopefully, the case will get postponed, and he'll have an opportunity to run Zach and Jill down. She wants them to take guardianship over King. She should want to after the way her ungrateful ass betrayed me. That bitch knows she owes me."

"We have two more days, King. We're gonna pray that they hold off the case until Zach comes home from Jamaica. Only God can grant us a miracle."

"You and Gavin can pray and have faith and look for a miracle. I'm done with all that stuff. I hope the judge will delay the hearing until Zach's evil ass comes back. Then maybe if we're lucky, he'll stop being selfish and do right by me for once in his life."

"How does this look?" London twirled around for Jamal in a baby blue business suit. The skirt was knee-length and pencil straight.

"Expensive."

"It's Michael Kors, so of course it's expensive, sweetie, but how do I look in it?" London twirled again and posed with her legs open and both hands on her narrow hips. "Say something," she whined.

Jamal aimed the remote control at the home-theater unit to increase the volume before he inspected London from head to toe. "You look nice, baby. It's a perfect fit."

"Great! This is my court outfit. I want to impress the judge and the social workers. That's why I'm bringing my A game. Uh-oh, I should've tried it on with the shoes for you. I found a fabulous pair of Jimmy Choos at Bloomingdales. Wait, I'll be right back."

"Slow your roll, London." Jamal patted the empty space next to him on the black leather sofa. "Sit down. Let me holla at you for a minute."

"What is it? You think it's over the top? Yeah, maybe I should go for the conservative look. I know. I'll wear—"

"Expensive clothes and shoes won't make you appear to be a good mother. It's not about how much money we have or this big-ass house either. A good parent is someone who is totally devoted to a child, no matter what. That child's welfare is top priority over a parent's wants or needs. A baby isn't a trophy or a symbol. It's a tiny human being who depends on his or her parents for everything for eighteen years or more. Are you sure you're ready for that?"

"You know I am. We need a baby to complete our family. Your kids are older. They don't need you very much. Well, they need your money. Just imagine how much fun it'll be taking your little boy to the practice field, all dressed in his little Falcon gear. The camera loves that cute face. We'll be the talk of the team. We're the only married couple in the organization without a child together."

"When we first hooked up, you didn't want any babies. You said you were cool with my situation. Now you're going crazy over the idea of adopting King Jalen. I'm having second thoughts. I like our life just the way it is."

"But you promised me that you would be on board."

"I was, but now I'm not feeling it all that much."

London stood abruptly and stared down at her husband with her hands on her hips. "I love you with all my heart, Jamal. God knows I do. I have put up with your kids treating me like shit all these years. I've dealt with the baby-mama drama, the outrageous child-support payments, and your mother's blatant disrespect. Now it's time for you to put up with me and my desire to be a mother."

"What's wrong, Zachary? You're scaring me." Jill reached over and turned on the lamp on the nightstand.

"You've been restless all night. Tell me what is troubling you so."

"We've gotta go home. I know we're not scheduled to leave for another three days, but we have to leave tomorrow." Zach got out of bed and crossed the room. He sat at the desk and turned on his laptop. "I'm about to change our flights. Can you start packing our things?"

"Sure I can, but why? Why are we leaving Jamaica early?"

Zach looked up from the computer screen to face Jill. He rubbed his goatee like he always did when he had something on his mind. "I can't do it, baby. I can't let Jay's son grow up in a house with strangers. He has King blood running through his veins. He's innocent. It's not his fault that he has a fool for a mama and a pimped-out preacher for a daddy. I'm going to court to ask the judge to grant us custody of my nephew."

Reverend and sister Broadus tiptoed out of the room when they heard a sound that reminded them of a bear growling. The sedative that the home healthcare nurse had given Aunt Jackie had finally kicked in. She had drifted off to sleep. Aunt Hattie Jean had called them in a panic, begging them to come to the house. Aunt Jackie had fallen into a pitiful, emotional fit, crying and screaming over Jay's baby. Zach was still in Jamaica, and the hearing would take place in less than forty-eight hours. The thought of that baby being adopted into another family when he had one of his own was wearing her down.

Aunt Jackie had scared the crap out of her big sister when she clutched her chest with a shaky hand and started gasping for air. Aunt Hattie Jean thought she was having another heart attack, but instead she broke out into a hymn. Aunt Jackie ripped into "Father, I Stretch My Hands to Thee" with her strong soprano voice. She sang it repeatedly for close to an hour, holding notes and executing runs and riffs like she was a contestant on BET's *Sunday Best*. And then, from out of left field, she snapped. Her uncontrollable sobs shook her entire meaty body. She started yelling prayers for God to take her, because she didn't want to live without King Jalen in her life.

Aunt Hattie Jean thought she was losing her mind, so she snatched up the phone and called the nurse at Agape Home Healthcare Agency. She didn't know what else to do. Sheila, the on-call nurse, agreed to come over to give her a sedative, but in the meantime, Aunt Hattie Jean put in an emergency call to Reverend Broadus. He and his wife, Glenda, arrived at the house a few minutes ahead of the nurse. They prayed with Aunt Jackie and tried to encourage her, but it didn't appear to be doing any good. She kept crying and screaming and shaking until Sheila showed up. Once she gave her the injection, Aunt Jackie fell silent and listened to Reverend Broadus and sister Glenda take turns quoting Scriptures of comfort to her. Minutes later she closed her eyes and hummed herself to sleep.

Chapter Forty-six

Ivy put the piece of paper in her purse. She smiled at Pastor Monroe. She had so much respect for the man. She would forever be indebted to him. Once again, he had come to her rescue. He'd given her not one but two job referrals.

"Remember, the job at the recording studio isn't steady at all. They'll call you in only when they need you. My friend says country western singers, gospel artists, and rappers use his state-of-the-art facility and equipment all the time. I'm sure some of those musicians can use someone as talented as you at some point."

"I hope so."

"The hostess position at the restaurant is a part-time position. I'm sure they'll hire you on the spot."

Ivy stood up. "Thank you so much for everything, Pastor Monroe. You're a good man."

"You're welcome. Call me anytime, Ivy. My door is always open to you."

There was a knock at the door. They both burst out laughing. Apparently, the pastor's open-door policy applied to others as well.

"I'd better get going. I'm sure you have more important people than me to deal with."

The pastor came from behind his desk and gave Ivy a hug. Then he turned toward the door. "Come in."

In walked Sophia Mendez, wearing a cute red and white waitress uniform. "Ivy, is that you?"

"Yes! Oh, my God! Sophia, it's so good to see you, girl."

The two former Leesworth inmates grabbed each other and hugged. Pastor Monroe smiled at their very emotional reunion. Both women shed a few tears as they held each other.

"What are you doing here?" they asked each other in unison and laughed hysterically afterward.

"I'm on my way to check out a job," Ivy told Sophia.

"I was in the neighborhood and wanted to stop by and say hello to my pastor on my way to work."

"Hi, Sophia." Pastor Monroe waved. "I don't mean to be rude, but I'm going to have to ask you ladies to excuse me. I have an appointment across town."

Sophia and Ivy followed Pastor Monroe out the door, arm in arm. They were chatting continuously, trying to catch up. When they reached the parking lot of the church, they realized they were headed to the same place. Pastor Monroe had hooked up Ivy with an interview at the restaurant where Sophia worked as a waitress.

"You will love it there. The owners are good Christian people. They are very, very fair. And they love our pastor. They would do anything for him." Sophia unlocked the doors of her old, rusty Toyota Corolla. "Hop in, girlfriend."

"I hope they'll hire me, because my boyfriend is a little jealous," Ivy explained as she put on her seat belt. "He doesn't like the club I'm working at now, even though that's where he met me. I guess he thinks some other man will come along and steal me from him."

Ivy and Sophia talked nonstop all the way to Salvador's Bistro. They shared tales about life after prison. It hadn't been easy for either of them. Freedom was sweet, but a parolee had to be cautious about everything. One wrong move could send them back to Leesworth in the blink of an eye.

When Sophia killed the engine, Ivy turned to her and asked, "How were King and Dixon doing when you left?"

Sophia gave Ivy a detailed rundown on their friends. As expected, Ivy lost her breath and almost fainted when she learned that Jay had given birth to a child.

"King had a baby? By who?"

"Yes, she had a baby boy, and he is white as snow. I don't know who the baby's father is, though. Jay refused to tell me, and she wouldn't let Shanika say a word. His name is King Jalen, and he is pretty. I'll show you." Sophia searched through her purse and pulled out a picture. "Isn't he a good-looking baby?"

He was good-looking all right, with dark hair and gray eyes just like his father. Sophia was naive and sweet, but Ivy was worldly and had eyes like a hawk. Pastor Gavin Monroe was the father of Jay's son. The baby was the spitting image of the man. The pastor and Jay had fooled her and a bunch of other people at the prison. Not only had they played church at Leesworth, but they'd played house.

Ivy handed the picture back to Sophia. "He is a cutie pie. Is his father caring for him until Jay gets out of prison?"

"I wish. Unfortunately, the baby is in foster care for now, but tomorrow there'll be a custody hearing. I'm praying that Jay's brother, Zachary, will take him."

"Why can't his father get him?" Ivy pushed curiously.

"I think he's some married white man who works at Leesworth, and Jay doesn't want anyone to know who he is. Some people say the man raped her, but I don't think so. The warden knows everything, and he has helped Jay keep it a secret. You won't believe how close she and Callahan are."

"That's some twisted shit, Sophia. I can't believe holier-than-thou Jay had sex with a man. That chick has been a dyke since her early teens. I wonder why she decided to change lanes."

Ivy and Sophia got out of the car and went inside the restaurant. Salvador's Bistro was every bit as classy as Pastor Monroe had described. All the tables were topped with red linen cloth, and easy-listening music filled the relaxed atmosphere. There were expensive paintings hanging on every wall. Ivy had almost another hour before her interview, so she asked to be seated while Sophia went to the back to prepare for her shift. Ivy smiled and looked around, impressed by everything she saw, until her eyes landed on Michael.

He was sitting at a table with a woman and four children. The fine hairs on the back of Ivy's neck bristled. Right away, the identical twins reminded her of miniature, female versions of Michael. Watching the family-sitcom-like scene pinned Ivy in her seat, speechless, as time ticked by. The woman, who had to be Mrs. Stokes, stood up all of a sudden and took the older little girl by the hand. She kissed Michael's lips before she and the child left the table.

Ivy hadn't planned to, but she got up and walked over to the table where Michael sat playing patty-cake with his twin girls. His little boy was coloring on his children's menu activity sheet. As Ivy got closer, she felt dizzy as the air all around her turned warm and heavy. Her palms suddenly became moist.

"Michael," was the only word Ivy could say as tears filled her eyes.

When he looked up and their eyes locked, just as they did every time they made love, time stood completely still. Neither of them spoke. Michael's jaw dropped. The tears in Ivy's eyes fell, causing her mascara to smear down her face.

Michael cleared his throat and swallowed several times. "Can we talk about this later? I'll come by the club tonight and take you home. I promise I can explain all of this."

"Hello." Michael's wife and daughter returned to the table. "I'm Sherry. Who are you?"

As any mistress would, Ivy sized up the model-thin wife, who had obviously had a boob job. She had dark brown curly hair hanging down her back. Ivy had to admit that Sherry was an attractive woman, but apparently, she was lacking something, because her good looks and four children couldn't keep Michael out of Ivy's bed on the weekends.

Michael was about to speak, but Ivy interrupted him. "I'm Ivy. I serve your husband every Friday and most Saturday nights. Drinks and appetizers, that is," she added after a pause.

Sherry's expression softened, and she let out a fake laugh. Her eyes shifted between Michael and Ivy curiously. "Well, it's a pleasure to meet you, Ivy. Maybe one Friday night Michael will let me tag along. Where is it that you work?"

"I'm a singing waitress at a restaurant and lounge in midtown. I'll let y'all get back to your meal."

"I'll see you tonight, Ivy," Michael had the balls to say as she walked away. "Don't sing 'Killing Me Softly' until I get there."

Chapter Forty-seven

"Gavin, have you signed the baptismal certificates yet?"

He stopped and thought about it for a few seconds on his way to the front door. "I did. They're in my study in the center drawer. I'll be back in a couple of hours."

"Where are you going? It's almost time for dinner. I ordered Thai food. It'll be here soon."

"I promised brother Rob that I'd go by the nursing home to visit his mother. Sister Rebecca's uncle is a resident there, too. I'll visit and pray with both of them and anyone else who needs me. I won't be long."

Pastor Monroe left the house, and Holly headed to his study to get the baptismal certificates from his desk drawer. When she picked them up, she saw a picture lying faceup in the bottom of the drawer of a beautiful baby boy. He had the most angelic face she had ever seen. His head full of dark hair was thick and curly. The child was sleeping, so Holly couldn't tell what color his eyes were, but she imagined they were dark, too.

"Whose baby is this?" Holly whispered in awe. She picked up the picture and examined it intensely. Then she laughed. "This picture must be from the stack Family Solutions sent us last year. How on earth did I miss this one?"

She sat down at her husband's desk and picked up his phone to call Trudy. As usual, she answered on the second ring. "I just found a picture of the most adorable baby boy. It was in Gavin's desk drawer in his study. It's one of the babies from Family Solutions. Somehow, I missed him. If I had laid eyes on this angel, I would've pitched a fit until Gavin let me have him. Oh, and he would have eventually, because there's no way I would've given up on this one. I would've pressured him like he tried to do me about that little nappy-headed tar baby he wanted us to adopt from Jayla the convict." Holly threw her head back and laughed at Trudy's response on the other end of the line.

Pastor Monroe froze in midstride. He had doubled back to the house to bring in the Thai food. The deliveryman had pulled up as he was about to get in his car. Pastor Monroe paid for the food, reentered the house, and placed it on the counter in the kitchen. He was coming to give Holly a heads-up when he stumbled upon her conversation with Trudy.

Her words stunned him. He was deeply offended by what he had heard. What kind of Christian woman, a first lady at that, would speak such harsh words about an innocent baby? And it wasn't just any baby. King Jalen was his son. In addition to having a sharp tongue laced with prejudice, Holly was also a liar. She'd told him the only reason she didn't want to adopt Jayla's baby was because she was opposed to an open adoption. In reality, she was opposed to King Jalen's race. Pastor Monroe shook his head and stood in place in the hallway, still listening to the woman he had married but no longer knew.

Holly fingered the baby's face on the picture affectionately. "I want this baby, Trudy, if he's still available. My schedule is so hectic tomorrow. I won't have time to go by the adoption agency to ask about him. Maybe Gavin has some information. This baby obviously had some kind of effect on him, Trudy. Why else would he have held on to his picture out of the dozen others after all this time? I'll ask him when he comes home tonight."

***

Ivy screamed when she walked into her apartment and found Michael sitting in the dark in her living room. "Didn't I tell you I never wanna see you again?" She kicked off her shoes and dropped her purse on the coffee table. "Go home to your wife and kids, Michael. It's over."

"Everything I told you tonight at the club is true. I swear, babe. I'm only there because of my children. Sherry and I were separated when we found out she was pregnant with the twins. She begged me to come back home because she couldn't handle all four of the children by herself." Michael removed his wallet from his back pocket. "Look, I've been shopping for a car for you every day this week. I narrowed it down to these three. Which one do you want? Just say it, and I'll buy it with cash."

"You're married! You lied to me. No man makes a fool of Ivy Maxwell. I have been through enough bullshit because of lying, cheating, punk-ass men like you. All men are dogs. Pastor Monroe ain't no different."

Michael looked at Ivy like he was confused. "I thought you said he was a decent guy, the real deal."

"Well, he ain't nothing but a scandalous dog, just like you and every other creature with a dick and balls." Ivy walked to her front door and opened it wide. "Get the hell outta my house! If you don't leave, I swear I'll call the police. Get out!"

"What the hell is going on up there?" Zach honked his horn like a maniac.

"I think it's a wreck, Zachary. There are at least four police cars ahead. Please stay calm. The weather is terrible."

"Yeah, that's why our flight was delayed. We couldn't leave Jamaica as long as there was a thunderstorm here. This was the wrong damn day for bad weather."

Zach honked his horn again for no other reason than to express his frustration. The traffic was at a standstill, and the heavy rain was steadily pouring. The sky was dreary and black. He checked his watch. "The hearing started twenty-five minutes ago." He honked his horn again.

"Stop it." Jill reached over and swatted his hand. "What good will it do, eh? You must be patient. When the road is clear, you will be able to drive. Until then, please don't beep the horn. It's pointless."

Stubborn, impatient, and impulsive were the three words Uncle Bubba had used to describe Zach over the years. Once, when Zach was a teenager, Uncle Bubba told him flat-out that he was so much like Belva Jane it was scary. Like his mother, Zach would buck against a bull if he had his mind made up about something. And for months he had stood by his word that he wasn't going to take Jay's son, no way and no how. Then he'd had the nerve to take his ass to Jamaica to make sure that he couldn't change his mind even if he'd wanted to. His stubbornness may have cost him more than he could afford to lose.

If he didn't make it to the Fulton County Courthouse in time, King Jalen would be lost to him and the rest of his family forever. How the hell was he going to live with that kind of shit on his conscience for the rest of his life? Jill, Aunt Jackie, and Dex had begged and preached to him about laying his feelings aside for the sake of his nephew. "Fuck Jay!" Dex had slurred in his face one night while they guzzled down a fifth of Remy Martin in his den. He should've listened to his best friend of twenty years, even if he was drunk as hell. Dex, as usual, was dead on point. Regardless of what Jay had done to him and Jill, her son was innocent and deserved to grow up with his family.

The slow-moving traffic prompted Zach's attention back to the road. His foot tapped the gas pedal, and he followed the congested row of cars ahead of him at a snail's pace. The traffic was moving but barely so.

"We're moving again," Jill announced, sounding relieved.

"Yeah, but we ain't moving fast enough."

"Let's pray that we'll get there safely in time and everything will turn out fine."

Chapter Forty-eight

"Your Honor, sir, the adoptive parents have bonded with the child, having cared for him since he was two days old. Any suitable member of his biological family could've taken him into custody in the absence of his parents from day one. None of them wanted the responsibility. Since then, they've all had more than sufficient time to consult with an attorney and make the necessary preparations to gain custody of the baby if they were interested. I see no reason why this hearing should be postponed."

London looked around the courtroom, feeling confident. Mr. Alan Rice was one of the most highly sought-after attorneys in the state of Georgia. He had an impeccable reputation with a near-perfect track record to support it. He'd promised London that King Jalen would become a permanent member of the Price family, and he was making it happen before her very eyes. She was so excited she felt like doing a double cartwheel and finishing it off with a Chinese split, like she used to do as a cheerleader back in the day. Not even the stone-cold faces of some of the people in the courtroom could douse her fire. More than likely, they were relatives of the baby's mother. The records from the child welfare department listed her as a 34-year-old African American woman.

"Is there any member of the family of the baby known as King Jalen M. present today, wishing to be considered as a permanent placement for him at this time?" the judge asked.

"I'm the child's maternal grandfather, Your Honor. My name is Reverend Wallace F. King, sir," he announced, rising to his feet. "My wife, Patricia, and I are willing to take my grandson. We live in Raleigh, North Carolina, and—"

"Your Honor," Attorney Rice interrupted, "unless an interstate compact application has been completed between Georgia and North Carolina, I think it is in the child's best interest for us to proceed with the adoptive parents' request and the recommendation of the Fulton County Department of Family and Children Services today. The longer we allow this matter to linger without resolution, the more stressful it will be on this wonderful family and the child. King Jalen deserves a permanent family, and my clients are willing to provide him with one and so much more. You have the file, sir. As you can see, they're very wealthy and have access to unlimited resources. Their home was rated a ten by the social worker, which is superior. The report from the guardian ad litem will reflect everything I have stated. On behalf of the child, please grant permanent custody of him to my clients, the only parents he knows."

Judge Theodore Robinson looked at Wallace. "Has the State of North Carolina completed the interstate compact, Reverend King?"

"They're in the process, Your Honor. We applied late because I was certain that my son, Zachary, would take the child. Unfortunately, he and his wife are out of the country. If you could delay your judgment for a week or so, I know, beyond a shadow of a doubt, that our family will come up with a solution that's in my grandson's best interest."

"My clients are prepared to take permanent custody today, Judge Robinson."

"And so am I, Your Honor!"

All eyes in the courtroom shifted to the two individuals rushing through the double doors. A buzz of whispers swept across the room. London wiggled in her seat and tugged Attorney Rice's suit jacket. He bent down and motioned for her to keep quiet. Jamal sat next to his wife, stiff and emotionless.

"Thank you, Jesus! Thank you, Lord!" Aunt Jackie's emotions bubbled over.

"Kirk Orowitz, Your Honor," the fashionably dressed attorney announced, strolling coolly down the aisle. "I'm counsel for the biological father, Gavin Kyle Monroe. We apologize to the court for our tardiness. We encountered a three-car pileup en route, due to severe weather." He instructed Gavin to take a seat. "May I approach, Your Honor?"

Judge Robinson pursed his lips, clearly annoyed. He blew out a breath and gave Kirk Orowitz the go-ahead with a slight nod.

Attorney Rice scrambled from his chair and rushed forward. "Your Honor, what is the meaning of this?"

"I have no idea, but I'm sure we're about to find out."

"It's simple," the confident attorney said. "King Jalen Monroe was conceived under very sensitive circumstances. It was a rather sticky situation. Mr. Monroe was present at his birth and signed the birth certificate, which is very much a part of the record. He was under the assumption that Mr. Zachary King, his son's maternal uncle, would take custody of him temporarily until certain pertinent issues had been resolved. Regrettably, that was not the case, but it gives me great pleasure to announce to the court that all is well with Mr. Monroe now. He has legitimated King Jalen, and his personal legal issues no longer exist. I have documentation to share with the court and opposing counsel," Kirk said, searching through his briefcase. He placed a folder on the bench and handed another one to Attorney Rice.

"My client has more than adequate income and resources, suitable housing, and a long list of references
who all say he is the best placement for his son. He has
been certified by Family Solutions Adoption Agency as
an excellent adoptive parent. Certainly, the court can
trust him with his own son."

"But what about Mr. and Mrs. Price, Your Honor? They
have dedicated their lives to this child. Shouldn't their
feelings be taken into consideration?"

Judge Robinson stopped flipping through the file and
frowned at Attorney Rice. "Feelings simply do not count
in my courtroom. I base my decisions on the law. I have
no other legal choice but to grant custody of King Jalen
Monroe to his legal and biological father, Gavin Kyle
Monroe. So ordered." The judge picked up his gavel and
banged it once. "Court is adjourned."

A piercing wail followed by a loud thump caused everyone in the courtroom to gasp and stir. A bailiff and one
of the social workers scurried over to assist Jamal with
London. She had fainted. Her limp body had slumped
backward, causing her chair to topple over.

By the time Zach and Jill reached the courthouse,
Judge Robinson's courtroom was locked. There wasn't
a single soul in sight. The law clerk was unable to give
them much information about the case, but he told them
that the judge had ruled on it, and it was now closed.

Jill followed Zach over to a bench across from the
abandoned courtroom and sat beside him. They were
both drenched from the rain. They'd rushed in and out
of the children's school, with no umbrella, to drop them
off, trying to make it to the custody hearing on time. The
closest parking space they could find once they finally
reached the courthouse was several blocks away. Still

they'd braved the stormy weather, running through the wind and rain all the way.

"I fucked up, didn't I?"

"It took you some time to come around, but you tried, Zachary. Sadly, it was too late."

"I can't face Aunt Jackie. She'll never look at me the same again. I was supposed to be the good guy. Between Jay and me, I was supposed to be the one she could always count on. I let her down, baby. I let the whole damn family down. How the hell am I gonna tell Nahima one day that I'm the reason she'll never know who her little brother is?"

Jill wiped Zach's tears with the back of her hand. "I don't have an answer for that question. All I know is that your heart was in the right place. Your timing was just wrong. Come, let's go home now. There's nothing left here for us to do."

Chapter Forty-nine

"I got your note. Why you wanna see me? You threw me out like swamp trash when you got all holy and sanctified, but you didn't have a problem fucking some cracker around here. I heard you got a little white baby. Where he at?"

"Lock the door," Jay told Private Freeman. "Don't worry about my son or who I've been fucking. Just take your clothes off. I know you miss me."

Freeman smacked her lips and rolled her neck. "Who told you that? I am so over you. You must think I'm stupid. I ain't gonna come running back to you after the way you treated me."

"Then why are you here?" Jay got up from her desk and approached Freeman. "Something made you come. I think you want me," she whispered in her ear and pinned the guard's thick body against the closed door. She licked her face and ran her fingers through her short blond afro.

"Get off me, King." Her words were soft and unconvincing.

"You know you want me."

"Uh-uh, no, I don't," she croaked, falling under Jay's spell.

"Your mouth says you don't, but your body is telling the real story."

Freeman gave up the fight. She allowed Jay to undress her, and together they stretched out on the floor. The heat was on and rising fast. Freeman's moans and grunts were those of an appreciative lover. Jay had game when it came to the honeys, and she knew it. She hadn't lost her touch. Freeman was melting like butter on a hot plate as Jay kissed, licked, and fondled every inch of her bare flesh.

Freeman was a sensitive sista, physically and emotionally so, like most full-figured chicks. It only took one touch to get her juices flowing, and she would explode within seconds, but Freeman loved too damn hard. She fell in deep the first time Jay worked her mojo on her. That was why it was so hard to shake her loose. Jay had grown bored with Freeman a year ago because she was becoming overly possessive and needy. She started weaning her slowly over several months, only spending time with her when she felt like it. When Jay's health began to decline, she cut Freeman off completely. She sought comfort in the Bible and prayer services at the chapel, and eventually she and Pastor Monroe became close.

Now that she had lost her son to the system because of Zach's trifling ass, Jay felt she had nothing else to live for, and she definitely didn't have anything to lose. She was a damn convict, facing at least ten more years in prison. Aunt Jackie was still recuperating, and Jay and her father were once again estranged. She couldn't have Gavin. What kind of relationship could they really have now anyway? Sure, she loved him, and he claimed to love her. But if his love was genuine, why didn't he save their son, the symbol of what they felt for each other?

Jay was partially to blame because she'd wanted to protect Gavin. But where she came from, real men stepped up to the plate, owned their mistakes, and faced the consequences of their actions no matter what. He was supposed to have done the right thing, even though she had begged him not to. Because he was a man of God, Jay had expected Gavin to do the honorable thing for the sake of their child, despite what she had said. Unfortunately, he hadn't, and like every other man in her life, he had disappointed her. He was no better than her father, who had killed her mother, or his best friend, Claudius Henry, who had carried on an affair with her. Zach, the big brother she used to worship as a kid, had chosen Venus and Nahima over her. Then he betrayed Jay in the worst possible way by sleeping with Jill behind her back.

She no longer believed Gavin loved her or their son. He loved the spot between her legs and the rush he got every time they secretly hooked up in his office. Jay had been nothing but his forbidden side piece of ass. She had been such a fool, and that realization sliced through her like a jagged edge. It hurt like hell. Jay wanted to bury all of the painful thoughts about Gavin, Zach, and her baby boy somewhere deep inside so she would never have to deal with them again. She had hoped that being with Freeman would help her do just that, but it was missing the mark.

"I can't do this." Jay lifted her head and sat up on her knees.

"What's wrong?"

"I don't want you, Freeman. I was dead wrong to send for you, but you were stupid to come running like some desperate fool. Don't you think you deserve to be treated better?"

"You said . . . I thought . . ."

Jay shook her head and pointed down at Freeman's sad and confused face. "Don't ever let anybody use you or treat you like shit again, not even me. Love doesn't exist. It's some imaginary, fairy-tale type of bullshit that everyone is searching for in someone else. The whole idea makes you weak and stupid. Just look at your dumb ass. You're lying on the damn floor, buck-naked and spread-eagle, all because you wanna feel loved. You need to learn how to love yourself."

Freeman sat up and crawled around, gathering her clothes. "You're sick, King. I swear I ain't ever met a human being as cold-blooded as you." Tears spilled down her cheeks as she slipped her bra and panties on. "Whoever got your baby needs to keep him far away from you. He needs to be protected from your crazy ass. No baby deserves to have an evil woman like you for his mother."

"Put your damn clothes on and get the fuck outta my office."

Jay went back to her desk and started doing some work. As Freeman finished dressing, she blocked her out like she wasn't even there. When the door slammed shut, Jay looked up and stared into space. The room was symbolic of her life. It was lonely, empty, and cold.

"Jamal, I really love that baby. He's so perfect. It's going to tear my heart to pieces when he leaves in the morning. I wanted him to be ours so bad."

"His father wants him. The judge had no legal reason not to give the man his son, London." He sat down on the edge of the bed where she was resting. "The law was on the father's side."

"Who's on my side? It's not you. That's for sure."

"I went along with the foster parent training, even though my schedule was crazy. I put up with you not being available when I needed you while baby Destiny was here and the entire time we had King Jalen. Who just wrote out a huge check to Attorney Rice, huh? I did! And you have the nerve to lie here, all miserable and disappointed, and say I didn't have your back?" Jamal got up and headed for the door.

"Wait a minute. I'm sorry. You're right. You have been there for me. It's just that you don't seem upset at all that King Jalen is leaving. Didn't you want to keep him?"

Jamal returned to his seat on the bed. "I'm gonna give it to you straight, baby. I'm not too thrilled about becoming a father again. I was only gonna do it to make you happy, because I love you. You knew when we first hooked up that I couldn't make any more babies. I thought you were cool with it."

"I was. My plan was to be this super-cool stepmom to Jamal Jr., Jamilah, and Jamir. I bent over backward to make them love me, but it didn't work. They hate me. Those children treat me like crap, and I've put up with it so there'll be peace in our home. But there's a void in my heart, Jamal. Something is missing. Neither money nor all the expensive things we have can fill it. I want a baby. At first my reason for wanting to become a mother was all wrong. I was jealous of the relationship you have with your kids. I felt left out, but now I just want to share the experience of raising a child with you. And just maybe the children will accept their little brother or sister and me at some point."

Jamal enfolded London in his arms. "If you really want a kid, I think we should go to marriage counseling first to make sure we can handle it. Then we'll do family counseling with my kids. If the counselor gives us the go-ahead, I'll have my vasectomy reversed so we can have our own baby. Now when the social worker comes in the morning for King Jalen, it's okay if you cry. But don't you scream or faint. You got it?"

"Yeah, I got it."

Chapter Fifty

Dex tossed his cell phone on the coffee table and sat down on the sofa to relax. He'd been calling Zach all evening to give him the good news about the outcome of the custody hearing. Aunt Jackie had called him at work, shouting and speaking in tongues, with a detailed report. Charles had followed up later that evening with his version of the courtroom saga. He and Venus had gone to the hearing prepared to ask the judge if they could be considered as a permanent placement for King Jalen in the event that no one else in the Dudley or King families was willing to take him. Charles had made it perfectly clear to Dex that it wasn't about helping Jay. It was all about Nahima. Once again, she was a helpless and innocent victim caught up in Jay's mess. King Jalen was her little brother, and she had every right to be a part of his life. If that meant Venus and Charles would've had to take custody of him, they'd been prepared to do just that.

Pastor Gavin Monroe ended up being the hero of the day. He came in and took responsibility for his son, like any real father should have. Dex chuckled at the thought. He wished he could've been there to witness the pastor's dramatic courtroom entrance with cool-ass Kirk Orowitz, the hotshot Jewish attorney, by his side. Both Charles and Aunt Jackie had described it like a scene straight out of *Law & Order* or *The Practice*. No one had expected the father of Jay's son to show up and demand custody, especially not Zach. As far as he was concerned, the man was a pimp and a player who had violated ethics codes from the pulpit to the state board of licensure.

Dex wanted to be the one to tell his buddy that he'd not only been wrong for refusing to take custody of his nephew, but he'd painted an inaccurate picture of Gavin Monroe. Aunt Jackie said the man truly loved Jay, and he had apologized for getting involved with her when he was supposed to have been counseling her at Leesworth. He then promised to allow King Jalen to have a relationship with his great-aunt and any other members of his family who wanted to be a part of his life, including Zach. In Dex's eyes, the preacher didn't look so corrupt after all. He picked up the phone and dialed Zach's cell phone number again. This time he left a message.

"Hey, man. I know you, Jill, and the kids are over there having a ball on the island. But you need to holla at your boy ASAP. I've got some news that I know you'll wanna hear. Call me, Zach. I'm out."

"Who was that, Jill?" Zach yelled from the bathroom. He'd heard his cell phone ringing while he was taking a shower.

"It was Dex again. I think he left a message this time. Maybe you should check it. He and Aunt Jackie have been calling since early this afternoon. It's after nine o'clock."

"I don't wanna talk to either one of them right now." Zach emerged from the master bathroom, naked, and got in the bed with Jill. "I can wait to hear the bad news. I don't feel like hearing Dex's guilt lecture. And Aunt Jackie's probably upset, crying, and singing hymns. I can't handle that right now. Let me enjoy tonight with you before I return to the real world tomorrow."

***

"There you are." Holly kissed her husband on the cheek before she went to the counter to pour herself a cup of coffee. "I didn't hear you come in last night. I had a long, hectic day. I was pooped."

Pastor Monroe took a few sips from his coffee mug and continued skimming the newspaper. "I didn't want to wake you. I crashed on the sofa in the den. Come and sit down, Holly. We need to talk."

"Oh, Gavin, I was thinking the same thing!" She joined him at the table with a mug of hot coffee in one hand and the picture of the baby she had found in his desk drawer in the other.

Pastor Monroe folded the newspaper and placed it to the side. Holly then laid the picture of the baby on his place mat, right next to his cup of coffee, in plain view. He stared at the face of his son when he was only 2 days old. He was so tiny and beautiful. He wondered what the child looked like now. Had he grown much? Was the color of his eyes still the same as his, or had they darkened to look more like his mother's? Pastor Monroe's pulse quickened, knowing he would find out soon enough. He kept his eyes on the picture without saying a word. He was gathering his thoughts before he began the conversation that would change his entire life.

Apparently, Holly had grown impatient waiting for her husband to respond to the picture. Her excitement took over. "I found that in your desk drawer when I was looking for the baptismal certificates. I want this baby. I think you do too." She smiled.

His eyes shifted from the picture to his wife's face. "You want this baby?" he asked, pointing to the picture of his son.

"Yes, honey. He's the most precious baby boy I've ever laid eyes on. I understand why you held on to the picture.

You thought he was adorable too. Oh, Gavin, what do you remember about him from the adoption agency? Do you know if he's still available?"

"I know he's—"

The doorbell chimed, interrupting the conversation. Pastor Monroe gave the picture a final glance and stood up from his chair. He noticed a frown on Holly's face. She was obviously eager to discuss the picture.

"Are you expecting someone this time of morning? It's barely nine o'clock."

"Wait here. I'll be right back," he told her, walking through the kitchen door on his way to the living room. He unlocked the front door and opened it. "Good morning."

"Good morning, Mr. Monroe. I'm Kadijah Rashad, the social worker from Fulton County Department of Family and Children Services. My coworker Samantha Willard should be here shortly. I just need you to sign a few papers before she arrives, and then I'll get out of your hair. I'm sure you have a thousand things to do."

The pastor offered the woman a seat. He admired her colorful ethnic attire. Her dreadlocks were bundled in a bright orange elastic band at the crown of her head.

"Please sign here and here, sir," she said, pointing with the tip of her pen. "Initial here and sign one more time there. Give this document to Mrs. Willard and show her your driver's license. Then you'll be all set."

Pastor Monroe took the document and folded it before he placed it on the coffee table. He saw movement to his right with his peripheral vision. Holly was peeping through the kitchen door. When he turned to stare at her, she disappeared behind it, but she entered the living room when Ms. Rashad left. She confronted him as soon as he sat on the sofa.

"What's going on?"

Chapter Fifty-one

"I need you to sit down." Pastor Monroe patted the empty cushion next to him.

Holly's eyes narrowed at him as if she sensed something far beyond what she could imagine was about to take place. She took her time walking over to the couch to take a seat.

"Holly, if you really wanted a child, why couldn't we adopt Jayla's baby?"

She laughed nervously. "I told you why. I wanted the child to be completely ours. That would not have been the case in an open adoption. Can you imagine how complicated our lives would've become the moment Jayla was released from prison? The poor little boy would've been a candidate for intense therapy."

"That's not why you didn't want the baby. Tell me the truth."

"I've told you the truth! What difference does it make now anyway? And why do you care so much about some convicted lesbian's child?"

"I care because he's my son! The 'little nappy-headed tar baby' you didn't want is my son. And you rejected him because of the color of his skin."

"Oh, my God." Holly covered her mouth with both hands. "You actually had sex with some crazy black inmate? That woman is insane. She hired someone to murder her own brother. I can't believe you touched her. How could you do something so despicable to me? I have loved you and stood by your side through the good, the bad, and the ugly, like a good wife should. And you repay me by screwing one of your damn convicts? You could've caught some nasty disease and given it to me, you sick bastard! I hate you! I don't want you anymore. Get the hell out!" Holly jumped up from the sofa and slapped her husband across his face. She stood above him, crying and trembling, filled with emotions.

Pastor Monroe nodded. "I deserved that. I'm an adulterer. What I did was wrong. There is no excuse for betraying you and dishonoring our wedding vows. I'm sorry, Holly."

"You're not sorry yet, but you will be. I'll make sure of it. Forget about this house, the cars, and both investment accounts. The beach house in Florida and the cabin in Tennessee will be mine when I get finished with you. And do you really think the church members, deacons, and the trustee board will let you remain pastor?" Holly laughed with a maniacal look in her eyes. "If you do, you're an even bigger fool than I thought. You're going to lose everything."

"That's fine. I won't fight you. You can have it all. Take it. None of it matters to me as long as I have my son. He'll be here any minute. I'd like you to meet him before we leave."

The social worker's timing couldn't have been better. Pastor Monroe hurried to the door as soon as the bell chimed. Holly flopped down on the sofa, rubbing her hands up and down her folded arms as if she were freezing. Her eyes were glued to her husband's back.

"Good morning," he said. Then his breath got trapped in his throat when he saw his son in the social worker's arms. Whatever Mrs. Willard was saying to Pastor Monroe was lost. All five of his senses were held captive by King Jalen. He reached out and removed the child from the social worker's protective hold. "My goodness, you have grown." He shook his head. "I'm sorry. Please come in, Mrs. Willard. I forgot my manners. And if you could take him for a second, I'll show you my ID and get the document Ms. Rashad instructed me to give you."

Mrs. Willard followed him into the living room with a sleeping King Jalen in tow. "Good morning." She smiled at Holly but frowned when she didn't get a response.

"Here is the document and my driver's license." Pastor Monroe exchanged the items for his son. He rocked the baby in his arms with care.

"We're all done here. I'll get the baby's things from my car. His foster parents sent everything he owns. Here's your ID, Mr. Monroe," she said, placing it in his shirt pocket. "I'll be right back."

When Mrs. Willard went outside, Holly glared at the man she had married. He turned his head, refusing to engage in a childish staring game. He lowered the baby from his shoulder and cradled him in the crook of his arm to get a better look at him. He was wearing a cute little Atlanta Falcons hat. His entire outfit was red and black, including the blanket. Pastor Monroe stared at the face that looked so much like his, in awe for several moments. It felt good holding his son after being separated from him for what seemed like an eternity.

"This is everything except for the stroller. It couldn't fit into my car, so I had to leave it with the foster parents," Mrs. Willard announced as she made her way back into the house.

She was out of breath and lugging two suitcases. An overnight bag was hanging from her shoulder. There were two cardboard boxes and a fancy car seat sitting on the stoop behind her. Apparently, she had dragged all of the baby's belongings to the doorway in a few trips. Pastor Monroe wanted to help the woman, but his arms were full.

"Just leave them right there, Mrs. Willard. You've been kind enough. I'll take care of them."

"Are you sure, sir?"

"Yes, they'll be fine."

Mrs. Willard placed the luggage on the floor. "Okay then, I guess I'll be leaving now. Best wishes to you and your son, Mr. Monroe." She looked at Holly and wrinkled her nose. Then she turned and left.

Pastor Monroe looked at the suitcases and tote bag sitting in front of the open door. The boxes on the stoop were bulging. King Jalen had accumulated a lot of stuff in thirty days. His foster parents had been most generous indeed.

"I'll hold the baby, if you don't mind, so you can carry his things to your car," Holly said calmly. When he didn't respond immediately, she rolled her eyes. "I'm not going to hurt him if that's what you're worried about."

Pastor Monroe hesitated a moment or two before he walked over to the sofa and placed his son in Holly's arms. "Thank you. It'll only take me a minute. I promise." He hurried to the door and grabbed the luggage. He paused and turned around to look at Holly and the baby. She was rocking King Jalen, staring at Pastor Monroe with tears streaming down her face. "Thank you," he said again and carried the luggage outside.

Holly looked down at the baby. She recognized his face from the picture she'd found in her husband's desk drawer. She began to weep harder as she continued to rock him gently in her arms.

Zach and Jill decided to surprise Aunt Jackie with a visit. She wasn't expecting them to return home until the day after tomorrow, but since she had called several times—obviously wanting to tell him about the custody hearing—Zach thought it was a good idea to have the conversation in person. He unlocked the door with his key. Zachary Jr. and Zion burst into the house as soon as the door swung open, calling for their nana.

Aunt Jackie met them in the hallway. "What in the world are y'all doing here?" She bent down and scooped Zion up into her arms and kissed her pretty face. Then she set her back on her feet. Zachary Jr. hugged her around her ample thighs.

"We decided to come home early. I just don't think it was early enough."

"Hello, Aunt Jackie," Jill greeted her. "How are you?"

She rolled her eyes at Zach, dismissing him, but smiled at Jill. "I'm fine, darling. I missed you and the kids. Let's go in the den so we can catch up."

Jill turned around and looked at her husband before she followed Aunt Jackie and the children into the den. Zach just stood in the hallway, feeling like shit. He knew he was probably going to feel that way for the rest of his life. Every single day he would wake up wondering where King Jalen was. Who was he with? Were they treating him well? Was he being loved and properly cared for? He would never know his nephew. Nahima would forever be denied the pleasure of playing with her baby brother, protecting him, or bossing him around. An innocent little boy would grow up without knowing his true identity or biological family because of his uncle's stubbornness and stupidity.

Zach couldn't handle the mess he had made. He needed a stiff drink or two to help him shake off some of the guilt and sorrow for a few hours, but it was barely ten o'clock in the morning, and Floyd's spot didn't open up until noon. Plus, only alcoholics drank alone. He, Dex, and Charles considered themselves social or mood drinkers. They only tossed a few back when they were in a social setting or when one of them was in a foul mood. Both of Zach's buddies were at work, so he decided to go home and sleep through his funk. He would come back for Jill and the kids later.

Zach opened Aunt Jackie's door and was surprised to find someone standing on the other side.

Chapter Fifty-two

"May I help you?" Zach eyed the stranger.

"Um, I must have the wrong address." the man answered, looking completely flustered and confused. He moved his arm back and forth, swinging a baby carrier slowly. "I'm trying to find the Brown residence. Do you know which house belongs to Ms. Jackie Brown?"

Zach blinked a few times. "Who are you, and why do you wanna see my aunt?"

"Oh, please forgive me. I'm Gavin Monroe." He extended his free hand. "This is my son, King Jalen. Did you say you were Ms. Brown's nephew?"

Zach left the man's arm hanging and knelt down to get a look at the baby sleeping in the carrier. He touched one of his tiny, mitten-covered hands. Tears swelled in his eyes, but he willed them not to fall. Zach's emotions were all over the place. There were millions of questions crammed inside his head, but he only needed the answer to one at the moment. He stood to his full stature and looked Pastor Monroe square in the face.

"So, you did the right thing, huh?"

"Yeah, I did. I manned up, I guess you could say. It was the most important thing I've ever done in my life."

"And how does your wife feel about what you did?"

"I'll be raising my son alone until Jayla is released from prison. We'll do it together from that point on. Of course, your aunt has offered to help me in the meantime." He stared down at the baby's face. He was still sleeping peacefully, without a care in the world. "I was hoping that you and your wife would want to be a part of his life as well. I know that you and Jayla aren't close anymore, but your nephew doesn't know that. I'd like you and him to get to know one another if that's okay with you."

Zach reached out and removed the baby carrier from Pastor Monroe's grip. "We're gonna be best buddies. Come on in, man. Aunt Jackie will be glad to see y'all."

Warden Callahan gave Jay permission to return to her cell after her appointment with Dr. Yusuf. She deserved a break after landing the Kemp contract for him, and she wasn't feeling well. Jay had been complaining about back pain and swelling in her hands and feet for a few days. Shanika convinced her to go to the clinic. After some blood work and a few tests, Dr. Yusuf broke the bad news to her. Jay's kidneys were barely functioning.

He made a referral for her to travel off-site to see a nephrologist by the name of Dr. Yeman Samba. Jay had met him once before when she was hospitalized during her early days at Leesworth. Dr. Samba told her then that the next time she visited him, he would order her to begin dialysis treatment, because he didn't think her kidneys would ever improve. The time was drawing nigh, and there wasn't a damn thing Jay could do about it. The birth of her son, the most important event in her life, had been successful. Nothing else mattered now. Jay didn't care about anyone or anything. She wasn't fit to live, but she was scared as hell to die. All she could do was hope for a better tomorrow until she took her last breath.

"Close the door, Michael, and have a seat." Connor waited for his once trusted and efficient investigator to sit down in one of the chairs facing his desk.

"What's up, boss? Do you have a new case for me?"

"I'm afraid not. You see, I just got off the phone with a very disgruntled client. Holly Blake Monroe is demanding a total freaking refund because she says you failed to do your damn job! It seems while you were out sniffing chocolate panties, you snoozed on your assignment."

"Wait a minute. I'll admit I got tangled up with an informant. I told you that, but I conducted a thorough investigation. Sleeping with Ivy didn't keep me from doing my job. I stayed on top of things."

Connor smirked and then slammed his fist on his desk. "You stayed on top of Ms. Maxwell, obviously, but I think she took you for a ride. Yes, she's an extremely sexy woman, intriguing even. I can understand why she made you weak, but you lost focus between the sheets, Mike."

"Ivy was the closest connection I had to Monroe and his dealings with the inmates at Leesworth. She told me everything she knew. The man is a saint."

"She told you everything, huh?" Connor leaned back in his chair.

"Everything she knows. I'm pretty sure of that."

"Well, she must've forgotten to mention how the good pastor was boning one of the inmates. Evidently, like you, Monroe has a weakness for black women. He knocked up an inmate named Jayla King. They have a newborn son together. It appears that Monroe has custody of the kid. He chose his son over his wife of nearly twenty years. Poor Holly never saw it coming. The woman paid this firm seven thousand dollars to find out why her husband was spending long hours at Leesworth prison, and you dropped the ball! How the hell did you miss it, Mike?"

Michael had never seen his boss as pissed off as he was at the moment. He had screwed up royally. Either Ivy was truly oblivious to Gavin Monroe's sinful side, or she had made a complete fool of him. Michael had no idea what the actual truth was. His investigative nature made his curiosity spike, but Michael Stokes, the man, realized that Ivy didn't owe him an explanation. She didn't owe him a damn thing. He had initially used her for information on a case and later for his physical pleasure.

As their affair continued, Michael became emotionally attached to Ivy. The chemistry and passion they shared had unexpectedly turned into something more serious and meaningful. Michael fell for Ivy, and he fell hard. His affection for her was genuine. She'd sparked a fire inside of him that he never wanted to burn out. Regretfully, he'd hurt her in the end, but he didn't do it on purpose. All of his lies and excuses to cover up his miserable marriage finally caught up with him. If Ivy had played Michael by withholding information about Gavin Monroe and his prison mistress, he couldn't blame her at all.

"I'm sorry, boss. I screwed up. If you decide to give Mrs. Monroe a refund, have the payroll department deduct money from my salary every two weeks until it's paid off. I want to take responsibility for my mistake. I compromised the reputation of this firm. I have to make it right."

"Zach, put that boy down now. You're gonna spoil him. His daddy is gonna have a hard-enough time tonight getting up with him every three to four hours. That poor man ain't got a clue what he signed on for. Raising a baby ain't easy, especially if you don't know what you're doing."

Zach rocked his nephew and looked down at his tiny face. His gray eyes were wide open, staring right back at him. "He told me he's been reading books and researching on the internet. The foster mother wrote him all kinds of notes, giving him some helpful hints about the baby's routine. That was cool of her to do that for him. It should help the pastor out a little bit."

"It's not going to be easy for him," Jill said. "But I think he will manage somehow. We can check on him regularly and give him a break from time to time."

"I'm glad I'm strong enough to take care of him during the daytime. Hattie Jean said she'll come over and help whenever I need her to. I'm just worried about how Gavin's gonna handle the remainder of his day, especially at night."

"Y'all heard me offer him a guest room at my house for as long as he needed. That way Jill and I would be there to help him. He declined. The preacher wants to do it himself. He's gonna stay at the Seven Seas for two weeks until the landlord finishes getting the house he'll be renting in order. I'll make the offer again when he comes back from the prison. He went to clean out his office. In order to avoid criminal charges and hold on to his professional license, he was forced to resign from Leesworth. Having a sexual relationship with an inmate at a federal correctional facility is a serious offense. Dude risked a lot for Jay and this baby. The baby will grow up and thank him. I hope Jay is grateful. That man really loves her. I pray to God she's serious about him."

Ivy walked into her apartment carrying two grocery bags and her purse. A stack of mail was tucked under her arm. She was mad as hell because she had missed her regular bus and had to wait twenty minutes for the next one. Then it was smelly and overflowing with hood rats. It stopped every five minutes to let a few riders off, only to pick up more people. All of that madness had cut into Ivy's afternoon nap time. She needed to rest in order to be fresh for her evening shift at Salvador's. Thank God Sophia had offered to pick her up so she wouldn't have to catch the bus.

The highlight of Ivy's day had been her session in the recording studio at her other part-time job. She had absolutely nailed it! She smiled as she put her groceries away and thought about the praise she'd received from the producer on the project and the rapper. Ivy had laid down a perfect track, singing the hook for a rapper on the rise named Triple 6's. His hit single "Ballers, Beats, & Bitches" was number seven on Billboard's Hip-Hop chart and number one or two on all urban music charts. Ivy had sung the hook on the lead single on his CD *No Rules*. Her smooth alto voice had covered the lyrics flawlessly. Triple 6's had offered her more work and dropped a hint about her starring in the video and singing on other tracks. He told her if things worked out, he wanted her to go on tour with him. An opportunity like that sure would help out with the bills.

Michael was supposed to be her financial support. He had also promised to buy her a car so she could get back and forth from both jobs. That wasn't going to happen now that they'd broken up. Ivy was on her own now. She alone was responsible for her rent, bills, food, and transportation. It would be a challenge, but she was determined to make it at any cost.

She picked up the stack of mail and relaxed on her comfortable couch. Michael had bought it. It was black leather with a matching love seat and a recliner. It was time to add up her bills and make a budget. It was something Michael had promised he would assist her with, but a married man couldn't hold down two households.

An icy chill ran up Ivy's back when she found a letter from Michael behind the water bill. He wanted to see her to clear the air. The memories of all the time they'd spent together were constantly on his mind, or so he claimed. Michael said he missed Ivy, and he had a surprise for her. He planned to swing by Salvador's one night soon.

Chapter Fifty-three

A few taps on Jay's office door broke her concentration and pissed her off. Everyone knew she was busy and stressed out. She was working through lunch in order to finalize the tax information needed to complete the new payroll account for the Kemp Corporation contract. The warden was anxious to have it on his desk by the end of the day.

"Come in," Jay called out, massaging her temples.

Pastor Monroe walked in. "Jayla, I have missed you." He hurried to her side and pulled her from her chair. He wrapped his arms around her. "How are you?"

"How the hell do you think I am?" Jay freed herself from his embrace and stepped back. "Our baby is gone! We'll never see him again. I wish—"

"Ssshhh, it's going to be all right." He reached out and wiped her tears with the pad of his thumb. "Everything is going to be all right."

"No, it won't!"

"Yes, it will, sweetheart, because I have our son."

Jay froze and stared at Pastor Monroe, confused. "You do? How? I mean . . . what did you do, Gavin?"

"I went to court yesterday with an attorney your sister-in-law had recommended. We asked the judge for custody of King Jalen, and he granted our request." He took Jay in his arms when she began to sob and tremble. "Our son is with your aunt, your brother, his wife, and their children right now. He's surrounded by your family. It's a blessing, isn't it?"

"Yeah, it is. I'm glad you saved our son. My heart was broken into a thousand pieces because I thought he was gone forever. You're a good man, Gavin. I'm happy you stepped up to the plate, but you're gonna lose everything." Jay backed away from him and rubbed her hands together nervously. "That's why Zach should've taken the baby, the same way Aunt Jackie took him and me when we were orphans. He's so damn selfish. I don't want him around King Jalen after today. If Zach didn't care enough to save him from being adopted by strangers, he doesn't deserve to be in his life now that you have him."

"Wait a minute. Zach left Jamaica earlier than planned, trying to get back to Atlanta in time for the custody hearing. Bad weather detained him and Jill. Your brother has set his ill feelings for me aside for the sake of our son. He and his wife are committed to playing supportive roles in King Jalen's life. Isn't that what you wanted?"

"No! I wanted them to take my baby from day one. Our son should never have spent a single night in foster care when he has an able-bodied, financially stable uncle living in a fat crib. This time Zach took his beef too far. I don't want him anywhere near my son. Don't cross me on this, Gavin. I mean it. King Jalen Monroe is off-limits to Zach and his family."

Pastor Monroe stuffed his hands inside his pants pockets and stared at the floor. "I can't cut your brother off from our son. He has already bonded with the little fellow. You should have seen them together. They click. And besides that, I need Zach. I know absolutely nothing about babies. Your brother knows everything. He takes care of babies for a living. Fatherhood is foreign to me. Zach and Jill have volunteered to help me whenever I need them, and I've already accepted their offer."

"You're gonna take my brother's side over mine?" Jay lifted her chin in a bold challenge. "That evil bastard turned his back on our son when he needed him the most. And now that you have him, he wants to be the devoted Uncle Zach, huh? I ain't down with that! Uh-uh, you better not take my baby anywhere near my brother or your wife."

"I don't have a wife anymore. I chose our son over my marriage, my church, and my freedom. King Jalen means more to me than anything else. I risked it all for him, for us."

"Holly left you when you told her about the baby?"

"No. She asked me to leave, and I did without a fight. The board of corrections forced me to resign from Leesworth because of my actions, but I retained my counseling license. I can visit you and bring the baby along. Warden Callahan allowed me to come here today to give you the good news and clear out my office."

"What did your church members have to say?"

"I have a meeting with the governing board this evening. I'm sure they'll vote me out. The majority of the congregation will more than likely agree with the board's decision. Then the bishop will sign off on my termination. I'll get another job, though. That shouldn't be a problem. However, my life as a minister is over. But that's to be expected. I fell far from grace. God has forgiven me, and in time I'll be fully restored. But man will never forgive me or forget what I've done."

Jay nodded, acknowledging the accurate assessment of his future. It was sad, but there would be challenges ahead of him because of the choice he'd made. Pastor Monroe was a good man as far as Jay was concerned. Before their affair, he was as close to perfect as any man could be. He didn't deserve to lose all he had worked to accomplish and sacrificed for. Yet he had gambled for the sake of their son. Now he was standing on the brink of financial and professional ruins, all because Zach had once again been selfish and cold-blooded toward her. He only cared about himself. The rage slicing through Jay's body like the sharp edge of a sword made her dizzy and nauseated. Her knees buckled and she stumbled forward.

Pastor Monroe caught her and helped her regain her footing. "Are you okay, Jayla? You're warm. Do you have a fever?"

"I'm weak, but don't worry. I've been so busy that I worked through lunch. I'm fine." She stood up straight but collapsed again in Gavin's arms. "The room is spinning. Something is wrong. Please help me, Gavin. Don't let me die."

The ten-member governing board at Marvelous Light Pentecostal Church was already seated around the conference table when Pastor Monroe rushed into the room. All eyes followed him to the head of the table, where he took his designated seat. His genuine smile was met by accusatory stares from the men and women when he greeted them individually.

Holly rolled her eyes and remained silent when he acknowledged her. He was actually surprised to see her. It had been more than three years since she had attended a board meeting. The doors of the conference room were always open to the first lady, welcoming her to be an active part of the governing body of the church. Holly had not shown much interest in the past, her excuse being that she despised politics at all levels. It was obvious why she felt the need to attend the emergency meeting this evening. She would be one of eleven people deciding his fate as opposed to the usual ten.

"Forgive me for my tardiness. Something came up unexpectedly, and it required my immediate attention."

Holly snorted sarcastically and shifted in her chair. When the other board members at the table turned and looked at her, she gave them all a wicked smile. It chilled Pastor Monroe to the bone. He was in deep trouble. Holly had come to make sure that every detail of his transgression was exposed and that he was stripped of all of his authority. Why else would she have come to the meeting?

The chairman of the board, Dr. Wendell Napier, a portly gentleman, cleared his throat. "Now that Pastor Monroe is here, I will call the meeting to order. As all of you are aware, this is an emergency assemblage. Our pastor called sister Eunice McBride, our vice chairperson, and me to inform us of the very pressing issue at hand. She and I agreed that the matter should be brought before the body expeditiously. That is why we are here. Everyone received a copy of Pastor Monroe's signed confession. The first lady has offered additional details. At this time, I will open the floor for discussion."

"Everything is in my confession, Dr. Napier," Pastor Monroe said, standing from his chair. "I want to spare the members of this very dedicated and efficient body from the unpleasant details of what I've done. There's no need for a debate or discussion. It's quite simple. I had an affair that resulted in the birth of my son. All I care to say at this time is that I am very sorry for failing this board and the congregation as its shepherd. I seek your forgiveness and solicit your prayers. I move that the matter be resolved in a vote to determine whether I should remain pastor of Marvelous Light Pentecostal Church or be relieved of my duties. Thank you very much."

"Very well, sir, I move—"

"Are you serious? You owe these people more than just an apology. They have served you faithfully for thirteen years. I think they deserve an explanation. You owe them answers, Gavin."

Dr. Napier regained control of the meeting and restored order with his gavel after Holly's dramatic outburst. It had caused whispers and some stiff body language among the board members. Pastor Monroe took his seat and studied his estranged wife's countenance. She was hurt, and for that he would carry eternal guilt. But he had made peace with God and was prepared to move forward, leaving the sins of his past behind him. His son needed him to be emotionally stable. As a new father, he couldn't afford to allow Holly's mission of revenge to shake him and cause him to lose focus, but that was her goal. There was determination in her eyes. Holly wanted to pluck every morsel of meat from his bones and feed them to the vultures.

Chapter Fifty-four

"Does anyone wish to address Pastor Monroe at this time?" Dr. Napier asked, wiping his brow with a handkerchief.

His question was answered with deafening silence. He looked at each man and woman around the conference table, giving them an opportunity to respond. No one spoke as seconds passed. Finally, Holly stabbed her husband with her eyes. They were filled with tears behind her glasses. The sight of it broke his heart. He was sincerely sorry for being an unfaithful husband and hurting her.

"Why don't you make this easy for everyone? You should resign and spare the congregation the financial burden of giving you a severance package. We deserve that much consideration at the very least. If we fire you, we'll have to compensate you, and you're not worthy of that luxury. Resign, Gavin!"

Pastor Monroe opened his mouth to address Holly but was interrupted by the chief operating officer of the church, brother Oscar Pointer. "According to the bylaws, he has the right to fight for his job. I, personally, want Pastor Monroe to stay. He has been an exceptional shepherd of this flock and has done great things here at Marvelous Light. He is human and has expressed remorse for his shortcomings. I will not vote to accept a forced resignation. I move that we vote to terminate or retain him."

"I second the motion," a female member of the board chimed in.

"Will there be another motion on the floor?" Dr. Napier asked. "If not, I move that we vote to either allow Pastor Monroe to remain in the pulpit as our leader or relieve him of all his duties with a severance package as specified in the bylaws."

"Have you people lost your minds?" Holly slapped her hand on the conference table and shouted. "He has yet to say that he wishes to continue pastoring this church. It's understandable, though. God knows he's no longer capable of leading us. If Pastor Monroe wants to maintain his position here, he should be required to express his desire for the record."

"According to the bylaws, that isn't necessary. It doesn't matter if the pastor expresses his wishes one way or the other. We have the final say if he will be allowed to stay. We're all aware of his confession. It's time to vote to determine if what he has done is reason enough for us to dismiss him from the pulpit." Dr. Napier looked at his fellow board members one by one before he spoke again. "Madam Secretary, are you ready to record the vote?"

"I am, sir," Trudy replied.

It was an open vote, with each member voicing their decision for everyone to hear. Pastor Monroe watched Trudy as she recorded each statement. Holly boldly cast a resounding vote to terminate her husband as pastor of the church he had labored over with his blood, sweat, and tears. But she wasn't alone. Three men and one other woman did the same. The vote was tied five to five. Under normal circumstances, the pastor would be the deciding vote whenever the ten members were deadlocked on a matter. Naturally, he could not vote on his own fate. Holly's presence increased the attendance from the usual ten members to eleven.

Everyone who would be allowed to vote had done so with the exception of Trudy. She looked up from her notepad, where she was scribbling the tally and minutes from the emergency meeting. The entire board's attention was focused on her sitting at the end of the table. Holly smiled at her best friend of over a decade.

"Sister Trudy," Dr. Napier said softly, "it's up to you, dear. The vote is tied. Five board members wish to dismiss Pastor Monroe from his position, while the other five, including myself, want him to stay here. Have you made up your mind?"

"Yes, sir, I have." Trudy kept her eyes on her notebook. She tapped her pen a few times on top of it as she chewed her bottom lip.

"Well? We're waiting." The chairman's voice had a hint of agitation in it.

Pastor Monroe clasped his hands together on the tabletop and leaned forward. Out of the corner of his eye he saw Holly shift in her seat. She and Trudy had been allies and confidants for many years. They told each other everything. He turned boldly and looked directly at Holly. There was a smile on her face as she stared at Trudy. Her fingers were drumming on the table impatiently, counting down the seconds until her best friend booted her unfaithful husband from the pulpit.

"Trudy, we need your vote now," Dr. Napier snapped in an impatient tone of voice.

"Well, I've prayed about it," she mumbled, running her fingers timidly through her strawberry blond curls. "All of us have sinned and fallen short of God's glory. None of us are holy enough to cast stones. I vote to keep Pastor Monroe as our spiritual leader." Trudy continued to avoid eye contact with the other board members, especially Holly.

"You people are stupid!" Holly sprung from her chair with both her arms flailing in the air. "I can't believe you! This man has cheated on me and this church, but you want him to continue to pastor us like he's some kind of saint?"

"Calm down, sister Holly," Dr. Napier said calmly.

"I will do no such thing, you idiotic, pompous kiss ass! The congregation will never go along with this foolishness. I'll make sure that the decision made by you incompetent morons will be overturned in the general vote." With tears spilling down her beet red face, Holly pointed a shaky finger at Trudy. "Do not ever let my name appear in your thoughts. Do you understand me? We are no longer friends." She turned and eyed her husband. "This is not over! You better prepare for the fight of your life."

"That's enough, First Lady! I will have order in this meeting. There are other issues that we must address."

"Go to hell! You and everyone in this damn room can go straight to hell and take your whore-mongering pastor and his little nigger bastard with you."

Zach had returned to Aunt Jackie's house after taking Jill and the children home for the evening. He wanted to feed King Jalen and give him a warm bath before his father arrived. Zach figured the former pastor would be physically and emotionally drained after squaring off with the officials at his church. Memories of his father returning home frustrated after church business meetings were still fresh after more than thirty years. More than likely, those heated conflicts had been all about money. Pastor Monroe's problem was much bigger and more complicated than balancing a church budget. He was in the ultimate struggle for his survival. The least Zach could do to help him was to make sure King Jalen was settled for the night.

The little guy was full as a tick, smelling sweet, and resting peacefully on his uncle's chest. Zach was lying comfortably on his back on Aunt Jackie's sofa in her den. He'd left the front porch light on for Pastor Monroe. Zach's eyelids were drooping from exhaustion when the doorbell rang.

Zach sat up carefully and cradled King Jalen in the crook of his left arm. The baby sighed and wiggled but didn't wake up. Zach padded down the dark hallway toward the door. When he opened it and saw Pastor Monroe standing on the other side, he tried to read his expression. It was flat until he looked down at his son's chubby, angelic face. Zach smiled. The pastor was in love with his son. The change in his expression was a certain confirmation.

"Come on in. This little dude tried to wait up for you, but he couldn't hang. Four ounces of warm formula and a bath knocked him out." Zach stepped aside and allowed Pastor Monroe to pass over the threshold.

They went to the den and sat on the sofa. The television was on BET. An old John Singleton movie was playing. Zach handed his nephew over to his father and watched them. King Jalen was the spitting image of Pastor Monroe, with the exception of the full lips he'd inherited from Jay.

"How did it go? Did they burn all your stuff on the front lawn of the church?"

He shook his head. "They actually forgave me and voted to allow me to keep my position as pastor."

"Shut the f . . . I mean, shut the heck up!"

"They sure did." Pastor Monroe chuckled weakly and rocked his sleeping son in his arms. "But I resigned. I love that church and its members, Zach. I didn't want to divide the congregation. If I had taken the board up on their offer to stay put, that's exactly what would've happened. I didn't want to be at the root of a war between my supporters and those who wanted me gone. My conscience wouldn't let me. It was best that I step down with my dignity intact. I'll live off of my savings and an investment account I've had for many years. I'll look for a new job eventually, but for now I want to get to know my son. He's all I've got until Jayla is released from prison. I owe him all of my time and attention until then."

"I bet Jay went crazy when you told her you had custody of the baby."

"She's very happy." He paused as if gathering his thoughts. "Jayla isn't well, Zach. Her kidneys are barely functioning. She's weak. This afternoon she had to be rushed to the emergency room. The doctor can't delay dialysis any longer. Jayla will begin treatment Monday. She'll be dialyzed three times a week for the rest of her life."

Chapter Fifty-five

Zach and Pastor Monroe continued their conversation for a couple of hours, covering many different topics. Aunt Jackie came into the living room and offered them a cup of coffee and a slice of sweet potato pie. Zach didn't want anything, but Pastor Monroe was starving. He devoured three slices of pie and nearly a gallon of black coffee while Zach cradled King Jalen in his arms. Aunt Jackie had volunteered to take the baby to her room with her, but his uncle didn't want to share him. Around eleven o'clock, King Jalen began to twist and stretch in Zach's arms. He grunted and wiggled until his little gray eyes popped wide open.

"Take him while I warm his bottle." Zach handed the baby to his father. "It won't take me long." He left the room and went to the kitchen.

"Do you know who I am?" Pastor Monroe smiled down at his son. "I'm your daddy. I know that for sure because you stole my eyes. But that's okay. You can keep them. You can have anything you want from me. I don't know much about taking care of a baby, but I'm willing to learn everything so I can take care of you."

"You can start by feeding him." Zach had returned to the den with the bottle. "After that, you can burp him and change his wet diaper. He'll be ready to go back to sleep by then."

Pastor Monroe took the bottle and eased the nipple into the baby's mouth with care. He watched his son latch on and pull with powerful suction. "You're hungry."

"Yeah, he is, and he'll be hungry again in four hours. That seems to be his pattern." Zach looked at his watch. "That means around one-fifteen in the morning, he'll wake you up for another warm bottle and a diaper change. How are you gonna handle that at the Seven Seas, man?"

"I don't know. I haven't given it much thought."

"Aunt Jackie wants you and the baby to stay here with her for a few weeks or so until you get your routine down pat. She already set up my old room. There's a bassinet and changing table in there. I brought a mini fridge from my house. I set it up in the corner with the bottle warmer Jill and I used for Zion. Everything you need for King Jalen is in that room."

"I can't impose on your aunt. That wouldn't be fair."

Zach laughed and stroked his goatee. "Look, I'm just telling you what Aunt Jackie wants. If you don't wanna stay here, go in her room and tell her. I'll be waiting right here when you come back. But give me my nephew first. I don't want him in there when the gloves come off."

Holly paced the floor of her bedroom with a glass of pink Moscato in her hand. It was her fifth drink since she'd returned home, mad as hell, from the emergency meeting at the church. She had driven around aimlessly for two hours before she'd sped to the grocery store and purchased three bottles of wine and a *National Enquirer*. The moment she reached her lonely house, filled with memories of her life with only man she had ever loved, she showered and started her drinking binge. She'd been tossing back glasses of Moscato and blazing a path on the carpet ever since.

Holly turned around quickly in the middle of the floor. Some of the sweet pink liquid sloshed onto her black silk robe and the carpet. She became instantly annoyed. Her heart was broken because her husband had betrayed her in the worst possible way. God had denied her the one thing she desired above all others. Yet Gavin was now the father of a beautiful son. God had blessed him, even though he'd had an affair with a black prison inmate he was supposed to have been counseling. And on top of all of it, the church that Holly had sacrificed endlessly to help him build was willing to pardon him for his cruelty and infidelity. No one gave a damn about her. They didn't care about her pain, frustration, and suffering. She was humiliated and wanted revenge.

Holly drained her drink and stumbled to the dresser. She picked up the bottle of wine to pour herself another glass. The thought of Gavin and Jay making love in his office or some other undisclosed area at Leesworth was pushing her closer and closer to the edge. Her emotions were spiraling out of control. She was losing it, and not a soul cared. Holly gulped down her glass of wine and poured another. Her vision was blurry as tears flowed nonstop. She grabbed the cordless phone from its cradle and dialed Gavin's cell phone number.

"This is Gavin Monroe," he answered in a hoarse voice.

Holly's body stiffened when she heard the baby crying in the background. She clamped her eyes closed tight, but it didn't keep her tears from falling. Gavin's son's soft whimpers floated through the phone line. He sounded close enough for Holly to reach out and touch his soft skin. She imagined his father was holding him in his arms like he would've held their baby if God had blessed them with one.

"Hello. This is Gavin Monroe. Is anybody there?"

"Just tell me why. I need to know why you betrayed me. I was a good wife to you. I loved you more than I loved myself. I would've done anything for you, damn it! Why did you break my heart and rip out my soul?"

"I really would love to talk to you, Holly. We need to have a conversation to get to the heart of the matter. You certainly deserve answers, but I'm busy right now. Can I call you back? I'm changing my son's diaper at the moment, and then I have to rock him to sleep. Give me half an hour. Will you?"

Holly ended the call without giving Gavin an answer.

Jay was up and ready to return to Leesworth. She would never consider the prison her home, but at least she had friends there she could talk to. Her nine-day stay in the hospital had left her longing for her cell, believe it or not. She missed Shanika, Erica, Odette, and all of their gossip. They were probably worried to death about her. Jay wanted to assure them that her first week of dialysis had gone well and she was fine. The treatments represented the beginning of the rest of her life. She would die otherwise, and she wasn't ready for that. Jay wanted to live.

She had a reason to live now. Her son was the driving force behind her will to survive. King Jalen would be a big boy by the time Jay would be released from Leesworth, depending on her behavior. She planned to be the ideal inmate and stay close to Warden Callahan for the duration of her sentence. And with her serious medical condition, an early parole didn't seem impossible anymore.

Just thinking about walking out of Leesworth as a free woman and never looking back gave Jay a warm feeling inside. That day would be better than any fairy tale. It would be her rebirth. She looked forward to a fresh new start. Everyone deserved a second chance in life.

Jay wasn't sure what to expect though. The uncertainty frightened her. Would Pastor Monroe still love her and want them to raise King Jalen together after so many years? There was no guarantee that he would be waiting with open arms for her. Time had a way of changing people. And Pastor Monroe was a man. He was a very passionate and affectionate one at that. He had needs. Only a fool would expect him to be faithful and celibate. Jay could be described in many ways, but no one could truthfully say she was naive. She couldn't control Pastor Monroe from her prison cell just like Holly couldn't from their home. Every warm-blooded, virile man—pastors included—had a mind of his own. And wherever their minds strayed, their bodies would follow.

Honestly, Jay had no idea how she would feel about Pastor Monroe at the end of her incarceration. There was a strong possibility that she would move on. She wouldn't get involved with another man. That was one thing Jay knew for damn sure. Pastor Monroe was her first, her last, and her only. What had taken place between them was special and couldn't be reproduced with any other man on earth. But if the right woman came along at the right time . . .

"Ms. King, your escorts from Leesworth are here."

Jay looked up at the nurse and smiled. "I'm ready." She slid the handles of her overnight bag over her shoulder and followed the woman out into the hallway.

Chapter Fifty-six

"He's a real fine baby, Gavin." Wallace's eyes bore into his new grandson's bright gray ones in awe. He, Patricia, and Wallace Jr. had made a special trip to Atlanta to meet King Jalen.

Gavin, who no longer held the title of pastor, smiled proudly and stuck out his chest like a typical first-time father. "I think so too. He's perfect. He only cries when he's hungry or wet. I don't have to sit around and hold him all day. He'll sit in his swing and suck his thumb. Last night he only woke up once for a bottle. And every time I read to him, he gives me his undivided attention. He's a good boy."

"And you're doing a great job with him," said Aunt Jackie. "You've learned all the hard stuff. I'm beginning to think you don't need me anymore. Before long, you'll be packing my great-nephew up and moving him across town."

"Oh, no, I'd much rather stay here with you. There's no place in Atlanta where I can find soul food like yours. And I never would've made it if you hadn't insisted that we hang around here. You've taught me a lot. But King Jalen and I will have to move out at some point. We can't live here forever."

"Yes, y'all can. I wouldn't mind at all." Aunt Jackie stood from the recliner. "I'm going to check on lunch. Zach, Jill, and the kids will be here soon. He had to pick up Nahima first."

"I admire you, Gavin," said Wallace.

Patricia patted Wallace on his knee and smiled. "We both admire you. You made your son a priority. It was a risky move, but you did the right thing anyway."

"I had to. My son means more to me than anything else in this world. I love his mother, too. Jayla is a wonderful person. I was wrong to get involved with her. There is no excuse for my unethical behavior. God's grace and mercy spared me from major punishment. I chose my son, and if I had to do it all over again, my decision would be the same."

"Papa! Papa!" Zion bounced into the den, full of excitement. She stopped when she saw Wallace on the sofa holding the baby. "Is that your baby?"

Zachary Jr. and Nahima were on her heels. Three sets of curious eyes stared at the unfamiliar baby. The children were fascinated with the tiny little boy nestled in their papa's arms.

"He's so cute! Did you and Grammy Pat have a baby, Papa?"

Nahima's question made Zach nervous as hell. He and Jill had just walked into the den after stopping in the kitchen to greet Aunt Jackie. A few weeks ago, he and Venus had had a heart-to-heart conversation about Jay, Nahima, and King Jalen. Some important decisions were made over lunch at their favorite rib joint. Zach and Venus agreed that eventually Nahima would have to be told the truth about her parentage, as well as her connection to King Jalen, but it was too early. Charles didn't think his baby girl could handle the shock just yet. Zach felt the same way, so he decided to take control of the awkward situation stirring in Aunt Jackie's den.

"The baby's name is King Jalen Monroe, Nahima. He belongs to Mr. Gavin, the man sitting next to your papa. Say hello to King Jalen and Mr. Gavin, kids."

Zion kissed the baby on the cheek and offered his father a shy wave. Zachary Jr. didn't seem all that impressed with King Jalen, but he did shake Gavin's hand. Nahima was smitten by the little baby. She poked her index finger inside his tiny fist, and he gripped it.

"He likes me." Nahima giggled as she forced her body in between Wallace and Patricia on the sofa. She leaned in and kissed King Jalen on his forehead. "I wish my mama and daddy would have a baby. I want one just like this one." She looked over at Gavin, who was smiling at her. "Where is your wife? Did she let you bring your little boy to my nana's house by yourself?"

"You're too nosy, pumpkin. Daddies know how to take care of babies just as good as mommies. You know that. Don't I take care of you and your cousins?"

"I guess so."

"It's lunchtime!" Aunt Jackie yelled from the kitchen.

Zach was grateful for the interruption. Venus may have been the one raising Nahima, but she was more like Jay than he cared to admit. The child was too damn inquisitive and observant, and the natural magnetism she had toward King Jalen was scary. She was smitten by him. From the day Zachary Jr. came home from the hospital, she had been in love with him, and she still was to this very day. Zion was her sidekick. They were tighter than a fat chick in a girdle, but Nahima's instant attraction to King Jalen—a baby whom she didn't know and had never seen—made Zach's chest tighten with anxiety. They were bound to see each other again, because Aunt Jackie would be caring for the child regularly once Gavin found a new job and got up on his feet. Then there would be times when he and Jill would babysit him in their home.

As Zach followed the others into the kitchen, he made a mental memo to speak with Venus and Charles again soon. The situation concerning Jay, Nahima, and King Jalen would probably have to unfold earlier than they'd all anticipated.

Ivy blew out a stream of smoke and strutted right past Michael. Her petite frame jerked forward when he gripped her upper arm. "Get your fucking hands off me! Why are you here anyway? I don't need no drama on my job, Michael." She snatched away.

"I didn't come here to cause any trouble. I've been calling you, but—"

"And I've been ignoring your ass! Damn it, can't you take a hint? I'm done with you. I don't do married men. You were so stupid. Did you think you would be able to hide a wife and four children forever?"

"I'm sorry, babe," Michael apologized and took Ivy by her hand. He guided her under the light above the back door of the restaurant. "I was wrong. You have every right to be upset."

"Oh, I ain't upset, sweetie. I'm pissed the hell off! You played me, and I don't appreciate it." Ivy yanked her hand free from Michael's.

"I know. I'm so sorry for that. Let me make it up to you. I bought you something. I'll pick you up after you get off so I can give it to you."

"Uh-uh, you need to go home to your pretty little wife and all your damn crumb snatchers. They need you. I don't." Ivy pulled long and hard on her cigarette and tossed it to the ground. She pressed it into the pavement with the heel of her shoe. "My break is over. I gotta go back to work," she announced, grabbing the handle of the back door.

"I'll be here when the place closes. You can't avoid me forever, Ivy. I bought you something nice, and I want to give it to you tonight."

Ivy didn't answer Michael. In fact, she didn't even turn around. She went back inside Salvador's Bistro, letting the door slam shut behind her.

Ivy rushed to the bathroom. She leaned forward on the sink and looked at her reflection in the mirror. Her light brown face was fully flushed. Michael's unexpected visit had made her weak as watered-down liquor. Her hands and knees were shaking out of control. As much as she had tried to hate him over the weeks since he had broken her heart, she couldn't. Ivy had fallen in love with Michael.

She cursed the day she had fallen under his spell. It wasn't supposed to go down like it did. How had their simple friendship-with-benefits arrangement taken a sudden and serious twist? The deep feelings Ivy developed for Michael during their affair had crept up on her like the flu in June. She wasn't supposed to fall for another man ever. It was love that had caused her the most grief in life. She'd stayed with Sammy, through all of his abuse, in the name of love. Then, once she'd had enough of his bullshit and decided to fight back, she was thrown in prison. Ivy had vowed never to fall in love again. She was making good on that promise when she first got involved with Michael, but she slipped and caught feelings for the white dude. Then he broke her heart.

He was trying to ease his married ass back into her life with the promise of a gift. Whatever he had for her, Ivy didn't want it. And she no longer wanted him. She couldn't lie to herself. There wasn't a day that passed by when she didn't think of Michael. They'd had some damn good times together. The man could eat pussy like nobody's business, he had the stamina of a raging bull, and he was more generous than Santa Claus. Michael Stokes was the total package wrapped up in white skin. His only flaw was his status. He was married with four rug rats, and Ivy didn't consider herself jump-off material. No, she never wanted to be Mrs. Stokes, but she damn sure didn't want to be Michael's mistress either.

Ivy turned on the faucet and let the cool water run over the palms of her hands a few seconds. Another glance at her reflection in the mirror forced her to face reality. Her heart belonged to a married man, but her head was in control. She would not rekindle her fling with Michael, but she was going to take the gift he had bought her as a consolation prize for the pain he had caused her.

Chapter Fifty-seven

"How are you, Ms. King?"

Jay took a seat in the chair facing Warden Callahan's desk and smiled. "I feel all right. I'm slowly getting back into the swing of things. Thank God you didn't screw up any money while I was away. I see where the payroll for the sixty inmates working for the Kemp Corporation is accurate. Are you trying to go strictly legal on me?"

"I'm getting better."

"Well, I'm proud of you," Jay commended him with a smile. "If you keep your nose clean, it'll make my job easier. I don't need any stress right now. The doctor says it's not good for me. I'll see him in a few days for blood work. Hopefully, he'll have good news about how my body is responding to dialysis."

"I wish you the very best. I'll keep my fingers crossed for good luck."

"Thank you. I appreciate that."

Gavin looked at the door of the restaurant again and peeped at his watch. He'd agreed to meet Holly there to discuss the failure of their marriage and the terms of their divorce. She deserved answers to some of her questions, and Gavin was willing to be candid with her to some extent. He didn't see any reason why he needed to delve into the deep details about his relationship with Jay. It would only rub salt in Holly's fresh wound, and he had no desire to do that. Gavin simply wanted to help her find the closure she desperately needed to move on with her life. It would be a stretch for Holly to forgive him with so many unresolved issues still lingering, but he certainly planned to ask her to. In all honesty, he needed her forgiveness in order to gain a sense of freedom from the spiritual prison he had sentenced himself to.

Gavin had refused to make a single excuse for his affair with Jay. He'd taken ownership of his sins and was seeking penitence daily from God through prayer and Scriptures. As a part of his renewal of faith, he wanted to make amends with Holly, the person whom he had harmed more than anyone else. Gavin was anxious about expressing his remorse to her in a face-to-face conversation. It was long overdue.

As he sipped black coffee from his mug, he wondered why Holly was running late. He had allowed her to select the time and location for their meeting. It was the least he could do. But she was now a half hour late, which he hadn't expected. Aunt Jackie was taking care of King Jalen while he was away. He'd promised her that he would only be gone for two hours or so. He wanted to return in time to feed the baby and give him a bath before he put him to sleep for the night. Holly's tardiness was messing up Gavin's rigid schedule with his son.

"Where are you?" he mumbled under his breath after checking his watch again. "You wanted to talk, and I'm ready to do just that. Come on, Holly. I don't have time for games."

"I don't play games. I was never good at them."

Holly's ghost-like appearance startled Gavin. He jerked in his chair and turned to stare at her. She was standing beside him, looking down her nose over the rim of her glasses. Gavin watched Holly walk slowly to the other side of the booth and take a seat on the bench across from him. She appeared calm and free of emotional distress. A quick, professional assessment of his estranged wife was necessary to determine where he should begin the conversation.

Gavin was aware that Holly had been struggling emotionally with their separation and how it had come about. Martha, his mother-in-law, had called and blasted him for the devastation he had caused her daughter. The older woman claimed that Holly was on the brink of a mental breakdown because of his infidelity. Although she was careful not to lash out and speak insensitively about King Jalen, Martha made it her business to point out exactly what the child's presence represented. The baby's existence was a slap in Holly's face. He was the one gift that she had longed to give her husband but wasn't able to.

King Jalen was also the coveted possession Holly had prayed for, for nearly twenty years. Her desire to become a mother became an obsession, oftentimes driving her to do the unimaginable. That was how passionate she was about conceiving a child. Martha reminded Gavin about the hell her daughter had put her body through and all of the risks she'd taken. Holly had gone to extreme measures to get pregnant so that she could give her husband a child. Looking into her sad eyes caused some of those painful memories to replay in Gavin's mind. Once again, he was assaulted with guilt.

"How are you, Holly?"

"I'm as well as any woman who's been cheated on by her husband and mocked with an outside child can be. How are you and your son?" Holly swiped at a lone tear sliding down her left cheek.

"King Jalen is fine. When I left him with his aunt this evening he was cooing and kicking at the animals on his mobile. He's fascinated by the bright colors and music." Gavin placed his coffee mug on the table and sat up straight in his chair. "I'm well, but I'm more concerned about you. You're obviously hurting, and I'm to blame for it. Please believe me when I say that I'm very sorry for causing you so much pain. You may have a hard time accepting my apology anytime soon, and I fully understand that, but I'm being totally honest about my feelings. I never meant to hurt you. I'll regret betraying you for the rest of my life. You didn't deserve it. You were a good wife. Our marriage may have had its ups and downs, but that gave me no right to cheat on you."

"Why did you do it then?"

He sighed and rubbed his beard before he answered. "My heart went wayward, I suppose. There was an inner need for me to be needed for something other than making a baby or preaching or praying for someone. I am more than just a husband and a pastor. I am, first and foremost, a man. For years all you saw me as was a means to make a baby. You didn't embrace my vision to help others, especially those outside of our church. You failed to see my passion for anything that didn't involve you. I loved you, and a part of me always will. I simply got caught up."

"You could have told me how you were feeling, Gavin. I was your wife and partner in ministry. If I wasn't meeting your emotional needs, you should've told me. I would've changed to please you. There's nothing I wouldn't have done to make you happy."

"Would you have given up on having a baby?" Gavin asked, reaching across the table. He placed his hand on top of Holly's, which was resting on the red checkered cloth. "Would you have ever found contentment in our marriage without a child?"

Holly moved her hand away and stared at Gavin as if seeing him for the very first time. "I wanted to have your child. Our son or daughter would have been a symbol of our love and commitment to each other. If wanting to give you a baby from my womb was a sin, then I would have gladly spent eternity in hell." Holly laughed sarcastically. "It's funny, because after dedicating my life to you and being a faithful wife for two decades, I still ended up in a living hell. I had to watch you walk out of my life with a son you created with another woman. Tell me, do you love Jayla?"

"You don't need to know the dynamic of my relationship with the mother of my child. What good will—"

"Answer the damn question!" Holly snapped. "Don't I deserve a simple yes or no after all my suffering? You owe me everything that will help me reach some kind of closure in this mess. I need to know if you fell in love with Jayla, or if she was there at the right time to give you what I had failed to. Please tell me. I'll never work through this until I know the whole truth."

"I'm not going to lie to you, Holly, although I don't understand why it's necessary for you to know one way or the other. Yes, I love Jayla. I fell in love with her against all odds. It wasn't planned, and I never saw it coming. One thing led to another before I could stop it. I'm sorry. Please forgive me."

Chapter Fifty-eight

It would be the last time Michael ever had his way with Ivy's body, so she wanted to make it last forever. It felt damn good to have him touch her in all the right spots, sending her soul flying over the mountaintop. Every inch of her brown flesh was sizzling. Evidently, he had missed making love to her as much as she had missed having him buried deep inside of her.

Mr. Stokes was stroking for Olympic gold it seemed. He had flipped and twisted Ivy in every position physically possible without breaking her in two. They were heading down the stretch. Their moans and explicit sexual dialogue, filled with promises Ivy had no intention of keeping, had grown louder. She was damn near hoarse, screaming and singing Michael's name in a key three times higher than she'd ever performed any song in her alto voice. The dude was pouring out pure ecstasy on a sista.

Ivy closed her eyes tight and savored the last few moments of her final sexual encounter with Michael. It was bittersweet. With each long and powerful thrust into her body, she had to fight the urge to tell him that she loved him, but she also wanted to scream how much she hated him for stealing her heart and shredding it to pieces. She wrapped her legs around his waist, pulling him in deeper. She rotated her hips and met each movement like she was on a mission. Her body tingled from her micro-braid-covered scalp to her French-manicured toenails. In another life she could have easily shared him with his wife and kids, but the new and improved Ivy Maxwell deserved better than a piece of a man.

The only reason Michael was slipping and sliding between her thighs, fucking her into oblivion, was because she had been overtaken by an unexpected moment of weakness. He'd come back to the bistro, as promised, with a dozen red long-stemmed roses and a set of keys. As soon as he whipped out the title to the used Ford Fusion, and she saw her name on it in bold letters, Ivy melted. She needed that damn car, and her body was overdue for a tune-up. No man had licked her kitty cat since Michael. She made a lightning-quick decision based totally on impulse and need. She accepted the car and invited Michael back to her spot so she could thank him for his gift properly.

"Damn, babe, you're driving me crazy," Michael purred in Ivy's ear.

"Mmm . . . mmm . . ." was all she could offer in response. He was hitting the bull's-eye, and she was seconds from liftoff.

"I love you, Ivy. I swear I do."

At another time, another place, and in another situation, those words would've meant the world to Ivy. But that night they fell on insensitive ears and an unforgiving heart. She didn't believe Michael loved her, and it didn't matter much to her if he really did. He was married, and Ivy was no homewrecker. She was going to keep the car, and she was working hard on getting the last orgasm she'd ever feel under Michael's skillful touch. Afterward, she'd probably have a pity party and even go through sex withdrawals and a broken heart all over again. But she wouldn't die or lose her mind. In fact, the whole experience would make her stronger, smarter, and more cautious for the next man.

Thoughts of her future love life faded away when Michael licked her earlobe and eased his hands under her body. He gripped her ass and pushed deeper inside of her. That move caused air to seep from Ivy's lungs. The room tilted and started spinning like an amusement park ride. The sensations that wrapped around her body made her lightheaded. Ivy's walls began to contract around Michael's dick, and a mighty wave snatched her up. All ten of her toes curled. Spasms of pure pleasure hit her repeatedly, each more intense than the one before it. Ivy didn't want the moment to end. She raised her head slightly to press her lips against Michael's. He offered her his tongue in a sweet, slow, and satisfying kiss. It must've been the icing on the cake for him, because his entire slender body went perfectly stiff. Then he bucked out of control and belted out her name and a few curse words.

"Ivy, I love you, babe. I can't live without you," Michael whispered in her ear. "I'll leave Sherry today," he continued as he executed a few more short and gentle strokes to complete his mission. "I need you. Just tell me you want us to be together. I'll walk away and never look back. It could be you and me forever."

Ivy didn't know what to say. She hadn't expected a proposition from Michael. She'd definitely had no idea that he wanted her to be a permanent fixture in his life. No man had ever offered her his heart forever. That was a mighty long time. It didn't seem very realistic. Chicks from her neck of the woods only experienced happily ever after through characters in movies or in romance novels. This was real life, and she wasn't dreaming.

But Ivy didn't want to gain a man by robbing another woman of her husband. It wouldn't be fair to his children either. They needed him too. As wonderful as it felt to be in Michael's arms again, and in spite of how much she loved him, Ivy couldn't do it. She would not change her game plan, even after receiving some of the best loving she'd ever experienced in her life. In the morning she would be able to face herself in the mirror, knowing she had done the right thing. In the wee hours of the morning, she would send Michael home to his wife and kids . . . forever.

"I tried to keep him up for you, but he got a little cranky. He turned as dizzy as a drunk man after his bottle. I'm sorry you missed tucking him in. I know how important that is to you."

Gavin turned around and smiled at Aunt Jackie. She had tiptoed into his bedroom quietly. She walked up behind him and peered over his shoulder while he stood above the bassinette. They both watched King Jalen as he slept with his index and middle fingers stuck in his mouth. He was an adorable child, with hair just like his father's. The only difference between the two heads of hair was that the baby's was filled with curls, and Gavin's was short and straight. King Jalen's golden complexion was even and unblemished. He had the cutest button nose and thick, dark brows. The deep dimple in his chin got everyone's attention at first sight. He was gorgeous enough to be in commercials.

"I hate that I didn't get a chance to put him to bed. It's the first time that's happened since we've been together. I guarantee you it won't become a habit. Every minute away from him is a memory missed. I'm still trying to catch up from the time he spent in foster care."

"Don't worry about the time you've missed with him in the past, Gavin. You're making wonderful memories with him now and forever." Aunt Jackie paused as if contemplating her next statement. "I take it that your meeting with your wife lasted longer than expected."

"Yes, it went into overtime." Gavin chuckled. "And surprisingly, Holly was late. Anyway, can we discuss this over coffee? I'll make a fresh pot. I need it to stay up and work on my resume and a few other things."

"Coffee and my whipping cream pound cake always make a conversation better."

Once they'd settled at the kitchen table with mugs of steaming coffee and slices of moist pound cake, Gavin recounted his discussion with Holly to Aunt Jackie. He couldn't truthfully say that they'd reached a truce or that one day they would be friends, but he didn't foresee any delays in the divorce proceedings.

Gavin had pretty much agreed to all of Holly's reasonable demands. She had decided to sell their home and wanted to keep all of the money from the transaction. Gavin had outright refused to go along with such nonsense. He had worked hard to finance the construction of their dream house. Holly was a graduate student at the time. It wasn't fair for her to reap the profits from the sale of a house she had not contributed one thin dime toward.

Her pain had fueled her greed, but Gavin laid it to rest with a threat to fight her with proof that his money had afforded them the luxurious lifestyle she had enjoyed during their marriage. He had financial and legal documentation showing that he was the rightful owner of every bit of property they'd acquired during the course of their marriage. He had been a generous husband and provider. Gavin warned Holly that his attorney, Kirk Orowitz, was prepared for a showdown if necessary.

It was only fair that Holly receive a liberal settlement after being married to Gavin for two decades. He'd acknowledged her support of his ministry and professional career over the years. Everything he had accomplished was possible because of the sacrifices she'd made, but it didn't give her permission to exit the marriage with all of their assets, leaving him homeless and penniless. For his infidelity and the pain it had caused her, Gavin had offered Holly one half of everything they owned. He'd also agreed to give her a lump sum from the investment account he was now living off of. It had been converted from an enormous trust fund he'd been willed from his wealthy paternal grandparents many years ago. Gavin had never withdrawn a penny from it until the day Holly asked him to leave their home and their marriage.

While he and Aunt Jackie cleared the table after their little chat, he told her about his plans to change his will and beneficiary on insurance policies. He wanted everything he owned to go to King Jalen in the event that anything should ever happen to him. If Jay wasn't available to raise their son at the time of his death, Gavin wanted Zach and Jill to take him and become the executors of his trust fund.

Chapter Fifty-nine

"Dr. Yusuf told me not to worry, but I can't help it. I was sure that dialysis was going to fix me."

Shanika hugged Jay and rocked her. She squeezed her friend tight. "It will. Didn't he say it was too early to really tell?"

"Yeah, that's what he said, but he also told me that my blood work didn't show very much improvement. After three weeks of dialysis, he expected to see more positive changes in my system. Hell, I did too. It's not easy, Shanika. All of that sticking and pricking wears me out. I hate this damn shunt in my arm. Then I'm nauseated and tired as hell after each treatment. I'm wondering if it's even worth it."

"It's worth it. You'll see. The next time Dr. Yusuf runs those tests on you, your system will be as clean and clear as mine."

"I don't want to talk about kidneys and blood work anymore. How do I look?" Jay stood from her chair and raked her fingers through her hair. There was a silky shine to the curls cascading down her shoulders. One of the chicks from C17 had worked her magic on Jay's natural tresses. Everyone seemed excited about her upcoming visit with Gavin and their son later that morning. "Say something!"

"You look good, King," she said after fanning her face for a few moments. Shanika was fighting back tears. "You look really nice. Preacher man might sneak you off to a room and put it on you! I'll babysit and be the lookout for y'all."

Jay laughed at her friend. There was so much body and volume to her curls that they bounced when she laughed. "That ain't gonna happen. Callahan warned me to be on my best behavior." She looked around the laundry room, even though they were alone. The door was open. Jay sat back down and leaned in to whisper in Shanika's ear. "He said that maybe he can work out a plan for a short conjugal visit between me and Gavin in my office someday soon."

"Mmm, mmm, mmm. I ain't no freak, but I would love to be a cockroach in a corner for that. I bet y'all gonna be acting like Tarzan and Jane up in there. The pastor's gonna tear that ass up, but y'all better use protection," Shanika said, pointing her finger in Jay's face. "You're extra fertile, King. That's what happens to a woman after she has a baby. Her shit gets potent, and if a man looks at her hard, she'll get knocked up quicker than you can blink your eye. Be careful."

"We will if we ever get the opportunity to be together. You know how shady the warden is."

"I know. Come on. It's almost time for visitation. My ex is supposed to bring Malcolm today. I can't wait to see my boy."

Gavin watched the guards search through the baby's diaper bag. He'd made sure that he only packed bottles of formula, diapers, wipes, and baby powder. Aunt Jackie had checked as a precaution. King Jalen was wide awake and alert, as if he sensed something significant was about to take place. He was moments away from seeing his mommy for the first time since he had been pried from her arms and taken into foster care two and a half months before.

"You're clear to pass through, sir."

Gavin took the bag. "Thank you."

He entered the packed visitation room. It was noisy and busy. People were talking and laughing all around him. Flashes and the humming sound of cameras came from every direction. Gavin's eyes roamed about, looking for the one face that occupied his dreams at night and visions by day. He walked farther into the room, passing by tables occupied by other inmates and their loved ones.

"Gavin, I'm over here."

He spotted Jay standing near a table a few feet away to his left. She was waving her hand with a bright smile on her face. She looked gorgeous. Nothing could have prepared Gavin for the surge of emotions that caused his manhood to stiffen. He loved Jay, and if it had been possible in that moment, he would have shown her just how much. He walked faster, his pulse racing with anticipation. When they came face-to-face, he leaned over and kissed Jay's lips softly.

"It's good to see you."

"I'm happy you came. Oh, my God, look at him," Jay gushed, reaching for her son's small hand. "He has gotten so big."

Gavin placed the baby in Jay's arms and watched her rock him. "Yes, he has. He's getting bigger every day." He pulled out a chair from the nearby table. "Sit down, Jayla."

Over the next thirty minutes, Jay held her son securely in her arms, like he was the most precious creature she'd ever seen. When it was time for his bottle, Gavin allowed her the honor. Nothing brought him more joy than watching the mother of his son care for him. Visions of them being a family outside of Leesworth flashed before his eyes.

"This is how it's going to be for us someday, Jayla. Once you're released from this place, we're going to be a family. I look forward to taking care of you and our son. You won't have to ask for anything because I'll make sure you have whatever you need."

Jay looked down at her sleeping son resting on her lap. "I may not live to see my way out of this hellhole. My liver is stable right now, but the dialysis treatments don't seem to be helping much. I could die right here."

"Don't think like that. You haven't been on dialysis for very long. Give it a chance. Where is your faith, sweetheart?"

Jay shrugged her shoulders. "I don't know. Sometimes I feel like God doesn't love me. It's hard to pray when you don't think He's listening."

"He's always listening to our prayers."

"If that's true, then I should be out of here soon so I can raise my son. Every child needs his mother. I don't want him to grow up without me. I don't want him to experience what I did, growing up without my mother."

"I'm sorry."

"It wasn't your fault. Anyway, I don't want to dig up my miserable past as an orphan. I want to enjoy this time with you and our baby boy. He's so perfect. I've never seen a more beautiful child." Jay kissed the baby on his forehead. "He looks just like you, you know. Those are my lips, though."

"Everyone says that."

"Who are you talking about, Gavin? How can anybody say our son has my lips unless they know what I look like?" Jay snorted and pursed her lips. "You're talking about Zach. I don't know why you insist that he be a part of my child's life."

"King Jalen and I are living with your aunt temporarily. Zach and his family visit her often. I can't avoid him."

"Well, I want you to hurry up and move outta that house so you won't have to run into him so much."

Gavin lowered his head. "Your brother and I will still run into each other from time to time, because your aunt will be caring for the baby in my absence. It's inevitable. And besides that, your brother and his wife have been a blessing to our son. Your father and his wife have been too."

"How so?"

"They've all showered him with gifts and offered to babysit him whenever I need them to. Zach and Jill have kept the baby overnight just so he could spend time with their children and Nahima."

The tension in Jay's body and the sour expression on her face couldn't be ignored. Gavin picked up on her shift in attitude immediately. He didn't know the whole story about Jay's past relationship with Venus or the daughter they shared. She'd only told him that her eggs and the sperm donated from Venus's cousin had been used for the in vitro fertilization process. Gavin knew nothing about how Nahima ended up with Venus after their breakup. He'd been tempted to do a little research but feared what he might learn and how it would affect his feelings for Jay.

"How do you feel about that, Jayla? Tell me how it makes you feel to know that your daughter and our son are spending time together."

"What difference does it make? There ain't a damn thing I can do about it from this cage, is there? It seems like you and your new buddy Zach are determined to do whatever y'all wanna do, no matter how I feel. But be careful. My brother is selfish and evil. He doesn't give a damn about anyone but himself. He has an agenda. This situation with our son and Nahima could explode in your face."

Chapter Sixty

Watching Gavin walk out of the visitation room with King Jalen in his arms nearly destroyed Jay and knocked her to her knees. She felt like someone had reached inside her chest and ripped her heart out. The hurt and the desire to be with her son was more unbearable now that she had been reunited with him. His fresh scent, infectious smile, and the softness of his skin had awakened her maternal instincts again. It reminded her of the day he was born. The instant Gavin placed their son into Jay's arms, she experienced the wonderment of a miracle for the first time ever. Her belief that God really did exist was reconfirmed.

Strangely enough, Jay had never experienced such euphoria at any time when Nahima was in her presence. All happy thoughts of sharing a child with Venus faded during the pregnancy. The thrill vanished and never returned. But from the moment Jay learned that she was pregnant with Gavin's child, an indescribable sensation had settled in. Even with uncertainty and a potential scandal surrounding her pregnancy, Jay had fallen in love with her unborn child, and she loved him even more today.

She wrapped her arms around her knees and pulled them to her chest. It was dark and quiet on the block. All the other inmates, including Shanika, were asleep. Jay was restless. She was forced to sort through a multitude of thoughts. There was absolutely nothing positive about her circumstances. Her future didn't appear all that bright either. Gavin and their son gave her hope, but reality, like payback, was a bitch. Jay wasn't stupid enough to believe that she would leave Leesworth alive, and she sure as hell didn't think that Gavin was immune to falling in love with another woman while she was on lockdown.

Jay clutched the picture of Gavin and her son and rested her body on her cot. She rolled over to face the wall. It was time to do some soul-searching.

"What are you trying to tell me, Dr. Yusuf? Speak in plain English so I can understand."

The doctor touched Jay's shoulder gently and met her fearful gaze. "Your body is not responding to dialysis the way Dr. Samba and I had hoped. There has been some improvement, but not significantly so. I'm sorry, my dear. You are suffering from renal failure."

"What exactly does that mean?"

"Unless you receive at least one new kidney soon, you are going to die. I will notify the warden that your name must go on a transplant list immediately. Until then, you will continue dialysis and all current medications." He patted Jay's shoulder. "I'll leave you to get dressed now. I will see you next week."

The news of Jay's condition dealt her family a shocking blow. Gavin had been the messenger of bad news after receiving her emotional phone call. He was devastated. He and Aunt Jackie decided to pray together as they waited for the rest of the family to gather at the house. It was the middle of the week, so Wallace and Patricia could not join them. Gavin had given them a full report and promised to update them after Jay's next appointment with the doctor. Aunt Hattie Jean and Uncle Bubba arrived a few minutes before Zach and Jill did. Everyone settled in the den to talk.

"It's a complicated situation. Jayla is an inmate in federal prison. She is not a priority to a society of tax-paying citizens. They would gladly skip over her and allow an available kidney to go to someone else. It will be one less inmate they'll have to house, feed, clothe, and provide medical care for. That's why I'm going to see my doctor and be tested to determine if I'm a match."

"You can't do that, man. You have your son to think about now."

Gavin shook his head and rubbed both hands down his face in frustration. "I have his mother to think about as well, Zach. I'm strong and healthy. If I'm a match, I'm going to give your sister one of my kidneys. I refuse to let her die if I can save her life."

"What are Jay's options and chances of being matched with a kidney from a public donor list?" Jill wanted to know.

"Her chances are very slim. I can tell you that right now," Zach said pointedly. "Like Gavin explained, a noncriminal will be considered over an inmate anytime. Jay has a better chance at getting a kidney from a family member or a friend. Most of her family is right here. She doesn't have any friends."

"Well, it's settled then. We'll all be tested to see if we're a match for Jay." Aunt Hattie Jean faced her baby sister, who was sitting next to her on the sofa. She placed her hand on her knee. "What I meant to say was that everybody will be tested except you. I know you wanna try to help too, Jackie, but I ain't gonna let you. You're still trying to make your comeback from the heart attack. Ain't that right, y'all?"

Everyone nodded in agreement.

Aunt Jackie held her head down in obvious defeat, but she didn't put up an argument.

Taking up where his wife had left off, Uncle Bubba added, "I'll tell Bertha and Dolly Mae. Phoebe and her children will get tested too. I'm sure Wallace and his young wife will do the same."

"Nah, that ain't gonna happen," Zach rushed to say. "My daddy is too old. Plus, he's a borderline diabetic. And Jay hasn't reached out to him in over a year. It wouldn't make sense for Daddy to give her a kidney when all she's given him since the day he walked back into her life is her ass to kiss. Scratch Wallace King off the list and consider me as an alternate. I'll only give my sister a kidney if there is absolutely no one else in the world who can do it."

After a series of tests, Gavin's doctor determined that he was not a compatible donor for Jay's kidney transplant. Their blood types matched. Both had type O positive blood. For the most part Gavin was healthy and strong, but his cholesterol was high. It wasn't a major deal, but his doctor did prescribe medication and put him on a diet to get it under control. But even if his cholesterol dropped to a healthy level, he still wouldn't be able to donate a kidney to Jay.

Gavin had a history of kidney stones. His first bout occurred shortly after he and Holly returned from their honeymoon in Hawaii twenty years before. Once, during his early thirties, he had to be hospitalized because the pain was so excruciating and paralyzing. It took him a few days to pass the twenty-three small pellets of calcium compounds. Even after years of Gavin not having any symptoms of kidney stones, his doctor refused to allow him to be a donor for Jay.

Chapter Sixty-one

"Are you going to do it, Zachary? Will you give Jay one of your kidneys, sweetheart?"

"Yeah, I'm gonna give my crazy-ass sister a kidney. Don't I always clean up behind Jay? Whenever she fucks up, everybody looks for me to fix it. But this is the last time I'll ever do anything for her. I swear."

Hand in hand, Zach and Jill exited the doctor's office and headed to their vehicle. Just as everyone involved had expected, the best candidate for an organ donor to any recipient was a parent or sibling. A healthy kidney from Zach would possibly extend Jay's life. To Jill's surprise, he had decided without resistance to give Jay another chance at life. She had prepared a speech about forgiveness and love, hoping that it might influence him to have mercy on his only sister in spite of all she had done to him. Miraculously, there was no need for the speech or any other type of coercion. For some reason, Zach was going to commit a brave and brotherly act of kindness for Jay of his own free will.

Jill paused at the open door of the SUV and faced her husband. "Are you going to donate a kidney to Jay because you feel it is the right thing to do, or are you only doing what is expected of you?"

"What difference does it make, baby? Jay is gonna get a kidney from me. It doesn't matter why. But after I make this sacrifice for her, I hope all of the bad blood between us will disappear. I don't want a relationship with Jay ever again, but I want a clean record and clear conscience. Every morning when Jay wakes up, I want her to remember that the brother she once wanted dead did something to help her live."

"I knew it! I knew it! I told you, King. Your brother is a good man. Yeah, he betrayed you once, but he's still my kinda dude."

Jay looked at her friends huddled around her cot. They'd all crammed in her cell after the news about her kidney transplant hit the Leesworth gossip loop. Odette had to have been the bigmouth to leak it. Callahan had sent her to the infirmary with Jay to speak with Dr. Yusuf.

"Zach's kidney is a guilt gift, Shanika. Don't get all soft and sentimental on me. Hell, he's supposed to give me a kidney. It's the least he could do after everything he did to me."

"Stop acting like an arrogant bitch." Shanika took a seat on the side of Jay's hard and lumpy cot. "If Zach had decided not to give you a kidney, you would have something to complain about. The man is risking his life to save yours, but you're still talking shit. What the hell is wrong with you?"

"Ain't nothing wrong with me. You just don't know my brother the way I do. Anyway, I'm tired from all of that poking and pricking the doctor did to me today. Y'all get outta here and let me get some rest. We'll talk at chow."

Holly hung up the phone and picked up her wedding album from the coffee table. When she opened the dusty picture book, she was immediately transported back to a place in time when her life, and the world around it, seemed perfect. Gavin was the most handsome groom ever. Not even the irresistible character Luke Spencer, on the day he wed his bride, Laura, on the popular soap opera *General Hospital,* could compare to her young preacher man back then. Gavin—in a white dinner jacket, black tuxedo pants, and matching bowtie—brought life to Holly's fantasy of becoming a June bride. They were so happy and in love. And they had plans, too. Together, the newly ordained pastor and his bride were going to lead their church into the twenty-first century and have lots of babies. But after eight years in full-time ministry and several mercy missions around the globe without a child, Holly realized that something was wrong.

As she flipped through the worn pages of her wedding album, she began to mourn the end of a marriage that was supposed to endure the test of time. Her heart ached for the love of her life and the baby she never gave him. The pain was endless. After her meeting with Gavin tomorrow, it would be officially over. Life would never be the same. Holly wasn't sure if she'd ever recover from her loss. She closed the album and cried her eyes out.

"Hattie Jean, how are you and Bubba doing with the baby?" Aunt Jackie paused and listened on the phone to her sister carrying on about their great-nephew. "Well, they'll be coming to take Jay down to surgery soon, but Gavin isn't here yet. That chile is going crazy. She doesn't wanna be put to sleep without seeing him first."

Two attendants pushed a bed past Aunt Jackie. They went into Jay's room. Time was up, and Gavin was no-where to be found. Aunt Hattie Jean said he had dropped off King Jalen to her and Uncle Bubba over three hours ago. He had one stop to make before hitting the interstate en route to the hospital in North Georgia. He and his estranged wife had agreed to meet at her house to sign the final set of papers that would dissolve all assets and property they'd accumulated during the course of their marriage. Gavin promised he would get on the road after that brief meeting.

Aunt Jackie ended her conversation with her sister with an eerie feeling in her spirit. She couldn't understand why Gavin hadn't arrived at the hospital yet. Traffic and the narrow roads around the mountains had more than likely delayed him. Jay was going to have a hissy fit if Gavin didn't get there soon. Warden Callahan had been so kind to grant him permission to be there. Surely, he was on the way.

The door to Jay's room swung open, and the two attendants wheeled her out. She was afraid. Aunt Jackie knew her better than anyone. She took Jay's hand. "Everything is gonna be all right, baby. I prayed with Zach before he went to surgery last week and God brought him through. He's at home resting and waiting for updates on you. You're gonna be fine too, sweetie."

"Where is Gavin, Auntie? He should've been here by now. I want Gavin." Jay's voice was weak from the medication she had been given to relax her, but her will was still strong.

"He'll be here, Jay. Now close your eyes so Auntie can pray for you."

"They took Jay to the operating room about thirty minutes ago. Aunt Jackie called while you were sleeping."

"Was she praying and speaking in tongues when she called?" Zach let out a soft, raspy laugh but stopped suddenly because of the pain in his back and left side.

"Actually, she was disturbed. You see, Gavin never showed up at the hospital. Jay was very upset because of it. I hope he didn't have a car accident. That would be horrible."

"Those winding roads around those mountains are narrow and tricky. Did Auntie call Gavin's cell phone?"

Jill nodded. "It rang without an answer."

"That ain't like Gavin. He's the only fool on the planet who loves my sister and has no fear of her. I love her, I guess, but that bitch is so crazy that I'm scared to be in a room alone with her. She'd better enjoy that kidney I gave her. That's as close as she'll ever get to me again. I'm done with her for real this time."

"You will change your mind when Jay is released from prison. I believe you and she will find a way to coexist for the sake of her two beautiful children. You love Nahima and King Jalen very much, Zachary. They are a part of Jay. Nothing can ever change that. So, at some point you and your sister must come to a truce."

Chapter Sixty-two

Gavin raised both hands and backed up. "Put the gun down, Holly. You don't want to do this. Let's sit and talk about it."

"Shut up! Don't try to get inside my head. I am not one of your precious convicts. I am your wife, damn it!"

"I'm not trying to minimize your hurt or make excuses for what I did to you. I just want you to understand that killing me will not serve you any purpose whatsoever."

"What purpose did your affair with some crazy, evil black lesbian serve me or our marriage? You are such a fucking hypocrite! It was okay for you to screw around on me, but you don't think it's right for me to make you pay for it?"

Gavin's back hit the kitchen wall. There was no place for him to run. He was trapped. "If you kill me, what kind of life do you think you will have? Prison is not the place for you. You're too smart and talented. There is a man out there somewhere who is much better than I am. He will give you his heart and be faithful to you. Don't destroy your life because of my mistakes."

"I don't want another man! I want you! We were a team in every way. I tried to give you what you wanted. I did all I could to give you a child." Holly's voice broke, and she started to sob from her soul. Her entire body shook as she screamed, pouring out her heart to Gavin. Tears and mucus slid down her face. "We promised to love each other forever . . . until death do us part. Remember?"

Gavin swallowed nervously. His wedding day replayed in his memory. He thought about his son and Jay. Holly's wide-eyed gaze and jerky movements were those of a woman on the edge. He had seen it many times before, dealing with some of his clients in the past. The thin line between sanity and insanity had been crossed. Holly had lost all sense of reality and logic. Gavin's infidelity had pulled her into a deep, dark place. Holly was no longer in control. She had snapped. She was deranged.

"What do you want from me, Holly? What can I do to help you?"

Her shrill laughter frightened Gavin. She raised the revolver higher and aimed at his heart. "I want to take from you the same thing you took from me. You destroyed my life, Gavin. And now I'm going to destroy yours."

Gavin pushed away from the wall and lunged toward Holly in an attempt to wrestle the gun from her hand. He was stronger and faster, but she was more determined.

The first shot shattered Gavin's shoulder blade. Holly immediately fired again and again. Blood splattered against the pristine walls of the modern, state-of-the-art kitchen and dripped down to the floor. Gavin gasped, pressed his back against the wall, and slid down to rest his butt on the floor. He held his chest as more blood and spittle oozed from his open mouth. He tried to speak, but the sting and shock stole his words.

Holly sat down next to him, the gun still in her grip. Gavin's weak and wounded body slumped sideways toward her. He gurgled and gasped, choking on his own blood.

Holly kissed Gavin's lips. "I love you, my darling. For richer or poorer and in sickness or in health, forsaking all others until death do us part."

After a moment of complete silence, Holly stuffed the barrel of the gun inside her mouth and pulled the trigger.

***

"Zach is in the waiting area, Jay. He wants to see you, but he wasn't sure if you were up to it. He's very concerned about you."

Jay rocked her son in her arms and stared straight through Aunt Jackie. She didn't respond. The new mental health counselor at Leesworth had warned her aunt about her state of mind. Dr. Rhonda Sharif and the entire staff, under Warden Callahan's orders, had been keeping a watchful eye on her since Gavin's death. Jay hadn't displayed any suicidal tendencies, but she was withdrawn from her friends and quiet. Dr. Yusuf had not released her to return to work yet. He didn't think she was physically or emotionally ready.

"Jay, baby, would you like Zach to come in? The guard will get him for you. I think you and your brother need to talk. After all, he did donate a kidney to you, and he and Jill will be raising your baby now that Gavin is no longer with us."

"He's dead, Aunt Jackie. Go ahead and say it. I ain't gonna nut up. Gavin is dead. My son is gonna grow up just like I did. And Nahima is in the same situation. One parent is dead and the other one is in prison. When children miss out on the love of their real parents, they don't turn out right. Look at me. I never had a fair shot in life. My kids are gonna be fucked up, just like their poor mama."

"Stop it, Jay! You're talking nonsense. I was there for you. I raised you and Zach with all the love in my heart. It's time for you to take responsibility for your own actions. You created most of your problems yourself. And until you own up to all the things you've done to the people who love you, you will continue to screw up."

Aunt Jackie stood up. "I think I should leave now and give you some time to think. I'm so sorry about Gavin. He was a wonderful man and an amazing father. Having his unconditional love, even for a little while, is something for you to thank God for. Now should I send Zach in?"

"No. We don't have anything to talk about."